PRAISE FOR THE
WEATHER WARDEN SERIES

"The forecast calls for ... a fun read.... You'll never watch the Weather Channel the same way again."
—Jim Butcher, *New York Times* bestselling author of the Dresden Files

"With chick lit dialogue and rocket-propelled pacing, Rachel Caine takes the Weather Wardens to places the Weather Channel never imagined!"
—Mary Jo Putney

"A fast-paced thrill ride [that] brings new meaning to stormy weather."
—*Locus*

"A tale that's sure to keep fans at the edge of their seats ... a must read."
—Darque Reviews

"[Caine] invents new and interesting ways to ramp up the tension and the stakes ... another excellent entry in a series that's been consistently enjoyable all along."
—The Green Man Review

"The Weather Warden books are an addictive force of nature that will suck you in."
—*News and Sentinel* (Parkersburg, WV)

"Exhilarating.... The story line is fast-paced and filled with plenty of magical action.... Rachel Caine provides another terrific tale in one of the stronger urban fantasies on the market today."
—*Midwest Book Review*

"Chaos has never been so intriguing as when Rachel Caine shapes it into the setting of a story. Each book in this series has built in intensity and fascination. Secondary characters blossom as Joanne meets them anew, and twists are revealed that will leave you gasping."
—Huntress Book Reviews

"Rachel Caine is still ... strong, throwing one curveball af... o shake up the status quo. She ... of impending doom and esca... ever higher.... I really like this ...y that ... tell[s] something ex... ...nging."
—SF Site

continued ...

BOOKS BY RACHEL CAINE

WORKING STIFF

A REVIVALIST NOVEL

Rachel Caine

A ROC BOOK

ROC
Published by New American Library, a division of
Penguin Group (USA) Inc., 375 Hudson Street,
New York, New York 10014, USA
Penguin Group (Canada), 90 Eglinton Avenue East, Suite 700, Toronto,
Ontario M4P 2Y3, Canada (a division of Pearson Penguin Canada Inc.)
Penguin Books Ltd., 80 Strand, London WC2R 0RL, England
Penguin Ireland, 25 St. Stephen's Green, Dublin 2,
Ireland (a division of Penguin Books Ltd.)
Penguin Group (Australia), 250 Camberwell Road, Camberwell, Victoria 3124,
Australia (a division of Pearson Australia Group Pty. Ltd.)
Penguin Books India Pvt. Ltd., 11 Community Centre, Panchsheel Park,
New Delhi - 110 017, India
Penguin Group (NZ), 67 Apollo Drive, Rosedale, Auckland 0632,
New Zealand (a division of Pearson New Zealand Ltd.)
Penguin Books (South Africa) (Pty.) Ltd., 24 Sturdee Avenue,
Rosebank, Johannesburg 2196, South Africa

Penguin Books Ltd., Registered Offices:
80 Strand, London WC2R 0RL, England

First published by Roc, an imprint of New American Library,
a division of Penguin Group (USA) Inc.

First Printing, August 2011
10 9 8 7 6 5 4 3 2 1

PUBLISHER'S NOTE
This is a work of fiction. Names, characters, places, and incidents either are the product
of the author's imagination or are used fictitiously, and any resemblance to actual
persons, living or dead, business establishments, events, or locales is entirely coinci-
dental.
   The publisher does not have any control over and does not assume any responsibility for author or third-party Web sites or their content.

I was going to dedicate this book to my mother, but the fact is, I'm not sure she'd totally appreciate being named in a book that verges on the macabre (often). But I love her anyway.

So instead I'm going to thank Kelley W. I am withholding her last name to protect her, because the reason I am dedicating this to her is that, finally, I believe there is enough blood mist in it for her. (She loves the blood mist.) See why I withheld her last name? Love you, Kelvis.

And for Sarah Weiss, about whom I have nothing embarrassing to say but plenty to praise, for she is awesome.

To Cat for coming up with a brilliant title (again)!

ACKNOWLEDGMENTS

I wish I knew where to start, but I'll just jump in. Thanks to Kenneth McKenzie and Todd Harra, authors of *Mortuary Confidential: Undertakers Spill the Dirt*; to Amber Lenore Winckler, author of *The Final Bath*; and Tom Jokinen, author of *Curtains*. These books got me started flying down the road. The wild, strange divergences I took are entirely on me. If you're curious about the funeral industry, those books are a great place to start.

Also, I want to acknowledge and thank the unsung heroes: those true believers who work in the funeral business. It's important work, and these are the last people we will ever meet. They don't get thanked, and they should.

Chapter 1

Bryn's first embalming instructor had told her, straight up, that two kinds of people entered the death business: freaks and true believers. Bryn Davis didn't think she was either one of those. For her, it was a prime career opportunity—a genuine *profession*.

Oh, she'd picked up odd paychecks during college as an office temp, a dog walker, and one memorable afternoon at a chicken factory, but none of those had ever felt *real* to her. Joining the army after college had seemed like a good idea at the time (steady job, good wages), but four years in Iraq hadn't made her want to be a career soldier; it had, though, given her a bedrock understanding of the fragility of human life. After that, dead bodies didn't scare or disgust her.

One good thing she could say for her time in the military: it had led her to where she was now, to this job . . . a good, stable one, and even better, an *important* one.

Bryn smiled a little at the thought. Maybe she was a true believer, after all.

She smoothed the white lab coat—with her name stitched on the left breast—and felt a warm surge of accomplishment. *Bryn Davis, Funeral Director, Fairview Mortuary.* Her business cards rested in a neat little cardboard box on her shiny new desk, all sober black ink in raised type, with the Fairview logo embossed in the corner. They wouldn't stay in the box for long; Fairview had furnished her with nice wooden desk accents, including a business card holder, and just as soon as possible, she intended to make that desk her own. She'd never had an office be-fore.

The cards and desk were elegant, like everything here. The room was neat and clean, filled with sober antique fur-niture and soft, dark cloth. Deep carpets. Subtle fragrances. Not a lot of flowers to overwhelm the already raw senses of the grieving.

She was a little nervous, but she also felt proud and happy. In fact, she felt *ready*. She tried not to feel *too* happy, though; it didn't seem appropriate to be so glee-filled about starting a job that was all about someone else's loss. The mirror on the wall confirmed that there was still a smile hiding in the corners of her mouth that she couldn't quite get rid of, and for a moment, she wor-ried about the shade of her lipstick. She'd chosen a light pink, but was it too light? A little too festive? She'd spent too many years in khaki, far away from the fairy-tale world of Maybelline.

There was a knock on her office door, and before she could say *come in*, it swung open to admit the head man ... Lincoln Fairview. Mr. Fairview was the fourth Fairview to operate the funeral home, and he looked the part, from his sober, well-tailored suit to his impeccably cut gray hair and soft, kindly face.

She felt her whole body jolt with adrenaline when she saw him. *This* was the man she had to impress with her professionalism. *Hoo, boy*. She worried, again, about the lipstick.

He crossed the room with a confident stride and shook her hand. "Hello, Bryn. Good morning. How are you set-tling in?"

She unbuttoned the lab coat and put it on the hanger in the small closet. Even the hangers were solid wood, and nicer than anything in her apartment wardrobe. "Every-thing's fine, sir," she said, and glanced down at herself to be sure she still looked okay. Her business suit was new, and a little stiff, but it was a solid dove gray color, and the soft pink shirt seemed like a nice match. Her new gray pumps pinched her toes, and she was afraid she was going to have to endure the blisters they were bound to raise, but overall . . . she thought she was presentable. Except for the lipstick, maybe. "Am I properly dressed?"

He gave her an X-ray stare, up and down, and then nodded. "Perfect," Mr. Fairview said. "Soothing, professional, everything I could ask. Perhaps a touch less on the lipstick next time; a pretty girl like you really doesn't need to emphasize her youth and beauty. Go on, have a seat, Bryn."

Oh, she *knew* it: the lipstick sucked. Bryn tried not to seem nervous as she settled into her leather chair on the other side of the desk. Mr. Fairview stayed on his feet. He studied her for a few seconds, and then said, "I assume that in your course work, you did live role-play on handling difficult clients."

"Uh—yes, sir." What an odd way to start. . . . She'd at least expected to get a tour of the building, maybe an introduction to the staff. At least she'd thought he'd show her the coffee machine and the bathroom. *Pretend he's your new commanding officer*, she told herself, and that steadied her. She'd gone through plenty of those meetings, and she knew the drill. Impress them early, and a lot, and they'd never bother you again. Bryn felt her spine straighten to military correctness. "Shall I be—"

"You'll be you. I'll be your client. Let me go out and come back, and we'll get started."

She steeled herself as he left the room, hastily blotted her lipstick with a tissue. She missed her lab coat. Her lab coat had given her an air of . . . scientific detachment, and there was always something comforting about wearing a uniform.

This time, when the knock came at the door, Bryn stood and walked around her desk to meet him, shaking his hand and making and holding eye contact, just as she would have to establish her bona fides back in the war zones. Firm handshake, not too firm; chin up, eyes steady and straight. Convey a sense of solid competence and trustworthiness. "Sir, thank you for coming to Fairview. Please have a seat. How may I assist you today?"

She indicated the sofa and chairs grouped in the corner of the office. Mr. Fairview took a place on the sofa, looked around, and leaned forward as she settled into a polite, alert pose on the chair—within reach, but giving him space. "I'm sure that this is a very hard day for you," she said in her most soothing voice. This, at least, was something she felt confident doing, even on her first morning of the job. "How can I help?"

Mr. Fairview didn't even give her a nod of approval. He stared over her shoulder instead. "It's my brother," he said. "He passed away yesterday."

"I'm so sorry." Bryn knew how to steer the conversation; she'd been through the training, and she knew better than to ask the emotional questions immediately. "May I get you a coffee, or tea, or—"

Fairview's gaze shifted to her face. "He was hit by a truck."

She had an instant, vivid flashback of the armored personnel carrier, of a screaming face outside the dust-smeared window, of the crushing thump of the wheels. Of the body in the dirt, blood leaking dark onto the packed road, head crushed into a shape that was no longer human.

Bryn took a deep breath and forced the images away. *Focus*, she thought. *He's talking about reconstruction work.* That was pricey, a definite plus for the business. "That must have been a terrible shock."

"It certainly was for him."

Oh, God, was he trying to make her *laugh*? Bryn didn't feel any inclination to it; the memory of that body in the road had drained all the laughter out of her. Her voice, when it came, was just a shade too cool. "I meant for you, sir."

"I never liked him anyway. Now I'm stuck paying for him. Dumb son of a bitch never knew how to drive anyway. I want the lowest price you can give me, understand? I'm not spending a cent more on his drunken corpse than I have to."

Bryn opened her mouth, but nothing came out. She'd had a course section on dealing with aggressive customers, but those brain cells had shut down and were refusing to cooperate. Mr. Fairview was selling the angry brother for all he was worth, and her instinct was to fight back—which she couldn't do, in this position.

She took a deep breath. "I'm sure we can work with you to find something within your budget, sir," she said. *Oh, God, that was weak.* "Let's talk about some options...." She reached out for the brochures and books, and realized that she'd left them across the room, sitting on her desk. Of course. She felt her face grow a bit warm at the oversight, but covered it by calmly standing and walking to retrieve them, talking as she walked. "I'm sure you'll find the Paradise plan the one that fits your needs, sir; it's a good combination of quality and price. We can also work with you on floral choices, which can save you a great deal of money." She held out the brochure to him as she returned to her seat.

He didn't take it.

Fairview let her dangle and suffer for a moment, then suddenly sat back and relaxed, arms spread out across the top of the sofa. "Good," he said, and nodded with a warm smile. "Very good. You made me feel welcome, established trust, competence, and a human connection; you seated me where you wanted me, and offered me refreshment. You didn't let me throw you off when I showed you sarcasm and anger. That's always the worst part, I think."

"Did I forget anything?"

"Tissues," he said. "Always keep the tissues here, next to the sofa, where they're easy to reach. Make sure the trash can is visible, but discreet, so they know where to dispose of them. And, of course, you've already realized how important it is to keep sales materials at hand, but don't make it obvious; this isn't a furniture store. If you can't do the math in your head, keep a calculator close so you can quickly update your figures; they'll always want to make changes to standard packages, and that will require repricing."

She nodded. "Anything else?"

"Up-sell, my dear. Always up-sell. Higher-priced options may not be within their budget, but they're certainly factored into mine." Mr. Fairview rose and offered her his hand. "I'll introduce you to Lucy when she comes in, and of course you will have to meet Freddy downstairs, but later. For now, I think you're ready for your first intake session.

I'll be sitting in, so don't worry; if you go off script, I'll bring you back."

She wasn't fooled by that. He wasn't there to help—he was there to give her a job evaluation. Fairview had a reputation of being strict, a stickler for regulations, and for making the best profits in the industry. He also had a reputation for going through funeral directors like bags of dinner mints.

She took a deep breath, smiled, and stood as Mr. Fairview went to get her first real customers.

Up-sell. You can do this!

Right.

The first one wasn't too bad; it was a middle-aged woman making arrangements for her father, and she seemed crisp and businesslike about it, or so Bryn thought, until she realized that there was a glaze of shock and misery over the woman's apparently clear eyes. Still, she didn't cry, didn't argue, bargained reasonably, and walked away with a relatively modest coffin, middle-of-the-road funeral package, and a slightly better than average floral package, as well as the higher-priced memorial notice in the newspaper and online.

Mr. Fairview sat off to the side, saying nothing of any real substance, looking solid and helpful. After it was over, he saw the woman to the door and walked her out; Bryn watched from the window as he escorted her to her car, head bent down as if he were listening. Halfway there, in the lovely little garden grotto with its beautiful angel statue, the woman just . . . collapsed, as if she'd been hit in the solar plexus. Mr. Fairview didn't seem surprised. He eased her down to a bench and sat beside her. Bryn watched, fascinated by the silent drama of it. His body language told the whole story—warm, kind, understanding. After a few moments, the woman managed to stand up and walk to her car, and Mr. Fairview came back inside.

"Wow." Bryn sighed; she was half-admiring, half-resentful. She hadn't read the woman as being ready to drop, but obviously Mr. Fairview had much more experience at this than she did. She had a lot to learn.

And to think she'd come in hoping to *impress* him.

By the time he arrived back in her office, she'd already gotten a good start on the paperwork and opened up the new folder with the deceased's name on it. Everything was paper here, still; she thought maybe she could teach them a thing or two about going electronic with the process. Maybe if they all had tablet PCs they could do this at the initial meeting. . . . So much simpler to avoid all this laborious writing after the fact. . . . Show the pictures of the caskets and floral packages right there; zoom to show the detail. . . .

Mr. Fairview came back inside and took the chair across from her. Bryn looked up, brows raised. She wanted to ask, but she was humiliatingly afraid of what he was going to say.

"Relax," he said, and although she would have sworn she really wasn't *that* nervous, she felt some hidden tension deep in her stomach slowly release. *Wow*. That felt good. "You did well enough, Bryn. Not a perfect job, of course, but solid. If you continue to sell that well, you'll have a bright future in the business. Do you know what you missed?"

"Well, obviously, she was ready to collapse," Bryn said, and bit her lip. "I didn't see it. You did."

"I've had considerably more experience at reading the recently bereaved. Don't blame yourself." He smiled at her, and the striking gray of his eyes reminded her suddenly less of silver than of dead ashes. It was just a flicker, and then it was gone. Probably her imagination running away with her. Again. Her imagination had always been a problem for her, which was partly why she'd stubbornly decided on a job in the death business. . . . Because imaginative people didn't usually choose working with corpses and grief. Bodies didn't scare her—no, indeed—but she couldn't help but imagine the pain that had brought them to this last, painless end. Unlike most funeral directors, she'd not only seen death; she'd seen *dying* in many forms—quick, slow, painful, painless. It was the wrenching emotional process of that that she wanted to avoid.

The dead didn't feel.

"Thank you for taking care of her," Bryn said. "She seemed . . . kind."

"Did she?" There was something odd in his look, as if Bryn were speaking a foreign language all of a sudden. "Well, I'm sure we'll have time to get to know her better over the next few days and see whether your assessment is correct. She'll be back for the detail arrangements. I assume you're fine with handling those."

"Oh, yes, sir."

"That would include deciding on music, speakers, choosing the display room, liaising with her chosen minister—the family is Lutheran, I believe—as well as things like funeral dress and makeup."

There were a dreadful lot of details about being dead, Bryn thought. She'd never had to arrange a funeral herself on the buyer's end, but it seemed almost as complicated as buying a house, and just as prone to larceny. *Right, note to self*, she thought. *Don't ever care enough for anybody to have to do this for them. Oh, and don't die.* Two very silly thoughts, but they made her feel better.

Mr. Fairview seemed satisfied, because he checked his expensive Rolex watch and said, "Ah, I see it's time for lunch. Plans, Bryn?"

"I— No, sir." She'd brought her lunch. PB and J, just as she'd had all through high school and college. After MREs, having a simple peanut-butter-and-jelly sandwich seemed like heaven in her mouth. Her tastes were pretty simple, but she didn't really want Mr. Fairview to think that; he seemed more the filet mignon type of guy. She bet he drank Perrier water, too.

"Well, then, you must join me to celebrate your first day. Do you like French food?"

She'd no idea, so of course she nodded, smiling, and tried not to seem as out of her element as she felt. She was glad now that she'd gone with the nicer suit. *Another note to self: buy way more business clothes.* She hadn't thought about it back at her apartment, but now that she was here, she could see that wearing the same two suits five days a week was bound to get old—not just for her, but for her coworkers, who'd think she was a charity case. That was something that hadn't really occurred to her; she was used to having uniforms for work—same thing, different day, all crisply laundered and starched, but nothing individual.

Her credit card would withstand another couple of purchases. . . . Well, barely. That last trip to Crate & Barrel hadn't been strictly necessary. When was payday for this job? Oh, yeah, not for at least two more weeks. *Damn.* She hoped the bill wouldn't come due in the meantime. *Awkward.*

"Let me get my purse," she said. She retrieved it from the desk drawer—the bag was a cheap leatherette thing, but as nice as she could afford. She hoped he wouldn't look too closely, or judge too harshly. He seemed *very* well tailored, the kind of man who paid attention to designer labels and the little details. She'd never really been like that. If her shoes were cheap and made in China, well, so what, who cared . . . but she could already see that her attitude was going to have to change about such things. Permanently. She thought she'd left all that spit-and-polish crap behind her, but she should have known; once in the army, always in the army. This was just an army that wore business suits, and her new CO was almost certainly going to turn out to be a total pain in the ass.

They nearly always did.

Getting out of the funeral home was a shock, because Bryn still hadn't gotten used to the beauty of being *home*. Well, not *home* home—her family lived in the not-very-scenic town of Clovis, New Mexico—but being back in the States had given her a new appreciation of how lovely it could be.

Especially southern California. It was a land of contrasts—the cool blue of the Pacific rolling into the distance, shrouded with a cloak of mist at the horizon, and the pale desert hills studded with cacti and patches of scrub trees. Stark and lovely.

Bryn couldn't believe she was living here. Couldn't believe it was her home now. It still seemed like some kind of dream; any second now, she'd wake up sweating in her uncomfortable bunk and start another day of IED Russian roulette.

No, it's real, she told herself. *This is real.* She closed her eyes and took in a deep breath of sweet, clean air—dry, warm, but not the oppressive stinging heat of Iraq.

"Bryn?" Mr. Fairview was standing at his Town Car, holding open the passenger door.

"Sorry, sir," she said. "Just enjoying the view. It's beautiful."

Fairview smiled a little, and to her eyes, it looked cynical. "It's expensive," he said. "When my great-great-grandfather built this place, I'm sure he did it for the cheap land; today, the taxes alone are ruinous." She shot him a startled glance. "Oh, not that we're hurting for money, Bryn. One thing about the dead: they just never stop coming."

That was one of the more unsettling—and yet weirdly comforting—things Bryn had ever heard.

The drive down the winding road to the restaurant in La Jolla took only ten minutes, but it seemed longer simply because of the silence in the car. Fairview, Bryn discovered, was not prone to chat. That was fine; she was used to silence—loved it, in fact. Her family life had been full of noise and chaos, and most of her college memories were of loud hall parties and stereo wars, not studying. The army, though, had introduced her to a whole new scale of what it meant to be noisy.

She'd learned to sleep through anything, when she had the chance to sleep; she'd also learned to relish the calm, cool peace of silence.

It settled between her and Fairview like the fog on the ocean.

"Here we are," he finally said, and turned the car onto La Jolla's main drag, lined with colorful shops, restaurants, and high-priced hotels. It was beautiful, in a way that most other shopping districts couldn't quite pull off. Maybe it was the sea view, since the hill sloped right down to the rocks and the gently rolling waves. Fairview expertly negotiated the narrow parking space with the big car and shut the engine off.

As he reached for the handle of his door, Bryn said, "Sir, can I ask a question?"

He glanced over at her, surprised. "Of course."

"You have relatively few employees, sir. I mean, there

are only four of us that I'm aware of; is that right? The receptionist, you, me, and—"

"Freddy," he said. "Our downstairs man. Yes."

"That's a very small crew for even a small mortuary. I'm a little concerned about our ability to cover—"

"Don't you worry; we'll do fine," he said. "We used to employ a half dozen people in your position alone, but the fact is, even though people keep dying, our business has fallen off some. More people choosing cheaper corporate-run funeral homes; you know how it is. But that doesn't mean we don't have work. Some days it'll be hectic, but I'm sure you can handle it. I outsource body pickups. That's half of the work right there."

He walked her to the door, opened it gallantly, and the maître d' showed them to a table. It was all very fancy, to Bryn's eyes: real tablecloths, crystal, fine silverware, and china plates. The waitress wore nicer shoes than she had on.

Once served, Bryn stared doubtfully down at a plate full of what looked like weeds drenched in sauce, and picked around with her fork. She decided the green stuff looked safe enough, and tried it. Like lettuce, but with spice. Not too bad. *Mom would have called it yard salad*, she thought, and almost choked on a suppressed laugh. *Ain't we grand now?*

"How's your appetizer, Bryn?" Mr. Fairview asked. He stirred a cup of coffee, making it look like the most elegant thing in the world, with carefully ordered swirls of his spoon in the small china cup, never once making any uncouth noise about it.

She swallowed and managed a smile. "Very good, sir. Thank you." She'd let him order for her, and if the salad was this weird, she had no idea what she was in for with the main course—but she'd eaten worse overseas; that much was certain. It was part of why her tastes remained so damn simple.

"I have to admit, you're the first woman I've ever hired who served in the military," he said, and nodded to the hovering, perfectly dressed waiter who waited to refill their water glasses. The whole restaurant had that hushed, whispering elegance to it that made Bryn feel every thread of her not-designer clothes and Payless shoes. There were ladies in here wearing jewelry that cost more than her annual salary. "I'm very interested to hear about your experience. You served in Iraq, I understand?"

Baghdad seemed like it wasn't in the same universe as this place, and Bryn felt a creeping sense of unreality in even tackling the topic. "I'm afraid it's not very interesting," she said, hoping he'd take the hint. She quickly took another bite of the salad. Not so bad. She could get used to it. You could get used to anything, in time.

"On the contrary, I find it fascinating that someone like you would choose to sign up during a time of war," Mr. Fairview said. "That tells me quite a bit about your character, you know."

Not so much about her character as her upbringing, Bryn imagined, but she didn't see any need to tell him about growing up poor in a family with two parents on minimum wage and six brothers and sisters, and doing it in a semirural town where aspiring to go to an Ivy League college was looked on as suspiciously elitist. Joining the military was a good, proper thing to do—even for a girl, these days—and if it paid off those expensive college bills, well, that was all right. Her brother Tate had followed in her footsteps, right into the uniform. He was a smart kid, the only smart one in the family, really. She had hopes for him.

She'd taken too long to answer, she realized, and covered it with a smile that felt shy. "You flatter me, Mr. Fairview," she said. "The army seemed like the best option to help me pay off my student loans. It trained me, showed me the world, and gave me a good start for the rest of my life." That sounded straight out of the recruiting brochures, and it said nothing at all about the sheer hell she'd gone through—the merciless and constant hazing, the blatant discrimination, the harsh conditions and constant fear of her surroundings and even of her comrades. She'd learned a lot, all right.

Mostly, she'd learned she never wanted to go to war again, and to avoid those who *did* want to.

And to keep her mouth shut about all of it.

"You're a very private person, aren't you, Bryn?" her boss asked, and she got the laser examination from those weirdly cold gray eyes again. "Not that I mind that. I like to keep things professional at the office, of course. But one more question: working with the dead and the bereaved doesn't bother you? Because I find that a number of recent entrants to the funeral home profession aren't emotionally suited to the requirements."

It seemed a weird time to be asking the question; after all, he'd already hired her. But she remembered that Fairview was known—notorious, in fact—for going through funeral directors quickly. She had the feeling that every conversation, every seemingly innocent moment, was another evaluation.

Yeah, that was relaxing. She tried to breathe and eat her salad without letting him see her discomfort.

"I don't mind the dead," she said, after she'd swallowed her bite of who knew what kind of weeds. "Bodies are just shells built of muscle and bone. They smell, and they're messy—alive or dead. But there's nothing frightening about a corpse once you get over the idea that they're . . ." She couldn't think how to put it, and then it clarified in her mind. "Once you get over the fact that you're just like them. And will be them, in the end."

"Ah," he said. She'd surprised him, apparently, or at least that was how she interpreted the quick up-and-down motion of his carefully groomed eyebrows.

She looked down at her salad and continued, more quietly. "We shouldn't ever forget that, out of respect."

"No," he agreed, in the same tone. "No, we shouldn't."

The waiter arrived and whisked away her uneaten salad, and delivered the main course. To her relief, it was some kind of chicken in sauce. Delicious. She didn't miss her PB and J at all, and when Mr. Fairview poured her a glass of wine, she let herself drink it and enjoy the rest of the meal.

She almost regretted going back to work, in fact.

I could get used to this, she thought.

Especially if she didn't have to pay the crazy expensive bill.

*   *   *

There was a second appointment for her, two hours later, in the midafternoon. It was—oddly enough—almost exactly the way Mr. Fairview had role-played it for her—a man coming in to make arrangements for his deceased brother. Only this man was a whole lot younger than Mr. Fairview—Bryn put him at around thirty—and he had a blank, closed-in face and watchful eyes that really didn't look too grief-stricken to her.

Mr. Fairview apparently had other things to do, because he just introduced the two of them and then left. *I'm flying solo*, she thought, and instead of making her nervous, it made her feel steadier.

"Mr. Fideli," she said, and shook the man's hand. "How may I assist you today?"

"My brother," he said. "He's passed away. I'm looking around for a place to hold his funeral, take care of things, you know."

There was something about Mr. Fideli, something familiar. Not him, but his type. From the close-cut hair to the straightforward way he assessed her to the way he sat alertly on the couch . . . Military, or recently cashiered out. He wasn't in uniform, but you didn't have to see the clothes to know the man. He might have seen it in her, too; she knew it showed in her straight back and the way she held herself. If he did, he didn't comment.

"I'm so sorry for your loss, sir," she said. She did a lightning-fast glimpse around to be sure her materials and tools were in the right places. They were, although Mr. Fideli didn't strike her as the type to need much in the way of tissues. "Can I offer you anything to drink? Coffee? Tea?"

"No."

Bryn cleared her throat. "May I ask how he passed . . . ?"

"What does that matter?"

"I'm afraid it does matter when it comes to suggesting options," she said. "If he was in some sort of accident, Mr. Fideli—"

"Joe," he said, and smiled at her. It was a nice smile, a real one. She found that . . . odd. Most people were a lot less at ease. "He died in the hospital. Cancer."

"I see." So no restorative work. *Damn*. "Are you think-ing of interment, or—"

"Probably cremation."

Cremation wasn't much cheaper, when it came down to it, and she immediately zeroed in on the up-selling aspect of the urns. When people found out the cremains came in a plastic bag in a cardboard box, even the most cost-conscious of them usually opted for something better.

She reached for the brochures, but Mr. Fideli did some-thing unusual—or at least, she thought it was unusual. "Be-fore we talk about that stuff," he said, "can I take a tour?"

"A tour," she repeated. "Oh, you mean of the viewing rooms?"

"To start with, sure."

She'd been planning to do that, but normally one settled on the basics up front. The order of events didn't really matter, though, and she led him out of her office, down the lush car-peted hallway, out to the viewing rooms. Two were occupied, and they looked in from the doorways on the floral displays, the coffins like centerpieces, the grieving—or the bored, or the curious—who filled the seats. She took her time demon-strating the empty room, showing him all the features avail-able, describing the services. Mr. Fideli was a silent observer, patient and unhurried. He didn't check his watch once.

When she'd run out of things to say about the viewing room, she showed him the caskets, explaining that he'd need to choose one for the viewing even if he were opting for cremation. She was angling toward the urn display when he said, unexpectedly, "Could I see downstairs?"

She blinked and checked herself. "I'm sorry?"

"You know, downstairs. I guess you do your own em-balming on the premises?" He said it without a flicker of emotion. Bryn was thrown for a second, then decided he just wanted to be sure they wouldn't truck his brother's body all over the city.

"Absolutely," she said. "We have a very fine embalming facility downstairs. State of the art." Not that she'd actually seen it herself, yet.

"So I understand." Fideli's eyes fixed on hers, and stayed there. "May I see it, please?"

You never said no to a client, so she was searching for a way to turn it around when she spotted Mr. Fairview coming out of his office. He must have seen that she needed help, because he came toward them with a confident stride and smile, extending his hand to Fideli. They shook hands, looking oh so cordial. Bryn kept her own smile with an effort as she said, "Mr. Fideli would like to view the preparation area, sir."

Mr. Fairview sent her a quick glance, then guided Mr. Fideli back into Bryn's office with one hand casually placed on their guest's shoulder. "Oh, I'm very sorry, but I'm afraid that's not possible," he said, sounding like he'd *love* to take a recently bereaved on a downstairs tour of the one place they should never go. "It's strictly off-limits to anyone but licensed personnel. Health concerns, you understand. And, of course, we wish to treat those entrusted to us with the highest order of care. That means respecting their privacy at all times."

Something strange flickered over Mr. Fideli's expression; Bryn couldn't quite catch it, but she thought it might have almost been . . . amusement? "Of course," he said. "Sorry. I was just curious. I wanted to be sure my brother would be treated right."

"Perfectly understandable," Bryn assured him, although it wasn't. "Now, let's talk about the urn you'll want. . . ."

She didn't feel that she handled it all that well, but Mr. Fairview didn't step in for the rest of the meeting, and Mr. Fideli didn't seem unhappy with it, either. She shook hands with him at the end—he was taller than she was, with a very firm handshake—and Mr. Fideli walked off with a handful of information, but no contract or commitment.

"Don't worry, my dear," Mr. Fairview said, when she closed the door and looked at him in mute guilt. "Sometimes you simply can't close the deal. Mr. Fideli is what we like to call a comparison shopper. He'll come back eventually. Usually, the first place he stops will also be his last. He just wants to satisfy himself that he isn't getting ripped off. I'd be willing to bet that his brother hasn't even passed on yet."

"Oh," she said. "Wow. That was . . . strange. They're usually more upset than that, aren't they?"

"Mr. Fideli did seem unusually self-contained. But from the way he carried himself, I would assume he is ex-military, like you. That would probably explain it." Mr. Fairview looked at his watch. "I have a four thirty set up with a Mrs. Granberry. I'd like you to take the lead on that one as well, if you don't mind."

"Yes, of course." It was four fifteen. Bryn rushed to the bathroom, fussed with her hair, and applied just a touch of lipstick. She did some deep-breathing exercises, and smiled professionally at the mirror.

There was a little too much brightness in her cheeks. She really needed to work on looking less *happy*.

Bryn was standing right beside Mr. Fairview when the front bell tinkled its mournful note, and Mrs. Granberry—a neat, dry-eyed woman with an iron distance in her eyes—came in trailing a sad-looking teenage daughter who refused to raise her head.

Mr. Fairview immediately bent his head close to Bryn's. "Here we go," he said. "Just remember: stay focused on what we're here to do. Don't let yourself get carried away on the tide of emotion."

Bryn had no idea how he could tell the difference between Mrs. Granberry and, say, Mr. Fideli from this distance, but he seemed to know what was coming.

Well, that was all right. She was prepared for anything.

Whatever Bryn had been prepared for, it wasn't this. Not raw, real, personal emotion from someone only a few years younger than she was. The girl sitting across from her was eighteen, just out of high school. Now that she'd finally raised her head, she kept staring at Bryn as if somehow, if she hoped hard enough, Bryn could make it all just go away. As if the universe would right itself again. *It doesn't work that way*, Bryn wanted to say, and she had to fight against an impulse to reach out and hold the girl's hand. She'd worked as a grief counselor, but that had been phone-bank stuff; she hadn't been there in person. She hadn't felt the personal impact of it quite this way. Her parents were both still alive, thank God; she'd never lost anyone close to her—well, except for her sister Sharon, and that wasn't the same thing at all.

Looking at this girl was like looking in a mirror and seeing the future grieving that was coming for everyone, eventually.

The mother was both easier in one way, and more difficult in another—fortyish, solid, mostly impassive except when she dabbed at her eyes as if more concerned with her mascara than her grief. "My husband wanted a frugal sort of funeral," she announced as the opening shot. Although Mr. Fairview had introduced Bryn as leading the session, Mrs. Granberry dismissed Bryn and focused on him directly. "I just want a plain coffin, nothing fancy. And no viewing. No embalming."

Bryn cleared her throat. Mrs. Granberry's eyes moved to her, then back to Mr. Fairview. "How did your husband pass?" Bryn asked, and offered Mrs. Granberry the tissue box. The woman waved it impatiently away.

"He died in his sleep," she said. "Bad heart. I always told him it would do him in, but he never listened." For some reason, she then glared at her daughter, as if it were somehow the girl's fault. The girl flinched and looked down. "I don't know what that has to do with anything."

"It's very helpful to family members and friends if you hold a viewing; it gives everyone a chance to say their good-byes. Gives them a sense of closure," Bryn said. "We would, of course, make your husband look just as you want to remember him; it's part of our full service—"

Mrs. Granberry's head snapped around, and her eyes narrowed in sudden fury. "I said *no embalming*!"

Bryn took a deep breath. "Mrs. Granberry, I know you're very upset right now, but the fact is that embalming is a state requirement, unless you choose cremation."

"It is?" The woman looked at Mr. Fairview, who nodded soberly.

"I'm afraid so," he said. "Miss Davis is quite correct. The only exception to this would be if your religious beliefs did not allow embalming."

"Oh." The mother frowned at Bryn, as if the rule were her personal fault. "Well, we're Methodist; I don't suppose that counts for anything these days. All right, fine. I suppose if we have to go to that much expense, we should have the viewing too. How much?"

"Mom," the girl said faintly. "Please. This is about *Dad*. You're not buying a car."

"I know it's about your precious daddy, but if you want to go to that fancy school next fall and have clothes on your back, you'd better let me do this my way, Melissa!" There was real anger in that sharp, vicious tone. Bryn felt its snap even from the sidelines.

Melissa was shaking all over. Bryn had to bite her lip to stop herself from saying something that wouldn't be funeral-director appropriate to the mother, but despite her control, her tone dropped a few degrees in warmth. "We'll work with you to make it affordable," she said. "Let's take a look at some choices."

When she opened the binder that showed the coffin selections, and asked the delicate question, "Was your husband a large man?" Melissa Granberry burst into hysterical tears and ran out of the room. For a moment, Bryn was frozen in shock; then she looked at Mrs. Granberry, who was stone-faced and dry-eyed.

"My husband was a fat, sloppy frog," she said. "Don't mind my daughter. She brought him a bowl of ice cream yesterday, which definitely was *not* on his diet. She thinks she killed him. And she probably did, too. She always was his pet."

Bryn's palm itched to make contact with the woman's cheek. Instead, she managed a forced, artificial smile. "I'm sure you'll talk with her about that," she said. "Obviously, it wasn't her fault."

"No?" Mrs. Granberry stared at her for so long it felt like ice picks were driving into Bryn's head, and then she turned her attention to the coffins. "I like this one."

Fortunately, it was one of the more expensive plus-size models. *Up-sell.*

It was a very long hour's consultation.

While Mr. Fairview got the paperwork together, Bryn fought down the urge to smack the ever-loving *shit* out of

Mrs. Granberry. She excused herself and went to wash her hands and calm herself in the ladies' room—where she found Melissa.

To be accurate, she didn't find her at first—she saw the stain, trickling in red streams toward the drain in the center of the floor. *Nail polish*, she thought first, very irrationally, and then her military mind said, *Blood. Still fresh.*

The second of shock snapped with a physical sensation of electricity burning through her nerves.

Bryn banged on the closed stall door at the end. "Melissa!" No answer. Bryn slammed her shoulder into the metal door, but it didn't open. She tried again, then braced herself against the wall and kicked, hard.

The lock gave way, and the bathroom door slammed back. Melissa Granberry was propped on the toilet, leaning against the wall. Her eyes were open, still damp, and tears still stained her cheeks. Her skin had the awful, ashen look of the corpses lying in the prep room one floor below.

She'd slashed deep, all down the interior aspect of both arms, and finished it off with a deep cut to her left wrist. Couldn't do the right, Bryn thought with a cold, precise kind of clarity, because she'd cut the tendons in her left hand. It didn't really matter; she'd done the job well. The knife—a small folding thing, a man's pocketknife with a deer on the handle—lay in a shimmering pool of blood between Melissa's feet.

Bryn lunged forward, grabbed the girl, and put her on the floor. She leaned on both of the girl's arms, applying pressure with both her hands. "Medic!" she yelled, and then remembered. "Help! I need help in here!"

Melissa's pupils were already wide, and she showed no reaction at all. Bryn didn't feel any sign of a pulse, no matter how hard she pressed.

It seemed to take forever, but it probably didn't; the receptionist came running, then Mr. Fairview. Mrs. Granberry's stony calm finally shattered; she began screaming and had to be taken away. Eventually, there was an ambulance, and people in uniform, and Bryn was shuffled off to the back to stand helplessly as they loaded Melissa up on a gurney and wheeled her away.

It all seemed like some surreal nightmare. And at the same time, it was all weirdly familiar. She'd seen a fair number of loaded gurneys, after all.

The receptionist, Lucy, helped her wash up in the men's room, chattering all the while about how she'd once found a man who'd shot himself in a viewing room, and wasn't it funny how that didn't happen more often in this kind of business, where people were running on adrenaline and grief?

Bryn didn't really feel much. She supposed it was shock more than anything else; she'd seen plenty of dead and dying before, but not like this. Not in such antiseptic surroundings. Someone—Mr. Fairview?—brought her a nice hand-knitted afghan and sat her in one of the viewing rooms, pressed a glass of whiskey in her hands, and left her alone.

Bryn couldn't get it out of her head—the girl's dark, pleading eyes, her sobs, her guilt. She sipped the whiskey but didn't really taste it, even though she hated the stuff, and then all of a sudden it came through to her with absolute, crystalline clarity.

Melissa Granberry was going nowhere but to the morgue, and eventually she'd end up downstairs in the prep room, just like her father.

I could have done something. I could have stopped it. She was just a kid.

Bryn put the whiskey down on the side table and began to cry in helpless, silent sobs.

Mr. Fairview was right. The tissues were in just the right place when she needed them.

Chapter 2

"I've got to hand it to you, honey," said Lucy several hours later. They'd been interviewed by the police, Bryn had been escorted to the locker room to shower and change, and then there had been more whiskey, because Lucy had said she needed it. Bryn supposed it did make things better, or at least less connected to what she was feeling. "That was one *hell* of a bad first day. Worst I've ever seen. Good news is, it can only go up from here, right?"

"Right," Bryn said. She felt comfortably numb now—not peaceful, just not feeling much of anything. She especially could not feel hope for a better tomorrow.

"Then I think it's time for you to go on home. Hot bath, more wine, maybe get a massage." Lucy wheeled her chair back from the reception desk and pulled a Givenchy purse from the bottom drawer. She was a gorgeous woman with flawless dark cocoa skin, and she was generously curved in ways that shouldn't have looked good but did, especially the way she dressed. Bryn wondered how much time she spent every day on the carefully lacquered updo of her hair. Probably more time than Bryn spent all week, added together, getting her own ready. "You going to be all right on your own this evening?"

"I . . . Sure." In truth, Bryn didn't really know, but she *wanted* to be okay. "I'm going to talk to Mr. Fairview, finish up some paperwork. And I'm supposed to introduce myself to Mr. Watson in the prep room."

"Oh, don't let Mr. Fairview catch you calling it that. It's *preparation* room, always." Lucy's friendly expression took on a sharper edge. "My advice is, if you have to say hi to Fast Freddy, do it tomorrow. And whenever you go down there, you watch it with him. That man is trouble; I told Lincoln that from the day he was hired on. We used to have a great restoration man, a real artist. His name was Vikesh, but he moved off to Arizona. Now we got Fast Freddy. I have to tell you, I am not impressed. I saw Mrs. Salzman's viewing last week—I swear, it looked like she was on her way out to pick up sailors at the dock. No class, that man."

Bryn tried for a smile. "I'm pretty sure I've met worse."

"You may think so, but he's a slimy little shit, I don't mind telling you." Lucy gazed at her a moment, clearly undecided. "You got your car here, honey?"

"I took the bus. But it's okay; the last one runs in a couple of hours. I don't want to go home just yet anyway. I need to walk off the Scotch a little."

"Well, okay. And don't you worry about tomorrow. One thing about this business—it's steady. Every day, you get different sad people with the same sad stories. Sooner or later, you get used to it." Lucy reached over and patted her hand, a quick, impersonal little gesture. "You take care, Bryn. I like you. Hope you stick around."

The office felt really empty with Lucy gone. Bryn walked the hushed paneled hallways back to her office and found that Mr. Fairview had left the Granberry folder neatly in the center of her desk. She signed all the paperwork, filled out the cost sheets, and made a list of to-do items before setting it aside.

Fairview had also left a sticky note on the folder that read, *Don't forget to brief Freddy downstairs about the arrangements for Mr. Granberry; he needs to know as soon as possible.*

It was the last thing she had to do. Easy enough to pick up the phone—it had a clearly marked extension labeled PREPARATION ROOM—but she felt that she ought to get the lay of the land down there. She was already having the worst day of her life. . . . She might as well get the slimy Mr. Watson out of the way, if the introduction was going to come.

That way, tomorrow there would be nothing she had left to dread.

There were two realities in all funeral homes—the public space, which was all beautifully appointed and quiet and comforting, and the prep areas, which were medical and sterile and cold. The stairs going down were sort of a transition between the two—still carpeted, but with an industrial metal railing and an institutional fluorescent light fixture overhead. The bottom floor was all Formica, easily cleaned. There was a freight elevator in the back, and down the hall seemed to be storage and rolled-down loading-dock doors. Bryn stopped outside the frosted-glass door of the prep room. She breathed shallowly; the smell of embalming fluids always made her a little queasy at first, until she adjusted to it. The ever-present smell of decay was just the cherry on top. She knocked on the door, a hesitant rap of knuckles. She could see shadows moving inside.

"Come in," someone said, and she entered. There were four spotlessly clean stainless-steel preparation tables in the room, each with all the pumps and tubing necessary to the embalming process. Only one was occupied at the moment—Mr. Granberry, fat as a frog. He really wasn't that fat, Bryn thought. And he had a nice face. She was mildly religious, and she hoped that wherever Mr. Granberry was, he could comfort his daughter now. Poor Melissa.

Standing over Mr. Granberry's corpse, massaging fluids through his tissues, was a handsome guy only a little older than Bryn. . . . Golden hair, creamy skin, big blue eyes, and a devastating smile. Except for what he was doing at the moment, he was completely smoking hot.

The smile put her on guard. It was just a little too predatory.

"Hey," he said, jerking his chin up in welcome. "Bryn, right? Just a sec. Got to finish this; I'm almost done. He's pinking up okay, don't you think?"

She nodded, not sure she knew what to say, except, "You're Mr. Watson?"

"Fast Freddy, they call me," he said, and winked. "Don't

let it bother you. Everybody in this industry's got a nick-name, right?"

"Do they? I don't think I do," she said. She felt faintly ill, and she wasn't sure coming down here was a good idea, given the day she'd had. Her head was spinning a little from the drinks.

"I think you got one today," he said. "Double Trouble Davis."

"Oh. You heard?"

"About the girl? Of course I heard. It only *looks* like a cave down here. I don't actually live in one." He shook his head, and she expected the normal platitudes—*what a shame*, or *she must have been so distraught.* "What a dumb-ass bitch."

Bryn blinked. "Excuse me?"

"Look, well-adjusted people don't go offing themselves messily in funeral home restrooms. If she wants to take the easy way out, fine. I'm not standing in her way, but if she was going to do it, the least she could have done was do it at her own home, not our place of business. Now we're the ones stuck cleaning it up. Trust me. She was a selfish little bitch."

It wasn't so much what he said as *how* he said it that made her muscles go tense and quiet; Freddy looked ripe, but there was something rotten in the relish he took in diss-ing the dead girl. It was like biting into a juicy red apple and getting a mouthful of worms. "Her name was Melissa. And she was only *eighteen.*"

"Old enough to vote, fuck, and know better," Freddy said, and shrugged. "Like I said, she was a selfish bitch. End of story. So, you got any orders on Mr. Granberry, here?"

Freddy's callousness reminded her of some of the sol-diers she'd served with, the ones who'd lost all feelings of humanity, especially for the Iraqis, whom they saw as walk-ing meat ready for body bags.

She'd tried to avoid those people. Hadn't always been successful. And here was another one, thrown right in her path. "Yes," she said, grateful for the opportunity to deliver the paperwork and escape. She handed over the folder, which he took in his latex-gloved left hand as he continued his gentle massage of the former Mr. Granberry with his right, working the embalming fluid through his chest. "Thanks. See you tomorrow."

"Oh, man, you're going to dump and run? Not cool, Double Trouble. The least you can do is help me out, here. I've been stuck all alone in the dead room for days; I'm starved for the company of a pretty woman." He flashed that brilliant smile at her again. "You've had enough of all this shit, I'll bet. Tell you what. Instead of me giving you the grand tour of the freezers, how about going out for a drink, or preferably lots of drinks? Could be your lucky night." With one last squeeze of Mr. Granberry's puffy biceps, Freddy stepped back and peeled off his blue gloves, which he three-pointed into a biohazard bin. His plastic apron followed, leaving him in a lab coat with neatly pressed jeans showing beneath, and some shoes that Bryn was almost sure were Kenneth Cole, or at least that expensive. "Unless you want to spend the evening with Mr. Gran, here. I mean, he's not much of a talker, but he's working a nice after-death stiffy right now. You want to see?"

"No." Bryn tried to keep her voice even, her gaze straight. She had the eerie impression that Freddy was one of those men who would go for the slightest sign of weakness. "I'll be going now."

"So you didn't get into the business for the cold ones? Some do, you know. Lucky you, then. I'm nice and warm." He winked at her, and Bryn wanted to throw up. "Right, it's drinks, then. We'll see about what comes after."

Bryn took a step back as Freddy rounded the end of the embalming table, suddenly aware of everything—the chilly temperature of the room, the deserted mortuary, the fact that the alcohol had led her into what could be a *very* bad decision. "No. Thanks. Really, I was just . . . on my way out."

"Going home to what? A single-serving frozen dinner and a twin bed? You don't look like a woman with a boyfriend—at least, not a boyfriend who's keeping you satisfied, and I can always tell. So how about that drink? You can tell me all about how lonely you are."

Bryn was shaken, not that she'd let him see it. "Take no

for an answer, Freddy. You ought to know the word by now. I'm sure you hear it enough."

"Ouch." He seemed more amused than hurt. "Look, I don't really want to be seen in public with you either; you're not exactly up to my usual standards. So how about a quickie down here? Nobody here but Mr. Granberry; I don't think he'd mind. I could break out the wine coolers."

"If you come near me with a *wine cooler*, I hope you go both ways, because I will shove it up your ass." Bryn walked for the door, half expecting him to grab her and throw her to the floor, but when she looked back Freddy was still standing there, smiling at her.

"Don't know what you're missing," he said. "When you're ready for a good time, you know where to find me, sweetheart. You're welcome down here anytime." He blew her a kiss.

Bryn didn't even remember going up the stairs, or going into her office—only the slamming of the door let her know that there was a solid oak surface between her and Fast Freddy. She shuddered, locked the door, and backed off to collapse into her office chair. "Ugh, ugh, ugh," she said, and dropped her head into her hands. "Now I *really* need a shower." She'd met guys like him, of course. Lots of them. It came with the territory of working in a tradition-ally male area. And she'd learned to deal with them. She just hadn't quite expected to have to do it *here*, in *civiliza-tion*.

And not at the end of a miserable first day.

After taking a few dozen deep, calming breaths, she stripped off her lab coat and retrieved her purse from the drawer of her desk. *So* time to go home. Maybe Lucy had been right—a glass of wine and a massage—but if she couldn't get the massage, at least a glass of wine, a movie, something to take her mind off of things.

Bryn jerked at the sound of a thunderously loud knock on the door. "Hey, girl? You still here? Come out! Come out!"

She hadn't turned her fluorescent office light on, so as long as she kept quiet, Freddy wouldn't know she was there. Hopefully.

She could hear him breathing. There was something *very* creepy about that.

Finally, he muttered, "Man, you are one cold bitch," and she heard him walking away. She held her breath until she heard what sounded like the front door slamming, and then went to the window to look out. Carefully.

Freddy drove a silver sports car, and she watched him climb inside and drive away in a squeal of tires. *Oh, thank God.*

Just her, then. Her and the late Mr. Granberry downstairs.

She bet Freddy hadn't bothered to put him in the refrigerator. That seemed like the kind of slap-dash asshole move he'd pull.

Bryn unlocked the prep room door and turned on the lights, and yes, she was right: Freddy had left poor Mr. Granberry naked on the table. It was cold in the room, but not cold enough to properly retard decomposition . . . and besides, it was just disrespectful, leaving the poor man there exposed and alone.

Bryn walked over and looked down at his face. Bodies didn't scare her—never had, really. They were a sad remnant of a life already gone by the time she saw them like this—an impermanent memorial, melting like paper in water. Everybody—and every *body*—had a story. She supposed Mr. Granberry's was kind of tragic, given his wife and what had happened with his daughter, but he didn't look especially tragic—just absent.

"I'm sorry," she said, and put her hand on his cheek. He felt cool and utterly lifeless, like a rubber doll left outside in winter. "Take care of Melissa, wherever you guys are. I don't think she meant to hurt anybody. She just didn't want to live with all the pain. I'm sure she really loved you."

Talking to the dead was always useless. Mr. Granberry didn't hear, didn't feel, didn't care. But Bryn felt better for having said it, and that was really the point.

"Time to go to your room." Bryn spread a clean white sheet over him, then removed the brakes from the wheels and rolled his table into the walk-in refrigerator. "Sleep

tight, Mr. G. I promise we'll do our best for you. Oh, look—
you've got a friend." Mr. G had a neighbor, it seemed—
another body, still zipped in a dark plastic cocoon. She
supposed it was a late arrival from a hospital or the coro-
ner's office.

As she closed the door on him, she could have sworn
she heard something. Bryn paused, holding her breath,
but she heard nothing now but the hum of machinery. She
couldn't help but think of poor Mr. Granberry sitting up on
his tray. Corpses sometimes did that sort of thing. It wasn't
anything to do with zombies; it was just muscles contract-
ing. It seemed creepy, but it was just . . . biology.

Although biology could be pretty damn creepy, when
you came right down to it.

She looked inside, but nothing seemed to have changed.
As she swung the door shut, she heard it again. A faint
sound, but definite.

Kind of a scratching.

"Rats," she said, and shuddered. She'd have to tell Mr.
Fairview. The last thing any mortuary needed was a rodent
problem. That would get them shut down quickly, and ruin
their reputation forever.

Bryn clicked off the lights decisively and walked out the
doors, locking them behind her.

She was halfway up the stairs when the door at the top
opened. She was caught—nowhere to go. All she could do
was stand there and look alarmed. Of course, Fast Freddy
had come back . . . and this time, he had her where he
wanted her.

No . . . As the shock faded and her eyes adjusted, she realized that the man standing at the top of the steps wasn't
Fast Freddy, or Lincoln Fairview. For a second she couldn't
place him at all, and then she remembered.

It was the man who'd come earlier today to talk about
his brother's arrangements. Joe. Joe Fideli.

He lifted a finger to his lips, a clear shushing motion, and
Bryn took a step backward, slowly.

Mr. Fideli raised a pistol. Not just a Saturday-night
special—no, this looked like a very serious professional
semiauto. Not military issue, but a similar model, and just

as good. She raised her hands in mute surrender. Mr. Fideli gestured her down the stairs. She slowly went, feeling for each step as she took it backward.

Once she was at floor level, there still weren't many options. The elevator and loading-dock doors were closed, and she didn't know the maze of basement storage at the other end well enough to count on another exit. Still, she had the crazy impulse to run—but there was something about running into the dark that stopped her.

Well, that and the fact that she thought Mr. Fideli was probably a crack shot.

"It's Miss Davis, right? You're not supposed to be here," Mr. Fideli said. "Sorry. I don't mean to scare you, but I'm going to need you to do what I say for a while."

He sounded like he meant it. He also sounded completely different from the buttoned-up, blankly inquisitive man who'd been sitting across from her this morning. He was kind of relaxed, as if this were his job, and he was very, very good at it.

Also, she supposed an unarmed, first-day-on-the-job funeral director probably didn't pose much of a threat.

"What are you doing here?" Bryn demanded. Her voice was shaking, so it spoiled the confrontational words, but Mr. Fideli just raised his eyebrows and ignored the question anyway.

"Anybody else here I need to know about?" he asked. "Fairview? Freddy Watson? Lucy?"

He knew everybody's name. That was . . . strange. Bryn shook her head.

"Okay." He stared at her for a long second, and she sensed he was making some kind of decision. It might have been about her own life and death. "Upstairs. Let's have a seat in your office and talk. Might as well be comfortable."

She led the way, terribly aware of the gun he was aiming at her back; she supposed some movie action hero would have been able to spin around, roundhouse-kick the gun out of his hand, and martial-arts him into blubbering submission. She'd been through extensive unarmed combat training, and she knew that in no way was that a good idea.

Bryn lived in the real world, and in the real world, you followed a gunman's instructions, and waited for any opportunity that wouldn't get you shot.

Once they were in her office, Mr. Fideli locked the door and sat down in the guest chair opposite her desk with a relieved sigh. When she hesitated, he gestured with his free hand for her to take the chair behind the desk. She did, making no sudden movements.

"Long day," he said. She nodded. *You've got no idea, mister.* "So. You weren't on my briefing paper. I'm guessing you're the new hire?"

"Today's my first day," she said.

"Well, you picked a honey of a time to start, Bryn. Mind if I call you Bryn?"

"Mind if I call you Joe? If that's even your name?" She felt a little better sitting down. A little more in control.

"Sure. And yeah, it's my name."

"Do you even *have* a brother?"

"Had," he said, and tilted his head slightly, still watching her. "How the hell old are you, anyway?"

"Twenty-six."

"Damn. You ought to be an actress; you could do those teen shows. You look sixteen."

Bryn ground her teeth and said nothing. She was *so* tired of people assuming she was high school age. She supposed when she was forty, she'd be grateful for the baby face, but up to now it had been a total pain in the ass.

Probably not the most important thing on the radar at the moment, from a macro point of view.

"Anyway," Fideli said, "I'm just here to do some reconnaissance. You know what that means?"

He clearly didn't know her past. "Check out the lay of the land."

"Ding. I wasn't planning on running into anybody. Where's your car?"

"I don't have one. I ride the bus."

"No shit. Is that one of those save-the-planet things, or I'm-too-poor-to-afford-it things?"

"Both. Mostly the latter, honestly." Sadly.

"Well, good for you, I guess. Bad for me, though.

Tougher for me to get you out of here." Fideli fell silent, staring at her.

She felt compelled to say something. "What do you want? We don't have a lot here that's worth taking, if that's what this is about. I mean, the furniture, maybe, but—"

"I'm not a thief."

"Well, there's not a load of opportunity for industrial espionage in this business," she said. It was a joke, but he didn't smile. His eyes certainly didn't. "What did you want in the prep room?" *Preparation,* Bryn remembered, too late. *Fairview always wanted to be formal about it with the customers.* Not that Mr. Fideli was shaping up to be a customer, after all.

"I'm supposed to find out if Mr. Fairview and Fast Freddy are running drugs," he said. "Prescription drugs. Stolen."

"*What?* Of course not!"

"No offense, but you're what, a day into this job? How would you know?"

"This is a successful business. Why would they do something so stupid?" Then again, she'd met Freddy. And she wouldn't put anything past him. "Unless—maybe it's not Mr. Fairview? Just Freddy?"

Fideli's head came back upright, and there was a new tension in his body. "You know something about the guy?"

"Not that much. Just . . . he's a creep. You know the type."

"Explain it to me."

"He came on to me. Downstairs."

"Romantic."

"Exactly." She cleared her throat. "Look, I'm not Wonder Woman—do you think you could put the gun down?"

"What?" He seemed genuinely surprised, and then smiled. "Yeah. I already went through the drawers of your desk. Just in case you had a thirty-eight-caliber surprise in there. So I guess you're safe enough."

She was startled. "When did you do that?"

"While you were downstairs." His gaze shifted, and the easy friendliness disappeared instantly. "Hold up. Don't move." She didn't. He got up and went to the window, looking without moving the blinds. "You know of any reason why your boss and Freddy would come back here after hours tonight?"

"No."

"Well, they're parking cars right now." Fideli backed up next to her, and the gun made an unpleasant reappearance. "Not a word, Miss Davis."

"You're not going to kill me, are you?"

"Why would I do that?"

"Because you're the one with the gun?"

He looked at it. "This old thing? Family heirloom. I hardly ever shoot anybody with it." He was lying, but he was doing it with style and a sense of humor, and whether she wanted to or not, she felt a little bit better about being held hostage. "You'll be quiet?"

"Absolutely."

He sent her a sassy wink, which wasn't nearly as creepy as when Fast Freddy did it. "Good girl."

Fideli moved to the closed door and listened with great concentration—but still keeping an eye on her; she was sure about that. Bryn didn't move. Straining her ears, she heard the front door opening and the door chime faintly making the announcement. Then nothing. Soundproofing worked in bad ways, too.

Fideli, however, had heard something she hadn't. "They're heading downstairs," he said. "Okay, let's get you out of here, miss."

"Excuse me?"

"No place for bystanders right now. Up and out."

Not that waiting in the dark for the bus was going to be her favorite thing, either. "Can't I just wait here? You know, until you're, ah, done?" Whatever that might mean.

"No," he said. "Get your stuff, Bryn."

The kinder Joe Fideli was gone again, replaced by one highly mission-focused. She got her purse and coat and followed him as he cat-footed it down the hall to the lobby door.

She grabbed his arm. "The bell!" she whispered. "They'll hear it!"

"You've got reason to be here, and reason to be leaving," he whispered back. "Play it cool, whatever they do. Just pretend like everything's normal, and leave. Go catch your bus."

Then he opened the door, the bell dinged, and he disappeared into the shadows, moving so fast that Bryn was left standing there, openmouthed, with the door swinging back shut against her outstretched hand.

Nowhere to go but out.

Bryn didn't get far. She was less than ten feet from the door when she heard the muffled chime of the bell again, and looked over her shoulder to see Mr. Fairview standing there.

"Bryn," he said, still using that soothing working-hours voice. "Well. This is a surprise. We thought you'd already left, especially after the day you've had."

"I got caught up in reading over the materials. There're a lot of things to learn. I'm sorry if I broke any rules. . . . I'm not putting in for overtime, I promise."

She felt nervous, and she knew he could see it—but hopefully, he'd put it down to the natural uneasiness of a new employee caught doing something slightly odd, and *God*, how had she gotten herself into this, anyway? Working with the dead was supposed to be *peaceful*. That was the whole point.

The silence seemed to stretch on. Bryn felt sweat break out under her arms. She had a choice to make—tell Fairview about Joe Fideli's quiet infiltration, or stay quiet and risk being wrong about him. *He's a man with a gun, skulking around at night. You should tell Fairview*.

And she would have . . . except that he said, "Did you go into the preparation room after Mr. Watson left tonight, Bryn?"

"Why?"

"We have a silent alarm that operates when we're off premises. To prevent any, ah, tampering with the bodies. I've turned it off now, since we're here." Fairview's eyes were in shadow, his face rendered into a blank mask by the lighting in the parking lot. There was nothing in his voice, either, but Bryn's instincts screamed that there was something wrong. Very wrong.

"I realized that Freddy left Mr. Granberry out on the table," she said. "I just went in to put him in the freezer. I hope I didn't do anything wrong. I do have the keys. Nobody told me the area was off-limits."

"Oh, it's not—not normally, of course. I was just concerned, based on the alarm." Fairview smiled. "Why don't you come on back inside, my dear? It's chilly out here at night, and the fog's coming in."

He was right; she was shivering, and the gray mist had rolled over the coast and faded out the lights of the town in the distance. Even the bus-stop lights seemed smeared and indistinct.

"I need to get home," she said. "The last bus is on the way any moment."

"Oh, no need to worry about that," Fairview said. "I'll drive you home, Bryn. But come back inside; have some coffee. I have something I need to discuss with you first."

She swallowed. The night felt dark, deep, and icily empty; she was fifty feet from the bus stop, but the shelter was empty at this hour, and although there were cars going by on the road, they weren't going to notice anything happening here. Running seemed stupid. At best, it would let him know she suspected something was going on inside; at worst, at least Joe Fideli was somewhere nearby, with his gun.

She wasn't sure why, but she felt that she trusted Fideli more than the man who'd hired her. The man she'd admired so much for his compassion and composure just this morning. Standing here in the chilly dark, watching his face, she thought he might be more of a killer than the guy with the gun.

The thought of lying cold on one of those trays robbed her of the will to run—not that there was anywhere to go; the bus wasn't even in view. She stayed where she was as Mr. Fairview descended the steps and came toward her. He took her arm and escorted her back into the mortuary.

"Nothing to worry about," he said, still using that soothing professional tone. "I just want to explain about some of our procedures, Bryn. You're in no trouble, I promise. If you'd wait in your office for a bit, I have to meet with someone else first. I'll come right up, and after we've talked I'll give you a ride home. I hate making you wait out there in the dark. It's just not safe."

"Okay," she said. This was a really bad idea, but she couldn't think of anything else to do except go along with him. Mr. Fairview hustled her, quietly and irresistibly, back into the mortuary and down the hall to her office. She fumbled with the keys and opened it, and Mr. Fairview gave her a reassuring smile.

"Just a few minutes," he assured her, and closed the door. She listened, but couldn't hear a thing . . . and then she heard his footsteps on the stairs leading down to the basement.

I really need to get out of here. Whatever the hell was going on, it wasn't her business. Not at all. In fact, Bryn decided then and there that she was officially quitting. She could get another job, and she could get it at some big-city mortuary where there were lots of people coming and going.

Someplace *sane*.

She was heading for the door when the bell rang, and a new person came in the front. Bryn ducked into the shadows, holding her breath, and a man and woman she didn't know walked into the foyer. The woman didn't look well; she was sweating, trembling, and had to be supported as she moved. *Terminally ill? Maybe a late-night consultation?*

The couple went straight for the basement stairs. Bryn frowned, watching them, and then looked at the front door. It was like Grand Central; one more bell ringing wouldn't matter now, right? And she could just run. Run like hell, flag down a car, get out of here . . .

Except now she was curious. Deeply curious. Was Fideli right? Were they running some kind of drug lab down there? Fairview had talked about how trade had fallen off. She supposed he'd do almost anything to keep the family business going.

She walked over to the basement door and eased it open a crack. Just to listen. The problem was, although she could hear voices, they weren't very loud, and she missed more than half of what was being said.

She came out onto the landing.

Down a couple of steps, very quietly.

Then all the way down, drawn by what the voices were saying.

"...need it!" a man's voice was saying. Not Freddy or Mr. Fairview, or even Joe...She was hearing the man who'd come in with the sick lady, Bryn guessed. "I know that's not the amount we agreed on, but it's all we have; please, she needs the shot right now...."

"This isn't a charity hospital, Mr. Jones," Mr. Fairview's voice said, rich with regret and sympathy. "I'm afraid that miracles are, by their very definition, rare—and rare means expensive. The terms were spelled out for you clearly, weren't they? Ten thousand up front, and five hundred dollars cash per shot?"

"I can get it for you; it's just ... it's thirty-five hundred a week...."

"Thirty-five hundred a week to keep your beloved wife alive," Mr. Fairview said. "I have to believe that you value her life more than the money, sir. And I must urge you to act quickly. She's clearly missed at least one dose, possibly two, and she is looking very distressed. After four days, the skin begins to slip; muscles loosen. It's a very nasty process."

Bryn couldn't quite believe what she was hearing. Joe Fideli had been right: her boss *was* selling drugs—bad ones. And they were extorting money from sick, desperate people.

It was *horrible*.

"I'm very sorry," Mr. Fairview continued. "But I really must have cash in hand before I can give her the shot. This was made clear to you from the very beginning."

"I lost my job," the man said. It sounded like he was crying. "I can't ... We already had to give up our house. I can't afford to pay you this much. Please. Please don't let her die! We've got *kids*!"

There was a second of silence. "I'm afraid that even though we talked about this, you still don't understand. She's *dead*, Mr. Jones. We haven't made her living. I explained to you that you were simply delaying the inevitable dissolution, and now it appears that the inevitable is upon you."

Not only were they selling some hard-core drug; they were bilking people. How could Fairview possibly be telling people he was bringing back the dead? Who'd believe that? Maybe the drug induced some kind of coma, then woke up the addicts. . . . It didn't really matter. Bryn felt deeply sickened. She'd been trained to *help* people in their darkest, worst moments, and this was an obscene, horrible perversion of what she'd believed. A betrayal of the worst kind.

She turned to go back up the steps, but a shadow blocked her path at the top of the stairs. She had a moment of déjà vu, but it wasn't Joe Fideli.

It was, unfortunately, Freddy Watson.

He descended the stairs faster than she could scramble backward, and grabbed her by the arm in a crushing grip. She tried to knee him in the groin, but he was obviously an old hand at that one; her patella caught the meaty part of his thigh instead, and then he was shoving her off balance, turning her, and locking his arm around her throat. She tried to stamp on his feet, but her Payless heels weren't that sturdy. He just laughed in her ear and dragged her, off balance, through the double doors into the prep room.

"Surprise visitor," he said, and it obviously was, to the three people standing there. Mr. and Mrs. Jones, and Mr. Fairview.

Mr. Fairview looked wearily disgusted. "I left her upstairs. And, Freddy, I thought you were supposed to scare her off from snooping around down here."

"I did," Freddy said. "I played the Big Bad Wolf as hard as I could, but she's tougher than she looks. I caught her listening on the stairs."

"Really? What did you hear, Bryn?" Mr. Fairview asked.

"Nothing," she said, and tried to jam her elbow back into Freddy's ribs. That worked well enough that he let up on the grip, and she slipped away and put the prep table between them. "He attacked me!"

"Yes, well, he does have impulse-control issues," Mr. Fairview said. "It's the reason I can't have him doing intakes. He doesn't inspire confidence in others. And I don't believe you, Bryn."

"You *saw—*"

"Not about the attack; about what you overheard. You did hear something. The question is what, and how much you understand."

On the second prep table, Mr. Fairview had a leather case open, with a small bottle of some injectable drug nestled in padding, along with a syringe.

Mr. Jones was taking advantage of Bryn's entrance to edge closer and closer to it. Now he grabbed the case, ripped the cap off the syringe, and quickly filled the chamber from the vial of liquid.

Mr. Fairview slapped it out of his hand. The syringe skittered across the floor, and Mr. Fairview stepped on it, cracking the plastic and leaving a wet smear on the tile floor as the drug leaked out.

Then he took out a gun from a drawer next to him and aimed it at Mr. Jones's chest, and pulled the trigger three times, the booms shockingly loud in the tiled room.

Before Mr. Jones fell, Bryn bolted for the door. Freddy grabbed her and pressed her up against the wall just as Mr. Jones hit the tile floor, light already fading from his wide, surprised eyes. His wife cried out and dropped down next to him, but after a second of horrified staring, she scrabbled for the vial of the drug held loosely in his dead hand.

Mr. Fairview scooped it neatly away. "Freddy," he said. "Stop playing with the new girl and take care of all this mess, please."

"Yes, boss." Freddy let go of Bryn and hit her. Hard. She saw darkness and flaming stars, and the world tilted sideways on her.

Cold floor.

By the time she got her eyes open again, Freddy was at the shelves. He yanked open a drawer and pulled out two body bags. Then, after a glance at Bryn, he added a third.

He unrolled the first one on the floor, dragged Mr. Jones over, and zipped him inside.

Bryn scrambled in slow motion to her feet, fought for balance, and staggered for the door, but Mr. Fairview was already there, and the sight of the gun made her slow and stop. She knew he'd shoot her.

She'd already seen the proof.

"How much do you know?" Fairview asked her. "Who are you working for?"

"I don't know what you're talking about! *Let me go!*" Her heart was hammering. Fear screamed at her to stay still, but she knew fear was going to get her killed. She needed to go back to her training. She needed to *think*. She had no idea what had happened to Joe Fideli, but if he hadn't already shown up, she had no reason to think he'd come riding to the rescue in time to save her now.

Freddy finished zipping Mr. Jones into his storage bag, and then unrolled a second one. Bryn caught her breath as he grabbed Mrs. Jones by the arm and dragged her over onto the plastic. The woman slapped at him weakly, but she just couldn't fight back.

He was zipping her into the body bag, *still alive.*

"No!" Bryn blurted, and lunged toward them to let the woman out. Freddy punched her, a true, no-holds-barred impact that sent another wave of blackness over her in a sticky, cold flood. She stayed upright somehow, and raised her fingers to her mouth. They came away bloody.

And just like that, her training came back to her, like a ghost returning to her body. The fear went away and the pain got blocked. She altered her balance, wishing for body armor, for boots, for a knife and a gun and all the things she didn't have. Then she let that fall away.

She'd manage.

Freddy's eyes were cold and avid. "She's not like you thought. Look at her. She's a fighter."

"I can see that, Freddy."

"I'm going to have to kill her."

Fairview sighed. "I really can't keep replacing people. It's just impossible, the recruiting fees; you have no idea."

"So don't replace her," Freddy said. "Kill her and give her the shot. She'll be just as reliable as I am, after. Bonus points—you get to have special fun with her, too."

Mr. Fairview smiled, but it looked bitter and pinched. "I

hardly have enough to keep you fresh, plus our retail stock. You know that. And I still have Mr. Garcia to contend with, which is entirely your fault."

Garcia. That name rang a bell, something immediate. . . . They'd mentioned, during her hiring process, that she was replacing a man named Cesar Garcia, who'd left town.

Maybe he hadn't left town at all.

"He's nearly done." Freddy shrugged. "It's been five days since his last shot. He won't last the night."

"Check him," Mr. Fairview said. "I don't want an unpleasant surprise."

Freddy opened up the walk-in refrigerator and wheeled out the other body that had been in the freezer, the one in the body bag. And Bryn, to her horror, heard that sound again.

That scratching.

Not rats. She could see the bag moving, very slowly.

"Oh, God," she whispered. She couldn't seem to move as Freddy unzipped the body bag.

The smell spread through the room, sickly sweet and foul, and from all appearances, what was in the body bag was at least several weeks dead and decomposing. Bryn was used to the stench, but what made her eyes widen and her throat close up was the fact that this corpse, this decomposing *thing*, was *still moving*. Not involuntary biological twitches. Real, directed movements.

The lipless mouth opened, and air scraped out—not a scream, because the vocal cords were gone, but she understood.

Deep inside, she knew it was a howl of utter horror.

"Christ," Freddy said in disgust. "He's hanging on better than I'd expected. I may have to disassemble him."

"No," Mr. Fairview said, and came to stand next to Freddy, looking down on the remains of Mr. Garcia . . . Bryn's predecessor. "This is fine. We can document the progress, until he's too far gone to be of any use to us. Five full days is the longest anyone's lasted, right? Maybe he'll go to six. Or Mrs. Jones will. I suppose we can give up any hope of a payday on her as well."

"What—" She hadn't realized that she'd spoken until the word slipped out, and then it was too late. She'd drawn their attention.

Bryn grabbed a scalpel from the tray of sterile instruments and menaced Freddy as he came her way. "Back off!" she said. "I'll kill you, you son of a bitch."

He laughed. "Late to the party, Double Trouble. Fairview got me first."

She was fast, but he turned out to be faster, slapping the scalpel out of the way and slamming her face-first into the wall. Everything went vague, except for the pain, which remained cuttingly sharp, and then she was on the floor in a heap, watching her own blood crawl red over the tile. *Just like Melissa.*

The voices came at her smeared and disembodied, from what seemed like a great distance.

"Do you want to keep her?"

"I'm not sure. Maybe. It's a bother to set up her disappearance properly. Let's do it and get her in storage. I'll decide later, once we dispose of Mr. Jones."

Bryn felt herself being lifted, then settling into place on a stiff, cold surface.

A preparation table.

"No," she whispered, and Mr. Fairview looked down on her with that distant, professional compassion she'd thought was so wonderful before. Adrenaline surged through her, and she tried to get up. He had leverage, and muscle, to keep her down.

"Sorry it didn't work out," he said. "You really did have a lot of promise, Bryn. I hope you don't take this personally."

He nodded to Freddy, and Freddy snapped on a pair of latex gloves, then lifted up a clear plastic bag.

He put it over her head.

Bryn involuntarily gasped, but the plastic filled her mouth and nose and blocked off her air. Freddy made sure of it by pressing his hand down over her face, and all her struggling didn't make any difference at all. It seemed to take forever, and the panic was so extreme that it was painful, like needles in her skin. She was screaming, but the sound couldn't get out. Her lungs ached, then hurt, then shrieked for air. *God*, it hurt. It hurt so badly.

Then it all started to go softly gray at the edges, and the edges pushed in, and in, until it was all a hazy mist, and she couldn't remember why she was fighting so hard, and it was all pain, all of it. Dying was supposed to be easier.

Something crashed in the room, loud enough to penetrate even her fading senses, but she couldn't make sense of it. Nothing made any sense. Everyone was yelling, and there was smoke, and fire, and the sharp pops of gunfire. Freddy's chest exploded in a red mist, and he fell away. Blood splattered the bag over her eyes, and she couldn't see anymore.

None of it mattered as she gasped, and gasped, and the taste of plastic was the last thing she knew as the shadows slipped over her and drowned her.

And it hurt, all the way to the very last scream of the last nerve.

"Crap, crap, crap," a voice whispered, from a very long distance away. "Goddamn it. *Shit*. Come on, Bryn. Come on back."

Someone was patting her face, which felt cold and clammy with moisture. She felt . . . numb. Cold to the bone. And oddly disconnected, as if she weren't quite inside her own body.

Then, with a harsh, electric snap, she was back, and everything woke up.

Bryn's body arched, and a scream raked its way up from her guts, out through her throat, and burst out of her mouth with so much force that she felt something tear inside of her. It didn't even sound human, that scream: certainly nothing she could imagine coming out of her own body.

And then the pain drowned her in a thick, stinging wave, and she knew why she was screaming.

There was a murmur of voices, and she saw a glimpse of a face in the haloes of bright lights.

Joe Fideli. He looked grim and sad, and he was holding her hand. "Relax," he said. "I know it hurts. Just relax now. You'll be okay."

She reached out, but it was too hard, too far, and whatever liquid they were injecting into her arm made her fall very far, very fast, into a hot, airless darkness.

Waking up the second time was both easier and worse. Easier because she no longer felt all the pain and horror; worse because she didn't know where she was. It was a featureless room, very clean. She was tucked in a narrow bed with rails, and there were portable medical monitors, cabinets—the usual hospital room accoutrements. Nothing else that she could see. She didn't even have an IV in her arm, only an oxygen clamp on her fingertip. The place smelled of antiseptic.

As she sat up to get a better look around, the door at the far end opened, and Joe Fideli came in. He was followed by another man Bryn didn't know—younger than Joe, with black hair and brown eyes and skin a few shades darker than Bryn's. He was wearing a tailored black suit and a sober-looking tie, and both he and Joe had ID badges clipped onto their pockets.

Joe's face was very, very calm, blank, and bland, and from the first look at him, she knew she was in trouble.

She just had no idea why, or how.

"Hello," Bryn said. The two men didn't say a word. She wet her very dry lips. "Where am I? What happened?"

Joe exchanged a look with the unknown man, then said, "You're in a safe place."

"Safe . . ." That didn't seem to make sense to her. There was no safe place. Not anymore.

The other man, the one she didn't know, walked forward, pulled up a single aluminum chair, and sat down next to her bedside. Close up, he was handsome in a quiet kind of way, and a little older than she'd thought—probably midthirties.

"Your name is Bryn Davis," he said. She nodded, waiting for him to offer his own. He didn't. "What do you remember about what happened to you?"

"I—" She stopped, because there was a black curtain between her and those memories, and she didn't want to walk through it. She knew instinctively that it was there for a reason. "I'm not really sure. I remember going to work; there was a girl who killed herself—"

"Yes," the man agreed, without any emotional weight on the word at all. "Go on."

"I worked late. I met Mr. Fideli. . . ." Bryn looked past her inquisitor to Joe, who was leaning against the wall by the door, still looking neutral and distant. He nodded at her. "And then I tried to leave, but Mr. Fairview took me back inside. . . ."

Her voice faded. Whatever had happened to her after that, before Joe Fideli had slapped her face to wake her up, she didn't remember, or want to remember. It made her stomach churn with anxiety to think about it.

"Something bad happened," she whispered. "Something . . ."

The man didn't blink. "Yes," he agreed again, exactly the way he'd agreed to her earlier statement. "Bryn, I need to know what you know about the business Mr. Fairview and Mr. Watson were running from the basement."

"The embalming?"

"Not the embalming."

"I don't understand." She really didn't, and her head hurt. Her mouth felt dry and tasted of metal, and she desperately craved a drink. "Could I have some water, please?"

"Not yet. I need you to tell me what you saw, Bryn."

"I can't." She meant it. She was shaking all over, ice-cold at the thought of even trying to pull up those memories.

He studied her for a moment, then pushed back the chair, stood up, and walked over to murmur with Joe Fideli in the corner. It was a quiet, fierce argument, and finally Joe turned and left the room. He didn't look happy.

The man in the suit looked at Bryn, and she felt vulnerable, fragile, and cold.

"I'm afraid I have to give you some very bad news," the man said. "Please, I want you to stay calm."

Bryn's hands clenched into fists around the sheet that was draped over her body. "I'm calm."

"You've suffered an attack," he said. "Unfortunately, you didn't survive."

She blinked. What the hell had he just said? "Excuse me?"

"You're dead, Bryn. You were suffocated with a plastic bag over your head."

"I'm not *dead*." But what he was saying made the darkness in her head ripple and threaten to tear and let those awful memories come out. "Obviously, I'm not dead; I'm talking to you. It's not true."

"I'm sorry, but I have no choice but to explain this to you. You've been treated with a proprietary drug, a drug that can bring a subject back from death for a limited period of time."

"Limited," she echoed faintly. "What do you mean, limited?"

"Without another injection, the nanites in your bloodstream will shut down in twenty-four hours. They're all that's keeping your body running, Bryn. They can repair damage and maintain your body at a certain level, but they don't restore life permanently. It's a facsimile of life, not sustainable on its own." He clasped his hands behind his back and met her eyes steadily. "You're a problem, Bryn. *My* problem. I made the call to bring you back, in the hope that you could give us some information about what was going on at the Fairview Mortuary, where they were obtaining the drugs stolen from our company."

She didn't understand. She didn't *want* to understand. Her heart was pounding—if she were dead, her heart shouldn't be beating, right? But she could *feel* it. She could feel everything. She was thirsty, for God's sake.

She was *alive*.

"You brought me back," she said. "From the dead."

He said nothing.

"To ask me questions."

"Questions you haven't yet been able to answer," he said. "Which is a problem for us both, you see. I made a substantial investment that isn't paying off. As things go, I really don't have any justification to give you a second shot. Unfortunately, that means you face a very difficult five or six days while the nanites completely shut down, and you . . . continue on the natural path of decay. We don't really know if consciousness survives during that process, but

I'm afraid it might, for a time. We'll do everything we can to make you comfortable."

It burst in on her with a blinding light: Mr. and Mrs. Jones. The drug. Mr. Fairview demanding all that money.

Mr. Garcia's rotting corpse, moving weakly in its bag.

That's going to be me.

"No!" she burst out. "No, you can't do this to me! You son of a bitch, you can't just let me *rot*!"

"Then tell me something that I can use to keep you alive," he said, and for a second, his hard shell of reserve cracked. "Please, Miss Davis. Tell me *something* I can use. Anything."

She swallowed hard, squeezed her eyes shut, and then opened them. "Mr. Fairview was charging ten thousand dollars, and five hundred per shot. I saw him with someone named Mr. Jones. His wife needed the shot. And . . . he'd lost his job. He tried to grab the drugs, but Mr. Fairview shot him." The world went too bright, and wobbly around the edges for a moment. She grabbed a deep breath to steady herself. "They put Mrs. Jones in a body bag. She was still alive. Still moving, anyway."

There was a flash of horror across the man's expression that made him seem, at least in that moment, human. "I'm sorry," he said, "but that doesn't help us. Did you hear Mr. Fairview say anything about where he was obtaining the drugs . . . ?"

"No," she said. "I don't know anything about that." And she realized, with a sinking sensation, that she'd just doomed herself. She had nothing left to tell him. Nothing he didn't already know.

He seemed to know it, too. He looked at her for a long, silent moment, and then he turned and headed for the door.

"Wait," she said. "At least tell me your name."

She didn't think he would. It was probably easier for him if he didn't. But he surprised her. "My name is Patrick McCallister," he said. "I'm the chief of security for Pharmadene."

"What's Pharmadene?"

"The company that created Returné," he said. "The drug that we gave you to bring you back."

"You mean the drug that's going to take five days to kill me again," she said.

He unclipped his badge and swiped it through a strip reader next to the door. The door clicked open. "Unless I find a good reason to give you the next shot," he said. "Yes."

She watched the door slowly close, and then lowered her head to the clean, soft pillow.

I'm alive, she thought. *Damn it, I'm alive.*

For five more days, anyway.

Chapter 3

There was no way to tell time in the sterile little room Bryn was trapped inside. She wasn't restrained, at least; that was something. There was a small, bland little toilet area off the main room, and she visited it regularly. Being almost alive came with toilet duties, apparently. She kept wondering whether they'd lied to her, if maybe there was nothing at all wrong with her; she didn't *feel* different. She felt fine.

She *was* alive; screw what McCallister had said. This was all bullshit, and they were just trying to scare her. She'd blacked out when Freddy had been suffocating her with the bag; that was all—someone had gotten it off of her in time, and she'd been unconscious for a while, but she was okay now. Nothing weird about any of it.

In fact, she was no longer sure she'd even seen what she thought she had. Mrs. Jones had probably just been a junkie, sick with need. And the body in the bag . . . No, that had just been a decomposing murder victim, nothing special about it. It hadn't moved. It hadn't.

It couldn't.

Bryn flexed her hand, staring down at it. Same smooth skin. Same fingernails, topped with the same chipped pearl-pink polish. Same flexors and extensors and muscles and bones. Same scar, there on the wrist, where she'd caught a piece of flying shrapnel from an IED. The only scar she'd brought back from the war.

Not dead.

There was a camera in the corner of the room, and Bryn stood and faced it, head raised. She felt cold, but defiant.

"McCallister," she said. "I'm not dead. I'm not. So you can stop all this crap; I'm not buying it, all right? Just let me go. I'll sign whatever forms you want. Nondisclosure. Whatever."

No answer. And the camera never blinked.

She found plain but serviceable clothing in the cabinet, neatly folded—they'd included a shirt, pants, socks, even underwear in her sizes. Bryn took everything into the bathroom to change, and as soon as the stiff, new fabrics slid over her skin, she felt better. More in control, even though she knew that was an illusion.

The room was small, and it got smaller the more she paced, arms folded, stopping to glare at the camera. She didn't speak again. There didn't seem to be any point.

Twenty-four hours, he'd said. It was all nonsense, but still, she couldn't help but wonder how much time had passed. Hours. Was he going to just keep her here the whole time, with not even the courtesy of a meal? Was this psychological warfare?

Well, she wasn't worried. She could outlast some soft corporate drone, and if they wanted to do any serious psychological damage they should have left her naked, not given her perfectly fine new clothes and shoes. (The shoes were, she had to admit, actually nicer than what she'd been wearing with her suit. Although she missed the pink blouse.)

They'd taken her watch and, of course, her cell phone. Nothing to read, watch, fiddle with, or do. She methodically explored the cabinets and drawers, finding nothing that could help, and set the water dripping in a rhythm as close as she could get to one second per drop. She set the plastic cup under the tap and occupied herself marking off minutes, then five minutes, then ten, thirty, an hour.

Voilà. Instant water clock.

She was two hours into the exercise when she heard a harsh buzzing sound from the other room, and left the clock to see the door swinging inward. *Rush him*, some instinct said, so Bryn moved toward the exit, fast.

She skidded to a stop when Joe Fideli pointed a gun at her. He shrugged apologetically, but there was nothing but business in his blue eyes. "Sorry, Miss Davis," he said.

"We're back to Miss Davis, Joe?"

"Bryn. Sit down on the bed, please. No crazy stuff."

She backed up and sat, well aware of the disadvantage at which he'd placed her. The hospital bed was high, and her feet dangled off the ground. No leverage for any sudden moves.

Bryn folded her hands and tried to seem as inoffensive as possible. He'd already mentioned how young she looked; that was an asset in a situation like this. One she hated to use, but still, she wasn't exactly awash in options here.

Joe settled comfortably against the wall, still holding the gun steady on her. "Pat," he said, "we're good here."

It bothered her how careful they were, because even then, Patrick McCallister surveyed the whole room before entering. Like Fideli, she was sure he'd had some kind of military-style training. Mercenary, if not traditional. He was way too good at checking corners.

He also secured the door, closing off her line of escape, before dragging over a chair and sitting down across from her. He did not, Bryn noted, block Fideli's line of fire.

Close up, without the adrenaline and fear to blur her focus, she was able to spot some interesting things about Mr. McCallister. First, the suit he was wearing wasn't just any off-the-rack thing; it was tailored, and silk, and every bit as nice as what the late Mr. Lincoln Fairview had worn to work. McCallister looked tired, as if he'd missed a night's sleep, but he was handsomer than she remembered. She'd missed how warm his dark eyes seemed, for one thing.

"Miss Davis," he said. "How do you feel?"

"Not like I'm dead."

"You think I'm lying to you."

"Obviously. You have to be."

He shook his head slowly, and leaned back in the hard-backed aluminum chair. "Joe," he said, "show her the video."

There was a flat-panel TV set flush into the wall, and well out of Bryn's reach; Fideli pulled a remote control out of his pocket and punched some buttons. Cue music and intro titles, and a logo that resolved into the words *Phar-*

madene Pharmaceuticals. It all looked very polished and corporate. High production values.

But what followed was cold and clinical. There was a corpse lying on a morgue table, clearly and obviously dead; the skin was chilly blue, and still smoking a little from being removed from the refrigerator. The eyes were closed. It was a man, nothing special about him except that he was dead, probably from the two black-edged bullet holes in his chest.

Enter a medical team, hooking him up to monitors that read exactly nothing. No heartbeat, no respiration, nothing.

And then the injection.

It took long minutes, but then Bryn saw a convulsive shudder rip through the body, saw the ice blue eyelids quiver, saw the mouth gape open, and heard . . .

Heard the scream.

She knew that scream. She'd felt it rip out of her own mouth, an uncontrollable torrent of sound and agony and horror and fear. It was the lost wail of a newborn, only in an adult's voice.

The corpse's filmed eyes opened, blinked, and the film began to slowly fade. The skin slowly shifted colors from that unmistakable ashy tone to something less . . . dead.

And the bullet holes began to knit closed—but not before bright red blood trickled out and began running down the heaving, breathing chest.

The monitors kick-started into beeps. Heart rate. Oxygen saturation. Blood pressure.

Life.

He stopped screaming and looked at the doctors. His voice, when it came, sounded hoarse and dry. "Did it work?"

Nobody answered him. They were all busily noting details, murmuring instructions, taking samples.

It was like the living man, where the corpse had been, didn't exist at all except as a clinical miracle.

Bryn felt a horrible chill inside, but she put on a brave face. "Nice special effects. Really nice—"

She would have gone on, but another video started, brutally fast.

That was *her*. Ash gray, lying dead in a hospital bed. Her

eyes were swollen and bloodshot and blank, pupils completely blown. She'd bitten her lip, and blood had dried on her face. Her head lolled limp on the pillow. They cut away her clothing, reducing her to just another shell, another dead thing, pitiful and cold and naked, and Bryn couldn't move, couldn't do *anything*, not even demand for them to stop the video.

Fideli wasn't watching it. He and McCallister were watching *her*. She was peripherally aware of that, but she couldn't tear her horrified gaze away.

"Right, give her the full dose," said the crisp voice of a doctor in the video. "Start the clock ... now."

It took long, torturous minutes, and then ... then ... Bryn's body stirred. Gasped. Spasmed.

But there was nothing else.

"Vital reactions," the doctor said. "Note the time in the log, please."

A nurse spread a sheet over her naked body. They seemed to be waiting for something, and Bryn realized that the video-Bryn hadn't opened her eyes, or taken another breath after that first, convulsive one.

The doctor glanced up at a clock on the wall. "She's not responding. I'm going to have to call it."

"Wait." In the video, Joe Fideli moved out of the shadows and put his hand on her face. "Come back," he said. "C'mon, Bryn, don't do this. Come on back. Come back."

He slapped her, a stinging blow, and Bryn saw her blank eyes finally blink, slowly.

And then she screamed.

The same scream.

Fideli held her hand through the rest of it. Bryn didn't listen, couldn't over the rush of blood in her ears. She felt dizzy and sick and very, very strange.

She looked at Fideli, who shifted his gaze away. Then she moved her mute stare to McCallister, the cool corporate drone, who leaned forward and took her hand in his. Squeezed, silently, and waited until the video finally ended.

Fideli shut the TV off. In the silence, Bryn heard some rational voice in her head screaming, *It's fake; it's all fake, special effects. This isn't happening; this can't be happening.*

The only problem was that she knew it *was* happening. She'd seen, and she finally, horribly, *believed*.

She looked up at Patrick McCallister's face and saw emotion there, quickly hidden. Pity, maybe.

He was still holding her hand. He'd been holding it through the whole ordeal, though she'd forgotten he was even there.

"Joe," he said, "I don't think we need the gun anymore."

Fideli put it away without a word. Bryn realized that she really ought to say something, *do* something, but for the moment, all she could think of was to sit very still, holding to the warm anchor of another human being. She felt like all the world around her had turned into a black, sucking whirlpool, and she was afraid that if she let go, even for a second, she'd drown.

Go back to . . . that. That empty ashen thing on the hospital bed.

Oh, she believed, all right. And it terrified her.

"What did you do to me?" she whispered. She was staring right into McCallister's eyes now, looking for that spark of connection again, but it wasn't there. He'd shut down. Maybe he had to, to deal with the emotion pouring out of her just now. She'd never felt so scared, or so alone. So *empty*.

"There's good news," he said, in a soothing, quiet voice that unpleasantly reminded her of Lincoln Fairview, with his nice suit and cultured palate and nasty lies. "You need a daily shot, but apart from that one thing, you're in the best shape you'll ever be in. No sickness, no aging. You won't change, because the nanites returned you to a template of what you were just at the cessation of life, and holds you there."

"I'm dying. I'm *dead*."

"You're dying less than the rest of us," he said. "You're . . . *on hold* would be a good description. And there are positives, believe me."

"Positives!" She couldn't control the bitter, shaky laugh that burst out of her, and put her hand to her mouth to muffle it. "God."

He didn't tell her it was okay after that. He just let her sit and think for a while.

Finally, she wet her lips and said, "How in the hell does a company set out to create . . . this?"

"They didn't," he said. "Returné was an accident, a side effect of an experimental drug for the treatment of cancer. It would have won Mercer and Sams the Nobel Prize, if it had worked the way they thought. Or if they could ever actually talk about it again, but of course now it's highly classified."

That made her laugh again, but it wasn't a laugh she recognized. It sounded wild and ugly, and very not-Bryn. Of course, she wasn't Bryn anymore, was she? The Bryn from yesterday, that girl had her whole life ahead of her. A career, love, a family—those were the things she'd wanted. And she was gone.

So who was *this* Bryn? No, not who. *What* was this Bryn?

She wasn't a person anymore. She felt like one and she looked like one, but what he'd just shown her had stripped that away.

She was an animated, breathing mimicry of life.

"Bryn," he said, and drew her attention again. She hadn't even realized it had wandered. "Bryn, please listen to me. You're in the danger zone right now. It's not just that your body has to survive; *you* need to survive along with it. If you withdraw, if you go catatonic, I can't help you. Stay with me."

Bryn pulled in a deep breath. "Do I have a choice?"

"Always. But I'd rather you didn't pick the other option," McCallister said.

"Decomposing?"

He ignored that, didn't blink, kept his focus straight on her. "I have a proposition for you."

She laughed again. Still not a nice laugh. "They lock you up in this state for necrophilia."

"*Bryn*. Listen to me, because what I have to say is vital to your continued existence. Pharmadene wanted answers out of you, and I wasn't able to get them. But together, we can offer the company something else. Something better, possibly."

She didn't answer, because there didn't seem to be much point. He was talking, but she didn't understand what he was getting at. Not at all.

They were never going to let her out of this room. Her

water clock was going to fill up and spill over and she was
going to sit here and rot. Literally. She imagined that it was
going to hurt.

"Bryn."

"I'm listening," she said. She didn't want to, but she
couldn't seem to block out his voice. Her own sounded remote and odd, disconnected from the rest of her, but it
seemed to reassure him.

"I'm going to put you back in Fairview Mortuary."

That called for another laugh, but she couldn't dredge
one up. "As a corpse in the prep room?"

"No," he said. "As the new owner. Inheriting it from Mr.
Fairview. You're his niece."

"I'm not."

"You are now, on paper; he didn't have any other living
relatives. You'll go back to work, oversee the necessary repairs, start up the business again. Make it known you're
carrying on your uncle's work in every way." McCallister
glanced over at Fideli. "You'll hire Joe as a funeral director.
He'll help you out if you have any trouble, and make sure
you get your shots on time. Your job is to go through Fairview's records, and try to make contact with Fairview's underground supplier of Returné and bring him—or her—out
into the open so we can shut down the leak who's selling
the drugs, quickly and quietly."

"And then what?" Bryn asked him. "I go back to being
dead?"

"Bryn—let's just take this a step at a time, all right? I'm
doing what I can for you. This gets you back into the world
and gives you a kind of normal life. Do well on this, and I'll
fight to keep your drug regimen in place. Deal?"

She didn't answer. She stared at him mutely, feeling as if
parts of her were just . . . shutting down. Falling away. Important parts of her, already gone.

Hope, for one. A sense of who she was.

All gone now.

"All right," she said softly. "Deal. On one condition."

McCallister hesitated, frowning just a little. Maybe he
felt the increase in her pulse through her fingers. "What
condition?"

"I get to have the gun. Not Fideli."

"Joe's trained—"

"So am I," she interrupted him. "Four years surviving in Baghdad. And I get the gun, McCallister. Or you can sit here and watch me rot."

He pulled back, baffled, frowning in earnest now. "Why do you want it?"

Fideli answered for her, face gone still and hard. "Because she wants to be able to end it," he said. "Put a bullet through her brain. Do damage the nanites can't repair. Right, Bryn?"

She didn't answer, but it sounded pretty good to her.

There was a moment of silence, and then McCallister sighed. "Not a bad plan, but it won't work. The only things that will truly end you are fire, dissolution, or dismemberment, and I can't see you sawing off your own head. You're tough, but nobody's that tough." McCallister tried for a smile, and almost made it. "If you put a bullet through your head, you'll just be wasting bullets and screaming a lot."

She felt her teeth bare in something that didn't feel like a smile. "How about if I use one on you? Would that work?"

"Are you asking if I'm like you? Revived?"

"Revived," she echoed, testing it out. It sounded innocent, like she'd just had a long rest. "Yes. Are you revived?"

"No. I've never died."

"Him?" She glanced at Joe Fideli.

"No. The drug's still highly classified, and highly experimental, not to mention expensive. Finding a way to keep you stable and on the drug constitutes extraordinary measures." His dark eyes locked on hers, demanding a straight answer. "If I give you a gun, are you going to hurt yourself? Or others?"

She imagined doing it. First holding the gun to her own head . . . but if what they were saying was true, it'd just be painfully inconvenient. And temporary. And messy.

So could she shoot Joe Fideli? He'd brought her back to this. He probably deserved it. Or McCallister. Shoot him right in the heart, if he even had one, which she doubted. She *could* imagine it, but it didn't hold any emotional warmth for her.

She'd just be spreading around misery.

"No," she said, and for the first time, her voice sounded like her own. "No, I wouldn't do that. I just want to be able to protect myself. It'd make me feel . . . safer."

"Gee, thanks," Fideli said drily. "I'm all flattered and shit."

"Joe," McCallister said. Just that, and Fideli went back to being a statue. "All right, you get a gun. And you get paid, Bryn. You run Fairview, and you spread the word that you're continuing *all* of your uncle's business ventures, including the one running out of the basement. I'll supply you with a stock of Returné, both for yourself and for whatever unfortunates still need the shots, but you have to find his supplier quickly. I can't guarantee an unlimited supply."

"I'll need more," Bryn said.

"More. More what?"

"Money. If I'm taking over Fairview, I need clothes. Better shoes. A real operational budget."

"You've got it. We'll be depositing money in an account in your name. Joe will bring you the details. It'll come through a network of shell companies, out of an annuity. You were left the money from your great-aunt Tabitha."

"Tabitha? Seriously?"

"Tabitha Quick. She was a real person in Fairview's family tree, just like you." McCallister stood up, looked at her for a moment, then went to the door. It buzzed open for him, and he was outside for only a few seconds before coming back and shutting it again.

He had a small pneumatic injection gun in his hand, loaded with a clear vial of . . . something. "Your arm, please," he said. When she angled her shoulder toward him, he cleared his throat. "Doesn't work through cloth."

Oh. In retrospect, dressing might not have been the best choice, because now it meant she had to slip off the button-up shirt; the sleeves were tight, and wouldn't roll up that far. She unbuttoned it down the front and said, "I guess you've both already seen it anyway."

Fideli promptly looked down at his feet. McCallister kept his gaze carefully on her face as she pulled the blouse aside and bared the flesh of her upper arm.

"What we saw was a body. It wasn't you. You, of all people, should understand the difference," McCallister said, very quietly, as he put the pneumatic gun to her arm. He pulled the trigger, and there was a star-sharp pain in her skin, then a heavy kind of warmth. "Done."

She pulled her blouse back together, holding it in place until he'd turned away, then did up the buttons with fast, shaking fingers. "How many others have you done this to?" she asked. "Like that man in the video?"

"He was number four in the trials."

"So four."

"No," McCallister said. "He was the first to make it. There have been six since then. Not including you, and whoever Fairview brought back. I told you, it's top-secret and highly experimental."

She met his eyes and said flatly, "Why me, then? Why did you bother?"

McCallister exchanged a look with Fideli, who shrugged guiltily. "I thought there was an outside chance—"

"You knew I didn't know anything. You knew I'd just started."

This was evidently news to McCallister, who straightened his already straight posture to give Fideli a long, measuring look. Fideli shrugged again. "No excuse, sir. She was a good kid, and I thought there was an outside chance she could be useful. My fault she ended up dead in the first place. I should have gotten there quicker."

"We're not in the business of cleaning up your conscience," McCallister said, and then shook his head. "Done is done, but we're having a conversation later."

"Well, that'll be fun."

While he was distracted, Bryn slipped in the question she really wanted to ask. "So you wouldn't have brought me back if I hadn't been of some potential use to you? Even though you got me killed?"

For the first time, she got an unguarded reaction from Patrick McCallister. It was written all over his face, just for a second, and then the corporate drone was back, smooth and seamless. "Of course we would have tried," he said.

Liar. But what was interesting to Bryn was that what

she'd seen flash over his face hadn't been the logical match to the lie—not impatience, or disgust, or superiority. What she'd seen had been pure, weary guilt.

Patrick McCallister, she thought, didn't really like his job very much. Well, how many corporate drones actually did? *Brilliant deduction, Bryn*, she told herself. *You could get federal funding for a research project on that.*

Still, it made him just a touch more human to her.

"When can I get out of here?" she asked. She rubbed her arm where he'd given her the shot; it felt warm now, and a little tender.

"Soon," he told her. He went back to the door and opened it again; this time he was gone longer, and Bryn took a deep, convulsive breath of fresh air that drifted in. Well, not *fresh*, but new. She felt stifled in here. What she could see of the hallway outside looked like more of the same, though—white tile, clean-room sterility. She couldn't see any natural daylight, just fluorescents. It felt like they were underground, but they might just as easily have been fifty stories in the air, sealed off from the outside.

McCallister came back with something that looked like a tablet PC, something he made a few taps on and then handed to Joe Fideli, who examined it and nodded.

"What is that?" Bryn asked.

"A lot of things, including an audio/video recorder, infrared detector, secured Internet connection, and tracking device."

"And it's got blackjack on it," Fideli said, straight-faced. He tapped the screen, then turned it around to show her a map, with a blinking light superimposed on it. "That's you. I can track you anywhere with this. There's an app for everything, apparently."

"Is that supposed to make me feel better?"

"The nanites in your bloodstream represent a significant financial investment," McCallister said. "We'd prefer it if we knew where you were at all times. And, obviously, we need to be able to find you to get you the shot."

She hated the first part of that, but the second wasn't unreasonable. "Where's the tracking device?"

"Inside you," Fideli said. "It's a smart device; it went in with the nanites and is attaching to your bone right now. Won't come off easily. Long battery life, too."

"It's not something we would use on a living person," McCallister said. "The battery sheds toxins, and can lead to metabolic bone problems, but the nanites can easily deal with it."

"You people are *crazy*!"

"We're not *you people*," McCallister said, and handed her a clipboard full of paperwork. "You're one of us now. Officially."

She looked at what he'd handed her. Employment forms, including—of all the crazy things—a full application and I-9 form. He shrugged.

"I'll need to see some ID, too. Welcome to the corporate world," he said. "I never said it would make sense."

Fideli drove her home about six hours later, in a big, black SUV with dark-tinted windows that just screamed *covert operations* to her. She felt a little queasy, and rolled down the window enough to get a cool breeze on her face. It was night again. She'd been dead most of one day, at least.

The first day of the rest of your so-called life. That almost made her smile. Almost.

"Hungry?" Fideli asked her. " 'Cause I could murder a burger right about now."

She wasn't, but she wasn't sure whether that was biology or just depression. "Do I eat?"

"Sure. Same as you ever did."

"Oh. Okay. Burger sounds fine. Whatever." She closed her eyes and leaned her head back. The SUV smelled like leather and cologne. A guy car, definitely. As she shifted to make herself more comfortable, something dug painfully into her hip, and she reached behind her to find it.

She pulled out a brightly colored plastic toy gun. Day-Glo orange and yellow.

Fideli glanced over at it, rolled his eyes, and grabbed it away. He tossed it in the backseat.

"So ... what is it, some kind of well-disguised stealth weapon, or—"

"My kids," he said. "Can't ever get them to clean up after themselves. Sorry about that."

Kids. She looked around the SUV with fresh eyes, not assuming anything this time. It was clean, but there were definitely signs she'd missed the first time . . . the most obvious being the infant car seat strapped in behind her.

She couldn't help it: she laughed, and kept laughing. It felt like a summer storm of pure, frantic mirth, and when it finally passed she felt relaxed and breathless. Fideli, making a right-hand turn into the parking lot of a burger joint, sent her an amused look. "What?" he asked. "It sounded good, whatever it was."

"I had you pegged for some corporate James Bond," she said, and shook her head. "Licensed to kill. Driving some kind of high-tech armored spy vehicle with rocket launchers. Jesus, you have a *car seat.*"

"Wouldn't let my kid ride without it," he said. "I've got three. Oldest is Jeff; he's seven. Then Harry; she's five. Juliet's the baby."

"I guess you've got a wife to go with that."

"Kylie," he said. "Best wife in the world. Best mom, too." He sounded quietly proud. "Here. Pictures." He opened the glove box, and there was an honest-to-God brag book in there, of charming kids and a pretty wife. Fideli looked like a different person in those pictures, relaxed and happy, a little goofy. It was . . . adorable.

And it reminded Bryn, with a cold shock, that her life was never going that way. Not now. She stared down at the picture of Juliet, a happy, giggling little baby in her mother's arms, and her eyes filled with tears. "I can't have kids now, can I?" she asked.

Fideli said nothing. When she looked over at him, his mouth was set in a pained, grim line, and his knuckles were tight where he gripped the steering wheel. She closed the picture album and put it in the glove compartment. The silence held until they were pulled up in front of the glowing marquee with all of the not-healthy choices.

"I'll have a Monster Burger with fries and a Coke," he said to the speaker, and then glanced at Bryn. "How about you?"

"Same thing," she said, and tried for a smile as she wiped her eyes. "Guess cholesterol's not an issue, right?"

"Bright side," he agreed, and conveyed the order. "Might as well get extra cheese with that."

The smell of the food filled the cab as they pulled away from the payment window, and Bryn realized that she was actually hungry. Funny, she hadn't expected to feel that at all, for some reason. Sensation, yes, but needs? It just seemed strange.

French fries still tasted as salty-delicious as ever. She munched on them as Fideli drove the last two miles to her apartment. It wasn't much, a lower-middle-class kind of neighborhood with hardworking people. The apartments were generic and cheaply made, but affordable. Fideli didn't ask what building she lived in, which indicated a little more knowledge about her than she felt strictly comfortable with; he parked the big SUV and said, "You mind if I take off? I like to eat with the family when I can."

"Sure," she said. She felt strange, suddenly, as if she were looking at a building she didn't know, facing an evening with a total stranger: herself. She took her Coke and bagged food, but made no move to get out of the truck. It idled gently, waiting. Fideli watched her in silence.

"Hey," he finally said. "Better idea. How about you come with me?"

She jerked a little in surprise, because she really hadn't expected that. She'd been waiting for him to impatiently order her out. "What?"

"Home," he said. "You look like you don't need to sit alone and watch your burger get cold, Bryn. It's been a pretty full couple of days for you, I'd say." What he wasn't saying was that he saw the fear in her. Fear of facing life alone, the way she was now. Whatever she was.

"Joe . . ." She didn't mean to use his first name; it was just instinct. She bit her lip. "Mr. Fideli . . . there's no chance I could be . . . contagious, is there? I mean, I don't want to put your family in any danger."

He shook his head. "Can't share the nanites, even through an open wound. They're keyed to your DNA, cease to function outside your body. I wouldn't let you around the kids if there were any risk, believe me."

"And you're sure that I'm not going to get a craving for brains or anything."

He laughed this time. "You let me know if that happens. But no. It ain't your zombie apocalypse scenario, not this time. You're just . . . you. On permanent, portable life support." That was a sobering thought, and even he stopped laughing. He put the truck in reverse. "No arguments— you're eating with us. We've got a guest room, too. Kylie's got some stuff that'll fit you."

Bryn wasn't really in the mood to stand her ground, not tonight. She was, deep inside, sobbingly grateful to him for the kindness. If she'd faced those blank, generic walls of her apartment alone . . .

She wasn't sure what she would have done.

"Hey," she said. "Can I bring my dog?"

Fideli raised his eyebrows. "Sure."

The messes inside the house really weren't something Bryn wanted to face, but she forced herself to clean up the worst of it. It wasn't the dog's fault, after all; she'd been busy getting herself killed and revived for almost a full day. In fact, Mr. French, her bulldog, was well behaved even in Fideli's wildly interesting SUV; he contented himself with sniffing the interior door and then poking his head out of Bryn's passenger window, tongue out and ears flapping all the way.

Fideli's house was a rambling ranch style in a typical suburban neighborhood, nothing really special about it except the old-growth trees that made it seem hidden and protected. There were more signs it was a house with kids that she spotted as soon as she drove up—the mommy van in the driveway, a boy's bike lying on its side in the grass, a brightly colored Big Wheel nearby. A candy-colored plastic playhouse made for a little girl.

The windows of the house glowed with warmth.

Bryn put Mr. French on his leash and carried her own food as she followed Fideli up the walk to the side door— the kitchen door, as it turned out, and the kitchen was busy.

Bryn had to immediately back up against the wall to avoid a pair of running children, a boy and a girl, who whizzed by. The girl stopped to awkwardly pat Mr. French on the head, then dashed off.

Mr. French woofed and sneezed, then sat down with his head cocked, assessing his new situation.

"Jeff, Harry, I'm *warning* you, one more time. . . ." The woman from Fideli's picture book rounded the corner carrying a stack of dirty dishes and stopped, glancing from Joe to Bryn and back again. The hesitation lasted for only a second, and then she came up with a bright, nearly genuine smile. "Hey, honey. Who's this?"

Joe took the dirty dishes from her and put them down in the sink, then kissed her. It was a warm, comfortable kind of kiss, not self-conscious at all, and then the kids came racing back around yelling and flung themselves on his legs, and he hugged them.

Bryn stood there clutching the leash, her Coke, and her bagged food, feeling like this had been a massive mistake, feeling more isolated than ever . . . until Kylie came forward, wiping her hands on a towel, and took the Coke and bag from her to put them on the counter. "My husband doesn't know how to introduce people," she said, "so I'll just jump in. Kylie, and that's Jeff and Harry. Harriet, but we all call her Harry." The two kids, one blond, one dark, waved. "The baby's still in her chair in the dining room—honey, check her, would you?"

"Yep," Joe said, and walked out of the kitchen trailing children.

The noise level dropped to almost nothing, and Bryn felt awkward again. "Hi," she said, and held out her hand. "I'm Bryn. Bryn Davis. I, ah . . ." How was she supposed to explain any of this? How top-secret was it, anyway? "I work with Joe. Oh, and this is Mr. French. I promise he's housebroken."

Kylie smiled at the dog, then shook hands. She had fine blue eyes, and Bryn sensed a sharp, lively intelligence behind them. "I never heard him mention you before."

Joe appeared in the doorway again with a baby on his hip, comfortably braced in his big arm. "She's new," he said.

"Honey, take her a minute; I have to lock up the boom sticks."

"Jesus, Joe, you're walking around with her and your guns?" Kylie rolled her eyes and took the little girl, who cooed and nestled against her with more trust than Bryn thought she'd ever had shown to her in her entire life. "Go. Shoo. Get less dangerous."

"Impossible," Joe said. "I'm a lethal weapon, baby."

"Shut up."

He blew her a kiss and disappeared again. Kylie jiggled the baby—Juliet—on her hip and exchanged another smile with Bryn. "So," she said, "he talked you into the heart-attack special, right? I hardly ever let him eat that stuff, which is probably why he's running late. Here, let me get you a plate; go on into the dining room." She raised her voice to a yell. "Jeff, come in here and rinse the dishes!"

"Mooooooom, the show's starting!"

"It's recorded, honey; put it on pause and just do what I tell you." Kylie handed Bryn a plate, picked up the food and drink, and followed her into the dining room. It was a warm kind of room, all earth tones and wood, with family photos on the walls. Bryn felt a little odd eating fast food there, until Joe Fideli came back, plunked his own down on the table, and began digging in. Kylie settled in across from him.

Bryn found out quickly that she wasn't just hungry; she was *ravenous*. The burger disappeared, and so did the fries. The fizzy sweetness of the Coke tasted so good it almost made her weep.

She didn't feel quite as dead anymore. Especially when Mr. French stretched himself out in a warm blanket across her feet.

Kylie and Joe chatted about family stuff, occasionally asking her a question or two; it was all unforced and comfortable, and Joe finally got around to telling his wife that he'd invited Bryn to use the guest room. That got another second of hesitation, as if she were trying to figure out his motivations, and then a quick agreement. Kylie got up to fix the room while Joe slurped the last of his drink.

"Do they know?" Bryn asked softly. "I mean, about what you do." Whatever that was.

"They know I'm in corporate security," Joe said. "And that my work is top-secret. So she won't ask you any questions. She's just going to assume you're someone I'm protecting. Which is true."

"Do you usually bring people you're protecting home to meet your family?"

"Not ever," he said. "Hope you feel special about it."

He started to get up from the table. Bryn put a hand on his arm, holding him in place. "Joe." She got his full, alert attention. "Thanks. You're sure I'm not putting anybody in danger by being here?"

He smiled, but it didn't quite reach his eyes. "You really think I'd bring you within a mile of my kids if I thought there was any chance at all of that? Bryn, you're a nice girl, and I admit, I got you brought back mostly because I felt I'd let you down. But you ever pose any danger to my family and I'll make you permanently dead, and I won't hesitate for a second."

She believed him. She let go, and Joe picked up her empties and cleaned up the table, just like a normal guy.

"If I ever did pose a danger to them, I'd want you to do it," she said. "You've got a lovely family."

"You say that now; wait until you spend a couple of hours with the little terrors," he said. "Come on. I owe Jeff a video game or two."

Normal life.

Bryn wondered if she would ever have this again, this taste of a future, of life, of family.

Well, she thought, *if this is all I get, I might as well enjoy it.*

Chapter 4

In the morning, the family had breakfast, and Joe drove Bryn to drop off Mr. French at her apartment, and then to see what was left of Fairview Mortuary.

It was a grim sight. Most of the building was still standing, but the other part was blackened and had collapsed in on itself. The serene little garden out front had been trampled into mush by firefighters and emergency crews.

"When you stage a rescue, you don't go about it subtly, do you?" she asked. Joe shrugged.

"I tried that," he said. "Fairview had hardened the doors. Only choice I had was to break down the loading-dock wall, and I had to use explosives to do it."

"And you just carry those around with you."

"Yeah," he said, "I do. In my job, it pays to be prepared."

"Like a Boy Scout."

"With C-four."

There were a substantial number of trucks pulled up in the driveway, unloading materials. Repairs, it seemed, were already under way, and a work crew in hard hats was swarming around the place looking purposeful. Bryn got out of the SUV and walked toward the building, then stopped. She turned to Joe. "What about the bodies?" she asked.

"Which bodies?"

"Fairview, Fast Freddy, Mr. and Mrs. Jones, Mr. Garcia . . ."

"The basement bodies. They were removed already." Joe cleared his throat. "Mrs. Jones and Mr. Garcia were special problems. They were, ah, cleared separately."

He meant dismembered. Or burned. Or both. Bryn felt

a little wave of faintness come over her, and had to grip Fideli's arm tight for a second until it passed. He didn't say anything about it, which she appreciated. Once she felt steady again, she started to walk on—and then stopped, stock-still. She turned to look at Fideli. "Just those two?"

"Yeah," he said, and his brows came down to a level, concerned line. "Why?"

"Because Fast Freddy was the same. Like me, I mean. Revived."

"Fuck," he spat, and pulled out his cell phone. He turned away and marched off, talking softly but quickly. She waited. He finally finished and came back, looking even grimmer. "Should have done a blood test. Damn it. Body's already been processed and sent off for cremation."

"Well—that's okay, then, right?"

"Would have been," he said, "except that nobody had any warning ol' Freddy might get all better, get up, and walk away. Which he did. He's in the wind." He shook his head. "Listen, Bryn, I've got to get back—"

"Yes, of course. I'll be fine, Joe. Thank you for . . . for everything." Including, she thought, the clothes on her back . . . a gift from Kylie of a butter-soft tan sweater and jeans that fit like a dream. Even the shoes—loafers again— were her size, or close enough. Kylie had gotten her sizes and gone on a midnight shopping run, and that woman had some clothing feng shui, no doubt about it. "I'm sorry. I should have told you about Freddy."

"You had other things on your mind, and I never asked. This one's on me," he said. He climbed in the truck and started it up, then leaned out the window. "Forgot to tell you, your ride's over there in the lot. It's the black one." He tossed her a set of keys, which she caught automatically, still not understanding. He grinned at her and backed out, then gunned the engine to a full roar on his way out of the parking area and onto the main road.

Bryn watched until he was out of sight, then looked around again. She wasn't quite sure what her role here was supposed to be, considering the damage that had been done—or she wasn't, until a big Cadillac sedan made the turn off the road and pulled up in the lot near her.

Lucy, the receptionist, got out and stood there, staring. "Lord," she said. "I was told, but I didn't believe it. Is it true? Mr. Fairview, gone?"

"And Freddy," Bryn said.

Lucy tore her gaze away from the damaged building and glanced over at her, lifting an eyebrow. "I'm not crying over *him*. Oh, you didn't meet him, did you?"

"No," Bryn lied. "I went home. After . . . after what happened to Melissa." That, Fideli had told her, was the official story, and it made sense. More sense than what she'd done. "I guess Mr. Fairview and Freddy were working late. They say it was some kind of explosion and fire."

"Some of those chemicals are real nasty," Lucy agreed. "It's just awful. Well, I suppose both of us are out of a job."

"No." Bryn took a deep breath. "I . . . I was Mr. Fairview's niece."

"You *what*? Why didn't anybody tell me?"

"He wanted me to make it on my own. Without any special treatment. You know."

"Well, that's just like him, fair as always," Lucy said. "What a good man. But still . . ." She let it go. "I guess you'll be inheriting the place? I know he didn't have a wife or any children."

"Yes," Bryn said. "I'm going to get it up and running as fast as possible. You still have a job, Lucy—if you're willing to work for me, I mean. I really need your help. You know so much, and I have so much to learn."

"You *must* be related to Mr. Fairview. You flatter just like him." Lucy tilted her head slightly, her expression gone calculating. "So you want me to be more of an administrator, then."

"Of course, there's a raise," Bryn said.

"How much?"

"How much do you want?"

Lucy seemed startled by that, but she didn't let it throw her too far off. "Thirty percent," she said. "That's only fair. There's a lot more to really running this place than just answering the phone and handing out tissues to the bereaved."

"I'm starting to realize that. Yes, that sounds fair. Shake

on it?" She held out her hand, and Lucy took it for a brief squeeze. "I don't think we'll get much done today. Maybe we should make lists of what we need to find first."

"First thing, you'd better start looking for a good down-stairs man; they don't come cheap. I do wish we'd never let Vikesh go. And we'll have to make sure these construction crews know which permits they're supposed to get."

"Do you think you can handle that last part?"

Lucy smiled. "That's what you're going to be paying me for, Ms. Bryn."

"Did we have anything scheduled for this week?"

"We had Mr. Granberry down there in the freezer—good Lord, we're going to get our asses sued off for that, I'll bet. I'll be in touch with our lawyer to see if he can get ahead of that and offer some kind of settlement. It'd just be the meetings you had yesterday we have to worry about, and I'll take care of that." Lucy thought for a second. "Hmm. I think Mr. Fairview had some private meetings booked. I only know that because I worked late a couple of times and people came in looking for him."

"Do you remember any names? Maybe I can contact them."

Lucy leaned against her car and patted her carefully lacquered hair as wind skirled through the parking lot, picking up ashes and random trash and stirring them ankle-high. "You think he was doing something illegal?"

"Do you?"

Lucy was quiet a moment; then she crossed her arms and stared off at the wrecked building with a distant expression. "I don't know. He was a good man, but he had his darkness, Mr. Fairview. I know that. Those folks that came in at night—they seemed scared. And desperate. But he seemed to be helping them."

"Lucy, do you remember the names? It may be important."

She shook her head. "He was right there, soon as they came in. I didn't even have a chance to ask. There was a man and a woman; she looked familiar but I couldn't place her. I saw them twice. She didn't look so good the second time. You think he was selling drugs?"

"Maybe," Bryn said. "We need to find out what was going on. Is there *anything* you can tell me that would help?"

Lucy hesitated this time for so long Bryn thought that she wouldn't bite, but finally she said, "You're going to think I'm crazy."

"No, I promise I won't."

"I think . . ." She took a deep breath. "I said the woman looked familiar. She did. She looked like one of the clients we had. And the man—I *know* he was a paying customer. The bereaved husband."

"By client you mean . . ."

"Corpse," Lucy said. "Deceased. Gone on to glory. Must have been the dead woman's sister, I guess."

"Probably." Bryn wondered how much Lucy really knew, or guessed, or didn't *want* to guess. "What about the other person you saw? Could it have been . . . a paying customer? Or a client?"

"Clients don't go walking around."

"Lucy."

She didn't look happy about it, but she finally said, reluctantly, "Maybe one of them looked familiar, too. Bryn, what the hell was going on?"

"Is," Bryn said softly. "*Is* going on. I don't know, but we have to find out. Is the phone still working?"

"I tried the number this morning, and it rang through to voice mail. I changed the message to say that we were closed for repairs."

"Good thinking. Were there any messages?"

"I'm not supposed to check the messages. Mr. Fairview always liked to do that himself."

"Lucy," Bryn said, and smiled. "Come on. You checked them, didn't you?"

"Well . . . only because of the accident. There were a couple from hospitals about pickups, but I took care of those."

"Anything else?"

"Two that were strange," Lucy said, "but strange calls to a funeral home aren't exactly breaking news. Half the ones we get are pranks during the day. Can't imagine how many end up on the voice mail during drinking hours."

"Can I hear them?"

Lucy pulled out her cell phone and dialed, then handed it over. Bryn listened as the recordings played. The first one was definitely a prank, complete with giggling and drunken college come-ons. She deleted that one. The second, though, was interesting. It came with a long leader of silence, followed by a shaky voice saying, "This call is for Mr. Fairview. I-I need to meet tonight; it's important. I have the money." A phone number followed, and Bryn quickly rooted in her purse for paper and pen to write it down.

"What are you going to do?" Lucy asked.

"Find out what he wanted," Bryn said. "Wait. There's another one."

This voice didn't sound at *all* shaky. It was a man's voice, and it sounded hurried and sharp. "You were supposed to meet me," it said. "Don't stand me up again. You know where. Tonight, nine." Nothing else. Bryn would have assumed it was a wrong number normally, but not this time. *That's him*, she thought. *The supplier. The Pharmadene leak.* He hadn't said his name, or left a number, or even specified a location. Fairview would have known.

But Fairview had taken it to his grave. Still, it was a lead. And if the number could be traced, maybe they'd have a name.

That fast? Bryn felt a surge of unease. If it had been that easy, McCallister wouldn't have bothered to bring her back at all ... and if she presented him with the solution on day two, what was there to keep her alive?

"Anything else?" Lucy asked, clearly interested now. "That one must have just come in. I only heard the prank calls, and that weird one to Mr. Fairview about having the money."

"Just a wrong number," Bryn said. She erased the message and handed Lucy's cell phone back. "Thanks. Listen, why don't you take the rest of the day off? Nothing we can really do here. Tomorrow, we'll go in and see what we can salvage. Wear something you can get dirty; I don't know how much smoke damage there is in there."

"All right. See you tomorrow, Bryn."

"Bye."

Lucy got back in her Cadillac and drove off; Bryn watched her go, then looked around the lot.

Mr. Fairview's car was still there. He, of all people, would be most likely to have GPS installed in his private vehicle, and GPS kept a record of destinations.

The car was locked, of course. Bryn tried the keys Fideli had given her, but they didn't work. She peered in through the heavy tinting and saw that sure enough, there was built-in navigation. Perfect. The only problem was getting in. An alarm light was flashing on the dash, and she didn't want to attract the attention of the construction crew.

If Joe Fideli had been here, he'd probably pop the lock in two seconds, using a harsh look and a bobby pin. She was not the car-theft expert.

But she knew enough to come back later, when nobody was around.

Nothing left to do here, then. She examined the car keys Fideli had given her, then looked at the choices. The lot was mostly empty, except for Fairview's other parked vans, hearses, and limousines, but tucked over in the far corner, next to Fast Freddy's sports model, sat a long, sleek Town Car. Bryn unlocked it with the remote and slipped inside. Warm, buttery leather interior. It was an automatic transmission, which was a relief, and when she poked around in the pockets she found that the car was registered to Fairview Mortuary, and she was listed as the principal driver. It was brand-new, apparently.

It started up with a purr that was hardly audible at all, but it grew to a low growl as she pulled out of the parking space. The acceleration on it was alarming, and she had to hit the brakes, fast, to avoid overshooting the stop sign at the top of the rise that led to the road. Pulling out into traffic wasn't just easy; it was *scary* easy. She'd expected it to be less ... powerful.

Somewhere, a phone rang. A cell phone on the seat of the car. She tried to fumble for it, but she didn't need to; a speaker inside picked up the call and magnified it for her. "Ah ... hello?"

"Bryn, it's McCallister. How are you doing?"

"Doing?"

"Feeling."

"Fine, I guess." She looked at the clock on the dashboard. "Uh, I guess I need to come in for a shot?"

"Yes. No later than three p.m. We've programmed in Pharmadene as a destination for you on the navigation system. Head this way. I have some things to show you, and something you have to sign for."

"What?"

"Your gun," he said. "You did ask for one, didn't you?"

He didn't say good-bye, just hung up on her. She glared at the console, then pulled over to the side of the road and punched commands into the nav. Pharmadene was code-named DOCTOR, she guessed; it was the only destination programmed. Surprisingly, it wasn't that far away, and even if it had been, the Town Car was a pleasure to drive. There was something amazingly simple and Zen about letting everything fall away and concentrating on the road, the view, the ride.

At least until her phone rang again, and she heard her sister Annalie's voice say, "Bryn? Bryn, I'm in trouble. Bryn?"

You could live, you could die smothered with a plastic bag, you could get brought back by some sci-fi nightmare robots in your blood, but some things just never, ever changed. "What is it this time, Annie?" Though Bryn could have made book on what the problem was, actually. Annalie's emergencies were always one of three things: men, money, or a combination of the two. The only good thing was that Annie didn't drink and didn't do drugs; that would have made things so much worse.

From the tone of Annie's frantic voice, Bryn guessed money, and she was right. "I don't know what happened; I was so careful, but I'm short. I think maybe somebody stole money from my account. . . ."

"How much are you short?"

"Only about a hundred bucks."

Of course, Annie rarely had more than two hundred in her checking account, ever. Bryn shook her head and said, as she always did, "I'll send you the money."

"Uh, today? Because, you know, rent and stuff."

"Can't you get Walter to give you an advance?" Walter being her boss, and an old friend.

"He already did," Annie said. "Uh, last week. I swear, I don't know how I got so screwed up this time."

Annalie never did. She was hopeless with money in general, and she skated by on check floats and loans—always had. If she weren't her sister, and honestly so good at heart, Bryn would have cut her off, but Annie didn't have a mean bone in her body. She had a job, a steady one, working the bar at Hooligan's Tavern, and Walter was pretty tolerant of her money problems so long as the till didn't come up short. Which, curiously, it never did. Annie could add like a fiend when she was on the clock.

"I'll send it to you today," Bryn promised. "Overnight mail. Okay?"

"Okay. You're a doll, Brynnie. I love you."

"Love you, too. Hey, did you hear from Tate?"

"Nothing since the last cryptic e-mail. Guess he's still in country." Their brother Tate, only a year older than Annalie, was in Afghanistan now, halfway through his rotation. They all tried to keep track of the casualty lists, just in case, but so far Tate had demonstrated the same trademark luck he'd always had. Drop that boy in the thick of the battle and he'd emerge unscratched.

Nothing like Bryn. She'd managed to get herself killed in a *morgue*.

"Okay, give Mom and Dad my love, okay?"

" 'Kay."

Short and sweet, that was Annie. She never chatted when she asked for money; Bryn guessed it made her uncomfortable. The next call would be about her latest boyfriend, and what she'd bought with Bryn's loan, and the latest frantic night at the bar . . . normal life.

Bryn wondered what the hell she was going to have to say during that conversation. Because her life right now wasn't exactly . . . something she could chat about. Family get-togethers were going to be odd and awkward from now on. Mom would be asking about when Bryn was going to give her a grandchild, which had always been a little bit weird, but was now going to hurt, a lot, for reasons Bryn couldn't possibly explain. Her oldest sister would be full of advice about that, most likely; she was the fertile one. Bryn never saw George or Kyle, which was a relief; Kyle was a criminal, and George was an asshole, despite being her brother. Bryn felt closest to Annalie, for all her screwups, and Tate, for all his absences.

Hey, guess what, guys. I'm dead. Apparently forever. But, you know, still hanging around. Cool, huh?

That would be one to drop into conversation over the barbecue grill and beer.

Oddly, hearing Annalie's utterly normal crisis had made her feel better, steadier, more herself. *Life goes on. Bryn's undead, but Annalie's still overdrawn.*

She found herself smiling as she pulled into the drive leading to Pharmadene, following the green line on her nav system. She hadn't noticed, leaving in the dark the night before, but this place was *huge*. The driveway was probably a half a mile, with two guard posts, both of which she had to pass with video conversations between the armed security presence and McCallister before being allowed to proceed. Her car was searched. *She* was searched, in a pat-down worthy of airport security. And finally she was allowed into a parking garage, which was the size of an office building on its own.

She was directed to the basement, which seemed weirdly appropriate, and, of course, armed security met her at the elevator. She wasn't given a choice where to go, but she was issued a badge with her picture on it—creepy, because she was sure she'd never posed for it. *God*, had they taken it when she was dead? No, this looked more like a hidden camera had snapped her from a distance. The badge had a red stripe at the top, and some kind of holographic image superimposed on it. Pharmadene's logo, she guessed.

"Miss Davis," the security man said who was escorting her. He had on a blue sports coat with the Pharmadene logo on the breast, and a badge with a green stripe. "Let me familiarize you with the rules. You're not supposed to be here from this point forward, but I'll go over the rules in any case. You will go only to your designated floor, and proceed straight to the person with whom you are meeting.

You're authorized for that person's office, the common break-room areas, and the restrooms. Nowhere else. Understood?"

"What happens if I go to the wrong place?"

"Alarms go off, and we go Code Red. Not a good thing. Please mind the rules."

Well, that was good to know. Code Red didn't sound like much fun, at least for her. "I'll be careful," she promised. The elevator doors opened on the seventh floor, and the guard walked her down a plushly carpeted hall that seemed to stretch on forever, to a door with no number, just a sliding nameplate that said MCCALLISTER, P., DIR. SECURITY.

The guard knocked, waited for the okay, and ushered her in. He didn't follow, and when Bryn looked back she saw that the door had closed behind her.

Patrick McCallister, wearing a fresh (but still beautifully tailored) suit and tie, came around the big modern desk and offered his hand. She took it, not sure why they were so formal all of a sudden, and took the square padded guest chair he indicated. "You're looking better today," he said, which was a backhanded compliment, at best. "Slept well?"

"Yes," she said. She wasn't sure if he knew she'd been at Joe Fideli's house, and didn't say, in case there were rules against it. "Surprisingly, I did. Maybe the nanites come with a Valium setting."

That surprised him into a smile, a genuine one. He was entirely different in that moment, and it caught her off guard. She looked away. When she checked, he was back to his old, unsmiling, very corporate self. "Let's get the obvious out of the way," he said, and reached in his desk drawer.

She was expecting to see the gun he'd promised, but instead, out came the pneumatic syringe. *I'm really going to get tired of this,* she thought, but rolled up the sleeve of her sweater and took the shot without complaint.

"Now. More forms for you to sign."

"Lovely." Bryn picked up the pen and clipboard and began flipping through, trying to glean from the legalese what exactly was being promised. It looked like the standard sort of safety disclaimers. *Shoot anybody with the weapon we provide you and we're not liable.* Whatever. She signed. "I would have thought being undead came with less paper-work."

"Not in the corporate sector."

"So am I a real Pharmadene employee now?"

"Unfortunately, you're not only official; you're my responsibility." He opened his desk drawer again, took out a box, and passed it across to her. She swung open the hinged top. Nice. A Beretta 92F S, basically the same as the weapon she'd been issued in the military. He'd included two boxes of ammunition as well. "It's registered to you personally," he said. "No direct connection to Pharmadene, as a security measure."

"Plausible deniability."

"Exactly. Should you go shooting up the town on Saturday night, the company won't be implicated."

"Am I likely to do something like that?" Bryn asked, checking the slide on the pistol. It was smooth as silk.

"Are you asking me if the drug makes you go insane? No. Not in any of our clinical trials."

"Well, that's reassuring."

"And I think we already established that it doesn't make you crave raw meat or brains."

"Even better." Bryn put the gun back in the box. "Still, this is quite a statement of trust, all things considered."

McCallister cocked his head slightly, watching her with those secretive, slightly sad dark eyes. "Not really," he said. "Pharmadene owns you now, Bryn. They control your access to the drug, and that absolutely guarantees your loyalty and service. Doesn't it?"

That was a harsh way to put it, and she felt a bright surge of anger inside. "Or it guarantees that I want to punish them for it," she said.

"Not advisable to take it there."

"Because you'll stop me?"

"Yes," McCallister said, and she was suddenly aware of his stillness. It wasn't quite human, the way he could shut down like that. And the look in his eyes . . . She'd been in the military, and she knew a stone killer when she saw one. "That's what they pay me to do."

She understood that; it hadn't been any different being a PFC in Baghdad. Whatever your personal feelings were about what you were ordered to do, you did it, unless it was illegal or immoral. And sometimes, she had to admit, you did it even then, because the gray areas were pretty broad.

"Good to know," she said softly.

McCallister relaxed in his chair, as much as he ever relaxed. "Good to have it clear between us," he said. "I understand you spoke to your sister on the way here." That was another unpleasant little jolt, and Bryn let him know she didn't like it without a word being said. McCallister gave her one of those little half smiles again, the kind that meant he didn't really mean it. "You're the property of Pharmadene now, Bryn. You won't have a personal life we won't know about. Sorry if that upsets you, but you're now carrying top-secret information, and we can't afford to let you just roam around without checking up on what you're saying."

"And what did I say?"

"Nothing specific, which is exactly what we'd like you to say. Nothing to anyone. Your family's not close geographically, which is good; we'd like you to limit your interaction with them to phone calls for a while, and discourage any kind of visits. Having your sister get curious about this unknown out-of-the-blue uncle you've just acquired would be . . . awkward."

"My family wasn't planning any get-togethers until the holidays," Bryn said coldly. "Is Big Brother going to spy on me on dates, too?"

"Probably," McCallister said. "At the very least, your gentlemen friends will be checked out thoroughly. Or lady friends, if your tastes run that way." He lifted an eyebrow, as if mildly curious.

"I thought you'd probably already know that, since you know so much about me."

He shrugged. "I try not to pry except where strictly necessary."

Which was so ridiculous that she wanted to hit him with a blunt object, preferably a bullet. "Didn't you have something to show me? Or was this just an opportunity to humiliate and frighten me again?"

"And give you a loaded weapon."

"That, too."

McCallister stood up and came around the desk, passed Bryn, and opened the office door. "This way," he said, and left. She scrambled up and after him, because he wasn't waiting on her. "Well, that's rude," she muttered, and hurried down the hall to catch up. "You know, if I go somewhere I'm not supposed to, this badge thing goes off."

"I know. I designed the system. If you're in close proximity to me or someone else with a green badge, you'll register as being escorted. Of course, until you try to open a door. *Then* you'll set off a Code Red."

"And what exactly happens during a Code Red?"

"You get thrown to the ground, handcuffed, and Tasered. If you're lucky." He sent her a half-amused glance. "Oh, and don't think that you can randomly shadow someone with a green badge, either. We're all well trained to challenge intruders and hold them for security. You wouldn't get far."

They rounded a corner—and this hall looked pretty much exactly like the last one, Bryn thought. Pharmadene wasn't big on decorating. Now that she thought about it, McCallister's office had been one big pile of modern nothing, too. No photos, plants, desk toys, the usual stuff people gathered around them. Not even a nonstandard paper clip tray. Of course, that could have just been him; he didn't seem like a cube-toy-and-kitty-poster type of person.

But as she glanced into a couple of nearby open offices, Bryn thought it might have also been corporate policy, because she'd never seen such personality-free workspaces. Everything matched, everything alike, everything company owned.

Like her.

"In here," McCallister said, and swiped his card to open up a closed door. No nameplate, she noticed, but didn't have time to ask what they were doing here. He ushered her in with a light touch at the small of her back, not quite a push. The fluorescent lights overhead flickered and came on automatically, revealing . . . an unoccupied office. Completely bare, except for the same stripped-down glass-and-chrome desk McCallister had, only this one was without accessories, a computer, or anything else except a desk chair in a plastic dust jacket.

In the desk chair sat Joe Fideli, who reached into his pocket and took out a small device. It looked like a black plastic pyramid. He pushed the top of it, and it glowed red in slow, hypnotic pulses.

"What—" Bryn started to ask, but McCallister put his finger to his lips. She subsided, waiting, until Fideli checked something on his smartphone, then nodded.

"We're good," he said. "Just keep your voices down. I can't do much about the soundproofing in here."

"What the hell is going on?" Bryn asked.

"I wanted to tell you something," McCallister said. "Something that shouldn't be on Pharmadene's public record."

"So talk to me after hours." *If you ever stop working*, she thought. She couldn't imagine McCallister without his suit and tie. He wasn't an off-duty kind of guy.

He and Fideli both shook their heads. "Doesn't work that way, sweetheart," Fideli said. "You already know you're being followed. Thing is, we're *all* being followed, monitored, tracked, you name it. You work for Pharmadene. You're their property, twenty-four-seven. Having any kind of private conversation is a real effort." Fideli looked at the red glowing device, which was pulsing just a bit faster now. "Enough chitchat. We've got about two minutes before I have to shut it down. Talk fast."

McCallister turned to Bryn and said, "When you get the name of the person selling the drug to Fairview, I want you to tell Joe that you need to see your sister Sharon."

Sharon. That sent a shock through her, and made her take a step back. "What do you know about Sharon?" Sharon had walked out of the house at nineteen and never been seen again. She might have run away. She might have . . . not. Privately, Bryn had always thought that something terrible had happened, something they might never fully understand, but the rest of her family carried on talking about Sharon as if she were still alive, still just absent.

"Nothing," McCallister said. "It's a signal to let him

know we need to meet off book and exchange information. This is for your own safety, Bryn."

She blinked and looked at Fideli. Him, she felt she could trust. "Joe?"

"He's playing straight with you. Listen to him."

"Why can't I just do what you told me to do? Find the seller and turn him in?"

"Because," McCallister said, "once you do, your usefulness to Pharmadene is over, and they're not going to waste one more dose of Returné on closed business. Understand? Succeed, and you're dead."

Her mouth opened and closed, but she couldn't think of anything to say. The look on his face, anxious and earnest, convinced her that he meant what he said. Her life—whatever it was—hung by a very slender thread, and Pharmadene's faceless bureaucrats and accountants held the scissors.

"I'm an investment," she said. "Once I no longer pay off . . ."

"Exactly. They'll let an investment mature, but a useless tool . . . gets discarded. Play for time. Give me a chance to find a way to keep you alive after that objective is achieved."

Fideli held up a finger, watching the now rapidly strobing pyramid. "Thirty seconds, man."

McCallister glanced at him, then focused back on Bryn. "Please," he said. "Do what I'm telling you. And be careful."

"Why do you care?" she asked, mystified.

He hesitated, then shook his head. "I don't think you'd understand even if I told you." His cell phone buzzed for attention, and he pulled it out and checked the screen. "I'm due for a meeting in fifteen. We need to wrap this up."

The little flashing-red device was really working now, clearly warning them failure was approaching. Bryn quickly looked at Fideli. "One more thing: did you find Fast Freddy?"

"Not yet. But I will, no doubt about it." He glanced down. "Time." He tapped the top of the pyramid, and it went back to a lifeless black plastic object. He waved silently at the two of them, shooing them to leave. McCallister nodded, opened the door, and ushered Bryn back out into the hallway. As they left the empty office behind, it was like the whole thing had never even happened.

"You have a full understanding of your position with us, Bryn?" McCallister asked, back to the poised, confident corporate exec. She had no choice but to nod. "Excellent. If you have any questions, my number's programmed into your cell phone, as is Joe's. If we need to meet, you can call me and ask me out on a date."

"*Excuse* me?"

"Was that unclear? Ask me to coffee. Or dinner. Whatever seems convenient. Simply to ensure you're maintaining your cover in the field."

"You are unbelievable."

There went that tiny little smile again, tight and controlled, meaning nothing. "I do date, Bryn. Occasionally."

She bet he did it on a schedule. *1900 to 2100 hours, dinner. 2100 to 2115, drive the girl home. 2115 to 2130, sex. 2135, shower, kiss good-bye. 2140, drive home.*

"I don't date jackasses," she said. "Just so we're clear."

If she'd expected to hurt his feelings, she was disappointed. "You express yourself with great clarity," he said, as if it couldn't have mattered less to him. They were back at his office again, and he opened the door and went inside. When she tried to follow, he held out his hand to stop her at the door. "Your escort will be with you in a moment."

"What about the, uh, Code Red?"

She was already talking to the wood, which had closed decisively in her face.

She needn't have worried. By the time she'd finished the sentence, there was someone at her elbow wearing a green badge and a Pharmadene blazer, mutely inviting her to proceed toward the elevator, please.

"Jackass," she muttered to the door, and followed orders. She had the feeling there were going to be a lot of orders to come, and she wasn't going to enjoy it.

At all.

With nothing better to do than wait for the construction, Bryn went back to her apartment. It felt *very* strange pulling the big, shiny Town Car into a slot in the very working-class parking area; she felt like a total fraud. Her neighbors would be gossiping like mad, dying to know how she'd come into such a windfall. She'd have to get her story together.

Right. Rich dead uncle, inherited the business, blah, blah.

Bryn climbed the stairs to the second floor and unlocked the door, not even thinking about any of it; she was focused instead on the heavy weight of the box in her arms that McCallister had given her. *Have to get a holster for this sucker*, she thought. Having a heavy handgun like this rattling around in her purse or stuck in her waistband, gangsta style, wasn't going to cut it.

She hip-bumped the door closed and reached for the light switch, then hesitated, because her instincts suddenly woke up and screamed. She didn't know why for a second, and then she heard the subtle whisper of breathing in the dark.

Oh, God. Fast Freddy. He's here!

No time to get the box open and the gun ready for use.

Bryn dropped her purse to the floor, flipped the light switch, and swung the heavy box in a short, powerful arc that connected perfectly with—

Nothing.

It didn't connect at all, because the breathing wasn't human, and there was no head in the way. Her bulldog, Mr. French, looked up at her with sleepy, disappointed brown eyes, snorted, and shook himself in a ripple of loose skin and fur. He turned around three times and plopped down on the floor next to his empty food bowl.

"Holy *crap*, dog, you scared the hell out of me!" Bryn gasped, and staggered over to the small card table she had in place of a dining room set. She put the box on it, retrieved her purse, and clicked the dead bolts firmly shut before coming back to glare at Mr. French. He snorted again. "So this is how it is, huh? You lurk in the dark and creep me out, and expect to be fed? Is that it?"

He put his head in his bowl and gave her the melting puppy-dog eyes. Bryn groaned and gave up. She kicked off her shoes and opened the pantry, pulling out the sealed bin of dog food; Mr. French obligingly and politely moved out of the bowl for her to pour, then sniffed the food. He always did that, as if he were in doubt about its quality, but this time, again, it passed doggy muster, and he began digging in with sharp little crunches. She refilled his water bowl, too, and checked the papers in the corner of the apartment. No messes. Mr. French had his standards about that, but now that he'd supped a bit, he looked up and her and wiggled his butt to let her know he was ready. She sighed and reached for the leash, and he padded over with great dignity to be harnessed for the trip outside.

Once his business was finished, it was back to the food bowl for more. Bryn watched him eat, mindlessly soothed by his happiness. Food consumed, Mr. French waddled over and jumped up in her lap, where he leaned against her, a solid little weight of muscle and fur. She petted him and scratched where he liked it and talked to him about nothing in particular, until suddenly tears were streaming down her cheeks and Mr. French was staring up at her with concern on his old-man face and trying to lick the sadness away. She hugged him. He had dog-food breath, and he needed a bath, but it was good, so good, to have someone love her right now.

"I'm sorry, baby," she said, and kissed him on the top of his furry head. "Was your day better than mine?"

Mr. French barked, just once. He knew when she asked him a question, and although his reasoning skills were a little suspect, she had the feeling that on this one, he'd almost certainly agree.

It felt so good to be home, with her clothes in the closet and her robe hanging on the hook in the bathroom. The shower felt great, and as the hot water beat down on her head, Bryn Davis, dead girl, sat down in the tub and let it carry away all the tears, the sweat, the fear, and the anger. And if she cried a little more, it didn't bother Mr. French, who did sentry duty curled up on the bath mat until she shut off the water, dried off, and got into her robe. Then he padded his way into the bedroom and hopped up on the unmade bed.

Routines. She'd come so close to never making it back here to this, to the dog, to her *life*. Maybe it wasn't much; maybe in Patrick McCallister's terms this didn't constitute a useful existence, but she liked it. Her apartment was spare, but nice; she had what she needed, and a few things she wanted.

"But everything's changed," she told Mr. French as he curled up on the bed beside her. Her hair was still damp, and she fluffed it as she leaned back against the stacked pillows. "I'm not the same as I was. You know?"

He huffed a little, which she interpreted to mean, *Oh, well, nothing stays the same.* And as always, the dog was right.

Bryn rested for a while, then checked the clock. It was seven p.m., and the voice on the message had said to meet at nine. The only question was, where?

Time to go back to Fairview and find out.

She blow-dried her hair and dressed in dark jeans and a black sweatshirt, tied her hair back in a ponytail, and rooted around for her most comfortable running shoes. As she strapped them on, Mr. French watched with troubled interest. He whined softly as she stood.

"No, you can't go," she said, and patted him on the head. "Tell you what: we'll go for a run in the morning, okay? You stand guard here."

He licked his chops and sat down next to the bed, and she felt a surge of love for this one relationship in her life that wasn't even a little bit complicated.

Then she went to perform some crime.

Driving to Fairview Mortuary at night was a special kind of creepy. Not the drive itself; that wasn't so bad. But getting out of the car in the growing shadows . . . not so great. The place looked like a classic Gothic nightmare waiting to happen, from the silent, lightless, ruined building to the undertone of tragedy that still vibrated in the air, like smoke.

She'd just walked over to Lincoln Fairview's silver Town Car when the last rays of sun faded, and the touch of darkness felt claustrophobic. The tire iron from the extremely clean trunk was in her hand, and as she raised it to smash the driver's-side window, a voice behind her said, "You sure that's a good idea?"

Bryn spun around, tire iron held in a death-tight grip, ready to defend herself, but it was only Joe Fideli. She hadn't spotted his truck anywhere, but Joe himself was now lounging on the fender of her car, arms crossed, looking calm and a little amused.

"Noisy," he said. "Glass everywhere. Alarms. Even out here, you run the risk of attracting attention; plus someone's going to report the break-in later."

Bryn calmed the panicked rush of her heartbeat with slow, steady breaths, fighting the push of adrenaline, and lowered the heavy steel bar. "You followed me."

"Bryn, my job is to make sure you don't do anything stupid. So yeah. I followed you. When you leave your house in the middle-class version of ninja clothes, I pay attention. You didn't look like you were running out for milk and kibble." He walked over, moved her gently but firmly out of the way, and reached into his coat pocket. He had a set of keys, and when he pressed the button, the Lincoln flashed its lights and the door locks disengaged.

"You've got his keys," she said, and pressed her eyes shut. Of *course* he had the keys; Fairview's body had been taken to whatever secured facility Pharmadene had designated, and McCallister and Fideli would have access to everything. "Thanks."

"No problem. What are we looking for?"

There was no point in pretending she was just indulging in some random destruction. "The GPS," she said. "There was a voice mail today on the company's line. It sounded like he stood somebody up last night whom he was planning to meet, and it was rescheduled for tonight. Apparently, Fairview knew where the meeting was to take place. . . ."

"And you figured he'd been there before. Decent call. Let's see what's what." Fideli slid into the driver's seat, fired up the car, and began checking the computer as Bryn slid in on the passenger side. "Home, strip club, home, strip club . . ."

"That's something I really didn't need to imagine about him."

"You and me both, sweetheart. Here's something. He went to an unknown address two weeks ago at eleven o'clock at night." Fideli pulled out his own phone, entered the coordinates, and studied the results. "It's a warehouse," he said. "Currently unoccupied. Good bet that it's where he was meeting his contact; industrial areas are nice and deserted that time of night, especially ones not being rented. What time was the caller saying to meet?"

"Nine," Bryn said. She glanced at the dashboard clock. It was eight. "There's something else—another caller. It sounded like a customer, you know, an illegal one. He left a number to call."

"We'll get to that one later," Fideli said, and fastened his seat belt. "If our supplier is expecting Fairview, I don't want to disappoint him, so we'll take this car. Strap in."

Fairview's car didn't drive quite as smoothly as hers, but it was still a lush ride. Bryn didn't enjoy it, mainly because she still smelled Fairview's cologne trapped in the upholstery, and couldn't help but think about how coldly he'd ordered her death. She'd so totally misjudged him, and she'd thought her judgment about those kinds of things was solid.

Thinking about Fairview led her to ask, "Any sign of Freddy?"

"Not yet," Fideli said. "He'll turn up. He has to, unless he's got his own supply of the drug stashed somewhere. . . . Even then, the nanites degrade fast. Two weeks is the longest you can keep the stuff out in the wild, unless you've got nitrogen freezers. He'll have to get to the supplier to make a deal."

"Or make a deal with Pharmadene," she said. "Like I did."

"True that, but I can't see McCallister getting all warm and fuzzy about hiring Freddy."

"McCallister would do whatever gets the job done."

He sent her an unreadable look and said, "You don't know him that well."

They drove in silence for a while longer before Fideli reached the turnoff to the warehouse. "Right," he said. "Here's how this will go. You've got your weapon?"

"Yes." It was in the pocket of her sweatshirt—not the

best place to keep it, but the only one she had, at the moment. She wasn't going to go all street-corner and stick it in her jeans waistband. She'd seen too many stupid accidents with guys clowning around in the army.

"We roll up and stay in the car." He pulled off to the side of the road and killed the lights. "Switch. You're driving."

"Me? Why?" Too late to ask; he was already out of the car and walking around. She scrambled over the seat and buckled in as he took her spot. "Okay, fine, I'm driving. Now what?"

"Follow the directions." Fideli took out his gun and checked it with professional calm. "You park somewhere with the passenger side up against the building, preferably out of direct lighting. I'll get out and into the shadows, and wait for him to pull up next to you on the driver's side. Then I go around to his passenger door, game over. If things get hairy, hit the gas and get out of the way."

"I thought I couldn't die from a bullet wound."

"You can't, but it'd hurt, and as the one who *would* die, I'd rather avoid the whole gun battle. You understand the plan?"

"Yes." She glanced down at the map. They were at the entrance to the warehouse complex. A turn took her down a deserted, well-maintained road. Four gigantic buildings on the left. Two were occupied, with semi trucks being loaded and forklifts whizzing around. The last two were completely dark, except for security lighting in the parking lots and over the shuttered entrances.

She turned in at the last entrance, made a big circle, and parked as directed with the passenger side close against the building, near the corner. "Joe," she said, as he turned off the overhead light before opening the door. "Be careful, okay?"

"It warms my heart that you care."

She tried for a smile. "Well, you're better than McCallister."

Fideli leaned in and gave her that odd look again. "Like I said, you don't know him very well. Lock it."

He shut the door, and she hit the lock button. He was out of sight in seconds. *Damn*, the man was stealthy. She supposed she should be happy about that, in these circumstances.

The minutes ticked by, and she watched the clock. Eight thirty crawled by, and then eight forty-five. She fidgeted and wished she dared to play the radio, but she didn't want to miss anything, even the slightest noise. If Joe Fideli could creep up on her, so could the enemy, and Bryn kept a constant watch on the mirrors around the car.

At eight fifty-eight, she saw headlights on the road. A car turned into the parking lot and glided almost silently across the empty space. It was black, with heavily darkened windows, and it looked fast.

It pulled to an idling stop with the hood facing her, lights boring into the vehicle. Bryn wasn't sure, but she thought the driver could probably see her through the tinting—at least her silhouette, which looked nothing like Lincoln Fairview's. The headlights were blinding, and she couldn't see a thing.

She heard Fideli suddenly shout, "Bryn, *down!*" and flung herself sideways, clicking out of the seat belt, just as a hammering chatter of gunfire filled the air. *Full auto*, she thought, ears rattling and burning from the onslaught of sound, even as she scrambled for the handle of the passenger door. *Damn it—locked!* She didn't know where the buttons were, but she flailed at them as bullets shattered the driver's-side window into bright, flying shards. One sliced a bright red line across her hand, but she didn't feel any pain through the rush of adrenaline. When she glanced back she saw light shining through holes punched through the metal of the door. The air was full of drifting particles of dust and fluff from the upholstery, and the firing was still going on.

Bryn found the lock release, opened the door, and slithered out to the ground. She scrambled over and put herself behind the engine block, the safest place, as the Lincoln shuddered under the impact of more bullets.

She heard more shots, measured and of a different pitch, coming from the rear of the car, and looked over to see Joe Fideli crouched there as he returned fire. There was a screech of tires, and their attacker pulled out after one last burst of bullets that rang and echoed against the concrete.

Then the car was gone, speeding for the exit.

"Bryn?"

"I'm okay," she said. "Are you?"

"Fine." Fideli sounded frustrated as he changed clips on his gun, chambered a round, and holstered the gun. He took out his phone and dialed. "Pat? You got him?" *Pat?* McCallister? Bryn waited tensely, and Fideli turned away and talked in too low of a voice to be overheard. She stood up on shaky legs. It finally occurred to her that she hadn't even drawn her gun. Hadn't fired a single round at the fleeing car. *Stupid.*

It seemed to take forever, but Fideli hung up and came back to her. He didn't look happy.

"What happened?" Bryn asked.

"We had the exits from the industrial park covered, but he dumped the car at the next lot over. He may have had another car stashed, or gone on foot. We don't know where he went from there. There are a lot of trucks coming and going from the other warehouses; he could be hitchhiking on any one of them, and we can't stop and search them without triggering a lot of questions. He could also have gone on foot; it's an easy run across the park area over there, and there's a mall on the other side."

"What about the car? Can you trace it?"

"Stolen less than two hours ago from a bar," he said. "Our friend isn't taking any chances, even at a supposedly friendly meeting. I think he's a little paranoid."

"You're not paranoid if they're out to get you."

"True," Fideli said, as a dark sedan pulled into the lot, and two Pharmadene security men, in the traditional blazers, got out and walked toward them. "Nothing we can do tonight. Let's get you home. I'll see you at work tomorrow. Oh, and Bryn?"

"What?"

He smiled and winked at her. "Good effort. But next time, tell me about your stealthy plans first. Not that I wouldn't be onto them, but it's nice if we can talk about it."

The next day, Bryn dressed in a practical gray pantsuit with a shell-pink blouse, minimal makeup and jewelry, and sensible flat shoes to go out to see the progress at Fairview. She took Mr. French with her, because hey, as the boss, she *could*. Besides, he loved the car, and sticking his head out the window. His doggy joy lightened her mood considerably.

Joe Fideli was already in the parking lot when she arrived, leaning against the hood of his big truck. He nodded to her, and smiled when he saw Mr. French padding along at her heels. "Is it bring-a-friend-to-work day?" he asked.

"He's not my friend. I never saw him before," she said, as the dog sat down next to her, regarding Joe with suspicious dark eyes. He growled a little. Joe growled back, which seemed to settle the matter to Mr. French's satisfaction. "Did you get any sleep at all?"

"Enough. Besides, I didn't want to be late for work," he said.

"Any progress on our gun-happy friend from last night?"

"Nothing. We're pulling security footage all over the place, but right now it looks like he's a ghost. And I'm guessing he won't be back in touch for a while."

That sounded ominous. "What . . . what does that mean for me?"

"I don't know." At least he was honest about it. "For now, we just continue with the plan. You've still got a lead on one of the revived. We can work that. Pat's keeping last night's little fiasco under wraps for now from the higher ups; his guys won't talk. There's got to be another angle we can work."

She hoped so, because suddenly it felt like her time—already short—was rapidly running out.

Fideli tried to sound positive. "Never mind all that. I've got your shot for the day; probably ought to take care of that about noon. My team has cleared the office area for entry, and they tell me they should be finished with the repairs on the prep room and that end of the building soon. You can plan for the grand reopening."

"Maybe we should rent one of those giant inflatable advertising things," she said.

"Gorilla?"

"Dracula," she said. "With the coffin."

"You might want to go with something a little more subtle."

"You're no fun."

"You know, that's exactly what my wife tells me, too. Especially when I stay out all night getting shot at."

Somehow, she doubted that. Fideli, lots more than McCallister, had the makings of someone who understood the meaning of *fun* without looking it up in the dictionary. "Hey," she said, following that train of thought, although admittedly with a strange twist, "can you get me a holster for my new, ah, accessory? It's pretty awkward to carry in my purse."

His eyes crinkled at the corners, and he walked around to the passenger side of the truck, opened up a lockbox in the bed, and came back with a bag. "Happy birthday," he said. "If it doesn't fit, let me know; I'll return it."

Inside was a shoulder holster and harness, and she smiled in genuine surprise. "You really think of everything."

"That's what they pay me for." That drained a little of the warmth out of the moment. Fideli turned instead to the main building and made an after-you gesture. "Guess we ought to get started, boss."

"I guess so," she said, and walked with him toward the front door, dodging the continuing ant march of construction materials and workers around the front. "What do you know about up-selling?"

Chapter 5

The first thing Bryn did, once she'd checked her office for damage, was pull out the paper on which she'd scrawled the phone number from the voice mail, and dial it. Joe Fideli hadn't left; he took up a post in the chair across from her, and even though she made significant motions for him to leave, he shook his head and made himself more comfortable with a steaming cup of coffee. He'd gotten her one, too, which was nice. Mr. French was waddling around the room busily sniffing things, which included a close inspection of Fideli's socks and shoes.

As Bryn dialed, Fideli said, "Put it on speaker."

She did, and they listened to three rings before the connection clicked in and a shaky voice said, "Hello?"

"Hello," Bryn replied. "This is Fairview Mortuary. I'm calling on behalf of Mr. Fairview."

There was a brief silence, and then the man said, "Is he there?"

"No. There's been . . . an accident. I'm afraid Mr. Fairview is dead."

"Oh. Oh, God." She heard him take a damp, shaking breath. "What am I going to do?"

"Sir—what's your name?"

"Spiro. Spiro Kanakareides. Look, Mr. Fairview, he was . . . doing something special for me—do you understand?"

"Yes. Yes, I understand." Bryn glanced at Joe, who nodded encouragement. "Mr. Kanakareides, why don't you come in to talk to me? I'm sure that I can help with your problem."

"You can?"

"Yes, I can." She tried to sound soothing, professional, and utterly reliable. She must have succeeded, because after a moment he agreed, and hung up the phone.

"Good," Joe said. "Let me know when he gets here. I'll have a team ready to take him."

"Take him *where*?"

Fideli frowned. "I thought you understood, Bryn. We're in the cleanup business. We get Fairview's contacts and his clients. Mr. Kanakareides has to be brought in and debriefed, and we have to decide what's to be done with him."

"But you'll probably let him die, right?"

Fideli looked away this time. "Yeah, probably, unless there's a real good reason to keep him maintained," he said. "Look, I'm not wild about any of this, but it's got to be kept inside the company. That's what we're here to do: seal the leak, repair the damage. People will get hurt. Can't be avoided. The good news is that we'll have all of them within a few days; they can't be skipping too many shots in a row, and they'll be contacting us. This isn't the hard part."

"Isn't it?" she asked softly. "He preyed on people who were scared and desperate, and made them even *more* scared and desperate. And now we're going to victimize them all over again. That doesn't bother you?"

"If it did, I'd be in the wrong line of work. Look, I'm as compassionate as I can be, but there have to be limits. These people weren't supposed to live. They're only here because Fairview got greedy, not because God came down from on high and granted them a miracle."

"And what about me? I'm only here because *you* had a spasm of conscience, right? Now I'm marking time, because you already told me your mysterious supplier was done with us. I'm surplus goods. After the last one of these . . . these revived checks in for their shot, I'll be dealt with, too."

He didn't deny it. "Theoretically. But in practice, there may be other ways you can be useful to us."

She laughed, and it sounded empty. "Forgive me if I don't feel reassured by that. It's not very theoretical to *me*."

"Bryn." He leaned forward and took her hand in his.

"I'm not going to let you down. Pat's not going to let you down. You can count on that, okay?"

She didn't believe him—not that he wasn't sincere at the moment. She *did* believe that. But Fideli wasn't a rogue; it wasn't in his nature. He'd do what he was ordered, even if he didn't like it. Sooner or later, Patrick McCallister would order Fideli to walk away while she was put in some sterile little room again, to die. And Fideli would feel bad about it, and probably carry guilt for a while, but his life would go on.

And hers would not.

There was absolutely no point in saying all that, she realized. Nothing was going to change her fate.

So Bryn smiled and said, "It's okay. What do we do now?"

"We get this place running," Joe said. He seemed relieved that she'd accepted his reassurances. "So let's get started."

Going through the files was empty work, but at least it passed the time, and that was all Bryn was doing now . . . passing time.

Mr. Kanakareides—Spiro—showed up two hours later. She knew only because she was looking out the window, sipping her coffee; he never made it to the building. Joe Fideli had a car there, and two plainclothes security men, and Spiro was intercepted and put in and driven off without a single ripple of alarm. That was how easy it was to end someone's life, she realized. All it took was being polite and efficient in public, until you didn't have to be polite anymore.

The phone rang.

Bryn looked at it with dread and misery, and picked up the receiver. "Fairview Mortuary," she said. "Bryn Davis speaking." She fully expected it to be another of the desperate revived, and it made her sick to her soul—if she still had one—to think that she had to lure these people into the trap. But she had no choice, and really, *they* had no choice. Fate. It was a bitch.

But this time, the call wasn't from one of those people. There was a silence, and then a strangely modulated voice said, "Now I know your name. Good. I'll be seeing you, Bryn Davis."

The call ended. Bryn stared down at the phone, frowning and a little creeped out. It *could* have been a prank call, but it felt . . . different.

"What's wrong?"

She looked up to find Joe standing in the doorway, watching her. Full of concern, just like those men had been down in the parking lot, calming down poor Mr. Kanakareides.

"I had a call," she said. "Caller ID was blocked."

"Do you think it was one of our revived friends?"

"It didn't seem like it."

"Our supplier?"

"Maybe," she said. "And now he knows who I am."

Joe hesitated for a second before he said, "Well, that was bound to happen. And it's what we want."

"Maybe what *you* want!"

"Bryn, we may still have a shot at luring him in. You can still make the case that you went to the meeting to fulfill Fairview's obligations, since you took over the business. You can convince him that you know everything, and you're willing to deal with him. It can happen."

"You're kidding, right? You *shot at him*! I'd think that would cancel any deals."

"Nah, people in this line of work expect to get some return fire when they shoot up a car. So you have a bodyguard. He'd expect that, too. I'll bet Fairview never met him alone. Fast Freddy was probably his muscle."

She thought it over, because it did sound logical, and somewhere inside, she was still struggling for hope, *any* hope. "So what do you want me to do?"

"Wait," he said. "He'll call back, or he'll contact you some other way. Stick to the story. Make sure he believes that you want to deal. He hasn't got too many moves right now, if he wants ready cash; this guy is too cautious to take it to the street. Fairview Mortuary is a known quantity."

"He'll recognize that your goons are *in the parking lot*!"

"They're contractors, not Pharmadene employees. Even if he's watching and makes their faces, he can't trace them back. We're good." He gave her a warm smile. "Relax, Bryn. I'm not taking any chances with your safety. I promise."

That, Bryn reflected, made her feel both better and worse, because she really didn't want to like Joe Fideli any more than she already did. But as the day went on, as the two of them found reasons to talk, she couldn't help it. He was just . . . likable.

The last call came in as she was gathering up her things to leave, and Mr. French let out a mournful whine as he stood at the door. "I know," she said. "We're going, I promise. Hang in there." She picked up the phone. "Fairview Mortuary, Bryn Davis speaking. Can I help you?"

"Maybe." It was the modulated voice again. "You surprised me last night. I was expecting my usual contact."

Bryn put down her purse and sank into a chair. Mr. French came over and flopped down onto the carpet beside her, looking depressed but resigned. She hardly noticed when he laid his warm, heavy head over her feet. "Well," she said, fighting to keep her voice even, "you have to admit, I think you surprised me a little more, what with the gunfire and all. I was just keeping my uncle's appointment."

"Your uncle." She couldn't tell if he meant that to sound suspicious; the modulation ironed all expression out of his voice. In fact, she wasn't even sure it *was* a him. "You're telling me you're related to Lincoln Fairview."

"Yes. And I inherited his property."

"Let's pretend I believe you. How did you know where to meet me?"

"Honestly? I didn't. My uncle's car had a nav system. I thought it was probably the warehouse, but it was a guess. He didn't leave me your contact information."

"He didn't have it."

Bryn waited, but he didn't say anything more. Still, he hadn't hung up on her. That was something. "So," she said. "You were supplying him with . . . a certain drug. And I'm going to need new stock, obviously. Whatever my uncle had on hand burned up with him, and I've got clients. Desperate ones. I need something to sell."

"I don't trust you," he said.

"My clients don't have a lot of time to wait around for us to develop a relationship."

"That's too bad for them. My advice is to recruit new clients. This is going to take some time, and you're going to show me some goodwill to start or this conversation ends now."

Bryn's office door opened, and Joe Fideli stepped in, moving in his usual ninja stealth mode. She pointed at the phone, and he nodded. Luckily, Mr. French had already gotten used to Joe; he raised his head and stared at him, but didn't bark or even growl. "What kind of goodwill?" she asked.

"You're going to do a wire transfer of a hundred thousand dollars into an account that I will name in the next call, and you're going to do it without bargaining."

"Really," she said flatly. "What do you take me for, an idiot? You think I'll just hand over that kind of money for nothing?"

"Not for nothing," he said. "You'll hand it over so I don't put a bullet in your head the next time you go home to that crappy apartment, Bryn, or the next time you go out walking that ugly dog of yours—and I'll kill the dog for free. A hundred thousand buys you a week for me to look you over and decide whether or not I want to deal. No negotiations. I know Fairview's coffers are deep."

Click. She waited, but he was gone.

Bryn hung up the phone and took a deep breath, feeling strangely violated—not so much that he knew so much about her, but that he'd mentioned her dog. *Dogs are off-limits.* "He threatened to shoot me," she said to Joe. "And my dog."

"Fucker," he said, and bent to pat Mr. French, who allowed it with regal indifference. "What does he want?"

"A hundred thousand dollars. I suppose it's an introduction fee. Black-market deals in Iraq used to be like that— you pay to play."

"And you know about black-market deals in Iraq how, exactly?"

She smiled grimly. "I was in supply, on the ground, in a war zone. How do you think I know? We couldn't always get what we needed when we needed it. My job was to get it, period."

"You're just full of surprises, kid. Okay, so you pay the hundred thousand, and . . . ?"

"And maybe he'll come back for more. Or maybe he'll just shoot me and walk away."

"Well," Joe said, "the good news is that if he does, you'll just ruin a good outfit."

He was, Bryn thought, always looking for the bright side.

The next morning, she got a modulated voice on the phone, reciting a string of numbers, which she took down and read back. There was no conversation, and no additional threats, by which she understood he wasn't screwing around. She gave the info to Joe, and he made the transfer using some method she didn't know about, and didn't want to know.

She got another call that simply said, "You're not dead yet."

Which almost made her laugh, because, hey, she really was.

It took exactly the amount of time Joe had said for the construction work to finish, and during that time, she got no more calls, except from two more of Fairview's extortion victims; those were quietly spirited away by Pharmadene, but away from Fairview's premises.

The grand reopening arrived, mostly thanks to Lucy's hard work; Bryn honestly didn't know what she would have done without her. Lucy knew absolutely everything about everything, including things Bryn had never imagined would have to be done. Plus, she was a complete sweetheart with inspectors, all of whom went away charmed and delighted with Fairview's new, improved looks.

Bryn had settled into a little bit of a routine—wake up, shower, breakfast, pat Mr. French on the head, drive her new car to Fairview, and get her coffee there. Joe Fideli had morphed into a totally acceptable funeral director, which did not surprise her much; in putting on the dark suit and tie, he'd also put on an air of gravity and seriousness. The only time he dropped it was when they were alone in her office, and even then, he used his little black pyramid device to give them a few moments' privacy.

"Done," he said on the morning of the grand reopening, as he emptied the contents of a syringe into her arm. She'd gotten used to choosing blouses that rolled up easily, determined not to have to go half-naked before him, and particularly McCallister, ever again. Fideli disposed of the syringe in a red biohazard sharps container, which he put in a second red biohazard bag. She watched this process, frowning, as she slipped her jacket back on.

"Is the syringe dangerous?"

"Nah, but it's proprietary. So I try to keep it double-bagged until I can get it back to the mother ship. I'm responsible for every one of these bastards."

"Have you found Fast Freddy yet?"

"No." Fideli seemed peeved about it. "He must have had a stash of the drug somewhere, and was able to make it there safely before too much damage was done. Otherwise he'd have shown up by now. People tend to notice shambling, decomposing—" He checked himself and looked at her. "No offense."

Bryn cleared her suddenly tight throat. "Uh, none taken, I guess. So what do we do now?"

"Same thing you were doing before, while we wait for our mysterious friend to get over his stage fright."

"I need another trained mortician before I can open for business."

"Luckily, I already got that covered. You've got an appointment in"—he checked his watch—"half an hour. Applicant's name is Riley Block."

"But I didn't even put out an ad yet!"

"Actually, you did. You're paying pretty well, too. Oh, and you offer medical and dental. Lucy's already prepared all the paperwork for you." He stood up and smoothed the creases out of his pants as the front bell sounded. "That'd be your applicant, I guess."

It was. Lucy bustled in, marched up to Bryn, and gave her a sassy grin and a thick sheaf of paperwork. Bryn took it and tried to smile brightly in return, but she must not have fooled anyone. Lucy gave her a concerned look. "Boss, you look pale. You need to stop working all day and night. You spend too much time inside this place."

The more she came in contact with real human sympa-thy, the more isolated Bryn felt. "I'm okay, Lucy. Thank you. I have to say, between you and Joe, you've done an amazing job pulling this place together. I really don't feel like I've done anything."

Lucy smiled. "Well, that's just nonsense. You pay me to know what I'm doing, and I know more about the death business than anybody you'll ever meet. I've been through *all* the wars."

"I'd love to hear some of those war stories," Joe said.

"Why, let me tell you ..." And she was off, chattering with Joe about her favorite mortician story, which was not just shocking but downright perverted, and hilarious. Bryn got herself a cup of coffee and left them to it as they walked from her office. She'd decided not to take Mr. Fairview's palace of a workspace, but had kept her own; she felt more comfortable there. Less haunted by what had happened. Now she sipped her coffee, then got up and put on her white lab coat and modeled it for the mirror. *How did I get here?* She could still remember the echoes of how proud this coat had made her, how excited she'd been to dive into the new job on that first day.

It seemed like a million miles away now.

Bryn started a little as a brisk knock sounded on her door; she couldn't help but flash back to Mr. Fairview, and her first morning with him. She took off the lab coat and hung it up, straightened the line of her jacket over the hol-stered gun, and went to greet her prospective new employee.

Riley Block was not what she'd expected—mostly be-cause she'd expected, well, a man. Riley was a woman, older than Bryn by about ten years; she was taller, blonder, and had a square face with a prominent jaw that seemed all business, all the time. Even the smile she gave Bryn seemed artificial and businesslike as she held out her hand. "Miss Davis," she said. "Nice to meet you."

"Nice to meet you. Please come in."

They settled in the same comfortable area where Bryn would have placed a prospective customer, and Bryn tried to gather her wits. She'd never interviewed anybody else for a job; she'd expected Joe Fideli to be here and guide her through it. *How do you tell if someone's a lunatic, anyway?* There had to be some kind of clue, but as she studied Riley Block, she didn't catch one. She finally, somewhat desperately, said, "So, tell me about yourself."

Luckily, that seemed to be the right thing to say. Riley whipped out an impressive résumé, which Bryn studied as Riley described her training (excellent), academic record (also excellent), references (ditto), and goals.

One thing was certain: she was no Fast Freddy, and Bryn loved her on the spot just for that.

Fideli finally showed up during the tour of the premises, but he let Bryn take the lead—just what she didn't want, but she toughed it out. Riley seemed to have a good grasp of the prep room; she did a fast and thorough inventory of the restocked supplies and suggested a couple of additions, which Bryn added to her notes. All in all, it wasn't a warm experience, but then, morticians weren't generally known for their social skills.

Riley seemed perfectly competent, and after a quick consultation with Fideli, Bryn hired her.

Fairview Mortuary was back in business.

If Bryn didn't feel especially great about that ... well, she hoped it didn't show.

They booked their first client the next morning: mercifully, it was a natural death, a ninety-year-old grandmother of four kids, twelve grandchildren, and twentysomething great-grandchildren. It was a sad experience for the family, naturally, but nothing traumatic. Bryn didn't think she could deal with trauma anyway, not yet.

Fideli carried the bulk of the work, and was surprisingly good at it; for someone who'd initially seemed so alpha-male-soldier and intimidating, he could really empathize when it counted, or at least give a damn good imitation of it. Riley received the body later that afternoon and started her work, and Bryn was surprised to find that she, too, was efficient and capable.

I'm the only one with a learning curve, Bryn thought. It didn't make her feel any better. Neither did her daily shot, administered by Fideli in the privacy of her office; it still stung, every time, and she was starting to really hate the sight of a needle.

What alarmed her, though, was that after his usual ritual of bagging up the syringe, he reached in his pocket and took out his little black pyramid device, switched it on, and checked its effectiveness against his phone app, which led her to wonder, again, whether there was a countersurveillance app store somewhere.

Probably.

"Okay, two minutes," Fideli said, and leaned forward, looking at her with unexpected directness. "Need to give you a heads-up. You're going to get a visit today from Irene Harte."

"I don't know the name."

"No reason you should. Ms. Harte is a vice president at Pharmadene, in charge of the division that makes our little wonder drug."

Bryn frowned. "What does she want from me?"

"My guess? She's going to try to shut all this down. And you." He didn't say it, but Bryn understood the subtext instantly—*shut down* was code for *death*. "McCallister had to make a situation report, and apparently Ms. Harte didn't take it too well. So you get a personal inspection. We need you to be on your toes, Bryn. She's got the power to destroy a lot more than just you."

"You mean McCallister."

Fideli nodded. "Patrick put his neck on the line when he brought you back, on my say-so," he said. "And it's still on the line, because he didn't terminate your revival as soon as he knew you weren't going to be an instant gusher of information. Harte likes results, fast, while McCallister prefers to invest time and get things right. It doesn't make them buddies." He glanced at the red indicator on his device, which was flashing a fast warning. "Time to wrap up. Be ready for her, and don't let her intimidate you."

Bryn nodded, and he tapped the top of the pyramid and shut off the surveillance jammer. It went back in his pocket, and he resumed talking about funeral arrangements for their new client as if they'd never stopped.

It set Bryn on edge. She was feeling a little odd anyway;

maybe it was her imagination (and it probably was), but she felt jittery and warm, and she wanted nothing but to go home and sink into a hot bath with a glass of wine. Spend the evening curled up with Mr. French watching a shamelessly romantic movie. That kind of thing. She forced herself to cut down on the coffee, but that didn't seem to help.

She thought they'd actually make it to the end of the day without the mysterious Ms. Harte making an appearance, but at ten to five, a whole *entourage* pulled into the parking lot—a sleek black limousine, flanked by two Pharmadene-issue black sedans. McCallister was driving one of those, and he was the one to open the limo's back door and offer a hand to the woman getting out.

Even from the perspective of Bryn's office window, Irene Harte seemed formidable—tall, attractive, with clothes that Bryn could never hope to afford (or pull off) and the body language of someone who went through life absolutely confident of her place in the universe. Which was almost certainly at the center.

Her bodyguards hustled to get ahead of her, open doors, check hallways. She didn't slow down for them. McCallister trailed her, and Bryn had the impression he was doing the rearguard work. Either that, or he just didn't care to be too close to Irene Harte.

Her phone rang, making her jump; it was Lucy, announcing—in a doubtful tone of voice—that Bryn had visitors. Bryn was actually pretty proud that her reply sounded calm and steady as she told Lucy to send them in.

She wished Joe Fideli were here, maybe just sitting quietly in the corner, but he was a no-show, probably for good and sensible reasons of self-interest. *And I hope our mysterious supplier doesn't freak out about this.* He might, if he were watching; she couldn't do anything about that.

The first man to open her door—without knocking— was the Fideli type: big, well muscled, with a shaved head. The difference came in the eyes; Fideli's always seemed to hide a sense that he knew how ridiculous the world was and was secretly amused by it, but this man was deadly serious as he looked around the office, nodded to Bryn, and then stepped out of the way to assume some kind of guard position in the corner. A second guard, identical assessments, parade rest in the opposite corner.

And then Irene Harte strode in.

Bryn's immediate first impression was that she was in the presence of someone whose face she ought to recognize—a high-powered politician, actress, royalty. Someone who was *important*. The smile Irene bestowed on her confirmed it—it was warm and professional, but somehow also definitely superior.

Bryn came around the desk as Ms. Harte held out her very well-manicured hand and said, "Miss Davis? Irene Harte, Pharmadene Pharmaceuticals. Very pleased to meet you."

The handshake that followed was brief and impersonal, and Bryn managed a polite smile and indicated the chair opposite her desk. Ms. Harte ignored the offer to sit, and instead stood there in her six-hundred-dollar pumps and studied Bryn with the impersonal intensity of an accountant reading a spreadsheet. "I understand that you've been briefed on the trouble we had with Mr. Fairview and his operations," Harte said, "and that you are unable to provide us with the identity of the person from whom he was obtaining his . . . supplies. Is that correct?"

Behind her, Patrick McCallister quietly entered the room, closed the door, and took up a post with his back to it—at parade rest, like the other security men. But as Bryn met his eyes, he gave her a slight nod and what was almost a smile.

Bryn cleared her throat. "No, ma'am, that's not correct."

"No?" Harte's eyebrows climbed in astonished, perfectly shaped arcs. "Please enlighten me."

"I'm not unable to provide you with that information. I just don't yet have all the facts."

"Excuse me?" Harte's smile was gone now, and her strong, beautiful face had gone still and expressionless. "Either you know or you don't, Miss Davis."

"I'm in a position to get that information for you. It will just take some time. I'm in contact with the supplier."

"Time is something that I don't like to spend, not on something as volatile and sensitive as this. Pharmadene has a significant intellectual capital risk at stake, and I can't afford to fund your fact-finding expedition. Nor can I afford to spend valuable supplies of Returné in hopes that you can one day provide some small return on my investment." Harte's eyes were ice-cold, so cold that Bryn didn't actually register them as being any particular kind of color. "I'm afraid that Mr. McCallister overstepped his authority in green-lighting this project. I'll have to terminate the funding."

"Why don't you say what you mean?" Bryn asked, feeling her fists clench at her sides. "You're not terminating *money*. You're terminating *me*. Personally."

"All right. You're in a very unfortunate position, Miss Davis, there's no doubt about that, but this is a business decision. Your life ended in a brutal and unnatural way, but Pharmadene is not a charity, and even if it were, extending your life support indefinitely is something even charities are reluctant to do when no hope exists for recovery. You won't recover, you know. Ever."

There was, Bryn realized, no reaching her on any human level. Irene Harte had no emotional buttons to press; her control and the smooth, untroubled way she said these things made it clear that Bryn's play was over.

So change the game, Bryn thought. "How much is your leak inside the company costing you?"

"Excuse me?"

"You're losing product. I'll bet it's costing you plenty, but that's not the real problem, is it? If your competitors get their hands on it, they can do some reverse engineering and come out with a cheaper version, undermining your patent opportunities before you really get the drug out there. Right? That's worth millions. Billions. Bill Gates money."

Harte still didn't answer, but Bryn definitely had her attention.

"What's it worth to you in the boardroom to save the day instead of being the one to fall on your sword? A few millions in bonuses to you, personally? A promotion? I'll bet you're at the level that it's hard to get another step up on the ladder." No reaction still, but Bryn kept going. She had, she realized, nothing at all to lose. "And how many of the men above you are looking for an excuse to kick you down a rung or two?"

That created a flicker in Harte's calm, just a second of real emotion, and Bryn felt an immense surge of relief. Not that she'd won, far from it. But she'd actually reached her.

Whether it would matter was a different thing altogether.

It took an obscenely long time for Harte to say anything, but when she finally did, it wasn't to Bryn at all. The woman turned to stare at McCallister, and said, "Patrick, this was your idea. Will you stand by it?"

"Yes," he said. Just the one word, as solid as concrete. He didn't try to explain, or coax, or threaten. He just gave her the certainty of his conviction, and waited.

It took a while, but Harte nodded. "All right. Miss Davis has a point; solving this problem may be worth a minimal investment of time. *May* be. I'll give you two weeks, fourteen doses, from today. If nothing solid happens in that time, I'll roll this up, and everyone involved will be rolled up with it. Are you clear on that, Patrick?"

"Yes, ma'am," he said. He wasn't looking at Harte; he was, Bryn realized with a shock, watching *her*. "Will there be anything else?"

"No." Harte checked her very expensive diamond-encrusted watch. "I have a dinner engagement. Keep my assistant informed daily on progress."

She didn't wait for any good-byes; she strode toward McCallister and the door, and simply assumed that it would swing open for her, and he'd get out of the way.

Which was exactly what happened. McCallister made it look as if it were his idea, which was an excellent trick, Bryn thought. As the two guards quickly left, ghosting Harte's sharp, staccato footsteps, McCallister stayed behind. Bryn took in a deep breath and sat down in the nearest chair. Suddenly, her legs felt weak, and she thought she might actually pass out. She lowered her head and sucked down deep breaths, but still felt as if she were suffocating.

McCallister's warm hand touched her shoulder lightly. "Breathe," he said, and she squeezed her eyes shut and tried to bottle up the black genie of panic that was expanding inside her. She was shuddering now, as the alarm that had been flooding her veins began to subside, and she felt absurdly cold and nauseated. Something warm settled over her shoulders, and when she clutched for it with shaking hands, she realized it was McCallister's suit coat.

Bryn looked up and saw him crouched down level with her, making needless adjustments to the jacket he'd draped over her. He wore a shoulder holster, one that appeared to be a match to what she had, and there was not a wrinkle or stain on his perfect white shirt. Even now, he looked calm, composed, absolutely in control of himself and everything around him.

Bryn said, "She just said she'd kill you, too, didn't she?"

And McCallister shrugged, such a small movement that she almost missed it. "I doubt she'd actually try, and if she did, she certainly wouldn't succeed. You made a good pitch," he said. "And we've got two weeks. It's something."

"She's going to *kill you.* And Joe."

"Not a chance, and she won't try to kill anybody if we find the answers, Bryn. Including you."

"But—"

McCallister cut her off. "We got ourselves in it, and I'm not sorry we made the choices we did. Don't be afraid for us. Concentrate on what you were brought here to do. Relax. Breathe."

She did, big, slow, trembling breaths that she dragged in through her nose, blew out through her mouth, until her heartbeat slowed and her nausea began to subside.

As he started to get up, she said, "Thank you, Mr. McCallister." And she meant it—not for dragging her back into this—God, no—but for not throwing her to the wolves when he could have. When he *should* have. He was in it with her now, all the way to his neck. And not just him—Joe Fideli, a family man, too. *Not my fault.* No, it wasn't, but that didn't matter anymore. They'd all go down together.

Perversely, that made her feel better. Maybe it was just having someone, anyone, at her back.

McCallister smiled, just a little, and there was a ghost of something warm in his eyes. He was surprisingly nice when he smiled. "Don't thank me yet," he said. She started to take off the coat, but he put his hands over hers, stilling them. "Keep it until you really feel better. I'll be down the hall, talking to Joe. Take your time, Bryn."

She watched him leave, and felt a frown grooving its way across her forehead. McCallister didn't actually *care*, did he? He couldn't. Not possible. And, of course, she had no reason to care about *him*, either. Absolutely none.

But she did. Hugging his jacket close, she felt the warmth not just of the fabric, but of his body, and when she held the collar closer to her nose she caught a ghost of his cologne, rich and dark. Like his eyes.

I don't like him. I'm not going to like him.

But she kept the coat on for far longer than she needed to, in the end, and when McCallister asked her if she wanted a drink, after dropping off her dog, she found herself saying yes.

I should have known it wasn't a date, she thought, as McCallister pushed her cosmo across to her, along with a thumb drive, and said, "I need you to study all of the material on this, and see if you spot anything out of the ordinary." At least, that was what she thought he said. He was drowned out by someone's drunken horse laugh at the next table.

She reached for the cosmo, not the portable storage device. "Why? What is it?" She had to raise her voice to be heard, because the bar was loud, trendy, and full of yelling and thumping music. He'd chosen the highest-volume pickup joint within easy driving distance. At first, she'd thought it had been some sort of odd date thing, but no. McCallister was never off duty, really. He was just using old-school noise canceling to discourage surveillance.

The taste of the cosmo, sour-sweet, lingered in her mouth like a kiss as McCallister pushed the drive closer. Their fingers brushed when she reached for it, and she glanced up into his face for one quick instant. Lights flashed in her eyes, blinding her, and then the moment was over and he was sitting back, as remote as ever.

"It's surveillance we've compiled on Fairview," he said. "Video, phone taps, e-mails, chat logs—"

"Mr. Fairview *chatted*? Online?" She honestly would have bet he couldn't manage a computer at all.

He raised his eyebrows. "Brace yourself for that, if you still had any illusions about his character; it's not pretty. We've also included his known associates. We've been through it, but you've got a better chance of spotting something we didn't."

She nodded and slipped the drive into her purse's zippered pocket, and toyed with her drink for a moment before downing a courage gulp. Then she said, "You had a choice, didn't you? Which of us who died in the prep room to revive?"

"I don't understand the question."

"Me or Fast Freddy. Or Mr. Fairview."

"Mr. Fairview had a head wound. He wasn't revival material from the start."

"You couldn't bring him back?"

"Not in any condition that would allow us to question him. There are limits to what the drug can do."

"But . . . Fast Freddy. You could have brought *him* back."

"We didn't know he was already on the drug, so it's a good thing we didn't."

She gazed at him, not blinking this time despite the bright lights strobing in her eyes. He was still just a shadow against them, but she caught the random outlines of his jaw, his mouth, his eyes. All in flickers. "You chose me over Freddy. Knowing he probably had a better shot of telling you what was going on. I know Joe asked you to do it, but you didn't have to. You must have had another reason."

McCallister was quiet for a long moment, the pause filled with the thunder and howl of the music around them. Then he tossed back the rest of his drink—she didn't know what it was, except it was light amber—and stood up. "I have to go," he said. "Tell me what you think about the files, and if you have any leads that come out of it."

She wanted to tell him to wait, to come back, but he walked out, weaving around the drunken, laughing crowds, and disappeared.

Bryn stared hard at her cosmo, frowning, and took another sip. No sense letting it go to waste.

A man slipped into McCallister's abandoned chair—not her type, an aging surfer whose tan was starting to curdle, wearing a chest-baring open shirt. He looked sweaty, and a little mean.

"No," she said, before he opened his mouth. "Just go. Don't waste your time."

He grinned, all teeth. The gold chain around his neck shot bright reflections at her eyes. "No, pretty lady, *you* are definitely coming home with *me.*"

And the oddest thing happened. Bryn blinked and said, "Okay," although that wasn't at all what she was thinking or feeling. *"Okay"? What the hell was that?* "No," she said, quickly. "No, I don't think so."

"Well, which is it? Okay, or no?"

"No. Ugh."

"Let's try this again." The man leaned over the table, looming over her, and fixed her with a stare. "You. Are coming. Home. With me."

And again, Bryn immediately and uncontrollably said, "Okay," and this time—this time . . .

This time she *reached for her purse.*

No, she thought in utter disbelief. *I'm not doing this. I can't be doing this. What the fuck?*

She forced herself to stop, and looked at the man with furious intensity. "What are you doing to me?" she demanded.

He said, "All right, enough screwing around. Condition Sapphire. Verify."

"Yes," she said, although she had no idea why. "Verified."

"Stand up and take your purse."

She obeyed immediately, and the man took her elbow and guided her through the crowd. Her body was on autopilot, and her brain was shrieking, but there was nothing, absolutely nothing, she could do to fight it. She passed laughing people, bright eyed and chattering, and wanted to scream, *Help me, God, please*, but nothing came out.

Something in my drink, she thought frantically. But what kind of date-rape drug did this? She didn't feel drunk, or sick, or woozy—she was just out of control.

The bouncer eyed her oddly as they left the club, and she wondered what he saw in her face. A terrified, desperate woman? Someone who needed help? Or just another sad hookup?

The man put his hand at the small of her back and steered her away from the bouncer, from the lights, from people, from safety, and her feet obediently made the steps. "You have no idea what's happening to you, do you?" he asked, and moved his hand up to stroke the sweating nape of her neck. Disgustingly intimate. "Oh, sweetheart, you've got so much to learn. They didn't tell you, did they? Didn't warn you? Typical corporate bullshit. Come on; walk faster. Don't speak."

She couldn't have, even if she'd wanted to. It was as if she'd become a puppet, completely under his control, and it made her want to vomit. Something was going on far bigger than she could understand, but she clung to one, burning thought: *Typical corporate bullshit.*

Patrick McCallister must have known about this, whatever it was. And hadn't told her.

The man fished in his pocket and came up with a set of car keys. He pointed the remote at a row of cars ahead, and one beeped and flashed lights. "Now, you're going to get in the car and be a good girl," he said. "Say you understand."

"I understand."

"Oh, and before I forget, give me the drive that McCallister handed over."

Bryn's fingers moved quickly and precisely to the zippered pocket in her purse, retrieved the storage device, and handed it over. He slid it into his shirt pocket and opened the passenger side of the car. "In," he said. He wasn't trying to sound charming anymore. He just sounded impatient.

Bryn's body, oblivious to the consequences that were bound to be coming, complied, and she settled into the soft leather interior. He was a smoker, and the cabin reeked of it; the metallic, burned taste filled her mouth as completely as if she'd licked the ashes off the floor. She felt wetness on her cheeks. She was crying. Some part of her body, at least, was still operating outside of his control—not that it would help her in the least.

As the man started to shut her door, she heard a sound from outside. It wasn't loud, but it was a crisp, metallic snap, followed by a solid, meaty thud.

Her door swung open again as the man stumbled, cried out, and turned.

Patrick McCallister stepped out of the shadows, face pale and very tight. He had always been so self-contained, but now, Bryn saw something blazing in him, something so full of rage that it scared her.

He had a riot baton in his hand. That had been the metallic snap she'd heard—the baton extending. The thud was pretty obvious, as the man who'd been abducting her yelled, "You fucker, you broke my ribs!"

McCallister didn't bother to say anything to that. He stepped forward, swung the baton again, with precision, and put the man down on the pavement. There was some groaning and twitching, but the fight was over, and as the man slipped into unconsciousness and his blood trickled out onto the concrete, McCallister moved around him to crouch down next to Bryn, still in the car.

"Bryn, can you get out?"

She tried. Tried desperately. "No," she whispered, and felt the tears overflow again. "I can't."

He didn't seem surprised. "Cancel Sapphire," he said, and she fell forward with a surprised cry, almost smacking herself into the dashboard. She'd been fighting so fiercely for control of her muscles that when she regained it, they tensed with crippling force. Bryn sucked in deep, whooping breaths, shuddering, gagging on the stale taste of cigarettes until McCallister reached in and helped her step out and over the fallen man. He was still holding the baton, and when she looked at it, he snapped it back to its original collapsed length.

"What the *hell*?" she managed to gasp out. Her whole body felt violated, even though she'd hardly been touched. She yanked free of McCallister's hand and put a lot of empty space between them.

Then she reached to her shoulder holster and pulled the weapon that still nestled there. She hadn't bothered to take it off for the club because they'd just been going for a quick drink; now the weight of it in her hand felt like salvation.

She aimed it first at the man unconscious on the street, but he wasn't a threat, so she focused the muzzle squarely on McCallister's chest. Her pulse was pounding so hard it was giving her a headache, and she still wanted to throw up, though her nausea was starting to subside with the clean taste of the outside air. "What the *hell*?" This time, beyond her control again, it came out in a raw scream.

McCallister slowly put his hands up. "Easy, Bryn. Easy."

"*Fuck* easy, you son of a bitch. What just *happened* to me? What did you put in my drink?" She shot a burning glance at the unconscious guy between them. "Is he one of yours?"

"No," McCallister said. "And I didn't put anything into your drink. Neither did he."

"Then what the hell just happened to me? *What?*"

McCallister glanced around. The bouncer at the club had walked out into the street and was staring their way, attracted by the raised voices. "We shouldn't talk about it here," he said, "and if you keep waving that gun around, we'll have a lot more problems than we already do. Come on, Bryn; my car is across the street. We need to go before the police arrive. Please."

"And if I don't want to go with you?"

"Then you don't have to," he said. "You can choose to put the gun up and walk away. I understand how you feel, Bryn. I won't tell you what to do."

She realized, as he said it, that he hadn't *ordered* her to do anything. Not like before. And she didn't feel that her will had been taken away from her.

You can choose to put the gun up and walk away.

Or she could choose to go with him.

He didn't try to convince her one way or the other, just waited as the seconds ticked by. A distant wail of sirens made him stir, just a little, but he still stayed quiet.

Bryn relaxed her stance and put the gun back in the holster under her shoulder. "I need to understand what just happened," she said. "You need to tell me. *Now.*"

He nodded. "Then please, let me help you."

*   *   *

He drove her—to her surprise—to a familiar house, glowing with lights. She recognized the kid's bike up against the hedge, and the leaning, weathered mailbox.

"Why here?" she asked.

"Because I don't think you feel safe with me," McCallister said, as he put the car in park and killed the engine. "Joe and his family have a . . . calming effect."

"You bring a lot of people here?"

"No," he said, then hesitated for a second before getting out of the car. "Never, in fact."

Bryn pondered that as she followed him up the walk, and as he rang the bell. Joe's wife, Kylie, answered the door, drying her hands on a dish towel; she blinked in surprise, then smiled in genuine delight and opened her arms to McCallister for a hug. "Patrick, you've been avoiding us," she said. He stepped into the embrace, briefly, and then pulled back to glance at Bryn. Kylie did, too, and if her smile faltered just a touch, it quickly warmed again. "Bryn. Nice to see you."

McCallister said, "I'm sorry to drop in on you like this, but—"

"But you need to see Joe?"

"I'm afraid so."

"He's out back in the workshop. Follow me."

Kylie led them through the warm, comfortable house, past the playing kids (who stopped to wave, or to stare, or, in the case of the baby, to gurgle), and out the back door. She pointed to a structure twenty feet away across the yard. "Out there," she said. "Pat, you know how to get in?"

"I know," he said. "Thanks, Kylie."

"Visit us for dinner sometime."

"I will."

His smile disappeared as soon as she closed the back door, and in its place was a moment of unguarded emotion. Sorrow, Bryn thought. She didn't need to be told that McCallister dreaded bringing danger here, as much as he enjoyed the company. It was written all over his face.

"It's this way," he said, and walked across the yard. He held out a hand to stop Bryn as they approached the closed door of the respectably large wooden shed, and a motion-activated light came on to bathe the area in a mercilessly bright glare. "Wait here."

She couldn't see why, but she nodded, and then, just to test that she *could*, disobeyed him and followed him as he climbed the three steps up to the door.

He shot her an irritated look and shielded a keypad from her as he punched in a series of numbers . . . a *long* series, longer than usual for these types of locks. She heard a musical tone sound, and a click as the lock disengaged.

Then McCallister knocked. "Joe? Coming in."

"Come ahead," said Joe's voice from within, and McCallister opened up and entered, with Bryn at his heels.

Joe Fideli was sitting at a desk that was absolutely loaded down with monitors, computer equipment, storage drives—and it took Bryn a second or two to realize that he was putting away a gun. A serious weapon, too, not a pistol but a semiauto rifle, which he put back on a rack behind him.

The man had more guns in here than an armory. In fact, Bryn was fairly sure that she couldn't even identify many of them, and that was a statement, after four years of supply duty in Iraq. That wasn't even counting the shelves of other types of weapons—knives, Tasers, throwing stars, and brass knuckles in tidy order.

"Close the door," Joe said to Bryn. She didn't do it—another test, to see if she could. She *did* feel a weird impulse to move, though, and that worried her. Badly.

McCallister stepped back and shut it, and the magnetic lock snapped closed. Only then did Joe truly relax in his chair. "So," he said, and laced his hands behind his head. "Nobody looks happy. Were the drinks watered? I hear that place ain't much for quality."

"Someone invoked protocol on her," McCallister said, and sat down in one of the other two chairs on the opposite side of Joe's desk.

Fideli immediately straightened up and got serious. "Deliberately?"

"Apparently."

"Which one?"

"Sapphire."

"Crap. That means whoever our friendly leaker is, they know way too much. And now so does our supplier."

"Excuse me," Bryn said sharply, "but could we please talk about *what happened to me*?"

The two men exchanged looks, and McCallister nodded to Joe. "Seriously," Joe said, "this is my job?"

"It is tonight."

Joe sighed and opened up a drawer in his desk. He took out a bottle and three glasses, and poured liberal shots all around. He handed one to Bryn as he said, "Tell me how it happened."

"I was . . . finishing my drink," she said. "And then a man sat down and came on to me. He said I was going to get up and go home with him."

"Just like that."

"Pretty much."

Fideli cast a look over at McCallister. "Any leads from him?"

"He's been taken in by my guys, but I doubt it'll go anywhere. According to what they've learned, he was paid to grab her and drive her to a drop point; he was told the protocol information, but I don't think he knows who paid him, or why, or what was going to happen. And he was paid at a dead drop, in cash, no surveillance available on that area. Dead end."

Fideli nodded, and transferred his attention back to Bryn. "And then what happened?"

Bryn felt herself blushing, and hated herself for it. "I . . . I said okay, I'd go with him. I didn't mean to. I didn't *want* to."

Joe nodded. "Drink up." He passed a glass over to McCallister, and sipped his own. Bryn tentatively took a taste, and almost choked on the rich, smoky liquor. Scotch. Serious Scotch. But it warmed the chilly places inside. "Go on."

"He said it again, and said something about *sapphire*—"

"He specifically triggered the protocol," McCallister said. "He knew what he was doing."

Joe said nothing. He just waited for Bryn to continue,

and she swallowed hard and did. "He made me go outside with him and get into the car. It felt like . . ."

"Like you had no control," Joe said, when she paused. "You couldn't stop yourself."

"Yes." It had felt that way right until the moment Mc-Callister had broken the spell. "*Please* tell me it was some kind of a drug."

"Afraid not, Bryn." Joe turned his glass in slow circles as he watched her. "There's a side effect to the drug you take, Returné. It has some fail-safes built in, and one of them renders you extremely susceptible to following orders. We call these fail-safes protocols. This one is Condition Sapphire. It was developed for military purposes."

"You mean it could happen again?"

"It can happen at any time," he said. "And it's real damn dangerous, because it means that if someone orders you to reveal things, you won't have a choice. You'll just talk."

"You said military. What kind of military purpose?"

"You could be given a covert assignment—like, say, an assassination—and you would carry it out without question. You couldn't talk if they ordered you not to do so. Not even to save yourself," McCallister added. "It's the most easily perverted use of the drug we can think of, and we've been trying to find a way to turn off the protocols."

"Wait. Wait just a minute. Who is *we*? You two?" Bryn laughed a little desperately. "The three of us don't make much of a mastermind conspiracy, guys. I'm just saying."

The two of them exchanged a look, and McCallister said, "For security purposes, I can't answer that."

"Which means it's *not* just the two of you?"

"Bryn—"

"Why didn't you tell me about this? Warn me?"

"Wouldn't have done any good," Joe said in a neutral, calm voice. "Warning you doesn't mean you could do anything to prevent it. Once a protocol gets invoked, you've got no choice. And no resistance. It would have just made you paranoid, not safer."

She downed the rest of the Scotch in a fiery burst, blinked away tears, and said, "You've got no idea how this feels. First I'm dead. Then I'm hooked on your stupid *drug*, and now I'm some kind of mindless robot zombie *freak*. What if he'd ordered me to screw him? Would I have done that, too?"

They didn't answer. McCallister looked down into his glass, but she saw how tight the muscles were in his jawline, and remembered the raw burst of fury she'd seen in him. So that answer was definitely a yes, then.

"There has to be *something* I can do about it. *Anything!*"

"We're looking into it."

"So until then, if some asshole comes up and talks about sapphires, I'm a slave? That's all you can do for me?"

"There may be something else," Joe said. "Give me a day to look into it."

A day. The prospect made Bryn shudder, going out into the world again with that kind of astonishing vulnerability. "I can't," she said. "I can't wait that long. I need help now!"

"One of us will stay with you at all times," McCallister said. "You'll be safe, Bryn. And we *will* find a way to neutralize the protocol."

Fideli nodded. "But, Pat, this changes things. It either means the leak ain't the same guy as the one who knows about the protocol, and someone inside Pharmadene is trying to use her freelance, or—"

"Or the leaker knows about the protocols as well. That's a very small pool of knowledge. And suspects. It may help us." McCallister finished his Scotch and put the empty glass on Fideli's desk. "How's your security here?"

"Damn good. Blocking technology built right in for data and physical surveillance countermeasures. And as you can see, firepower's up to the challenge." Fideli shrugged. "As panic rooms go, it's all right."

"And you can get the family here in an emergency."

"They know the drill. It's as safe as anyplace we could go. We've got internal sources of food, water, sewer, medical supplies."

"Airflow?"

"Three sources, one damn near impossible to block. Plus oxygen for emergencies." Fideli's usually cheerful expression went suddenly cold and blank. "You think they're going to come after Kylie and the kids."

"I think if this heats up, we've all got bull's-eyes on our backs, from both sides. So watch out for trouble."

Fideli inclined his head, just a little. "What about her?" Meaning, of course, Bryn. "Her apartment's not exactly a hardened bunker."

"I'll do personal security tonight. Tomorrow, it's your turn. And, Joe—check on the progress of our consulting friend. I think our time line's been moved up."

"Affirmative on that; I'll see if I can get an update. You two crazy kids have fun."

With McCallister?

Bryn was fairly certain that nowhere in the universe was that possible.

Chapter 6

McCallister drove her home, and they didn't talk. Not at all. He cast her glances occasionally, but he seemed to understand that Bryn wanted silence more than comfort. She did like that about him; he wasn't afraid to just let her think, and having him there soothed the constant roil of terror inside her.

Except that he can make me do anything he wants, she thought, and shivered, even in the blast of the car's heater. *Anytime he wants it.*

McCallister glanced her way and turned up the heater.

"It's not that," she said.

He nodded slowly. "You're realizing how vulnerable you are," he said. "I'm sorry. I wish I could tell you there was something I could do, but for now, we have to wait and see."

"I thought having a gun would make me feel better, but if you order me to put it away, I have to do that, don't I?" Her voice sounded soft, but bitter. "I have to do anything you want. *Boss.*"

"I'm not going to take advantage of that."

"But you could." She turned her face toward the passing dark streets. "Some would."

He was silent for a moment, and then said quietly, "Yes. Some would." That was it. He didn't race to reassure her again, or to argue that he wasn't like that. He just let it go.

And strangely, that made her trust him, just a little bit. If he didn't need to defend his character, there was a lot better chance he actually had one. "Why did you bring me back?" She'd asked it before, but somehow, she didn't feel he'd really answered.

"Would you rather we hadn't?"

"Yes. I think I'd be better off dead. Don't you?"

"No," he said. "And if you want a real answer to that question . . ." He stopped, as if he were weighing his answer carefully. "You must have fallen next to the far wall, and a table tipped over and covered you. We had no idea you were suffocating until Joe realized you weren't where he thought you were, and started looking for you. We were *right there*, and we let you die while we screwed around securing the scene. I was the one who moved the table and found you. I was too late. You were gone. When it came down to a choice, I really didn't have one."

There was so much going on in his voice, although he was trying to keep it bland and even. She could imagine how that had felt, to find someone like that—someone you might have been in time to save. Someone whose chance had slipped away while you were only feet away.

"So it's guilt," she said. "You did it out of guilt."

He looked at her and said, "Would it make you feel better if I said yes?"

Obscurely, it did. A little. "Would you do it again?"

"Yes," he said. "And I wouldn't even think about it. Not now that I know you. And it wouldn't be guilt if I made the choice now."

"No?" She smiled a little, intrigued despite her weariness. "What would it be?"

He avoided that question neatly. "We're here," he said. "Home."

The apartment complex looked shabbier than ever; the wind had blown some trash out of the overflowing bins, and it lay heaped against parked cars like dirty snow. Mc-Callister found a parking space, and Bryn led the way up to her door.

He took her keys and edged her out of the way. "Let me check it first," he said.

"It's fine. Mr. French is on guard inside."

He gave her a slightly baffled look, but eased the door

open and hit the light switch. The bulldog inside stood up on the couch, growling, staring at McCallister with murderous beady eyes.

"Mr. French, I presume," McCallister said. He sounded amused. "Call him off, please."

Bryn whistled, and Mr. French's ears perked. He stopped growling and sat down, but he still looked concerned until Bryn pushed past McCallister and came over to pet him. "Good boy," she said, and scratched him behind the ears. "You just stay on guard against all the bad men."

"Me included?" McCallister shut the door and locked the dead bolt.

"I have to walk him, you know."

"Not until I check the other rooms."

"There's no need. Mr. French—"

"I'm not doubting his abilities. I'm just double-checking."

It didn't take long, really—the kitchen was tiny, the bedroom disorderly and almost as small. Closets held no surprises, and neither did corners or the dust bunnies beneath the bed. McCallister was methodical; she had to give him that: he not only checked every conceivable hiding place, including the bathtub, but made sure every window was firmly secured. She was vaguely worried about what he thought of her housekeeping.

"All clear," he said. "I'll take the dog out."

"He's *my* dog."

"And I don't want you outside alone," he said.

"Fine. Come with." Bryn clipped the leash onto Mr. French's collar. "It's a nice night for a walk, right?"

McCallister clearly didn't like the idea, but he didn't argue the point. Together, they walked the dog down the stairs and out to the grassy area on the other side of the parking lot. It was the common pet-walking area, and Bryn had brought her poop bags; Mr. French did his business; she cleaned it up. It was all very normal except that she had a solid male shadow who kept watching the shadows as if waiting for an army of ninja assassins to appear.

The only thing that happened was that a rat scrabbled out of the trash container and raced across the parking lot, making Mr. French bark and lunge to the end of his leash.

Bryn struggled to hold on to him; he had a lot of muscle packed into his small body.

"Let's get back in," McCallister said. His body language was almost as tense as the dog's, and Bryn finally surrendered and let Mr. French drag her back partway on the rat's trail before she tugged him toward the apartment stairs. He went willingly enough, confident he'd driven off the invader, and by the time they were back inside, locked in, he stretched out and looked supremely self-satisfied.

McCallister checked the apartment *again*.

"We should eat something," he said, coming back to find her still on the couch with the dog.

"I could call out for pizza."

"No deliveries. It's not safe."

"Oh, come on, it's *pizza*."

"And if someone wanted to get to you, and me, it's easy enough to doctor a pizza. No. We make something here."

Bryn scratched the bulldog's ears. "Okay, well, I hope you're one of those amazing cooks who can make a feast out of two dried cranberries and a lemon, because that's about all I have."

McCallister looked at her in complete bafflement, as if she were making some kind of an obscure joke, and then checked the fridge. He stared a moment, then let the door swing closed. He repeated the exercise in the pantry, and pulled out a moldy half loaf of bread, which he threw out, and finally an open package of crackers and a peanut-butter jar.

"You don't cook," he said.

"Are you sure you're not Sherlock Holmes? Because the way you notice subtle clues . . ."

"I thought everyone was capable of cooking at least a can of soup. How do you survive? Not on pizza."

"They also deliver spaghetti, and sub sandwiches. And Chinese food."

McCallister shook his head and sat down across from her with the crackers and peanut butter and a butter knife. He handed her a paper plate, which was the only kind she owned. Mr. French stood up, curiously examining the peanut-butter jar until Bryn shooed him off the couch. He obediently sat down, staring at the two of them, and the peanut-butter jar, from a different angle, and doing his best to convey that he was, in fact, starving.

Bryn ate in silence, casting glances at McCallister from time to time; chewing crackers and sticky peanut butter didn't make for much conversation. By the end, though, the silence had begun to feel oppressive, and as Bryn swallowed the last of what was clearly a highly inadequate meal, she thought she ought to at least try to be social. "Thanks," she said. "For, ah, making this."

He gave her a trace of a smile and took her empty plate into the kitchen, along with the rest of the crackers and peanut butter. While he was in there, he opened a couple of other cabinets, apparently looking for a second course. Which wasn't there, Bryn almost told him; she'd been out of everything, planning to make a run to the store for at least a few basic things. He must have decided that the saltshaker didn't have much potential, because he began to walk around the apartment, checking the view out the windows.

"I'll take the couch," he said, still not looking directly at her. "It'd be nice if you had an extra pillow, but it's not required."

"I'm not *that* bad. I have an extra pillow. And a blanket."

"One the dog hasn't slept on?"

She blushed. "Come on, am I that horrible?"

McCallister glanced in her direction and, for the first time, allowed the look to linger. It was almost . . . human. "No," he said. "You're not."

"Coming from you, that's nearly a compliment." Bryn swallowed hard, suddenly feeling the pressure of tears growing behind her eyes. "I'm not feeling anything *but* horrible lately. Like an alien in someone else's skin."

"I can understand that," he said. He hadn't looked away from her, and she felt that spark of warmth take hold between them. "What you've been through . . . But you're still an attractive woman, Bryn, if you have any doubt of that."

"That was *definitely* a compliment."

He smiled with genuine amusement. "I hoped you'd

take it that way. I didn't only ask you out for a drink to pass
on information, you know."

"Could have fooled me," she said. "You're very . . . professional."

"Never off the clock," he agreed, and turned back to the
windows. "Especially not tonight."

Great.

Bryn walked into the kitchen, opened a cabinet, and
pulled down a bottle of wine. It was cheap, because that
was all she could afford, but it was decent. And open. She
poured half of the contents into a jelly jar without asking
whether he might want any, drank some way too fast, and
then moved into the bedroom. She came out with a pillow
(the extra from her bed) and a blanket, which she put on
the couch. McCallister watched this in silence, leaning
against the wall, and as she finished off the giant glass of
wine and poured the rest he said, "Don't you think you
might want to slow down on that?"

"Why? It's not like I haven't had a fucking awful day.
Week. Month. Life. *Death.*"

"Because of that," he said. "You'll get reckless, and we
don't need that."

"No, we sure don't want that," she said. She felt better
now, with the wine. Glowing inside. Belatedly, she thought
he was probably right; she'd had a cosmo and a Scotch tonight, and most of a bottle of wine wasn't going to help her
keep her head together. But she wanted to be out from
under the tension and fear, at least for now. Let McCallister be responsible for keeping her alive. It was all his fault,
anyway.

She reached for the glass again.

Bryn hadn't seen him move, but now he was right in
front of her, taking the drink from the counter and moving
to the sink, where he poured the rest of it out. "Hey!" she
blurted, but it was too late by then, and he was running the
water to swirl the last purple stains down the drain. "You
jerk, that was mine!"

"You'll thank me in the morning."

"I doubt I'll *ever* have any reason to thank you!" Rage
ignited inside her, sudden and shocking and utterly beyond

her control. "You left me to *die* on the floor; isn't that right?"

He turned on her, and suddenly he was *that* Patrick McCallister again, the one who'd burst into that white fire of anger on the street and put a man down with two scientific strokes of a riot baton.

The scary one.

"Sit. Down," he said. It was quiet, but she had no doubt that there was an *or else* clause attached to it. But it was the phrasing that triggered something inside her—an almost compulsive wish to do as he said.

And it made her even more enraged.

"Or. *What?*" she spat back, taking a step toward him, not away. "You think you can invoke your creepy protocol and make me your little living doll? She walks, she talks, she does whatever the hell you want? *No. Never going to happen!*"

The thought seemed to shock him out of his own anger, and McCallister's eyes opened wide. "That's not what I—" He stopped himself and took in a deep breath. "That's not what I meant," he said. "I would never do that to you. I wouldn't take away your choices."

"You already did. You brought me back. You took away my choice to live or die—and what choice do I have now? Don't take the shots? *Decompose?* You think this is some kind of freedom you've given me?" Oh, she was feeling dizzy now, off balance with both alcohol and pure, sweet rage. "Don't tell me you won't take away my choices; you take more away from me every day!"

"Bryn . . ." He didn't seem to know what to say now, and instead, he did the last thing she expected.

He reached out and put his hands on her shoulders.

She stiffened and started to pull away, but there was something vulnerable in his face just then, and she stilled herself and returned his stare. Seen this close, he was much more handsome than she'd realized—fine soft skin, a dark shadow of stubble stroking his cheeks. His eyes weren't just dark; they were a rich, complex brown, rimmed with dark green. There were strands of silver in his hair.

He started to say something, then checked the impulse,

and for a moment it was just the two of them, feeling something odd and powerful pulling between them. Attraction, yes, but more than that.

Shared desperation.

"You didn't answer me before, at Fideli's house," Bryn said. "About how many of you were working on—"

He covered her mouth with his hand, stepping closer. He bent so that his lips were very close to her ear, close enough that she felt the hot stroke of his breath against her skin, and he whispered, "Say nothing you don't want overheard. We're being monitored. We're always watched. Remember that."

Oh, *God*, she felt a sudden flush of heat, one that transmitted directly from the warmed area on her neck down through her body to pool . . . lower. He was right up against her, his chest brushing hers, and she felt the tension in his hands as he continued to hold her. Instead of pulling back, he stayed where he was, as if he had more to say.

But he didn't.

"If we're going to be this close, can I call you Patrick?" she whispered, and it broke his tension, shattered it into a startled laugh low in his throat, and *God*, how exactly had she stopped hating him? Maybe it was the fact that he was fighting to stay professional; she could feel it.

Just then, Mr. French barked, a single, sharp, angry sound that hit Bryn like a slap. She looked down. He was standing belligerently at her feet, and he glared up at McCallister with possessive zeal.

McCallister looked down, too, and this time, his soft laugh had a little bit of despair in it. "You should probably go to bed before he takes all this personally," he said to Bryn, and their eyes met again just for a raw second before he moved back, leaving her cold and alone. "I don't think he likes me."

She started to say something, and fell silent when he shook his head. "Better we don't start anything between us," he said, very quietly. "We have enough to worry about already without making our situation more . . . complicated."

"Right," she said. "We'll just . . . keep things simple. That sounds"—*awful*, she thought, but managed to change it to say—"awfully sensible."

"That's me," McCallister said, with a bitter twist to his lips. "I'm nothing if not sensible."

He sat down on the couch and fiddled with the pillow, clearly wanting her to go. So she did, with Mr. French trotting along in her wake.

She closed the bedroom door, leaned against it, and looked at the dog. "You are an asshole; you know that?"

He snorted, turned three times in a circle, and flopped down in the doorway.

"Now you think you're a chaperone? Fine. Knock yourself out. No treats for you."

It seemed unnaturally quiet as she prepared for bed; she found herself stopping, waiting for some hint of sound from the living room. Bryn made herself move briskly, brushing her teeth, her hair, slipping into comfy flannel pajama pants and a cotton tank top. When she got into bed, Mr. French abandoned his post at the door and jumped up onto the bed to curl at her feet.

She glared at him. "Don't even try to make it up to me, loser dog." He licked his chops, grunted, and put his head down on his paws. "And don't give me the sad eyes. I'm not going for it."

He whined softly, so she melted and petted him, and got rewarded with an affectionate lick before she turned off the lights.

Now it was quiet. Really, really quiet. Except for the always loud bulldog breathing, it felt like her apartment had been wrapped in soundproofing. She usually heard something from her neighbors—voices, smeared TV noise, *something*—but tonight it was like her room had been launched into outer space. Maybe they were on vacation. Or out to a late dinner.

Maybe they're dead. That morbid thought crept in unexpectedly, and Bryn fought to get rid of it. Not everything had to have an awful explanation. Not every shadow had a threat.

But it was *really* quiet.

Bryn turned, twisted, sighed, flopped over on her back.

It felt hot in the apartment. Almost stifling. She considered getting up to adjust the thermostat, but it was in the living room, and no way was she going out there. Better to sweat.

She drifted, almost asleep, and found herself sighing happily as a cool breeze dried the sweat on her face. Felt good.

Breeze.

Mr. French suddenly bolted off the bed, barking furiously, louder than she'd ever heard him, and the shock threw her off the opposite side in instinctive reaction. She fumbled for the gun she'd left sitting out on the nightstand, found it, and crouched behind the bed as her eyes adjusted to the darkness.

The pale square of the window. Billowing curtains. The cool breeze moving over her skin.

Mr. French, snarling and barking.

There was no one at the window. *I didn't open that. Someone else did. He may already be inside.*

No. If someone had gotten in, Mr. French would have gone after him.

The next second, her bedroom door slammed open, and McCallister stepped in, took cover next to Bryn, and said, "What happened?" He was still in his suit pants and shirt, but his tie and jacket were off—that was a minor, fleeting detail, though. What she mostly noticed was that he'd come armed. His voice sounded a lot calmer than she felt.

"Window," she said. "I didn't open it."

Mr. French was bouncing up and down, ricocheting off the wall and snapping at the blowing curtains.

"Call him off," McCallister said. "Let me check it out. Maybe you did and forgot."

"I didn't! And it didn't open itself!"

"I know. Just let me check."

She whistled, but Mr. French wouldn't heel; he was fixated on the window, angrier than she'd ever seen him. McCallister shook his head and stepped out and moved like a ghost to the side of the window. Mr. French, apparently realizing he had backup now, stopped barking and stood at alert attention, watching as McCallister eased back the curtain and looked out. His body language stayed tense, even after he gave Bryn the all-clear sign and slid the glass closed. He checked the lock. "Not broken," he said. "Someone must have slipped the catch and opened it. Not that hard to do, with these kinds of cheap locks. I just didn't expect anyone to come up the wall. It's a pretty rigorous climb."

"Could you do it?"

He shrugged, which she assumed meant *yes*. Bryn sat down on the bed and imagined someone climbing up that wall—and without her will, that image morphed from a shadowy figure to Fast Freddy. She imagined him raising his head and grinning as he did it, and it was the memory of his weird, lewd smile that made her shiver. "Jesus," she whispered. "He didn't get in . . . ?"

"Mr. French says no," McCallister said. He reached down and patted the bulldog on the head; the dog growled in response, lifting his lips to show teeth, but didn't bite. Just made the point. "I think the dog stopped him."

If she hadn't let Mr. French into the bedroom—which she usually didn't, actually—he might have been in the other room, barking at the door. More time for Freddy—if it *was* Freddy—to get in and do . . . whatever he was planning to do.

Or—on the pleasant side—maybe it had been a garden-variety rapist/murderer. That, Bryn thought, would actually be a relief.

"I don't think you should stay here," McCallister said. "Please pack a bag." It was, she noticed, in the form of a request.

"I'm not leaving my dog."

"We'll take him with us. Please."

McCallister still seemed tense, and she wasn't in any mood to be obstinate, or to argue about the twinge of obedience she felt even though he'd phrased it politely as a request. He was one of those people who was so normally unreadable that when he flashed actual stress, it had to be a real crisis. Plus, someone really had jimmied her window—whether it was Fast Freddy or not. Getting out of here didn't sound like a bad idea at all.

Packing took about five minutes. Hell, as much as Bryn

owned, she thought she could have packed to move house in under an hour, depressing as that was. McCallister checked his car thoroughly, inside and out, for tracking devices, hidden passengers, or explosive parting gifts before he allowed her to come anywhere near it. He even checked out the trunk. She felt that little frisson of revulsion when she imagined Fast Freddy hiding in there, like a trapdoor spider down its hole.

They'd gone about a mile from her house, taking apparently random twists and turns, when McCallister finally said, "I don't see a tail."

"That's good."

"Maybe." He didn't sound convinced. "I'm switching cars."

"You're *what*?"

"I could have missed something. This isn't a game, Bryn. It's not television. I can't afford to take a chance with our lives."

"I thought I was hard to kill."

His voice, when it came, sounded grim. "You're not hard to *hurt*."

McCallister got on the car phone and ordered up a second car from one of his Pharmadene henchpersons. Within half an hour, they'd pulled into a parking lot and switched vehicles with another man driving a similar car.

"Where's he going?" Bryn asked.

"Anywhere but where we're going. If anyone's tracking him, it'll be a wasted and lengthy trip."

"Well, where are *we* going?"

"I'd rather not say."

"In case we're being monitored."

He didn't answer, but then, she really had stopped expecting him to make the effort to give her any actual information.

They left the downtown lights behind and drifted into suburbia, sleepy streets and darkened houses. He kept driving, and now that the adrenaline had worn off she found herself dozing, her head at an uncomfortable angle against the window. She must have faded out for a while, because when she jerked upright again McCallister was pulling to a stop in front of a massive stone wall pierced by an enormous, forbidding wrought-iron gate.

It slowly opened, revealing a moonlit blue-tinged gravel drive that was probably blindingly white in full day. The hedges were manicured and shaped as if they'd been taken to a high-end salon, not one leaf fluttering out of place. Bryn blinked as he drove up a long, winding path, past stately old trees and perfect rose gardens and a white gazebo large enough to host the New York Philharmonic for an afternoon concert.

A massive square block of a house appeared at the top of the next curving hill, illuminated with tasteful outdoor spotlights. The place was the size of a mall, Bryn thought, not to mention being so elaborate it could have been used in a movie with women in corsets and men behaving badly.

McCallister pulled up in front of the front steps, and the massive wooden door opened to reveal an actual *butler*. Well, she assumed he was, although he wasn't wearing a tuxedo. More of a dinner jacket, which was remarkable enough at this late hour.

"Where *are* we?" Bryn asked.

"Home," McCallister said. "Come on."

This could not *possibly* be someone's home. Not anyone who actually worked for a living. But McCallister walked around, opened her door, and she looked at Mr. French, who huffed something in dogspeak and jumped out to toddle along after him.

"Traitor," she said, and grabbed her bag.

The butler was an older man, well into gray hair, but with a kind face that put Bryn at ease immediately. He took the suitcase from her without hearing any kind of protests, and said, "Miss Davis, I'll take this to your room."

"Give her the Auburn Room, Liam. I want her in a defensible position," McCallister said. The butler nodded briskly and went up the stairs with her bag, leaving her and Mr. French to gawk at the huge, vaulted entry hall. It was some odd shape—octagonal, maybe—with three doors angled out of it, plus the staircase sweeping grandly into the shadows. She had an overwhelming impression of age, solidity, and above all, *wealth*. The paintings. The tapestries. The richly colored rugs on the floor.

"Welcome," McCallister said, "to the ancestral millstone around my neck. Before you ask, yes, it's mine. Or, more properly, it belongs to my family's trust, and I'm allowed to rent it for a nominal fee."

What did you say to that? Bryn finally settled for a sub-dued "Wow," and studied a painting close to her. She'd seen that image before. They sold posters of it at Wal-Mart. "So you're . . . rich." Evidently, that was an understatement.

"Not really. As I said, most of this belongs to the trust; I just act as the administrator. I'm . . . ." He thought for a second, and smiled. "A caretaker, I suppose. I avoid the place as often as possible, anyway. Liam is more than capable of running the enterprise without my interference."

"But it belongs to your family."

"No, to the trust. It belonged to my father. And my father didn't leave it to me." McCallister looked around for Mr. French, who was sniffing a low-hanging tapestry quite carefully, flat nose buried in the probably priceless fabric. "Ah, would you mind . . . ?"

"Come here, dogface," she said, and scooped him up. He squirmed, but she held him. God forbid the mutt should pee on anything in here; she'd be in debt for the rest of her life. "Who did your dad leave it to?"

"My brother," McCallister said. "He died." That was short, unemotional, and didn't invite any more questions. "Let me take you to your room."

"The Auburn Room," she said. "Is everything named that pretentiously around here?"

"Be nice. I could have put you in the Aubergine Suite."

"My God."

"I'm two doors down," he said. "If you need anything, you can press the button for Liam, or come get me. Don't go wandering by yourself."

"Ghosts?"

"None that would bother you." Again, there was that slammed conversational door. McCallister jogged up a few steps, then turned and looked back at her. "Something else?"

She paused, hand on the railing. "What is your room called?"

"Patrick's room," he said. "But it used to be called the Black Room."

Somehow, she wasn't at all surprised.

The Auburn Room was the most beautiful thing she'd ever seen.

Bryn paused in the doorway, staring at the graceful lines of the canopied bed, the massive gilt-framed mirror that stretched half the length of the room, the silks in muted orange, rich browns, harvest golds. *If the Queen of England has a favorite room, this is probably it*, she thought. Her cheap little suitcase looked particularly pathetic where Liam had put it on a folding luggage rack. The luggage rack was probably worth more than the entire contents, *and* the suitcase.

She'd been starting to like McCallister, but now ... now she couldn't honestly believe that they had anything at all in common. He came from a whole different reality than she—or anybody she knew—lived in. Why in the *hell* was he working as some corporate drone?

"I hope this is suitable, ma'am," Liam said, and gave her a warm smile. "Shall I bring a bed for your dog?"

"Um ... can I let him sleep with me?"

"Of course."

Yeah, what was a little dog hair on that national treasure of a bedspread, or the rug that the *Antiques Roadshow* appraisers would have orgasmed over? She let Mr. French hop down to run around the room sniffing excitedly, and tried not to think about the disaster that might happen next.

Liam was watching her, and clearly knew what she was thinking, because he smiled and said, "No worries about the dog, ma'am. We have seven here, including two rottweilers, three greyhounds, a poodle, and a pug. Your friend is quite welcome. I'll bring some food and water for him. Anything for you?"

"I'm all kibbled out," she said. "I think I just need to sleep, but thank you. And thanks for not making me feel ... second-class."

"You're assuredly not," he said, and nodded to her before closing the door behind him.

That lasted about two full seconds before there was another rap on the wood, and when she looked out, McCallister was there. He cleared his throat. "So you'll be all right." It wasn't a question, really. "As I said, I'm two rooms down. The panic button is next to your bed. Press it if you're in any way alarmed, and Liam will come running. So will I."

"Why do you work for Pharmadene?" she asked, as he reached for the doorknob. "You must have a reason. It's not like you need the job. If I lived here, I'd never clip on some corporate badge and wear a monkey suit."

He considered giving her an honest answer—she could see that in the way he looked at her—but then he shook his head. "We'll discuss all that some other time; it's a long story. For now, please get some sleep. Liam will make sure you're ready for breakfast. We'll be leaving right after that."

"Going where?"

"Hopefully," he said, "to someone who can help you more than I can."

"Patrick?" She saw him glance back over his shoulder as he opened the bedroom door. "Back at my apartment, we—"

He shook his head, and left without a word.

"—didn't do anything," she finished softly, as the door shut. "Right. Professional relationship it is. No problem."

Despite the amazing down mattress and soft sheets and feathery duvet, neither she nor Mr. French slept much at all.

The morning dawned soft and bright, with those kind of cheerful chirping country bird sounds that Bryn thought existed only in the movies. She felt tired, but oddly at peace, and swung open the window to look out at the unbelievable view of the manicured, jewel-perfect gardens. That lasted about a minute, until Mr. French marched to the closed (and locked) bedroom door, whined, and she remembered that mansions probably didn't come with convenient doggy doors. She was pulling on her robe and slippers and wondering what the rules were about wandering around this place looking ratty when a soft knock came at the door.

She unlocked it and peeked out. Liam smiled politely and said, "May I take the young lad for a walk outside?"

Oh. "Well . . . if you don't mind . . ."

"Absolutely no trouble, Miss Davis. Will you want coffee or tea with your breakfast?"

Right on cue, she remembered her caffeine deficit, and her stomach rumbled. "Coffee," she said. "And just a bagel, please. Oh—Liam?"

"Yes, miss."

"What's the story about this house?"

Liam regarded her for a few seconds without replying, then leaned against the door and said, "I'm not sure that Mr. McCallister shouldn't tell you himself."

"Mr. McCallister has a policy of telling me absolutely nothing, and it's getting pretty old."

"He does tend to be very private," Liam agreed. "Very well. His great-grandfather was a hardscrabble railroad man who made a fortune, which his grandson set about squandering. Luckily, his granddaughter was more astute, and by the time Mr. McCallister's father was born, the fortune had been successfully defended."

"He said he had a brother."

"He did."

She waited, but he didn't expand on it. *"And?"*

"I believe Patrick told you that Jamie died."

"It sounds like neither one of you wants to tell me the truth about it."

"So it does," Liam said. "I should walk the dog, miss. Go down to breakfast when you're ready."

He left before she could think of any better way to pry information out of him. Not that she'd have succeeded. Liam and Patrick both seemed to have taken vows of silence on the subject.

Freshly scrubbed and dressed, she came downstairs to find Mr. French comfortably snuggled into a doggy bed near the door, looking deliriously happy. Liam showed her to the Small Room, which apparently was where the breakfast buffet was laid out; the room wasn't *small*, and it held enough food to take care of a fairly major armed camp. "I just wanted a bagel," she said weakly, surveying the ranks of gleaming serving trays. Liam pulled out a chair at the table, and she saw a steaming china cup and a bagel ready for her, just the way she'd asked. "Oh." She sank down, and was taking her first sip as Patrick McCallister walked in.

I made this man sleep on my ratty old Sears couch, she thought. *Covered with a Wal-Mart blanket. In my six-hundred-a-month apartment. I made him eat peanut butter and crackers off of paper plates.*

And he smiled at me.

She wasn't sure which emotion that boiled up in her was the most apt: a vague sense of shame for being . . . not part of this world; anger, for making her feel inadequate; or surprise, because once again, Patrick McCallister looked like a real person when he smiled.

Or a secret, unsettling sense of delight that there was warmth in the smile, despite everything.

Bryn shook it off and forced herself to look at him analytically. He looked like he was wearing an identical suit, shirt, and tie to what he'd had on yesterday, only these were spotless and wrinkle-free. Maybe Liam had some kind of overnight cleaning service, too. Even his shoes were shiny. He filled up a breakfast plate, moving fast but gracefully, and took a seat across from Bryn.

"Good morning," he said. "Did you sleep well?"

"Yes," she said. "Sure. Why wouldn't I? Fast Freddy rose from the dead and someone is apparently climbing sheer walls like a lizard to get at me. Nothing to keep me awake there."

"He won't be climbing them here," Liam said, sounding absolutely convinced of it. "Motion sensors on the walls, security at every possible entrance. Constant monitoring. You're quite safe here, miss."

Before she had a chance to feel better about that, McCallister said, "She's not staying. We'll be leaving right after breakfast."

"I see." Liam's eyebrows went up just a little. "Will you be needing anything in the way of supplies?"

McCallister flat-out grinned at that. "I'm starting to wonder if you think being a butler means that you're Alfred and I'm Bruce Wayne. Do we have a Batcave?"

"Once again, I'm not a butler, sir. I'm an estate administrator. And we do not have a Batcave that I'm aware of, but I can certainly check the basements just in case. I was speaking more of providing you with a packed lunch. Perhaps some coffee in a thermos."

"Ah," McCallister said, and took a bite of bacon, which Bryn was starting to regret not having. "Lunch and coffee would be fine. Thanks."

"And for the lady?"

"Whatever you're doing is fine," she said hastily. What did rich people eat for lunch? Finger sandwiches with the crusts cut off? Oysters? She had no idea. This place made Mr. Fairview's fancy French lunch look like the corner deli had slapped it together. "Where are we going?"

That last was directed at McCallister, and he chewed and swallowed a large bite of eggs before he said, "I told you that I had a contact who might be able to help with your . . . unique problem. A therapist. We'll be visiting him shortly."

Again, he was talking in code, and the reality descended hard on her shoulders, like hands pushing her into the chair: someone was always watching. Listening. Even here. No matter where she went, she couldn't shake off Pharmadene's leash around her neck.

She took a bite of bagel. It was probably delicious, but she tasted almost nothing. At least it would keep her going, along with the coffee. "I need my shot," she said.

"You'll get it once we're at the therapist's."

"You have it with you?"

"Yes. I keep two with me at all times in case of emergency." When she frowned, he continued. "If you get severely injured, you may require a booster shot. I don't want to be unprepared, as long as you're with me."

"In other words, I could knock you out and take them, and I'd be all right for two days."

The smile went back to a tight, controlled, almost humorless expression. "Your problem is assuming you could knock me out." She knew that glint in the eye; McCallister wasn't confident because he was arrogant. He was confident because he had historical evidence he was right. "And I don't think one more day of running would take you out of the reach of Pharmadene."

He was right about that. Without resources, she'd be delaying the inevitable, and very messy, end. Pharmadene wouldn't even have to chase her, unless they really wanted to. They could just literally let her rot.

Sucks to be me.

Bryn ate her bagel in silence, and by the time she was finished, Liam had already neatly packed her overnight bag and loaded it in McCallister's car. He even included a new dog bed for Mr. French to travel in comfort. Lunch was in modular little boxes. "I think he *is* Alfred," she said to McCallister, who was downing the last of his coffee as he watched.

"Actually, I often wonder if he's Batman." McCallister handed Liam back the cup and saucer and opened the passenger door for her. "Time to go."

She let Mr. French jump in and take his seat in the dog bed before slipping in herself. McCallister got behind the wheel, and in ten seconds or less they were heading down the gravel path. Bryn let the crunch of the tires fill the silence for another five seconds before she said, "Your family has a shitload of money."

"That's one way to put it."

"But it's not *your* money?"

"I told you. I'm the trust administrator. I decide where the money is spent, but I'm not allowed to touch it personally."

"Is that why you took the job at Pharmadene?"

"Even ex-rich people need salaries."

"But why *there*?"

He didn't glance at her. His focus stayed on the long, winding road down to the gates. "I don't think we need to discuss my job, Bryn. It's not healthy for either of us to dig too deep into the details."

"But back at Joe's you said—"

"Bryn." He cut her off, cold as a guillotine blade. "Change the subject. Now."

She hadn't been going to spill anything top-secret, damn it; she wasn't that stupid. It offended her that he thought she would. "Fine. Tell me about your family."

"Pick something else." He finally reached the estate's gates, which silently opened for them, and they hit the open road. She could sense his frustration in the way he edged the accelerator up past legal speed.

"Oh, no, you already warned me off of one topic. Liam said your family got its money the old-fashioned way."

"By oppressing others? Yes, there was a lot of opportunity for that around the early industrial age, and they took full advantage. Great-Granddad was a rival of Rockefeller for a while, only he lacked the civic responsibility. It's not a glamorous story, Bryn."

"It is to someone whose biggest family celebrity was a cousin who made it to the second round of *American Idol.* Nobody's ever going to mention the Davises in the same breath as the Rockefellers."

"That's almost certainly a good thing."

She laughed. "And you really don't have a clue what it's like to grow up poor, McCallister."

"I know what it's like to grow up—" He stopped himself, shook his head, and said, "Let's not talk about this."

"Why not?"

"Because it's not germane to the problems you face."

"I didn't think you wanted to talk about my problems. What with all the secrets."

To her surprise, he laughed. It was a strange, almost humorless little laugh, but closer than she'd ever heard from him. "You can be infuriatingly right; did anyone ever tell you that?"

"I can safely say it's not a problem that's really bothered me so far in my life."

"All right then," he said. There were crinkles at the corners of his eyes, and a ghost of a smile on his lips. "You tell *me* about your family."

"You're kidding."

"No."

"You probably know everything about all of them."

"I know facts. Tell me what they're actually like."

So she did, as the miles hummed by under the tires: Annie, her sweet but financially incompetent sister; her brother Tate's current deployment to Afghanistan; her older sister Grace, the know-it-all, working as a department manager at Wal-Mart, but with embarrassing secrets; George, the asshole Bryn never spoke to, who was still the apple of her mother's eye because he ran his own business; and, last, Kyle. "But you know about Kyle," she said.

"Do I?"

She sighed. "He's serving fifteen years for armed robbery. Don't tell me you don't know about my big brother. I barely know him, though. He took off when he was fifteen years old, and I was just a kid. He was smart, though. Smarter than George, for sure. He got in with bad people after he left home."

"Isn't this where you tell me he's not a bad guy?"

"No. As far as I know, he's a hard-ass Aryan Brotherhood member. It'd be stupid to say he's not a bad guy."

McCallister let that lie for a moment before he said, "What about Sharon?"

"What about her?"

"You didn't tell me about her."

"I didn't really know her, either." That was a lie, though; Bryn remembered Sharon well. Sharon was pretty, with flowing red-blond hair, a teasing laugh, big lovely eyes. "She was a lot older than I was."

"You refer to her in past tense, you know."

"I know. She's dead. I mean, the family party line is that she's missing, but she's been missing for a long time, and you know the odds on that. If a pretty eighteen-year-old girl with no history of behavior issues goes missing . . ."

McCallister nodded slowly. "Still, she could be out there somewhere."

"If she is, she's got no interest in contacting any of us. Not even Mom, and they were close right up until the day she walked out of our lives." Bryn took in a deep breath. "No. She's dead. Whether it was an accident or murder, she's lying out there somewhere, waiting to be found. I know it, and so do you."

"I'm sorry," he said. It sounded like he meant it.

"Then it's your turn," she said. "I've been talking for more than an hour, spilling my entire family history. What about you?"

"Bryn—"

"I'm not asking for classified secrets. Just tell me about your family."

He didn't want to—she could see it—but he finally said, "Nothing much to tell. Rich people are remarkably boring; they're either big philanthropists, like my mother, or self-absorbed, like my father. Either way, the effect was the same. They didn't spend much time at home. I had more in common with my tutors and nannies than I did with my parents." He shrugged. "I'm not trying to be poor-little-rich-boy about it. It's what it was. My mother was a good person; she just felt that the family's responsibility was to do good with what we had, so she was always out at fund-raisers, contributing to causes, attending charity events. She was beautiful, and I think she would have made a ruthless businesswoman if she'd been required to do that. She wasn't."

"And your father?"

Patrick just shrugged and said nothing, but she saw the skin tighten at the corners of his eyes. Not a smile this time—something else. Something darker.

"Liam said your brother's name was Jamie."

"That's right."

"And?"

"And what?"

"And what *happened*?" Nothing. He might have been a mannequin, for all the emotional response he gave to that. "Oh, come on. I spilled about everything, including Grace's secret adoption. I went all talk-show about it. And you won't even give me more than his *name*?"

McCallister said, "What made you go into the funeral business?"

"Oh, no, you're going to tell me *something*. No changing the channel. Was he older or younger?"

"Older," McCallister finally said, after what seemed like a pretty fierce internal argument. "Two years older."

"Did you get along?"

"I was the younger brother of a filthy rich family. The surplus child. No, we didn't get along." From the way McCallister's hands tightened on the steering wheel, then deliberately relaxed, that was putting it mildly. "Jamie died. That's all the story you're going to get."

"And you were disinherited." He didn't bother to answer that one at all. Silence fell, deep and uncomfortable, and Bryn finally sighed and said, "When I was in Iraq, I saw a lot of death. Not just our people, but the Iraqis, too. I didn't mind helping gather bodies after a bombing; some couldn't handle it, but I could. It felt like something I could do to restore some kind of dignity to them. So when I came back, I thought . . . I thought it might be a good thing to do for a living. There's something honorable about it. Something real."

McCallister looked over at her, nodded, and said, "I was in the military, too. I can kill, but gathering bodies—that always bothered me. It takes a special kind of strength to devote yourself to that."

"True believers," she said, and smiled.

"What?"

"Something one of my instructors said. Two kinds of people in the funeral business: true believers and freaks. I guess I'm a true believer, after all. Except that what you did to me does make me a bit of a freak, I suppose."

"Different kind of freak, perhaps, than what he was referring to."

"Yeah. Fast Freddy was the kind he was talking about. Me, I'm . . . life-challenged."

"I think that could apply to any of us, Bryn." McCallister downshifted, and the car slowed for him to make a turn onto the interstate. "We've got another hour, if you'd like to take a nap. Mr. French has already beaten you to it."

So he had; she looked back to find the bulldog snoozing away, comfortably curled in his fluffy new bed. And truthfully, she *was* tired. Aching, actually. She caught herself yawning. "What about the shot?" she asked.

"When we get there," he said. "Rest."

It didn't take much for her to drop into a dark, uneasy sleep filled with flashes of nightmares. Fast Freddy leering at her. The decomposing, impossibly moving corpse in the mortuary. Her own image, dead on a TV screen, until it screamed.

Last, she dreamed of her sister Sharon the final time she'd seen her—carefree, laughing, heading out on a normal afternoon and walking right out of the family's life, forever.

Only this time, Sharon wasn't laughing.

She was screaming as someone carried her away. Reaching out for help, while Bryn stood frozen and silent.

Life-challenged.

Chapter 7

The sound of voices outside the car woke her, finally.

Bryn yawned, made a face at the horrible taste in her mouth, and blinked to clear her eyes. She couldn't see much. *Is it already dark?* No, it couldn't be. A jolt of shock and fear went through her. *My shot. Is it late?*

Then she calmed down and realized that she could see daylight in the distance. McCallister had parked the car inside a windowless building, something like an open, deserted factory. She could dimly make out an empty expanse of concrete, some dilapidated wooden crates, and a few bolts where large machinery had once been installed.

It didn't look like anyplace she'd have voluntarily visited.

Bryn listened more carefully. She heard McCallister's voice, and saw him standing outside the car talking to . . . no one. Wait. He was addressing a speaker grille set into the wall next to a solid metal door.

". . . message, Manny. I know you don't like it when I bring strangers, but I didn't have a choice. Open up. It's dangerous to let her sit out here."

"No, it's not," the speaker said, with a faint crackle of static. "We intercepted the tracking signal half a mile out and jammed it. Your satanic bosses will be looking in all the wrong places by this time, especially since I ghosted the signal out to some repeaters. They'll get random blips through half the state for as long as I want."

"Thanks."

"Don't thank me, Pat. As far as I'm concerned, you can take her and go."

"Manny, we talked about this. You said you had something for me."

"I do. And I'll give it to you. But she's not coming inside— Wait. Pansy, *Jesus*, don't go and—" Manny fell silent, then sighed. "Well, crap."

A light switched on above the door, and it opened with a heavy scrape. On the other side was a small-framed woman with dark hair cut in a pageboy style; she had a lovely, heart-shaped face, and a wicked smile for McCallister. "Well, bring her in, Pat. I can't stand to hear the two of you yammering at each other anymore, and I know how stubborn you both can be."

McCallister leaned forward and kissed the woman on the cheek. "Thanks, Pansy."

"Don't thank me yet. He's going to pout for days about this, and he may not help you at all now. You know that, right?"

"He'll help," McCallister said, "once he meets her."

Pansy lifted a shapely eyebrow and shot an amused glance at the car. Bryn suddenly felt far too unprepared for whatever was going on. *Damn it*, why couldn't McCallister part with details once in a while? What was so hard about that?

He turned and motioned to her, and Bryn got out of the car. Mr. French woke up and started barking in confusion, but she shut him inside and told him to be quiet, for all the good it did. When she turned around the woman—Pansy, God, what a name—was offering her a hand to shake.

"Pansy Taylor," she said. "You must be Bryn."

"You know who I am."

Pansy smiled. "You've been a hot topic around here, believe me. Come with, and bring the dog. Oh, and ditch the guns, Pat; you know the rules better than I do."

McCallister sighed and took out his own guns—two of them—and placed them in the glove compartment of the car. He silently demanded Bryn's, and she handed it over. Reluctantly. Once the weapons were locked up, Bryn grabbed Mr. French, who wiggled excitedly, and Pansy led them up a narrow, featureless concrete staircase as the door boomed shut behind them, and at the top of the steps entered a complex code into the keypad, then put her hand on a scanner.

"In case you're wondering if you can cut my hand off and use it to get inside, you can't," Pansy said. "It checks pulse."

"I wasn't wondering," McCallister said. Bryn was, but she didn't say so.

"Who exactly are we going to meet?" she asked. There was something vaguely mad-scientist about all this, crossed with evil-villain. It was surprisingly disturbing.

"Manny Glickman," Pansy said, and frowned at McCallister. "What, you didn't tell her?"

"I didn't want to broadcast it to anyone who might be listening."

"Jesus, you're as paranoid as he is. Get help, man."

The door hissed open with a puff of cool air, and Pansy held it open as they passed before locking it behind them.

Bryn had expected a decrepit warehouse environment, like the floor below, but this was . . . high-tech. The floors were concrete, but clean and glossy; to the left she glimpsed a kitchen gleaming with tile and aluminum. Ahead was a series of tables, equipment, humming machines, and computers, all in clear-walled rooms.

At the far end hung floor-to-ceiling burgundy velvet curtains, which seemed very out of place for such a laboratory environment.

Pansy saw her looking, and winked. "The bedroom," she said. "Trust me—it's nice. Manny would crash on an air mattress in the corner if someone didn't keep him civilized, but I do my best."

Bryn had been so caught up in all of the busy detail of the place that she'd failed to see the man bending over a complicated-looking lab setup in the corner until he said, "Oh, come *on*. Really? A dog?"

Mr. French growled, right on cue, an aggressive reply that made Bryn wince and quiet him with a hand on his head. "Sorry," she said. "He'll be good."

The man sighed. "Dog owners are so gullible. 'Oh, he won't bite. He's perfectly friendly.' They say that right up until their pit bulls rip your throat out. Has she been searched?" He was, at first glance, not very remarkable. Frizzy dark hair, body swathed in a white lab coat. That was all she could tell about him, because he didn't turn around or even glance their way.

"I'm vouching for her," McCallister said. "She's all right."

"Just like her for the dog?"

"Manny, turn around and at least say hello," Pansy said. "They came a long way."

"Then they should turn around and go back." Still, the man straightened up and turned to face them. He was bigger than she'd expected, broad shouldered, with surprisingly green eyes. He didn't meet Bryn's gaze for more than an instant, though, before he transferred his attention to McCallister. "Pat, you can't just drop in. It's not safe. What if you were followed?"

"You jammed the trackers. You just told me that."

"*Physically* followed."

McCallister shook his head slowly. "In all the time you've known me, have I ever been that careless?"

Manny stared at him for a long moment, then turned back to his chemistry set, or whatever it was. "There's a woman involved," he said. "You're not the only man to forget to watch his back under those circumstances."

"It's not about that."

"It's *always* about that, and if you don't think it is, you're lying to yourself." Manny sent her another fast, scorching glance. "She's pretty."

"She's an asset. And you're making me wish I'd never come here, because you're embarrassing me."

"Then we're even, because I wish you hadn't come here either."

"Manny, come on. What's got the bug up your ass?"

"Nothing." Manny peered through a microscope and made some notes on a pad off to the side. "I've got business to do. Clients who need help."

"I'm paying."

"Damn right, you're paying. If Pharmadene knows I'm playing in their sandbox, they're not just going to send me a cease-and-desist letter, you know. They *kill* people. I've got Pansy to think about."

Pansy, who was gathering up used coffee cups that were scattered around the area, rolled her eyes, which made Bryn smile, even as she felt a twinge of uneasiness. Safety was obviously a very big concern for Manny Glickman. Bryn had met paranoid people before, but never anybody quite *that* far gone who wasn't under serious medication, in a locked-down facility. She had no idea what McCallister saw in this weirdo, or why he was expecting *Manny*, of all people, to be their ace in the hole.

"I need this from you," McCallister said. He took a step forward, grabbed Manny by the shoulder, and spun him around. Manny was taller, but in that moment, McCallister simply dominated the room, just by the intensity. "And you owe me."

"So you're finally going there."

"I will if I have to."

Manny stared down at him, eyes half-shut, and then nodded once, sharply. "I don't care how much I owe you; I took one hell of a risk even messing with this stuff for you. If you want the results, you've got to pay me for that."

"Ballpark me."

"It took weeks, you know. Your Pharmadene bioengineers are really good."

"Get to the point."

"All right. A hundred thousand for the single-shot prototype. To set up any kind of an actual production line for quantity, I'm going to need expensive equipment and raw materials. A hundred thousand more, minimum. Not including my fees, which will be twenty-five to start."

"Jesus, Manny. I thought you owed me."

"I do," Manny said. "Which is why I agreed to fuck around with your Pharmadene zombie drug in the first place. I'm giving you the friend rate, but I don't give freebies. Ever. You want me, you pay me. You know that."

McCallister hesitated a bare second before he said, "I'm going to need to see the prototype in action before I jump into that kind of money. I'm not—"

"I know how much you've got in the bank, Pat. Don't

kid a kidder. You may not have access to the trust, but you don't do so badly for yourself. Couple of hundred thou won't break you."

McCallister stared at him for a long, long moment, then nodded sharply, once. "It had better work."

Manny shrugged. "It's science, man. We fail before we succeed. I don't guarantee anything."

Well, *that* was comforting.

Pansy touched Bryn's arm, making her jump, and said, "Come with me. You're going to want to sit down for this."

It's just an IV, Bryn told herself, as she watched the clear fluid drip slowly from the bag into the flexible tubing. *Just saline.*

It wasn't just saline, and it was going into her veins, and that scared her so much her mouth felt dry. The shots, at least, were fast, over before she could really think about the implications. But sitting here like this as Manny's *prototype* whispered into her veins, that was something else entirely.

"So," she said, to take her mind off of things, "how long have you been working on this?"

Manny didn't seem to hear her, but he finally answered as he scratched down notes in a chart, referring to the machines she was hooked up to. "McCallister brought me a sample of Pharmadene's drug when it was first started in trials," he said. "He wanted to know the potential for abuse. I told him there was nothing but potential for abuse. So technically, I suppose almost a year since I started taking the thing apart."

"And this is . . . an antidote?"

"For what, death?"

"Manny!" Pansy called from the next room. "Behave."

"Sorry," he muttered. He didn't sound sorry. "As far as I can tell, your condition isn't fixable by any medical means. The drug maintains you. It doesn't bring you back to life, just supports your vital functions. If I wanted to get poetic, I'd say it replaces your soul."

That was . . . uncomfortable. Bryn looked at the needle going into her arm. "So what exactly does this thing do?"

"No pain at the entry site?" Manny asked. It wasn't that he sounded concerned, really, just inquisitive. All this was an intellectual problem for him.

Life and death, for her. Or whatever passed for life these days.

"It's fine," she said, and dry-swallowed. "I'm really thirsty."

"Yeah, that's a side effect," he said, and poured some water from a carafe nearby. He handed it over, and she gulped it down in three convulsive swallows. "Not too much. You'll vomit."

Comforting. She leaned her head back against the leather headrest and studied the ceiling girders high above. "I can't believe that I'm taking experimental IV drugs from some guy who bunkers himself in a warehouse."

"You left out paranoid. A *paranoid* guy who bunkers himself in a warehouse."

"I was trying to be nice."

"Don't waste it on me; I mostly don't notice. Or care."

"Do you have *any* qualifications?"

"Why, would it matter now? The IV's already in. If you wanted to see my Johns Hopkins certificate, you should have asked before."

"Do you have one?"

He shrugged. "Somewhere."

She eyed him curiously and wondered what his story was, but mostly what she was concerned with was what the hell was going into her body. Slowly. To no apparent effect. "I repeat—what the hell is this stuff?"

"If I tell you it could prejudice the trial," he said. "Just tell me if you feel anything."

"Anything like *what*? Because I'm feeling pretty damn unnerved right now!"

Manny, unruffled, checked his watch and the level on the bag above his head, then stood up and went to the door. "You can test it now; the solution should be filtered throughout her system."

"Try what?" she asked, feeling ridiculously exposed, as if they'd left her naked and defenseless. "Uh, could someone please explain *anything* to me?"

McCallister stepped into the room, shut the door behind

him, and exchanged a look with Manny before he said, "How are you feeling, Bryn?"

"Pissed off," she said. Her voice was shaking, and she was breathing faster than she should have been. The urge to rip the needle out of her vein was almost irresistible. "Terrified. How's *your* day?"

"Interesting." McCallister pulled up a stool across from her and said, "Your pupils are a little wide."

"Probably because whatever's in this stuff is making me high, but not in a fun way." She swallowed hard and lowered her voice. "I'm scared."

"I know." He leaned forward and studied her for another few seconds before he said, "What color underwear do you have on?"

"What?" She blinked at him, and felt a surge of heat in her face. God, she hated blushing. "None of your business!"

"Tell me."

"No!"

"Condition Sapphire. Tell me!" He'd raised his voice, shouting it in her face, and she felt all the tension, all the anger, all the *hate* she'd pushed down for days now suddenly boil up to the surface.

Bryn surged up out of the chair and screamed back, *"Go to hell, you son of a—"* The truth hit her in a cold rush, and she paused, staring into his eyes. "Oh," she said, in a much calmer voice. *"Oh."*

McCallister smiled—a real, relieved smile. "Manny," he said, "you are a genius."

"Is that news? I thought you knew that when you promised to pay me—let's see—two hundred and twenty-five thousand dollars. To start." Even Manny was smiling—or at least, he looked like he was tempted.

"Try it again!" Bryn said, and grabbed McCallister's hands. She squeezed hard. "We have to make sure! Come on; order me."

"Kiss me," he said, still smiling.

Maybe it was the smile that did it, but she felt a wild and uncontrollable impulse to follow *that* order. Bryn froze, stared at him a stricken second, and then said, "Something else."

The glow in his eyes faded, and so did the smile. For a second he'd seemed . . . so different. Almost human. But now . . . now it was just business again. "Walk to the corner," he said. "That's an order."

She didn't move. And didn't feel any impulse to, either. What she *did* feel was a corresponding need to slap him.

"Manny, if this stuff is supposed to counter that protocol thing, I think it works," she said, and sat back down in her leather chair. "So maybe it's a good time to explain to me what you just did to me."

"I didn't so much reprogram the nanites as chemically inhibit some of their functions," Manny said. "I've been working on turning off specific design features of the proprietary drug ever since Pat made it available to me for study, more than year ago; I've also been working to develop a protocol-free version. That one's a little tricky, but I thought the counteragent would work in the meantime. It's got a toxic side effect that would kill most people, but for someone like you, taking Returné, that doesn't matter. The nanites will clean up the mess. Does make you a little loopy, though."

"It's *toxic*?"

"Not so you'd really notice."

McCallister stepped in, fortunately. "We had to address your vulnerability to the protocols, especially Condition Sapphire. I thought you wanted that as much as we did," McCallister said. He seemed to have recovered his composure nicely; she couldn't see even a trace of emotion left in him now. "If you can be ordered to talk about anything and everything, you're useless to me as any kind of asset. Before I could tell you anything of note, I had to be sure the protocols wouldn't trigger if Harte ordered it."

Well, that just warmed her with the blanket of his concern. Or not. "So now I can lie about things."

"Just like you normally would."

Bryn stared at him with calm, level intensity until he looked away.

"Yeah, maybe we should sit down and have some coffee," Manny said. "You'll be good for about a week before you need another dose of the inhibitor."

"Great," she muttered. "More needles."

McCallister gave her a look. "Would you rather lose your free will on command?"

"No. But I'd rather do it without puncturing any more veins." She eyed Manny as he bent down, expertly slipping the needle out of her arm as he applied the cotton pad and bandage to stop the bleeding. He glanced up and gave her an awkward half smile. "Thank you, I guess."

He shrugged. "I don't get paid in thanks." But there was a glow in his eyes; he was pleased. "You start feeling faint or strange, you yell for me or Pansy. Loudly. None of this hero crap." He glanced aside at McCallister. "She stays put for a minimum of four hours before I let you walk out with her. Give me the syringe."

"No," McCallister said.

"She needs her shot."

"And she'll get it. From me." McCallister met Bryn's eyes briefly, then looked back at his friend. "It has to be that way. The syringes have sensors embedded all over the surface, and they're coded to two users—a primary and a backup. For Bryn, that's me and Joe Fideli. If anyone else, including Bryn, tries to administer them, the nanites inside self-destruct and become inert. Useless. It's a security measure to prevent theft."

Manny stared at him and slowly shook his head. "And here I thought I was the paranoid one."

"You are," McCallister said. "But you're just one person. Multiply it by an incredibly greedy corporation and you get some idea what we're up against."

He reached in his coat pocket and pulled out the syringe container; it looked exactly like a silver cigar tube, and he unscrewed it and removed the contents. *Great. Another stick.* Bryn didn't look at him as he walked over, took her bared arm, and punched the sharp chisel point into her skin. It was over in seconds, and it didn't hurt too much, though the lingering afterburn of the injection was annoying.

The two men were watching her with great interest. She frowned at them and said, "What?"

"We're waiting to see if there's any kind of unplanned reaction," Manny explained. "There's an outside possibility that the nanites could try to resist the secondary agent. That would be . . . bad."

"How bad?"

"Oh, you know. Decomposition." He shrugged. "Probably won't happen."

Bryn decided she was going to *hate* Manny Glickman. Forever. She waited tensely, trying to be alert for any sensations that didn't belong and trying not to overreact and invent them at the same time. Her two not very compassionate observers sat and waited as the minutes ticked by.

She got permission for a bathroom break at the two-hour mark, and on the way back ran into Pansy, who was coming out of the kitchen carrying a tray loaded down with sandwiches, tea, coffee, and a stack of magazines. "Here," she said, and handed it to Bryn. "No sense in your being stuck in there without anything to do. There's a sudoku puzzle book in there, too. And a pen."

"Not a pencil?"

Pansy winked. "Around here, we do them in ink."

"Of course you do. Um . . . thanks. For even thinking about it."

"That's why I'm here. To remind Manny to be human every once in a while. You've got your work cut out with Pat, though. I'm not sure someone didn't replace his blood with antifreeze some time ago."

"I don't care what's running through his veins. He's not my boyfriend."

"I know that," Pansy said calmly. "I just meant as a colleague. Of course."

She so very *didn't*, but Bryn let it go. She headed for the observation room, where McCallister silently rose from his chair and held the door open as she brought the tray in. "Pansy made us lunch," she said.

"Of course," McCallister said. "She's always the practical one."

"Ooh, peanut butter," Manny said.

"I rest my case." McCallister grabbed a sandwich from the tray—probably not peanut butter, Bryn guessed; he'd probably had enough of that at her apartment—and poured himself a cup of coffee. "You feeling all right?"

"You don't think I'd tell you if I had any doubts? I'm scared to death!"

"Point taken. Coffee?"

"God, yes." She grabbed a cup and held it while he poured, doctored it with sugar and cream to her satisfaction, and stood there with him downing caffeine. It almost felt . . . friendly. "I feel fine, just to make it clear."

"I'm glad."

"Yeah, I can tell you're overwhelmed." She blew on the surface of her coffee, watching him through half-closed eyes as he took a bite of sandwich. "You don't really work for Pharmadene, do you?"

"Of course I do. Want to see my pay stubs?"

"That's the most interesting pickup line I've heard this week, but no, I don't think so. You may get *paid* by Pharmadene, but you don't *work* for them. You've got another agenda. And maybe another boss."

"No, no other boss," he said. "But another agenda might be accurate."

"Pat," Manny said in a warning tone, but McCallister raised a hand to stop him. "Fine. Don't say I didn't warn you. You go around trusting people, you get a kick in the ribs every time. No matter how pretty they are."

"Do you say that to Pansy?" McCallister asked.

"Oh, no. I'm not crazy. She might wise up and leave me."

"If you've got something to tell me, say it," Bryn broke in. "Honestly, I'm so sick of this cloak-and-dagger *bullshit*!"

McCallister, of course, took a moment to think about it. Just when she was about to throw her coffee at him and tell him to go to hell, he said, "I have a reason for being careful. There have been two other prospects I've worked with from Pharmadene's program. They didn't work out. That's why we have the cloak-and-dagger bullshit; I came very close to being exposed by the last one I trusted. I thought that reviving you and being involved start to finish would give us the ability to guarantee you wouldn't be used and discarded by the company. As you noticed, that wasn't quite the case. The protocols were still in force, even though I specifically turned them off in your prerevival profile."

"You're blown," Manny said. "They've got to suspect you, if they countermanded that order."

"Not necessarily. All of my decisions are subject to review by my superior. She might just have done it as a precaution, not out of any suspicion. I could easily say it was a clerical error."

"Your superior's Irene Harte," Bryn said softly. The one who'd treated her like a walking, talking asset that had reached the end of its once-useful life. "*Does* she suspect you?"

"Irene suspects everyone. It's her job."

"You said you had an agenda."

"I didn't, at first," McCallister said. "I took the job in good faith, and for the first year, it was fine. Normal corporate security issues, a few employees diddling the books or stealing from the supply rooms or cooking expenses. Then two scientists invented Returné, and everything changed overnight. It wasn't a company anymore; it was an armed camp. The implications of what they have are staggering."

"Department of Defense," Bryn said.

"Oh, they'll sell it to the government, but Pharmadene has bigger plans than a defense contract. Before they jump, they want to be sure what they have, and what they can do with it. Why make an official deal when they can sell it under the table as a black-market terrorist's wet dream?" McCallister sounded grim, and certain. "I knew how it was going to play. Someone had to do something. I thought about blowing the whistle, but there's nobody I can go to who won't get sucked into the whirlpool. The government? It has to be destroyed from inside."

"How's that working out for you?" Manny asked. It sounded cynical, as if he already knew the answer.

"You know how it's working out. Pharmadene constantly monitors its own employees—computer activity, e-mails, phone calls, physical surveillance. I'm no exception to that. Harte will be suspicious today, after Bryn and I drop out of sight for a few hours and it's clear that I've covered my trail." Manny opened his mouth, but McCallister bulled straight ahead. "I planned for that, Manny. It won't lead back to you."

"The fuck it won't!" Manny said, and stood up to pace around the room in agitation. "All right, that's *it*. You're my friend, and I owe you, but I'm not getting in over my head with Pharmadene. Not with *them*. You take her and you go. Don't bother to come back. I'm moving the lab."

"Manny."

"No!" Manny swung around on him and pointed a shaking finger in his face. "No! You *know* how I feel about this. I *do not* take chances with my safety, or Pansy's. Not anymore." He left the room and slammed the door so hard the entire clear plastic structure of rooms rattled uneasily.

McCallister watched him go, and took another bite of his sandwich, which he chewed and swallowed before he said, "Pansy will calm him down."

"Is he always like this? Or is this just a really bad day?"

"Actually, it's a fairly good one."

"God. And you *trust* this guy?"

"Yes."

"Why?"

McCallister glanced at her, then went back to watching Manny stalk around the lab, randomly touching things as if it were a calming ritual. "Manny had a very bad time a few years back. He worked with the FBI."

"One of those profiler people?"

"No. He was a rock star in the lab. A genius, but a pure science geek. He never wanted to be out in the field, not for any reason."

"But something happened."

McCallister loosened his tie and sat back with a sigh. "He put a puzzle together, a serial killer's messages to the agents who were hunting him. That brought him to the killer's attention. As soon as Manny identified him, the killer grabbed him at his apartment, gave him a paralyzing agent, and buried him alive in a graveyard, with one air tank."

Bryn shivered. That was one of her nightmares now—being sealed in a body bag alive, being buried alive and conscious. That was all too possible a future for her, and she could well imagine the terror. "He got out."

"No," McCallister said. "He was found. The tank had run out."

"You found him, didn't you? That's what he owes you for."

McCallister looked away. "I helped find him. I provided information, and led the FBI to him."

"God, that must have been ... How long was he down?"

"Two hours. One hour breathing from the tank, one hour breathing the foul air in that coffin. He had to force himself to take slow, calm breaths, and he didn't know whether anyone would find him." He shook his head. "I honestly don't know how he did it. I would have died before help arrived. But ... he came out different from the way he went in—there's no question about that. He was always OCD, but now he's completely off the reservation about personal safety. He quit the FBI, took up private practice, and he moves around. A lot. He's got patrons. I don't even know how many, but enough to keep him funded."

"That's ... kind of horrible."

"It's a reasonable reaction," McCallister said, very quietly. "The coffin was already occupied. He was trapped in there with a body, in the dark, dying alone for two hours. It's a miracle he's sane at all."

Manny had stormed off into some private sanctum with what looked like a panic room door. Pansy came back instead. She opened the door and looked in at them, eyebrows raised. "Should I even ask what brought that on?"

"He thinks Pharmadene will trace us here."

"Does he have a point? Don't bullshit me, Pat. Even paranoid people are right sometimes, and I'm not risking his life. Not again. Not even for you." Pansy, Bryn realized, might look sweet and gentle and practical, but she had a core of steel that even McCallister might envy. "I will toss your ass out to the wolves before I let him go down. I've worked hard on this relationship."

"I know," McCallister said, and put all the warmth and conviction he could into the words. "I swear to you I will protect him. And you. They won't get to you through me, or Bryn."

She stared at him with such intensity that even *Bryn* felt the burn, and then slowly nodded. "All right. I'll talk him off the ledge, but if anything happens, swear to God, I *will* go nuclear-option on you, McCallister. He may owe you his life, but I'm more interested in preserving it." She swung the door all the way open. "Go. He won't come out until you leave, and I can't make him see reason until he's calmer."

"Pansy, I need him to keep making the inhibitor for her. It's important."

"I get it." Pansy met Bryn's eyes briefly. "And I'm sorry for everything that's happened to you. I wish we could help you more, but I'll do what I can to keep that going, at least. Manny's good at this. *Very* good. But he's fragile, you understand? And this Pharmadene thing—it's bad. You know that."

"I do. I woke up dead. I understand . . . a little of how that feels."

"Yes. Yes, I think you do. I'll do what I can for you, I promise."

That was the end of it. Bryn retrieved Mr. French from where he'd been snoozing in the corner of a very empty plastic-walled room, and five minutes later they'd negotiated the spy-quality security and were driving out into the sunlight. Mr. French wiggled into the front seat, onto Bryn's lap, and gave a pointed whine as he put a paw on the door.

"Oh—ah, we need to stop somewhere," she said. "Time for a walk."

McCallister was frowning, very inside himself, but that startled him into an even *deeper* frown. He said, "Do you trust me?"

"I hate it when you ask me that, because it means you're about to do something I won't like."

"Bryn."

"It depends."

"That's . . . not what I was hoping for."

"Look, could you please just stop the car?"

"Not yet. We have an alibi to establish."

"Which is . . . ?"

"You're not going to like it."

It took fifteen minutes for him to finish his drive and arrive at the destination, and he was entirely right: she didn't like it.

"Seriously," she said, as he parked.

"Take Mr. French for a walk. I'll check us in."

Bryn opened the door, and Mr. French hopped down and ran, loose skin flapping, for the small, straggly strip of brush and grass at the rear of the parking lot. "Wait!" she called, and hurried after him as McCallister headed in the opposite direction. "Stupid dog."

Well, it wasn't exactly his fault; he clearly had needs. So did she, as a matter of fact, and standing out here fidgeting from one foot to the other reminded her of it. Not that she was looking forward to exploring the bathroom facilities of the Hallmark Motor Court Inn, which looked like it had last seen any kind of upgrade in the 1970s. It was faded pink stucco, flat roofed, built in an *L* shape around a parking lot and a fenced-off, trash-filled dry pool that insurance issues had probably long ago rendered useless. There were six cars in the parking lot, mostly beaters, and it didn't look like a place anyone stayed for more than a couple of hours unless they were seriously down on their luck.

She was starting to get a sense of what McCallister's alibi would be, and no, she didn't like it at all.

When she blinked, she had an image of utter darkness, of being trapped in a coffin, like Manny Glickman; of gasping for each trembling breath, knowing that each one was one closer to the end. That would happen to her, too, when she missed a shot. How long would it take for the invisible little machines that kept her breathing to slow, drift, shut down? How long would it take for the toxins to build up and poison her? *God*, how long would she be able to feel it?

Mr. French watered a few dry spots on the ragged lawn, then wandered over to the edge of the building. The wilderness was thicker there, mostly knee-high grass and some very wild-looking shrubs, everything shrouded in shadow by the angle of the sun. Bryn patted her thigh. "Come on, boy. Let's go." He ignored her to sniff the concrete, intensely interested in some ghost of a prior dog or cat. "Oh, come *on*! Seriously?"

He waddled farther into the shadows, nosing out scents, peeing where he felt it might be necessary, and then squatting down at a modest distance.

Bryn was peripherally aware of a man coming out of a room a couple of doors down, but her attention was on the dog and her near-bursting bladder; when a shadow came into her peripheral vision she was sure it was McCallister, returning for her.

But it wasn't.

The shove caught her unprepared, sending her stumbling after Mr. French, and as she twisted to get a look at the man who'd pushed her she realized that she was in deep and immediate trouble. He was big, and his eyes were dead in an immobile, expressionless face. "Cash," he said. "Give it up, bitch."

She didn't have a purse, or anything in her pockets. "I don't have—"

He hit her, hard, in the face, and the pain exploded into black waves and red stars. Mr. French came charging out of the grass. He latched on to the man's pant leg, but was kicked away.

Bryn immediately went for her gun.

Too slow. Her attacker grabbed her by the shirt and punched her again, even harder, twice in the face, once with shattering force in the gut. She only managed to jerk her sidearm partway from the holster before he'd slammed her down on the ground, and then twisted, trying to throw him off to get leverage to draw it the rest of the way. No good. He grabbed the gun butt and pulled it free. She struggled with him for it, but the knee in her stomach was making her giddy and weak.

With a final wrench, he got control of the weapon.

She didn't hesitate; she slammed her fist into his balls as hard as she could, and he flinched, off balance. That let her throw him off, but he held on to the gun.

She could hear Mr. French's snarls, then a yelp, then more vicious snarling as he went back at her attacker.

The man aimed her own gun at her, and she knew in that second he intended to kill her, and the dog . . . and then he looked around, backed up, kicked Mr. French out of the way, and ran.

Bryn rolled over slowly to her side. Blood dripped onto the grass in vivid red globes, and when she coughed it sprayed out in a mist. It was all weirdly pretty, and seemed very remote. So did the pain. She was aware it was there, but a chemical firewall had gone up between her and her nerves, and that was a good thing. Very good.

Mr. French suddenly appeared in her field of vision, whining in concern, and licked her face anxiously. She tried to shove him away, but there was no strength in her arms.

"Bryn." That wasn't her voice; that was someone else's. Oh, it was McCallister, kneeling next to her dog, staring down at her. He didn't look remote anymore, or cold, or guarded. He seemed worried. "Can you get up?"

"Sure," she said, and tried. She couldn't. He pulled her up, and when her legs folded, he lifted her and carried her with Mr. French growling and whining around his feet as he walked. "Shut up, dog. 'M fine."

"No, you're not," McCallister said. "You've got a broken cheekbone, your nose is smashed, and that's just what I can see. Bryn, I left you alone for *one minute.*"

"Not my fault," she whispered. "Mugged."

"Why didn't you use the gun?"

"Tried." She swallowed a mouthful of blood, which tasted awful. "He took it."

"He won't have it for long." McCallister sounded grim and very sure. "I'm going to have to let you stand for a second. I'll hold you up."

"I'm fine," she said again, as if saying it could make it so. He let her legs swing down, and she concentrated on keeping her knees firm. And holding on, because the first plan wasn't working so well. McCallister slotted a key attached to a big plastic tag into the door that was facing them, opened it, and carried her inside over the threshold, which struck her as weirdly funny.

When she laughed and coughed, he looked down at her with a frown. "What?"

"Just married."

"Did he kick you in the head?"

"A little?"

McCallister slammed the door shut and put her on the bed. He probably did it as gently as he could, but all of a sudden, the firewall came crashing down in Bryn's brain, and the full force of her screaming nerves hit her in a wave. She couldn't bite back the cry of pain, and McCallister put a soothing, warm hand on her forehead. "Easy," he said. "Be calm. I'm going to give you a booster shot, but I have to wait. The shots have to be a couple of hours apart. You've got enough damage that the last one will burn off quickly." His fingers stroked her brow, smoothing back her hair, then withdrew. She felt Mr. French's warm weight drape itself across her legs, and heard him whining in concern. "How bad is the pain?"

She swallowed and lied, like a good soldier. "It's fine."

"You really need to look up the definition of that word. Hang on."

He put a hand on her nose, and pulled. A glassy, hot snap of pain bolted through her head, drawing another cry, and she felt her muscles tense and her back arch. McCallister grabbed her hand and held it as she squeezed. She gasped out, "What—"

"I had to reset your nose so that the nanites could heal it," he said. "You'll feel some pain when the bones start healing in your cheek, too. Hold on. I'll be back." He disappeared for what seemed like an hour, and returned with a glass of warm water and a thin washcloth, which he wetted and used to wipe the blood from her face in slow, soothing strokes. Her nose was still bleeding, and the rose red blooms spread across the washcloth, but she felt it trickle to a stop.

The pain built up along her cheekbone, like an unanesthetized root canal boring through bone. She grabbed for his hand again and held on, trembling, as the wave kept rising. It filled her head until she thought it would burst, and then there was that same glassy *pop* of bone shifting, and the pain began to recede. It left her weak and sick.

"Breathe," McCallister said. "The worst is over. Soft-tissue damage doesn't hurt as much as it heals."

"Says you," she whispered. Her whole midsection felt as if a truck were running over it, crushing and ripping things apart. But he was right; it faded fast. In five minutes, she was breathing easier, and the blood that had been choking her was just a nasty memory.

McCallister took the reddened washcloth back into the bathroom, and Bryn finally felt good enough to try to sit up a little. It was a mixed success. Mr. French watched her with unwavering attention, and if a dog could frown, he was definitely trying out the expression. She couldn't decide whether he was concerned or annoyed with her initiative.

McCallister, as it turned out, had the identical expression when he came back. "What do you think you're doing?"

"Sitting up." Sort of.

"Don't. Let the nanites do their job. You're at least an hour away from the next shot, and the more you move around, the less effective they'll be as they try to maintain additional activity. Understand?"

She did, but she'd finally gotten the thin motel pillow tucked where she wanted it, and it was more effort to lie flat again. "I'm—"

"If you say you're fine again, I swear to God, Bryn, I will drive you back to Pharmadene and dump you on the doorstep as a lost cause." He didn't mean it. At least, she didn't *think* he meant it. "Stay still. Do not open this door for anyone. Understand?"

"Sure," she said, and finally realized, as he grabbed the doorknob, that he was leaving her. "Where are you going?"

McCallister flashed her one of those rare, unguarded smiles. "I'm going to get your gun back," he said. "After all, I'm responsible for it."

She settled back, staring, as the lock clicked shut, then looked at Mr. French. He settled down across her legs, as if he intended to single-handedly hold her down. "How about you, dogface? You okay?"

He licked his chops and put his head down.

She rubbed his fur with trembling fingers, and knew just how he felt.

Chapter 8

Bryn didn't intend to drift off, but she woke to the sharp jab of a needle in her arm. Panic set in. For a second she thought she was back in that place again, that awful moment of screaming back to life. She jerked, but he was fast, and the needle was out of her skin in the next second, and McCallister's hand was on her chest, holding her still. "You're safe," he said. "Booster shot. How are you feeling?"

She felt ... well, weirdly enough, she felt *good*. Rested. Revived, if that wasn't too sick a word to select. "Okay," she said. "Better."

"No pain?"

"No." He took his hand away. Bryn sat up fully, expecting to feel a twinge from her abused abdomen, but the muscles contracted normally, as if she'd never been hurt. She put her hands to her face and felt carefully, but it was just smooth skin, and no bumps or complaining sore spots. Even her nose was straight. "Wow. That's—"

"Amazing," he agreed. "You have blood in your hair. You'll probably want to shower."

McCallister, she realized, also looked like he could use a rinse, and maybe a long, hot soak. . . . There was a livid red mark on his left cheek that was going to turn into a dirty bruise before too long, and his hands were bloody at the knuckles. His tie was crooked, his jacket torn at the shoulder and streaked with mud. His pants were filthy, too.

"What happened to you?"

For answer, he reached over and picked up a gun from

the bedside table, showed it to her, and put it down again. "I got it back for you."

Ouch. "It doesn't look like he gave it up without a fight."

He shrugged. "No significant damage." His lips stretched into a grim smile. "To me, anyway. I'm not as concerned about his welfare." The smile faded. "I'm sorry I wasn't backing you up."

"You're not my bodyguard, McCallister. I'm supposed to be *your* asset, remember? Not the other way around."

"I don't like my assets being damaged without any real benefit."

"Charming." She didn't believe it for a moment, though; she was starting to figure out McCallister, and she thought the man who'd carried her inside and tended to her was more real than the corporate persona. "So, your alibi for Irene Harte is that we've sneaked away to a seedy motel for some private busy time?"

"Yes."

"Do you know how stupid that is?"

He smiled again, this time a little more warmly. "You underestimate yourself. Or possibly me. No one at corporate will doubt it."

"Let me guess. You have a reputation."

"I've taken pains to build it. It gives me the ability to duck out of surveillance without too much notice being taken. You do enough legitimate philandering and no one questions you when you drop off the radar for a few hours with a girl."

"Wow," Bryn said. "You really are a man whore."

"I prefer the term *player*."

She had no response for that. For some reason, she could well imagine McCallister being familiar with these kinds of seedy roadside establishments, although she thought he probably preferred nicer accommodations. Which made her wonder . . . "Why here?"

"It has no wireless Internet or any other modern conveniences that make it easy to conduct off-site surveillance," he said. "It takes time for them to get organized and send real bodies out. Even the security camera in the office is state-of-the-art circa 1980, and I think it's just for show. If we'd checked in at a more upscale establishment, they'd have a much easier time keeping track of us."

Of course he had a reason. McCallister didn't do anything without a reason, and maybe two or three of them. "I really ought to be at work," she said. "Not that this hasn't been fun."

He checked his watch and said, "No hurry, it's already four o'clock, and by the time we drive back, it'll be well after closing time at the mortuary. Joe's been briefed. He'll cover for you. One thing about the dead—they'll wait."

His cell phone chose that moment to buzz like an angry hornet, and McCallister paused, checked the screen, and turned it off. "Harte," he said.

"You're not answering?"

"Would I be answering if we were doing what they think we're doing?"

"I don't know. Would you?"

He raised his eyebrows, smiled, and said, "Maybe." He switched the phone back on and hit a button on the TV remote at the same time. A porn channel popped up. *Why am I not surprised?* Bryn thought, and reached to change the channel. He shook his head and stopped her. Instead, he turned up the volume for the pants and moans. "McCallister," he said into the phone, sounding annoyed and distracted. "This had better be important." He listened for a second, then subtly altered his tone. "Ms. Harte. Sorry. I didn't check the screen." *Now* he turned the volume down. "Yes. Yes, I know." Another longer pause. "I'll alert my team to handle it. I'm not close to the office now." He locked eyes with Bryn, and mouthed, *Say something.*

What? she mouthed back. He shrugged.

Well, might as well have fun with it. She pitched her voice to a low, sexy range and said, "Patrick, this is no time to be on the phone."

He shushed her—loud enough for Irene Harte to hear it—and gave her a thumbs-up.

Bryn reached over, took his tie, and unknotted it. The rustle of fabric would sound good, she thought.

McCallister froze, staring at her, momentarily distracted

from his conversation. He reengaged with a physical jolt. "Ah, yes. Yes, that's fine. I'll be in later. Eight o'clock."

This was kind of fun. Bryn unfastened his collar, then slipped the second button loose. She was enjoying the rising confusion in his eyes. Thank God she actually had the upper hand in this very weird relationship, for once. *Stop*, he mouthed. She grinned and went for the next button.

He grabbed her hand in his, tightly, and pulled her closer—so close she could almost make out what his boss was saying on the phone. She froze, and he didn't move again either, until he said, "All right. See you then," and hung up the call.

He didn't release his hold. "What the hell were you doing?"

"I was selling your alibi," she said. "Let go."

"That," he said, "was not at all necessary, Bryn. I thought we agreed not to complicate things."

"You were trying to make her think we're having a mad affair. I was just helping."

"Helping," he repeated. "Bryn—trust me, you are *not* helping."

She met his eyes and held them. "Then why did you pick this particular alibi?"

He bent forward and kissed her. *Really* kissed her. The shock of his warm, silken lips pressing and sliding on hers made her tense at first, and she thought about resisting for half a second before her muscles melted in to warm jelly of their own accord. She didn't intend to kiss him back, but she couldn't help herself. He was warm and alive and strong, and the intense sensation of his mouth opening, of his hands on her back, of his tongue . . .

He let her go and stood up, very quickly. He took a giant step back from the bed, turned away, and began fastening the buttons on his shirt.

"Pretending that didn't just happen won't help," she said. Her heart was pounding, and she was vibrating all over with the intensity of what had just happened. He was, too. She could see it in the abrupt, jerky motions of his hands. "Patrick. Talk to me."

"Nothing happened," he said. His voice was tight and angry. "And nothing will ever happen again. I apologize."

"I don't want your apology; I want you to tell me what's going on between us, because there's been something for a while now. You know it. I know it."

"I told you. *Nothing*. Instinct." He lips twisted, and he turned away to do up his tie. "Hey, you're the one who called me a man whore."

"I didn't mean it." She got off the bed and touched his shoulder. "I didn't. And . . . thank you."

"For what?"

"For . . . stepping off." Even if, at this moment, she didn't want him to. Some desperate part of her wanted this, craved feeling *alive*, but she knew it was probably a terrible mistake. That was what he was trying to tell her. "I'll go take my shower."

She closed and locked the bathroom door, leaned against it for a moment, and then stripped off her clothes. The tub wasn't particularly clean, but the water was hot and plentiful, and the rough, cheap soap felt good. Not as good as she imagined other things might feel, but good enough.

She washed away the blood, and the desire, and by the time she came back into the cramped, cheap bedroom (and, God, she hadn't fully appreciated just how cheap and worn it was until that moment) she found McCallister stripped down to a white T-shirt and Joe Boxers, scrubbing mud out of his pants. He was still wearing his socks and dress shoes, which for some reason she found hilarious.

He looked up, frowned at her, and went back to what he was doing. Mr. French was sitting at his feet and watching with his head cocked, evidently fascinated, but he broke off and padded to Bryn. She leaned against the doorframe and crossed her arms. "You know, it's not going to help. That suit's pretty much ruined."

"I'll change on the way."

"Maybe you can tell Ms. Harte that I like it rough."

"Not funny," he said. He put the washcloth aside—a different one, she noticed; it didn't have bloodstains—and put the pants on. His shirt was wrinkled, but clean, and he buttoned up quickly. Even his jacket looked passable now, except for the torn seam at the shoulder. "If I don't have time to change, I'll tell her we had some problems in the field. She'll believe it." There was something wrong, some tightness around his eyes and mouth. He almost looked haunted.

Bryn took a wild, instinctive guess and said, "The appointment tonight. It's not just a business meeting, is it? You and Harte . . . ?"

He passed the loose circle of his tie over his head, popped his collar, and snugged the tie tight before he snapped down the points again. "We've got a long drive. Do you need me to walk the dog before we go?"

"No, he's fine. And you didn't answer me."

"I'm not going to answer," he said. He swung open the door to the setting sun, head down. "After you."

On the way back to her apartment, plans changed; McCallister got a phone call, said a few terse words, and then said, "Problem at your apartment. Joe is sure it's been compromised. You'll have to stay the night at the house."

It was funny that McCallister referred to the huge pile of a mansion as *the house*, because Bryn honestly couldn't imagine feeling that comfortable about it. "Why?"

"Because I don't have time to find you anywhere else. Liam will look after you."

"Then why exactly did we spend the afternoon in a cheap motel, when you have a swanky love nest all your own?"

He barked out a laugh at that term, then said, "Do you want to know the actual truth of it?"

"Sure."

"Our excuse is not so much the cheap, anonymous sex— which was great, by the way—but the drugs I buy there."

"Drugs," she repeated. "What kind of drugs?"

For answer, he reached into his coat pocket and came out with two plastic bags. Pills. Some kind of pills. "The kind that get a don't-ask, don't-tell pass from executives. I make a point to go out there once a month."

"Do you actually take them?"

"The only ones they see me take are gelatin-filled. I may be the only corporate employee who fakes a positive drug test."

"But aren't they going to wonder about you bringing me back here?"

"Joe's arranging for your apartment to be tented, as if for fumigation. It's as good as we could come up with on short notice." He smiled grimly. "And there really are bugs, after all. The electronic kind, anyway."

They ate the picnic lunch Liam had packed on the way back. There were, in fact, finger sandwiches without crusts. And delicious, too. McCallister was a font of utter silence. He answered when she spoke, but in monosyllables or utterly uninformative responses. Back to the same old Patrick, then.

She wondered if he was as uncomfortable as she felt.

Liam was standing on the steps with a suit coat on a hanger when McCallister crunched the car to a stop on the flawless white gravel, and Bryn's door was open before she could do more than cast a look Patrick's way. He didn't return it. He was staring straight ahead, through the windshield, at the growing gloom and the halogen glare cast by the headlights.

Liam gathered up the picnic basket and Mr. French's doggy bed, put the fresh jacket on the hook in the back, and shut the passenger door once she was out of it. McCallister, without another word, took his foot off the brake and continued along the rest of the circular drive leading back to the main entrance.

Bryn watched him go. When she turned, Liam was watching her with far too perceptive a gaze, but he merely said, "It's getting chilly, Miss Davis. Shall we go in?"

She let Mr. French follow up the steps; he needed the exercise anyway. He let out a *whuff* of recognition once they were in the door, and immediately went in search of his dog bed, which Liam had set against the wall. "I can see you've had quite a day," the butler—*estate administrator*—said. "I've kept some dinner warm for you. Mr. Fideli is waiting in the Small Room. If you'd prefer to change first, there are clothes in your closet upstairs. I took the liberty of buying a few things for you."

Implying, of course, that what she'd brought wasn't

suitable. She didn't feel at all offended, because, well, he was right. She'd never bitch about someone with exquisite taste—and he almost certainly had that—buying her something new to wear that was out of her budget range. *Liam* wasn't out for anything but upholding the good name of the McCallister trust. If Patrick had bought her clothes, that would have seemed . . . awkward.

"Sure," she said. "Thank you, Liam. I'll go change first."

Mr. French, the traitor, stayed in his bed and watched her go upstairs alone. Funny how quickly he was adapting to the good life. Her dog, she decided, was quite the social climber. She wasn't sure she was any different, and that made her feel a little dirty, somehow.

The things hanging in her closet were, predictably, amazing. She picked out a pale pink silk blouse and a pair of designer jeans and dressed quickly. When she walked into the Small Room, Joe Fideli—digging into an overflowing salad bowl—looked up and said, "I feel like I should get up or something. You look good, Bryn. Ladylike."

"Don't get up. You'll make me feel worse than I already do about all this." She got herself a plate and inspected the silver warming trays. Chicken, fish, salad, vegetables, dessert. It all looked amazing. She chose the salad and sat down with him, feeling hungrier than she expected. "What did McCallister tell you?"

"That the protocol inhibitor from Glickman is working," he said. When she frowned at him, he waved his fork vaguely at the room around them. "Room's shielded. You can say what you want in here. So, you met the crazy man. What'd you think?"

"He's the most paranoid man I've ever seen not locked up."

"Yeah, that was my feeling, too. He knows what he's doing, though."

"Yes, he does. Did my mystery guest call today?"

"No. He said he'll take a week to look you over, so I didn't expect it anyway. As soon as I get your apartment buttoned up, you're out of here, and you don't come back. In fact, you break ties with McCallister, at least in public. I'm going to be your shadow."

"You don't think our friendly supplier's going to notice *you* and trace you back?"

"I'm not on record at Pharmadene, as I told you. I'm a ghost who gets paid in cash. Besides, I think he'll think we're really, really close." He held up two fingers together, then crossed them. "You know."

"You can't do that. You've got a family."

"Yeah, and Kylie won't be too damn happy about my shacking up with a good-looking woman like you, but I'll martyr myself for the cause." He was, she realized, kidding her. "Seriously, Kylie's good with it. She knows the drill. This isn't our first rodeo, and she's met you. It's all good."

"So our cover story is what, *you're* sleeping with me on the side? *God.*" Bryn dropped her head into her hands. "If only my personal life were really this exciting."

"Sorry?"

"That was also McCallister's alibi for slipping off the chain today. I'm getting twice the reputation and none of the fun. I'm assuming that Pharmadene would also notice the sleepover."

"Oh. Right. Well, Pharmadene doesn't officially know me; I'm not on any corporate records. Pat pays his contractors off book. Shouldn't present a paper trail for our mystery guest to follow."

"My apartment . . ." Bryn bit her lip. "McCallister said you'd be making it safe."

"Well, safer, anyway; it's a cinder block box, only so good I can make the place. Tonight, you sleep here; this place is as solid as you can get. I'll go do some midnight renovations: sensors, motion detectors, upgraded doors and windows. Your neighbors might be a little pissed off about the noise, but I can do it in a couple of hours. Pat'll sign off on the expense, no problem."

"Maybe I should go with you."

"Trust me, you shouldn't. I don't want to be looking over my shoulder wondering whether somebody's creeping up behind you while I'm installing windows. Because it's all about me, obviously." Fideli fell silent for a moment, then said, with studied casualness, "What happened to you today?"

"Me? Nothing. Why?"

"Tremors." He pointed at her hand as she picked up her water glass. Sure enough, it was shaking. She could see the ripples spreading across the surface of the liquid, and quickly put the glass down. "I know Pat can be tough to take, but people don't usually get PTSD from a day with him."

McCallister was going to tell him anyway. She picked up her fork and ate a couple of leaves of lettuce drenched in heavenly balsamic dressing before she replied. "I got mugged. He beat me pretty bad. Broken nose, broken cheekbone, probably some broken ribs. It wasn't McCallister's fault. He was checking in for the room. I was walking the dog."

Fideli absorbed that in silence. "Just a random mugging."

"Yeah."

"You're sure about that."

It was a new thought, and a nasty one, and she took another bite and considered it carefully, before she said, "You think someone might have set it up? How? We weren't followed. Even I didn't know where I was going."

"Pat did."

She almost choked on her salad, and took a quick gulp of water to wash it down. "You think *he*—"

"No, no, but if he scouted this location before, or used it before, they might have made an educated guess and planted somebody on coverage at every possible stop. That would mean a big operation, big enough to scare me, and I don't scare easy. Of course, I could just be paranoid, but that's what they pay me to be." He shrugged and drank about half a glass of water. "Maybe it was random. Maybe you're just damned unlucky, Bryn."

She *felt* that way. "Why would they do that? Send someone to beat me up?"

"I can only think of one reason," Joe said. "Because they wanted to see if you'd heal."

"Oh, God. They just proved I was revived?"

"Look, our Mystery Guest must have already guessed at it; he sent that guy to protocol you at the bar. We got to the son of a bitch before he could report in; that meant he had to try something else. This could be it. And this could still be pure speculation." Joe finished up the last bite of his salad and pushed back from the table. "I'm going to need the keys to your apartment. Whether I'm being crazy or not, you need better security on that place. It's a kill box."

"Eat first. It's not going to get any worse before you get there."

"Yes, ma'am, boss. By the way, I up-sold two premium packages today, with full floral. Should net us about ten thousand in clear profit." He got up and speared a piece of chicken from the warming trays, then added rice and asparagus. "Of course, the bad news is I had to kill one of them myself. Anything to get business, I always say."

It was morbid, but he made her laugh, and as they sat together and ate, and Liam came in and out, and Mr. French wandered in with a pug she hadn't seen before, life seemed . . . temporarily normal. Death-and-taxes normal, anyway.

It was a good way to end the day.

"So," Joe said, "this is a panic button. There's one in every room, recessed, so you can't hit it by accident. If the electricity goes out, they light up on their own battery power so you can see them easily." He pointed to something that looked like a simple doorbell, recessed beside the interior frame of her apartment door. "It hits up police and robotexts me and Pat a nine-one-one with your address. I added break-resistant windows last night, with key locks and interior panic releases in case you have to get out quick. Here's the alarm keypad. You put in the code and you arm tamper sensors on the wall under each window and on the door outside. You want to leave motion detectors on; you just press this button after you arm it. I configured it to ignore anything dog-size."

He was *good*. Bryn, looking around the apartment, couldn't see any sign that anything had been done at all, except for the keypad next to the apartment door and the recessed button. Well, the windows might have looked a little less grimy. "Anything else?"

"Here's the deactivation code and secret panic code."

He passed over a sheet of paper. "Memorize and destroy; you know the drill. There's a video surveillance monitor in the bedroom that shows you the external door and the outside walls, so if you're worried about somebody out there, just check the feed. Got it?"

"Got it." She cast him a look. "Anybody else watching my monitors back at the mother ship?"

He laughed. "Yeah. Can't avoid that. They'll keep tabs and records. We all get used to it."

Or, Bryn thought, *we build ourselves fortresses of solitude in the backyard and arm up with AK-47s.*

"You're clear on how the system works?"

"Yes."

"Time to get back at it, then." He yawned wide enough to crack his jaw. Bryn winced at the noise; it sounded painful. "Don't worry; I'll stay awake. Couple of pots of coffee will fix me right up."

"Sorry."

"Part of the job. Sleepless nights just come with the territory." He dropped the apartment keys back into her hand and brushed a fleck of dust from his suit lapel. "How do I look?"

"Impressive." He did. In the suit, Fideli looked trustworthy, calm, kind, attentive—all the things you should be as a funeral director. "I guess I'll take my own car.... Oh, damn." Her car was probably parked in a lot near that damn bar where she'd been so humiliatingly introduced to the concept of *protocols.*

"I had it brought over," he said. "Don't want people thinking the boss got smashed and had to be driven home."

"Do you have *any* idea of the alcohol and drug abuse statistics among mortuary workers? It's not like anyone would blink at my getting drunk."

"It scares me that you knew that and still took the job."

"Why? What are the self-harm statistics in *your* line of work?"

He was silent, then shrugged. "Point taken." He bowed, elegant and formal, and yet warm in ways Patrick McCallister didn't seem he could ever be. "After you, boss."

* * *

Fairview Mortuary was now hers, Bryn thought. She stood there in the elegant lobby and greeted people, signed for flowers, assigned runners to take floral arrangements to viewing rooms and out to grave sites; she checked the clothing choices of staff to make sure everything was appropriate, and despaired, because she was *not* ready for this. She'd studied, she'd graduated, she'd apprenticed successfully, but this . . . this was different.

It wasn't even the grief. She quickly got used to the raw emotions, and the awful, gut-ripping stories of loss; funeral directors learned how to distance themselves from that, like police officers and therapists. By the third day of what she supposed constituted her normal life, she'd hired on two more funeral directors and three assistants. Two of those assistants had lasted about half a day before leaving and never coming back, which Lucy assured her was entirely normal. "We never stop running the ads," Lucy told her, as she helped get the death certificates filed and paged people for pickups out to residences, hospitals, and the county morgue. "Can't keep assistants. You're lucky if one makes it a few months, seems like. It's even hard to keep funeral directors; I guess because they like to move around to greener pastures. We went through three last year."

Well, Bryn thought, *I know what happened to one of them*. She'd seen him, still moving weakly in his body bag, body rotted into rags. The memory came back to her in a post-traumatic rush of sight, sound, and smell, and she felt herself waver. *That's my future*.

No. No, it wasn't. She just had to keep telling herself that.

It was lucky Riley Block was on the staff, because there was no one, *no* one, better than Riley at doing the delicate, artistic work of embalming. Bryn was astonished the first time she went down to do her own work at how meticulous and neat the prep room was kept; nothing was left out, except what Riley was currently using. Every surface gleamed. Unlike the creepy atmosphere the place had had when Freddy reigned, this felt oddly warm and comfortable, even though it had the usual chilly temperature. Riley had brought in some lovely art to put on the walls, and warm lighting in the corners, and there was a subtle scent of vanilla and jasmine in the air to cover the usual uneasy spoiled-meat tang.

Bryn said hello and went to the locker to grab a gown and mask, which she tied on with practiced ease, and gloved up before retrieving Mrs. Jacoby from refrigeration. This one was simple enough that there was no need to waste Riley's time, and Bryn needed the practice. She was discovering, as the days went by, that even as much education as she had left huge gaps in her practical experience.

Riley, she discovered, wasn't chatty when she was working, so Bryn kept her silence, too. There was something oddly Zen about the prep room; it was like a chapel, hushed and peaceful. As Bryn made her incisions and hooked the carotid out of Mrs. Jacoby's pale, fleshy neck, she concentrated on the details. *Don't break the surface* was the first rule; the dead did bleed, particularly from the carotid, and it was a mess that ruined the clear field of vision and made embalming that much tougher. If she screwed this one up, she'd have to go for the femoral.

She didn't screw it up.

The mechanics of the embalming went smoothly enough, and Mrs. Jacoby had died peacefully in her sleep. It was only a matter of pumping out the blood and pumping in embalming fluid, applying the hydration cream to keep the tissues supple, and suturing the mouth.

"You know the worst thing about this business?" Riley suddenly said. She stepped back from her table, sighed, put her hands on her hips, and stretched as if her back ached, which it probably did; Bryn's already had a twinge, even though she'd probably done a lot less standing and leaning. "You can get used to the bodies, the smell, the mess. I've picked up bodies that were melted into furniture, they'd been down so long. You can get used to the grief, too."

Bryn nodded. She'd already experienced that; after the first few days, she'd realized that the tearful stories still moved her, but not in a deeply personal way. She'd put up a wall to muffle the vulnerability. That was manageable. She'd seen the bad (Melissa) and the sad (most of the rest), and so far, only one that was crazy, but it was all a manage-able process now. A continuum.

"You get used to thinking of them as just skin, bones, flesh, to-do lists, but every once in a while you find some-thing that makes you realize they used to be just like you. Just like us." Riley stared down at the man she was working on. He was a tough one, a car crash victim in his thirties. Handsome, too, though Bryn had more reason than most to subscribe to the whole beauty-is-skin-deep theory. "He had plane tickets in his pocket. He was supposed to be headed to Hawaii today—can you believe that? First class. He probably paid extra so he could really enjoy himself, and somewhere, right about now, they're calling his name at the ticket counter and moving on to a standby because he hasn't shown up."

Riley was right. That made it uncomfortably real. There were so many layers of reality to the world. Nothing stopped for death; nothing stopped for grief or horror or tragedy.

As if she'd read her thoughts, Riley said, "The worst part of it is that it never stops. Death keeps coming. We get older; we get tired; we get sad and lonely because nobody understands what we do or why we do it. Police and fire-men, they're heroes. Us, we're pariahs. And every day, there are more bodies." She said it without any particular emo-tional emphasis; it was an observation, delivered calmly, but it chilled Bryn deep down.

"Then why do you do it?" she asked.

Riley turned and met her eyes. She didn't smile. "Be-cause I'm good at it," she said. "Because it needs doing. Why do you?"

Originally, it had been because the money was good and the job was stable, but Bryn understood what Riley was saying. There was a certain unspoken honor to this job, a certain quiet dignity. *We*, Bryn thought, *are the great dirty secret, the reality that runs under everything else.*

And Riley was right. It was lonely.

"Don't mind me," Riley said, and finally smiled. It didn't reach her sad eyes. "I've been at this awhile. I get maudlin. Some people drink; some get depressed; some run around having sex with anyone with a pulse. Me, I get philosophical. It's healthier."

"What do you do when you're not, you know, here?"

"I shower three times before I leave the building, and then I go out to dinner with friends. I watch movies and read books. I exercise. I live a normal life." Riley cocked her head and looked at Bryn with suddenly sharp, inquisitive eyes. "Don't you?"

"Well, I have a dog." That was just about the only normal thing in her life anymore. "Mr. French."

"Dogs are good. Pets are good. People will let you down." Riley shook her head and put her mask back on. "That's good work on Mrs. Jacoby, by the way."

"It's easy."

"Nothing's easy here. Just delicate."

As Bryn warmed the tinted wax in the palm of her hand and gently, gently applied it to Mrs. Jacoby's pale, lifeless lips, she had to agree.

Joe Fideli gave her shots every day. She didn't see McCallister at all, although she knew Fideli was in contact with him. By special arrangement, she and Fideli carpooled; he didn't like having her on the road alone, unprotected. So she had a bodyguard from the minute she left the fortress of her apartment until she arrived at the funeral home, with was always buzzing with activity until closing time.

And still, she felt very alone when the phone rang in her office, and the distorted voice said, "I got your good-faith money, Bryn. Very nice."

Him. Bryn sat very still in her leather chair. She was suddenly hyperaware of the paperwork sitting in front of her, the crooked angle of the pen beside it, the way light from the desk lamp fell across things in shadows and glares. She'd closed the door to work on files, and in here, it was so silent it might have been on another planet.

She spun the chair to look out the window. That was better. There was normal life out there: sun, trees moving gently in the breeze, clouds passing. Joe Fideli pulled up in the mortuary van and backed down the ramp that led to the downstairs loading dock, delivering more clients. She felt obscurely glad to have him here, somewhere close.

"Bryn?"

"I'm listening," she said. She cleared her throat. "Are you ready to do business?"

"How are your Returné customers doing?"

"They're dead," she said. "What did you expect? You know how quickly the drug wears off."

"They were already dead. Now they're just . . . normalizing their state."

She felt her free hand clench into a fist, and forced herself to stay calm. *Don't take it personally.* But it was tough, when all that stood between you and that awful future was a shot controlled by someone else. "Like you said before, I can always get new customers."

"Hmmm, any prospects?"

"I have a thirtysomething man downstairs with lots of money," she said. "He should be good for a few months of profit."

"Family?"

"He was single; no next of kin to speak of."

"Excellent. You don't have to worry about conscience nibbling away at you for robbing the wife and kids. See, I know something about you, Bryn. You're softhearted."

"I'm practical. You don't get into the death business if you're softhearted."

"You do if you inherit it." It was hard to pinpoint, but Bryn thought his tone had been sounding lazily amused, but now it changed. "Enough chat. You want to do business, bring another hundred thousand to the address you'll get in your e-mail. I pick up the money, and I e-mail you another address where the goods will be waiting for you."

"No way. I'm not leaving money and walking away. What do you take me for?"

"Bryn, I had a good working relationship with Uncle Lincoln, but I don't know you. And I don't trust you."

"Why not?"

He laughed. It sounded horrible and mechanical through the voice filter. "Because I don't have any hold on you. Fear is the basis of any good relationship, and you're not afraid enough of me. Not yet."

He hung up. Bryn stared at the receiver for a moment, then slowly replaced it in the cradle. She looked mindlessly at the paperwork for a moment more, then stood and walked out of her office, down the hall. There was a viewing in progress in the Lincoln Suite—the boy, Jake Hernandez, who'd been shot in a drive-by. She drifted through the people talking outside the room in hushed tones; some nibbled the cookies; some used the tissues. There were a few family members and friends who had that hardened, dead-eyed look; nobody had said Jake had been in a gang, but then, nobody had needed to. She'd seen the tattoos and the knife and gun scars.

Bryn passed through the door that led to the other world, the Formica-and steel-world, with a sense of actual relief. She came down the stairs just as the loading-dock door slid up, and Joe Fideli, standing in the back of the van with two sheeted gurneys, looked back at her.

"Hey," she said. "Need a hand?" She didn't wait for his answer. The metal ramp was off to the side, and she brought it over and put it in place to bridge the gap between the van and the concrete.

"What's up?" he asked her as he maneuvered the first gurney in line with the ramp.

"Our friend called," she said. "He wants another hundred thousand. He's sending me an e-mail with the address of where to leave it. Then he'll send another e-mail with the location of the drugs."

"Smart," Joe said. "Low risk for him, high profit. If we do anything out of line, he can cut and run and never contact us again." He pushed the gurney out, and Bryn grasped her end and pulled it over the ramp onto the dock's clean, firm surface. They repeated the process with the second body. "I'll run it by Pat, but it sounds like we need to play along a little more. Once he starts trusting you, it'll be easier to set this guy up for a personal meet. Once he shows himself, we've got him."

"Can't you just pick him up when he gets the money?"

"He's not stupid. He won't get it himself. We could spend all day chasing down handoffs."

Bryn concentrated on the logistics as they wheeled the gurneys down the hall and into the prep room; Riley was washing a body, and waved to them without speaking as the gurneys went into refrigeration. Each body had an ID tag and a plastic envelope of paperwork, which Bryn clipped to hanging boards above the appropriate stations.

"You look spooked," Joe said.

She laughed. "I'm standing in a cooler full of bodies, Joe."

"That doesn't bother you. Was it the call?"

Fear is the basis of any good relationship. "No," she said, but the lie wasn't very good, and she knew he'd see right through it, so she changed it. "Yes. He's ... There's something about him. Something that really scares me. He's not just in this for the money. He actually enjoys it."

"I know the type," Fideli said. "Look, we're doing everything we can to keep you safe. You're armed; you've got escorts to and from work; you're secured when you're here and when you're home. We've got remote surveillance working. You're covered, okay?"

"Okay," she said. She really *didn't* have any reason to feel so scared. Maybe it was the chill of the air, or the stale, never-quite-right smell of the refrigerator. Maybe it was her own inevitable end pressing down on her. She wanted warmth, suddenly, and remembered the man with Hawaii airline tickets in his pocket. *I could do that. Just ... go somewhere.*

No, she couldn't. Not without permission. Not without an escort carrying her shots.

She wasn't free, and she'd never be free again. She was owned by the ultimate corporate loyalty program.

"Hey," Joe said. He took her hand in his. "Look at me."

She did, and his earnest concern made her try for a smile. "I'm just having a hard day," she said. "No reason. You ever have days like that?"

"All the damn time," he said. "I get too involved. So Pat tells me. Come on. Let's get some coffee. I've got to move the van and—"

The pager on his hip went off. Ten seconds later, so did Bryn's cell phone, ringing a text alarm.

Both of them checked devices, and then looked at each

other. "My apartment," Bryn said. He nodded. "Someone tried to get in."

"I'll drive."

The police were already on the scene when Joe parked the mortuary van—a cruiser, light bars strobing, and a curious bunch of her neighbors dawdling and gawking. Bryn jumped down from the passenger seat and dashed up the stairs, with Joe right behind her. Her front door was open, and the alarm was still going off in wild shrieks.

A uniformed officer held out his hand to stop her from going in. "Sorry, miss—"

"I'm Bryn Davis," she blurted. "This is my place. Is my dog okay?"

Mr. French barked furiously from somewhere inside—full-throated roars of outrage.

"He's fine," the policeman said, sounding resigned. "We had to put him in the bathroom. Good little guard dog you've got there."

That eased the knot in Bryn's chest. "Thank God. What happened?"

The cop started to reply, but before he could, a slender hand grabbed the door and pulled it all the way open.

Bryn's sister Annalie stood there looking tired, stressed, and bedraggled. She was shorter than Bryn, and curvy in ways that men seemed to much admire, but right now she didn't look bouncy or sexy. Just shocked and frustrated. "Would you turn this damn thing off?" she shouted over the racket. "God, you could have told me you had an alarm!"

"Annie?" Bryn pushed past the cop and entered her code on the keypad. The pounding noise shut off, to the relief of Bryn's ears, and probably everyone else in a five-block radius. "Annie, Jesus *Christ*, what are you doing here?" There was a flower-patterned suitcase sitting on the floor next to a bright aqua purse that had to be her sister's. "How did you get in?"

"It wasn't easy. Do you know, the key you gave me last time doesn't work? What did you do, change the locks?"

"Annie—how did you get in?"

Annie grinned and shrugged. "I called a locksmith and got him to open it for me. I paid him triple. He wouldn't do anything about the alarm, though, and he took off."

Bryn rubbed her forehead. There was no system sophisticated enough that her sister couldn't find a perfectly obvious way around it, apparently. "He's supposed to check ID."

"Well—I paid extra."

"Don't take this wrong but . . . why are you here?"

"Well . . . I know. It was kind of supposed to be a surprise. I brought you a present to celebrate your new job," Annie said, and tried for a grin. "Surprised?"

"Bowled over." Now that her heart was slowing down to a more normal pace, Bryn hugged her sister, then looked at the waiting policeman. "Uh . . . it's okay; I'm so sorry. I didn't know she was coming, that's all. She's all right. Everything's all right."

The policeman had been joined by his partner, a woman. She seemed more amused than angry. "Happens all the time," she said. "Maybe you ought to let anyone with keys know that you've put in a new alarm system."

"Nobody else has keys." Well, Bryn imagined McCallister did, and Fideli, because that would be par for the course, but she'd never *given* out any other keys. "I am really very sorry about the bother."

"That's okay; you'll get the bill," the male policeman said, and nodded to her on the way out, followed by his partner.

Joe Fideli stepped in, shut the door, and leaned against it, looking *much* more amused than Bryn felt. "So?" he asked. "Going to introduce me?"

"I hope so," Annie said, and gave him a smile. "Bryn, you didn't tell me you had a cutie for a boyfriend. Holdout."

Bryn rolled her eyes. "Annalie, this is Joe Fideli. He works with me at the mortuary. He's a funeral director. Not my boyfriend."

"You're kidding. Really?"

"Tongue in mouth, please. He's taken, and not by me."

"Permanently?"

"Oh, yeah," Joe said. "Afraid so, darlin'."

"That is just Bryn's luck." Annie sighed dramatically and sank down on Bryn's couch. "Since when did you need an alarm system, sis? Scared ten years of life out of me!"

"Since I got robbed," Bryn said. "There's such a thing as crime, you know."

"Yeah, I bartend, doofus. I know all about it."

"It's really good to see you, Annie, but . . . why? What happened?"

Annalie shrugged and looked down. She seemed casual, but Bryn wasn't fooled; there was a subtle tension about her that only someone well versed in Annie-speak would recognize. "I just wanted to get away for a while. You know how it is. Mom was driving me nuts." Mom, it seemed, had always been hardest on Annie, but then, Annie had needed it. Bryn had skated by as the example against which everyone else was measured. It was a miracle, she thought, that she hadn't been shivved by her siblings by now. Annie came out of it and gave her a bright, sweet smile. "You want your present now?"

"You shouldn't be buying me things."

"I *didn't*. Well, I contributed, but Mom and Tate went in on it with me. I even got Grace to put in, believe it or not."

"Wow. How'd you manage that?"

Annie opened up her suitcase and took out a small, neatly wrapped box with curly ribbons dangling from the top. It looked very festive. "I twisted arms," she said. "You deserve a present, Bryn. You do a lot for us. Especially for me. I know I'm kind of a burden sometimes." A cloud came across her smile, dimming it. "And I should have called—I know that. I'm sorry."

That was typical of Annie—doing something thoughtful and thoughtless at the same time. The present, when Bryn unwrapped it, proved to be a beautiful, delicate watch, probably way too expensive; she put it on and loved it immediately. She hugged her sister, and Annalie hugged her back with fierce intensity. "There's a card, too," she said. "We all signed it. Even Kyle, if you can believe that."

"*Kyle?*"

"I sent it through his lawyer. It took a week to get it

back. Which is why I'm late, by the way; it was supposed to be a first-day-on-the-job kind of thing."

Well, thank God for small favors. Having Annie involved in all that . . . Bryn didn't even want to consider it. "I'm surprised Kyle even remembers who I am."

Annie gave her a wide-eyed look. "He's your *brother*. Of course he remembers!"

There were times, Bryn thought, when Annie could be kind of hopelessly naive. Not that it wasn't a little endearing, but she conveniently forgot what Kyle was like. Family first—that was Annie's motto.

Bryn felt a little guilty that she couldn't see it quite that simply.

"You want a Coke?" she asked, to cover the awkward moment. That was Annie's drink of choice, even at the bar. She nodded, and Bryn went into the kitchen to pour. "Joe? Would you like anything?"

"I'm okay," he said. "Rain check on coffee for later, though."

Bryn carried back two glasses, one for her, one for Annie. "All right. What's Mom done to make you come running out here? Because you could have just mailed the present, you know."

"I missed you!"

"I know, but come on. What happened?"

"She . . . Well, you know. She's being Mom." Annie drank, and fiddled with the glass. "She doesn't like me working at the bar. She keeps trying to get me to quit and go to college. I just got tired of the lectures. I needed a break."

"You weren't arguing about money?"

"What?" Annie choked on her Coke. "No. No, don't look at me like that! I swear, I didn't ask her for a dime." She sounded wounded. "I wouldn't do that. Besides, you bailed me out—I know. I remember."

"I've never been able to figure out where you spend it all. You don't drink; you don't, you know . . ." Bryn made a smoking gesture.

"Do drugs? Jesus, Bryn, we're not twelve; you can say it. No, I don't!"

"Then—"

Annie sighed. "I just like to buy things. I try, I really do, but I just . . . lose track. And then the banks make it worse. Did you know they process the biggest charges first, so you bounce the most checks and get hit with the most fees? It's awful."

"You know what solves that? Not spending so much."

"You sound just like her." Meaning Mom. Of course. "Look, I *know*, okay? I'm trying really hard to get better with money."

"Annie . . ." Bryn shook her head. "You say that, but you just spent too much on this present, and don't tell me Tate and Mom and Grace pitched in; I know you paid for most of it, right? And then you flew all this way to deliver it." The fresh airline tag was still on the handle of Annie's bag. And she must have gotten a taxi, which cost a fortune from the airport. "Well, you're here now, so it doesn't matter."

Annie seized the moment. "Yes! I've missed you, you know. We can go out—do you know I've never been to Sea-World? Or the zoo. I hear the zoo is amazing. We can go! And we can have so much fun. It'll be like when we used to share a room— Oh, it's okay if I stay, right? I didn't get a motel."

Joe gave Bryn a wide-eyed look of very clear warning. "Well . . . actually, there's not much room. How about if I get you a hotel room? We can do things at night if you want. I do have to work during the day." That clearly wasn't good enough; Joe gave her a tiny shake of his head. She glared back, trying to send the silent message of, *She's family, damn it!* He finally shrugged. Surrender.

"Oh," Annie said, subdued. "I didn't think . . . Okay. Right, a hotel is fine, I guess. And I can just do things on my own."

"Annie—"

"Maybe I should just see if I can get on standby and go home. I don't want to bother you. I just thought . . . I wanted to spend time with you."

Annie didn't exactly *mean* to make it a guilt trip; she really did feel abandoned and sad, and didn't cover it well. She never had. In some ways, Annalie was still a child, and

Bryn sometimes forgot that. Everybody had always indulged her. Protected her.

And Bryn was no different, because she gave up at the sight of Annie's sad, almost teary eyes. "Okay, I'll tell you what. You can stay here during the day. I'll give you the codes to get in and out. Mr. French needs someone to play with, anyway...." *Oh, crap.* Bryn felt a guilty shock. Mr. French—she'd left him in the bathroom. She jumped up and hurried into the bedroom, embarrassed by the fact that she hadn't made her bed or picked up the clothes on the floor, and the police had been in here staring at it. Too late now. She opened the bathroom door.

Mr. French was lying in a pile of snow, looking somehow supremely grumpy and self-satisfied. He let out a *whuff* of disapproval when she opened the door, and stood up to waddle regally past her.

No ... that pile wasn't snow.

It was the shredded remains of her full roll of toilet paper. He'd ripped it apart. Also, the towels were off the racks, although she couldn't imagine how he'd bounced that high. And the back of the door was gouged with scratches.

"Damn," Annie said from behind her. "Your dog knows how to party."

"You know what? You really should stay here," Bryn said, and shut the bathroom door. "He needs a walk right now. When you come back, you can pick up all that and clean it up."

"Me? He's *your* dog!"

"He was locked in because of *your* mistake. You clean it up." Bryn handed her the key, took a piece of paper, and scribbled down the code for the alarm, which she thrust on her sister before Joe could tell her what an awful idea that was. "Memorize it and destroy the paper, and I mean *destroy* it; don't just crumple it up, okay? Shred and flush."

"Seriously? Bryn, are you mad at me? I had a key; I didn't know it was going to be a problem. I mean, I know he made a mess, but I didn't think—"

"I know," Bryn said, and took a deep breath. Annie never meant to cause chaos. It just followed her around in a dark cloud. "It's okay. You stay here today. I'll see you tonight, and then we'll figure things out."

Annie brightened up into a smile immediately. "Cool. See you tonight. And I promise the house will be clean, your bed will be made, and I'll have dinner for you." Annie, bless her, *could* cook. And Bryn had just been thinking about how damn lonely life was becoming. Having family to come home to might be a blessing . . . just for a little while.

She hugged Annie, impulsively, and her sister hugged her back, then tenderly smoothed Bryn's hair back. "You smell like dead people," she said. "Confidentially, it's probably why you don't have a boyfriend."

"You are such a *bitch*."

Annie grinned. She had perfect white teeth, the achievement of years of dentist visits, rigorous brushing, flossing, and bleaching. She had a nice tan, too. "I'm not judging. I smell like airplane," she said. "I'm going to shower and lie out by the pool for a while."

"After you clean the place."

"Oh, absolutely. After." Annie assumed a saintly expression and crossed her heart, which made Bryn laugh; it was Annie's giveaway for lying. They exchanged another hug, a quick one, and Annie waved as she and Joe descended the steps.

"Lock the door!" Bryn called back. "And turn on the alarm!"

"Yes, Mom."

Joe held his tongue until they were in the van, buckled in, and driving away. "Do I even need to tell you what a terrible idea this is?" he asked. "Or how incredibly pissed off McCallister will be?"

"Nope," she said. She felt oddly very much steadier now. Annie might be a doofus sometimes, but she was an anchor to her past, to her family, and Bryn needed one right now.

Joe was a good guy, but there was no substitute for that.

Chapter 9

The day passed. Bryn kept her e-mail in-box active, waiting for something, anything from her mysterious would-be supplier; nothing arrived. She'd fielded about twelve calls, eight of them certainly pranks, three legitimate customers, and one from her sister about dinner.

She was checking out a suspicious e-mail message when her phone rang again; the e-mail, it turned out, was legitimate, but trash.

The phone call was odd.

At first, Bryn thought it was a prank call; she'd gotten used to those fast. Lucy called them their sex-chat clients, and joked that they needed to start charging $9.95 a minute to make some extra money off of it; they usually started out with breathing and vague noises, and that was exactly what this was. Some kind of labored, wet gasp, and undefined sounds.

"Hello?" Bryn said, just to be sure. "Not funny. I'm hanging up now."

Usually, that either brought some kind of obscene proposal, or a hang-up. She got neither, just more of the breathing. On reflection, it didn't sound sexual. It sounded slow and tortured.

"Hello?" Bryn glanced at her phone. Caller ID had brought up a name, which was unusual for a sex caller.

And the name seemed familiar.

Bryn felt a sinking sensation, listening to that whispering breath. She tried again, but got no response to her questions.

She hung up and called Lucy on the intercom. "Lucy, can you look up a contact for a customer for me?"

"Sure. Which one?"

"Sammons, first initial *V*. I think someone was trying to call from her number and got cut off."

"We get a lot of hang-ups, you know."

"I know. But look it up, would you?"

"Just a sec." Lucy put the phone down, and Bryn listened to keys clicking. "System's always so slow— Oh, there it is. Sammons, Violetta. She wasn't a customer, though. She was a client."

"A client." The difference, in Fairview terminology, was that customers wrote checks; clients filled coffins. "You're sure about that?"

"Maybe somebody kept the number switched on? Could have been a relative; she had a husband who made arrangements. She only passed a couple of weeks ago, right before you arrived here. One of Mr. Fairview's last personal preps, poor man."

Personal prep. Fairview seemed to do personal prep only on his special clients.

The ones who kept on paying.

She couldn't talk, Bryn realized. *Violetta Sammons was too far gone to talk, but she was trying to ask for help. My God. She's been without a shot for . . . how long? Why didn't her husband try to call us?*

The implications made her sick and light-headed. "Thanks. Can you read me the address?"

"Sure." Lucy recited it, and Bryn wrote it down. "You need anything else?"

"No," Bryn said. Her knuckles had tightened around the phone. "No, thank you, Lucy." She hung up and rang Joe's extension. He didn't answer at once; when he did, it was clear the call had switched to his cell. "Joe? Where are you?"

"At Atlantic Memorial, waiting on a pickup with Doreen." Doreen was the latest in this week's parade of assistants. "She's still with us."

"The pickup?"

"Doreen. What's going on?"

Her throat felt tight with panic. "I had a weird phone

call. I think it was someone Fairview . . . you know. She's in trouble."

"All right, give me the address; I'll send people."

"No. Joe . . . Joe, she called me. She needs help. We've got supplies, right? I want to give her the shot."

"Bryn, you can't. The syringes are ID coded. You know that."

"Then come back and go with me."

"You want me to leave Doreen here alone to do the pickup? Even if I did, I'm a couple of hours away."

"This can't wait, Joe. It can't."

"She's not going anywhere, right?"

Her eyes were burning now with unshed tears. She couldn't explain why she felt so oppressed by this; she couldn't understand it herself. "She needs help *now*. I'm going."

"Tell me where you're going first." She read him the address. "Seriously, wait for me. I'll be back as soon as I can."

"I can't leave her like that."

He was silent for a second, then said, "You know what you might have to do. She's probably too far gone to dose."

"I know," she said. "I can't let her suffer, Joe. That's why I have to go."

"As long as you know what you're getting into. I'll get Pat to meet you there; he's not far. No arguments, boss. This is how it's done." The *boss* was ironic; Bryn was almost sure. She was no one's boss, not even her own. He hung up before she could tell him not to call McCallister—not that he would have listened.

She hadn't spoken directly to McCallister since they'd parted ways in that uncomfortable fashion at the mansion, and she wasn't looking forward to it now. But mostly what she dreaded was what she was going to find at Violetta Sammons's house. Where was Violetta's husband? *McCallister will have the shot*, she thought. *We can do this. We can make it right and figure it out from there.*

I have to make it right.

She grabbed her preloaded removal bag from the locker room, added a few things, and took one of the mortuary vans—freshly cleaned out and smelling astringently of bleach. *Either I smell like dead people, or I smell like cleaning products.* Annie was right: boyfriends were probably out of the question at this point—presuming, of course, that she had any right to think about such real-life issues anymore.

She tried not to think about that, or anything, as she followed the navigation system's directions to Violetta's address up in the La Jolla hills. It was in a very posh neighborhood, with big, expansive houses and a breathtaking view. Not Patrick McCallister's price range, but even the smallest of these properties must have gone for a couple of million.

No wonder Fairview had chosen Sammons for his scam.

Bryn parked the van and got out, carrying her black canvas bag, just as Patrick McCallister's tinted black sedan closed in behind like a shark. He stepped out, and they looked at each other for a few seconds. His bruised cheek had mostly healed, and his suit looked clean and impeccable, as always.

He had a black bag, too. She didn't think his held the same things hers did.

"Bryn," he said, in a very careful, neutral tone. "What's the emergency?"

"I think she's one of Fairview's," Bryn said. "And I think she's been without a shot all this time. I couldn't just ... I have to help. I have to. You understand?"

McCallister hesitated, then nodded. "Let me go first."

"No," she said. "I have to do this."

"Not alone," he said. "We do it together, then."

That felt better, because she was terrified and trying not to show it. The house looked completely normal, nothing to sound alarms. Bryn rang the doorbell, then tried the front door, but it was locked.

"What now?" she asked. McCallister led her around to the side, to a kitchen door. She tried that one. "It's locked, too."

He stepped up and did something with a set of tiny tools—lock picks, she guessed. She expected an alarm, but when the door swung open, she didn't hear a thing. A house like this, there had to be an alarm. . . .

McCallister stepped inside and checked a keypad next

to the door. "It's off," he said. "Come in." He closed and locked it behind her.

She immediately caught the unmistakable smell of decomposition—ripe, sickly sweet, and dense. She wavered, and exchanged a wordless look with him.

"Bryn," he said. "Let me do this. You don't need to—"

She shook her head, waited to let her senses adjust, then went forward through a spotlessly kept white tile kitchen, down a hallway. The stench got more intense. She was achingly aware of McCallister sticking close beside her, silent now.

No turning back.

She expected a horror show, but there was nothing in the large, gracious living room, although a big-screen TV was still playing with the sound turned down. There was a glass of what looked like Scotch sitting on a coaster on the coffee table, and a book spread open, facedown, as if someone had put it away for just a moment.

McCallister touched her shoulder and pointed. She followed him out into the marble-tiled foyer. A curving staircase led upstairs.

The smell was worse here, and increased as they ascended. Halfway up, Bryn heard the first hum of insect activity. She hesitated just for a breath on the last step, gathered herself, and stepped over a busy line of ants that marked a trail right to where she had to go.

McCallister was right behind her, silent and solid. He was the only thing that gave her the necessary strength to keep going.

The bedroom door was shut, and Bryn touched the knob gingerly first, as if it might be hot. Instinct, trying to stop her from doing this. Seeing this.

She took a deep breath and opened the door.

The noise exploded in an angry buzz, and flies whizzed past her, heading out into the open air. She ducked. So did McCallister. He coughed and put his hand over his mouth; it was the first sign of weakness she'd seen from him.

Bryn stepped into hell.

The first thing she saw was the dead man, sitting in a

deep armchair at the end of the bed. There was a bullet hole in one temple, and a giant exit wound on the opposite side. The gun still lay on the carpet next to his feet.

He'd been gone for days.

The woman lying on the bed wasn't much of a human being anymore. She was covered in a moving blanket of flies, wriggling pale maggots popping through the slipping, discolored stretch of skin, and ants busily carrying away pieces for the good of the colony.

Her eyes were open. Clouded, discolored, decomposed, but *alive.*

Oh, *God*, still alive. They moved, very slightly, toward Bryn. The lipless mouth moved, but there was no sound, could be none. The phone receiver lay on the pillow next to her, and one desiccated finger was still resting on the redial button.

"Mother of God," McCallister whispered behind her. He sounded shaken, stunned, more human than he'd ever seemed. Bryn, on the other hand, felt . . . remote. Untethered. That was shock, she guessed. Useful thing, shock, at moments like these.

"Give her the shot," she said.

"Bryn—it won't work."

"Give her the shot."

He shook his head, but he opened his bag and took out the syringe. She saw him hesitate, trying to find enough muscle to inject, and watched as he did his best.

The liquid oozed back out through her skin and soaked into the bedding.

They waited for long moments, and Bryn finally turned to McCallister.

"She's too far gone," he whispered. "End stages. The drug won't help."

Then there was only one thing to do.

Bryn dropped her canvas bag, opened it, and took out a gown, a mask, surgical gloves. She handed those to McCallister, then took a second set for herself. They dressed in silence. The mask didn't block the eye-watering stench. There were ants crawling on her feet, over her legs, but Bryn didn't think about that. Couldn't think about that.

She took out a surgical saw.

McCallister took a step back. "What are you—"

Bryn didn't answer, because she couldn't. Talking required some kind of cognition she didn't think she was capable of at this point. There was only one thing that was important, one thing that had to be done.

She had to stop the woman's pain. There was no walking away from this, no choice. It had to be done.

She had to be the one to do it.

"I'm sorry," she whispered to what was left of Violetta Sammons, and stared into those clouded, desperate, terrified eyes for a second before she put one hand on the mandible of her jaw, pushed up, and exposed the rotten column of her throat.

It didn't take more than three strokes. The saw was very sharp. As the head rolled free, Bryn saw the life desperately continue in those filmed eyes, and then dim . . . and then, finally, mercifully, depart.

Byrne dropped the saw, staggered, and put her back against the wall.

That's me. That's me on the bed. That's me.

Not yet, but it was coming, as inevitable as death itself.

Across the bed, Patrick McCallister stood frozen, watching her. He finally reached down and grabbed the canvas bag, retrieved the saw, and took her arm. "Out," he said. "Come on."

Leaving that room was like walking out of a grave, and Bryn ripped the mask away from her face and gulped in deep breaths. She'd thought the air out here tainted before, but it smelled sweet now. Sweet as roses.

Her legs had gone numb, but McCallister helped her down the steps, past the line of ants, past the silent living room with its TV still playing, Scotch waiting.

Outside, into the clean breeze, and the sun.

Bryn collapsed against him, put her arms around his neck, and wept as if her heart were breaking. "Oh, God," she whispered. "Oh, my God. I had to do it; I had to. *I had to.*"

And Patrick McCallister held on just as fiercely. "I know," he whispered back. "It's all right. It's over."

"No." She gasped, and fisted her hands in the collar of his suit. "That was me. Going to be me."

"No. Bryn, you're alive; hear me? And I won't let that happen to you. I won't. I swear it."

"What if—"

"Don't."

"You saw; she could still feel—"

His voice turned fierce. "*I won't let it happen.* I will never let you suffer, Bryn. Believe that, even if you never believe anything else about me."

She did believe him. She believed that if he had to, Patrick McCallister would take up that saw and end things for her, once and for all. He had the strength of will.

She'd never thought she did. Not until the moment when she'd had to choose.

That terrified her, the fact that something like that was hiding inside her—something so strong, so cold, so *capable.* She didn't want to know that about herself.

She didn't want to know what it was going to be like in the end, either. She'd looked into her future, into the ruined, screaming eyes of Violetta Sammons.

McCallister held her until his security team arrived to sanitize the scene of the crime, and she was glad he did.

Fifteen minutes after they'd started the . . . removal proceedings, McCallister stepped back into the house. He donned an extra pair of coveralls stored in Bryn's go bag, a ball cap, a thin Windbreaker that had the Fairview Mortuary logo on the front, and said, "I'm going with you. You shouldn't be alone." His team had their orders. They also had come in disguise as renovation workers, with their own van, tools, coveralls—they even put a sign out by the curb. Anyone looking out would see nothing but normal life, although what was going on was far, far from sanity in there. "We need to get the van out of here. It'll raise questions."

The Fairview logo was small and discreet, but he was right; it was visible to anybody who really looked. Bryn, who'd finally gotten feeling back in her arms and legs, started to unlock the driver's-side door.

McCallister took the keys from her. "No. I'm driving."

She didn't feel able to argue the point. It felt good to let someone else take charge, at least for the moment. *Maybe the protocols are kicking in again.* But she didn't think so. It was just shock, and the drugged exhaustion that followed extreme emotional stress.

"Is it safe for you to do this?" she asked in a remote, tired voice as he piloted the van back toward Fairview. "What if he's watching?"

"He probably is. And yes, it's risky. But you go through staff quickly at the assistant level, so new faces aren't unusual. I'll keep my head down." He glanced her way. "You still with me, Bryn?"

"Yes." She could hardly keep her eyes open, but when she tried to let them drift closed, she saw jolts of images. Ants. Maggots. Flesh. Eyes. "I think I need a drink."

He laughed softly, and a little shakily. "That, Miss Davis, is a vast understatement. There has never been a single moment in my life when I more needed a drink, and I wasn't the one—" *Holding the saw*, Bryn finished silently. He let it go. "I heard your sister is staying with you."

"I thought you'd be angry."

"I was. It seems a little beside the point right now."

"Annie's okay," Bryn murmured drowsily. "She's just a kid; that's all. And we push her too hard."

"We?"

"The fam. Especially Mom, and my sister Grace. Grace is kind of a bitch. Not as bad as George, though."

"George is a girl?"

"George is a pissy little bitch of a man. He's not gay, which is too bad; he'd be a lot more fun that way. He's just a jerk. He runs a pharmacy in—" Her brain finally caught up to her mouth. "You already know all this. I told you all about them, in the car."

McCallister shrugged. "I like hearing you talk about them."

"Remember Kyle?"

"The one who's three years into a fifteen-year sentence for armed robbery?"

"Kyle is still more fun than George."

"Ouch."

Her brain was waking up. Small talk, it seemed, did wonders. "Anyway, Annie just wanted some space, so I'm letting her stay a few days. It's not a big deal, and I won't tell her a thing."

"She's a walking, talking security breach, and you should have run it by me, but what's done is done. I'm just concerned for your safety."

"From *Annie*? She grew up wanting to be a fairy princess. She's not exactly dangerous."

"That's what I'm concerned about."

She couldn't work that out, tired as she felt, so she let it lie. "You got me to talk about my family," she said. "But you never return the favor."

He glanced over at her, frowning, and shook his head. "It's not the time, Bryn."

"Come on. Humor me." She needed something else in her head besides . . . *that.* Besides the smell, the insects, the desperation in Violetta's eyes. The rasp of the saw. "Tell me about your brother."

"I can't." He paused, then let out a sound—not a laugh, more of a sigh. "*Can't.* That doesn't sound right either, considering . . . it's just words. All right, if you really want to know. Jamie was . . . different. My parents couldn't see it. He was a charmer, but he was cold inside. A sociopath with no real empathy or connection to anyone else. Including me. And I was his favorite target."

"You."

He shrugged. "I learned to cope. I had to. Jamie's little games were often meant to maim or kill. I couldn't complain; when I tried, he blamed it all on me, said that I was the bully. They believed it."

"My God."

"By eighteen, I wasn't going to let it go on anymore. I went to my father, but he didn't want to hear it. So I left. I went straight into the marines, enlisted as fast as I could, and got the hell away from the whole family."

"You told me Jamie . . . died."

"By the time I came home, eight years had passed. I think he was truly surprised. He fully expected me to die in the line of duty." McCallister's eyes were unfocused now, looking into something far away and not at all pleasant. "He was out on his own by then, with his own house out in the country. I came back from deployment and intended to just stop in and try to mend fences with him, as much as possible. But when I got here, he was . . . He'd found a new hobby. One that suited his personality." He swallowed, a visible bob of his Adam's apple above his collar. His hands gripped the steering wheel a little too tightly. "I found out later that he'd made a business of it, but I didn't know that at the time. I just knew that when I went looking for him, I found him upstairs in one of the rooms with cameras and a victim. I shot him. I had to, to save her life."

"What was he—"

"No," he said. "Don't make me tell you. Please. We've had enough today." He let the silence fall for a moment before he continued. "I'm not sorry I killed him. I'm just sorry that I let him walk away when I was eighteen. It would have saved lives if I hadn't been . . . weak." He smiled, but it looked painful and false. "My mother was already gone by then. My father passed on soon after that, thinking I was a murderer. Thinking that I'd set Jamie up and killed him in cold blood. I was written out of the estate, of course. I didn't really mind."

Bryn thought about her own family, with all its problems and squabbles; she might not totally love many of her siblings, but at least they weren't sociopaths. And, although he wasn't saying it outright, murderers. It brought back the haunting question of what had happened to Sharon, all those years ago. *Maybe she ran into another McCallister. The wrong McCallister.*

"I'm sorry," she said. "I'm sorry for making you tell me that."

"No," he said. "No, you needed to hear it. And I guess I needed to say it, too. It's all right. Now it's done."

McCallister drove in silence the rest of the way, parked the van, and walked with her into the mortuary through the back entrance. He kept his shoulders hunched and his hands in his pockets. It was as much cover as possible, but she still felt an uncomfortable, probably imaginary weight of eyes on them until they were safely inside.

Joe and Doreen weren't back yet from the hospital run, so Bryn took McCallister directly to her office, locked the door, and opened up a locked drawer in her desk. She set up six miniature bottles of liquor: Scotch for McCallister, vodka for herself.

"Did you raid the minibar somewhere?" he asked, but didn't turn down the tiny servings. He unscrewed the first and downed it in two gulps, then opened the second.

"Certainly not at the Hallmark Motor Court Inn."

That got her a shadow of a smile. He saluted her with the bottle, downed it, and sat down. She concentrated on the soothing fire of her vodka as it slipped over her tongue, down her throat, clearing away the taste of rot and despair. Somehow, she managed to drink her third before McCallister had properly started his, but then, as he hadn't quite said, she'd been holding the saw.

"So," she said, and leaned her head back against the leather of the chair. "Did you sleep with your boss?" Silence. She opened her eyes just a slit. McCallister continued sipping his Scotch without comment. "You're really not going to tell me."

"Is this the question that comes to your mind right now?"

"Evidently it is." She was starting to feel numbed again, but in a slightly better way.

"Do you have any more of these?" He held up the liquor mini. She opened the drawer, pulled out two more, and pitched him one. "This is bourbon."

"You're really going to complain?"

He upended it while she sucked down her fourth vodka. This one was lemon-flavored. Nice. "If I say yes, what does it matter to you?"

"It doesn't." It did. It did, and he knew it, the bastard. *Why* it mattered to her was a mystery she didn't care to explore at the moment; her emotions were confused, raw, and horribly tangled. "Was it good?"

"With *her*? Not likely."

She almost choked on her drink. "So you did do it."

"I didn't say I did. *If* such a thing had happened, for which there is no evidence and no admission, now or ever, then it would not have been a good time. Just . . . maintenance."

"Of your low reputation and your alibi."

His lips twisted into a brief, unhappy grimace. "Something like that." McCallister got weirdly funny and precise when he drank. If he felt anything like Bryn, he had to be at least slightly tipsy. Overcompensating, probably. "It's not all fun and games in my business."

She had a nauseating flashback, and suddenly she realized that she reeked of dead flesh; it had soaked into her clothes, her skin, her hair. The whole office stank with it.

Fun and games.

Violetta Sammons's disconnected head rolling free.

The rasp of the saw vibrating in her hand.

The vodka rushed up on her, and Bryn barely made it to her trash can before she threw up. Between the convulsions, she gasped for breath and sobbed, and McCallister came around the desk and silently handed her tissues, then helped her back into her chair as she covered her face and tried to muffle her wild, uncontrollable sobs.

He stroked her hair, very softly. He didn't say a thing.

Finally, she was able to shut it off, just enough to gather her voice together. "I have to shower," she said. Her voice was uneven and broken, but he nodded as he looked down at her. "Sorry."

"Don't be," he said. "I'll be there after you're done."

She grabbed another set of clothes and went into the locker room at the end of the hall; Riley was in there, changing into jeans and a comfortable sweatshirt with her hair still clinging damply to her face. She looked up, surprised, as Bryn dumped her stuff on the bench.

"Everything okay?"

Bryn didn't want to talk, but she had to try. "Bad one," she managed to say. "Major decomposition."

Riley nodded and opened her locker. She tossed Bryn a bottle. "Try this," she said. "Best I've found. Use it four times, you should be okay."

Bryn didn't even wait to thank her. The urge to get clean was so overpowering that even after she was standing in the hot spray, soaping herself from head to toe, she couldn't stop gasping and shaking from the pressure. Two passes with the shampoo and she still felt filthy. By the third she was calming down, and by the fourth she felt almost normal. Her skin tingled from the scrubbing, but that was a good thing; the greasy, horrible stench seemed to have finally rubbed off.

Bryn threw her old clothes into the incineration biohazard bag and dressed in the clean ones, dried her hair, and was just finishing when there was a knock on the locker room door, and McCallister looked in.

He looked rough—pallid, with dark circles beneath his eyes. He'd stripped off his coat and tie and unfastened the top button of his shirt. "All right if I come in?" he asked, and she suddenly felt very selfish for taking up the shower for so long.

"It's all yours," she said.

He nodded thanks and opened a locker—Joe Fideli's— and took out a pair of blue jeans and a clean white T-shirt. "We're about the same size," he said. "At least I won't look like I'm going for gangster style."

She passed him Riley's shampoo. "Four passes," she said. "It works."

He smiled, faintly, and said, "Good."

He was already stripping off his clothes before she closed the door, and in those fast, ruthless motions, she sensed that McCallister, too, was on the edge of losing control.

She let him do it in private.

Back in her office, Bryn turned on music, something soft and soothing, and nibbled some crackers to settle her still-restless stomach. Her skin and clothes smelled clean and fresh, but it was hard not to imagine the ghost of that stench still hanging around. She cleaned out the trash can, then used disinfectant spray around her chair and on her shoes. Probably too much.

Finally, she sat down and closed her eyes.

A soft chime made her open them again.

She had e-mail.

Oh, God. She'd actually forgotten all about it.

Sitting in her in-box was a new message from one of those throwaway account services, with the ominous moniker of *deadman*. There was no subject line, and the message was just an address and a time of day—ten p.m.

McCallister came back, still glistening with drops from the shower, and saw from her expression that something was up.

She mutely spun her computer around and showed him. He leaned over the desk to read it. "Can your tech wizards trace that?" she asked.

"Probably not, but we'll try it. That is the e-mail equivalent of a burner phone, and if he's got any sense at all, he hid his IP address through a randomizer." McCallister already had his cell out and was dialing.

"Don't you need my account password?"

"Already have it," he said, and got up to turn his back and talk to his resources.

Proof, once again, that there was nothing secret in her life anymore. Nothing sacred. She'd expected to feel some sense of burning betrayal, but instead, she felt . . . tired. And, weirdly, a little reassured.

McCallister stayed on the phone a while longer, and she contemplated opening up another set of drinks, but that seemed less like a necessary safety valve and more like a crutch, at this point. Bryn shut and locked the drawer, and looked at the clock.

It was coming up on six o'clock.

Four hours to get the money and deliver it to the address—or else what? Lose their potential chance at the supplier.

If they did, Bryn had no doubt whatsoever that Irene Harte would pull the plug on the project, and her, with pleasure. It was that, as much as anything else, that made her step back from the comfort of the booze. *I'm not giving you the excuse,* she thought. *Not you. You don't get to kill me.*

But it wouldn't be Harte, she realized. When it came to the end, it would come from the man pacing the floor on the other side of her office, talking quietly into his cell phone. He'd be the one told to withhold her drug, reduce her to that decayed, rotting shell. She'd be eaten alive. She'd beg for release until eventually the last of the nanites faded and died. . . .

Or until he dismembered her, out of sheer horrified mercy.

No. He promised. He promised me he wouldn't let that happen. She closed her eyes and took deep breaths and tried to think of something, anything less painful. He'd promised, and he'd meant it. He wouldn't let her linger on and rot.

McCallister finished the call. "I have a car and driver coming, and I'm on the way to pick up the money," he said. "Joe is five minutes out. Stay here, and he'll take you home. I'll come by here at eight thirty to pick you up for the rendezvous."

She nodded. "Thank you."

"For what?" he asked, and she held his eyes until she saw that he knew. "I meant what I said, Bryn. I won't let that happen."

"I know," she said. "Thank you." She stood up and hugged him. It was an impulse, and she didn't mean anything by it except gratitude, until she was in his arms, and then . . . then it was something else entirely. "Tell me you didn't sleep with her," she whispered, very quietly.

He didn't ask what she was talking about. "I didn't," he said, and something brushed her forehead, very gently. It might have been a kiss. "Stay safe."

And then he was gone.

Bryn arrived home at six thirty, feeling exhausted and not up for family drama of any kind. Luckily, she didn't get any.

The apartment was spotlessly clean, Mr. French was happy to see her, and the air smelled like rich Italian food.

"Hey, sweetie!" Annie said brightly from the kitchen. "Hope you're hungry. I think I cooked enough pasta for the complex!"

I can't do this. Bryn dropped onto the sofa and covered her face with her hands. In a few seconds, she felt Annie's weight settle in next to her, and her sister's arm went around her shoulders. She didn't look up.

"Hey," Annie said. "Hey, what did I say? You don't like Italian anymore?"

"It's just . . ." For an extremely unsettling second, Bryn thought the dam might just collapse inside her. If she said *anything*, she'd say *everything*, everything that she'd promised to keep secret. And that would unburden her, but doom her sister. McCallister's people were always listening, and someone was always listening to *them*. "It was a bad day. Really bad."

"Sorry, honey. Hey, does it have anything to do with the hottie who was here with you before?"

"No! Why would you even assume that?" Bryn looked at her sister finally. Annie cocked an eyebrow and shrugged. "It's not all about my love life. Or lack of one."

"I'm just saying, he's hot."

"What about *married* did you not understand?"

"There's married and *married*, in my expert opinion."

"Expert?"

"Honey, I work in a bar. I *am* an expert."

That was . . . a good point. Bryn let it pass. "It's not about Joe, and it had nothing to do with . . . It was work. Bad day at work."

"Oh. So . . . it was disgusting, right?"

"Very."

"I think I'd rather talk about your lack of a love life. Seriously, there isn't *anybody* you're interested in? Come on, Bryn. Humor me."

"Nobody," she said, but then she sighed and shook her head. "He doesn't care about me. Not that way."

"Is he male?"

"Obviously."

"Is he straight?"

"As far as I know."

"Then he cares, sweetie. You don't have any idea how sexy you are, do you?"

Bryn laughed, and it sounded a little wild, a little despairing. "I am so very far from sexy right now, Annie. And how did we get on this subject again?"

"Because you wouldn't discuss dinner?"

"Well, I'll discuss it now. I don't have much time, though.

I'm sorry, but I have to go out tonight. An appointment. I need to be there by eight thirty."

"Cool." Annie squeezed her and let go. "We can go out tomorrow night. I made bruschetta and pasta primavera; I walked over to the store and stocked your fridge. You'll love it."

And Bryn did. For the first time in a long time—since before that awful moment when her whole life had ended and restarted—she tasted food, really tasted it. Crisp, nutty bread, fresh chopped tomato, basil, garlic, balsamic vinegar, oil . . . and the pasta, perfectly cooked al dente. Annie offered wine, but Bryn refused, on the grounds of driving. They talked. They laughed. They mocked each other. They did dishes and splashed each other, half out of spite, half out of joy.

Sisters.

Bryn felt the darkness and horror slip away, just for a while.

It all passed in far too short a time. By eight, they were sitting on the couch again, and Annie was flipping channels on Bryn's TV. "What time do you think you'll be back?" she asked. She flipped her hair back over her shoulders. She'd showered, and her hair had fallen into golden brown ringlets, perfectly shaped. When Bryn was ten and Annie was eight, Bryn had given her sister a deliberately awful haircut with a pair of safety scissors out of sheer envy—and in truth, she still hadn't quite gotten over coveting those curls.

"Why? You going to wait up?"

"Are you going out on a date?"

"I wish. No."

"Are you going to be draining body fluids out of some poor dead person?"

"No, and God, you are morbid."

"Me? You're the one with the job in the death business." Annie made air quotes around it. "I'm sorry, and I don't want to judge, but it just seems really weird to me."

"It's not weird. It's . . ." Bryn remembered Riley's words, back in the prep room. "It's something sacred, in a way. We're the last people to touch someone in this world, and that's important. We're all going there, in the end. Wouldn't you like there to be someone there to care for you?"

Annie turned toward her, eyes wide. She didn't speak. Finally, she settled against the cushions and refocused her attention on the TV. "So you don't know when you'll be back."

"God, Annie, are you planning on throwing a party while I'm gone? No, I don't know. A couple of hours, probably. Stop questioning me."

"You always ask me these things."

"I'm your older sister. I'm supposed to."

"So who are you meeting? Your mystery man?" Annie nudged her with her shoulder. Bryn nudged back, harder.

"None of your business."

"Oh, come on. If I've never met him, what does it matter?"

"He's . . . complicated," Bryn said slowly. "And very . . . complicated."

"You are the worst. Okay, just answer this. Is he hot?"

"I don't know." She didn't, honestly. He was; then he wasn't. She didn't know how to view Patrick McCallister objectively at all. "I suppose so."

"What's his best feature?"

Annie probably wanted her to say his ass, or his abs, or his eyes, or something like that, but Bryn thought for a second and said, "His certainty."

Her sister laughed outright. "You are insane—you know that? No wonder you can't get yourself laid properly."

For answer, Bryn grabbed the remote and put on a reality show she knew her sister hated, and as Annie breathlessly chased her around to grab the remote, she knew, deep down, that it was all going to be okay. Somehow, it was all going to be okay.

It had to be.

Eight thirty came far too soon.

By nine thirty, sitting with Joe Fideli in his black sedan, she wasn't so sure of a positive outcome. McCallister was in the backseat, hidden behind the tinted windows; he'd changed the white tee for a black knit shirt, but kept the jeans. She'd expected him to be . . . different, but from the moment she'd entered the car at the mortuary, she'd sensed that McCallister's armor was back up, and in full force. He was polite, but cool and slick as glass.

"I don't like this," Bryn said. "What if he wanted me to come alone?"

Joe shrugged. "I think it'd be more suspicious if you *didn't* bring your bodyguard. If he'd meant for you to come alone he'd have said so. After all, you're a woman, no offense to your self-defense skills, and this is a nasty part of town at a dangerous time of night. You brought backup. That's acceptable behavior to him."

"You act like you know him." She meant it as a joke, but as soon as she said it, her brain fired off into wild, improbable directions, and she took in a sudden breath.

Joe interpreted all that flawlessly. "You think I'm the leak from Pharmadene?" He laughed outright. In the backseat, McCallister echoed it. "Way to think out of the box, Bryn, but no. No way I could pull it off, and I got no use for anybody who'd make money this way anyway. Patrick knows that."

"You know the system. And you could rip off the drugs; don't tell me you couldn't," she said, obscurely offended. "You'd probably get a kick out of doing it, too—stick it to the evil corporation and all."

That sobered him quickly. "Pharmadene's got some rot in it, no question about that, but it's also full of smart, idealistic people. They save lives, Bryn."

"I saw today what they do. It's hideous."

"This thing, this drug . . . it's *not* what they do. Or did. Returné was an accident that came up while they were trying to find a way to nonsurgically remove cancers. Now it's like a cancer of its own inside the company, eating away. And I—" He stopped himself—or, more accurately, McCallister's hand clamping down on his shoulder stopped him. Joe swallowed the rest of it. "I just think Pharmadene's got some good in it," he finished, which she was sure wasn't what he'd intended. "I think you should give it a chance, Bryn."

"You really think I have a choice?" Bryn muttered. "So am I doing this or not?"

"Yes," McCallister said from the backseat. "It's time. All you need to do is get out, walk into the building, and leave the bag in the first open place you see, then come right back. I don't care what you see or what you hear, you leg it back here as fast as you can. If you take more than two minutes before you're back in our field of vision, Joe goes in after you."

"Guns blazing," Joe added. "And nobody wants that. Gets real messy. On the upside, if I shoot you, it really doesn't matter."

"I thought you were on my side."

He winked at her. "Good luck."

Bryn took a deep breath, nodded to both of them, and got out of the passenger side. She retrieved the black canvas bag full of cash and began walking. She'd dressed practically—dark pants, dark sweatshirt, running shoes, her hair tied back in a sloppy knot at the nape of her neck—but even so, she suddenly felt very exposed, very vulnerable. Her gun was under the sweatshirt, one zipper pull away. And as Joe had so not-kindly said, she could take a bullet if she had to and survive.

So why was she so damned nervous?

Because I feel like a mousetrap tester, she thought. *And I'm the mouse.*

Not all of San Diego was shiny and tourist friendly; this area was inky dark, very few lights, and most of these feeble security lighting trying to protect what was surely a losing investment for some poor real estate company. Everything was graffiti covered, weed overgrown, and littered with trash and broken bottles. She felt the crunch of ground glass under her feet as she walked.

The address from her e-mail was on the right, behind a rusty chain-link fence with a No Trespassing sign on it. The sign had been defaced, mangled, and shot three times, and right below it someone had chopped a gash in the links big enough to squeeze through, if you were reasonably small and didn't care too much about tetanus. Bryn sucked it up and scraped by. The fence snapped back with a dry rattle, and a random breeze pushed trash past her feet in a postmodern snowdrift of cups, plastic bottles, and torn paper.

The building she was facing had started life as some kind of a factory for a product probably made with great success now in Asia; signs were long gone, and the paint was faded and covered in a thicket of colorful but also fading neon tags.

Bryn watched her corners, just the way they'd taught her in urban combat training, and kept walking toward the dark hole of the entrance. It used to have an accordion gate across the doors, but the doors were gone, and the security barrier was ripped off and dangling by one hinge.

Bryn heard a stirring inside the building, and paused at the threshold. This wouldn't even be a third choice for the homeless, but she still felt stiff with tension. *Rats*, she thought. This place was probably a playground for them.

Now that she'd stepped into the mouth of the beast, there was no particular reason to stay stealthy; she switched on the penlight she'd brought with her. The narrow, stark white beam didn't make her feel any better; if anything, it only increased her anxiety about what was in the ink-black edges of her vision. *In and out*, she thought, like a mantra. *Get in; get out*.

The clock was running.

The main entry room was large and had four doorways leading out. There was a metal desk left abandoned in the approximate middle of the room, bolted in place. It listed to one side like a sinking ship and was covered with rat droppings, trash, empty bottles, broken syringes . . . the typical treasure trove of an abandoned building. Everything stank like a molding sewer.

Bryn put the bag on the desk and turned to go.

"Hey," said a soft voice from the shadows.

She spun, pointing the flashlight, but the voice echoed weirdly in the empty room, and she couldn't pinpoint where it had come from.

"Hey," the whisper came again, closer.

Screw it. Bryn unzipped her sweatshirt and pulled her gun. The weight of it made her feel less off balance, less vulnerable, even though she knew that was an illusion; she'd seen comrades chewed up by small-arms fire even through ballistic nylon vests. Human beings were always vulnerable.

Not that she was legally considered *human* anymore.

The voice seemed to come from behind her this time, startlingly close. "Hey, sugar, where you goin'?"

Bryn spun, gun in a firing stance, just as something lunged at her from the darkness on her left. The man skidded to a stumbling halt, the muzzle pressed to his face.

"I'm leaving, *sugar*," she said. "Sit your ass down on the floor, cross-legged, hands behind your head. Now."

He sank down and complied without another word. Homeless, she guessed, and definitely high, from the way his pupils failed to contract in her flashlight beam. He was wearing faded surplus military khakis under layers of coats and dirt-stiff scarves. " 'Sup?" he mumbled. "Just tryin' to be friendly."

"Yeah, I can see how friendly you want to be by the bulge in your pants. Just your way of saying hi? Stay down." Bryn took three giant steps back, and then paused. She was leaving a hundred thousand in cash sitting there with a homeless would-be rapist. If she turned her back, he and it would surely be gone. "Okay, I'm going to need you to get up. We're going to take a walk."

"A walk?" He went from menacing to pathetic in the blink of an eye, and raised his hands over his head. "Please don't kill me; I didn't mean nothin'!"

"I'm not going to kill you. Stand up. I can't leave you here."

"It's my place. I got stuff. I leave it, it gets took."

"Get up, *now*, or I promise you won't need stuff ever again."

He scrambled up, awkward with fear, and she knew this wasn't the first time he'd had a gun pointed at him. His head was tucked down, his hands trembling, and his posture was totally submissive.

"Walk," she said, and circled around so that his path was clear and not within grabbing distance of her.

Her captive shambled out, hands raised, and she followed, careful not to close the distance as he slowed down.

"Move. Head for the fence." He glanced back, and she noticed something strange about him.

His eyes. They didn't look right. Still dilated, but . . .

Contacts. He was wearing some kind of costume contacts.

This was him. The one collecting the money. Maybe even the mystery caller himself. It was a great disguise, and she'd almost completely fallen for it.

"Wait," she said, but that tipped him off that the game was up, and he dodged, blindingly fast, out of the beam of her flashlight.

She lost him.

Bryn switched the light off—had to, to use the starlight effectively—but it took time for her eyes to adjust to the change, and in the second or two required, he just . . . vanished.

Bryn backed up toward the building, then plunged inside and turned the penlight on to illuminate the desk.

The bag was gone.

The whisper came again, raw and amused. "I think I like you, sugar. You can handle yourself."

"Show yourself!" she yelled. "I don't do business with jackasses in clown makeup!"

She got nothing in reply but echoes, but she heard a scrape from a side passage. Her blood was pounding in her head, and she knew the smart thing to do was withdraw, regroup, wait for backup . . . but he was going to get away clean if she did. *I had him,* she thought. *I had my gun in his face.*

She also knew that she'd never be able to identify him. She'd seen what he wanted her to see—the filth, the straggly hair, the clothes, the contacts hiding his real eye color. First rule of disguise was to distract, and he'd done it brilliantly, right down to the submissive body language.

There was another scrape, behind her, and she whirled with her gun ready and braced. She wasn't going to take another chance, not this time. . . .

And she barely stopped herself from putting a bullet center mass in Joe Fideli's chest.

He held his hands out to the sides, his gun pointed up,

until she came off the shooting stance. She started to speak, but he shook his head, and she fell back into military hand signals to show him where their suspect had gone. He pointed at the penlight, and she clicked it off, and for a moment she felt claustrophobic, swarmed by the dark, until her eyes adjusted enough to make out shadows and shapes.

Then Fideli went in the direction she'd indicated. He moved like the very best combat soldiers she'd worked with, or watched—smooth, calm, no wasted motions. He had some kind of extremely advanced training, whether it was Army Rangers or Navy SEALs or Marine Recon. . . . Bryn felt unavoidably clumsy next to him, but she kept up as he glided through the hallway, stepping over and around obstacles and trash as best she could. There was a faint clink from somewhere up ahead, off to the right—a bottle rolling? Fideli held up a clenched fist, and she stopped, nerves crawling. After a few seconds, he indicated for her to wait, and he glided a few more steps ahead, checking the exposed point where the hallway emptied into the next room.

Gunfire shattered the glassy silence. Fideli hit the floor, return-firing from a prone position, and Bryn decked it, too, to avoid any ricochets. It was over in a couple of seconds. Her ears were still ringing from the hammer blows of the shots, but she heard running feet somewhere beyond.

Fideli stayed in firing position, but he keyed a throat mike and said, "He's on the move, heading for the north fence—" He coughed, and rolled over on his back. "And I took one," he added. "Call nine-one-one, Bryn."

She saw the dark stain of blood on the filthy floor, and for a second she couldn't react at all—and then it all snapped together, and she flung herself across to him and pulled his jacket back, then ripped open his shirt.

"Be gentle," he said. "Got to"—a pause for an ominously wet cough—"explain to Kylie later—"

"Shut up." Bryn fumbled for her phone and hit the programmed button for McCallister. He answered on the first ring. "Fideli's down; he took a round in the shoulder but I think it bounced; he's got a lung wound." Time was of the essence; she knew that. Depending on the size and location of the puncture to the lung, it could collapse quickly or slowly, but it was bound to happen. "Get in here."

"I can't," McCallister said. He sounded way too calm. "Calling nine-one-one now."

"But—"

"Handle it, Bryn. Keep him alive until they get there."

"Wait!" But McCallister had hung up on her, damn him. She dropped the phone and began ripping up the clean portion of Fideli's shirt to make a pressure pad for his shoulder; it was freely bleeding but not pumping, so it was unlikely the bullet had hit an artery. Internally was another matter; the bullet could have done terrible things on the bounce. No way to tell.

His color was fading, but that was a normal shock reaction. She pressed the wadding of cloth into place, and he winced, turned his head, and spit blood. Not much, though. Not as much as she'd feared.

"Pat call nine-one-one?" he asked. His breathing sounded labored and damp, but not yet critical.

"Yes. I thought he was your friend."

"He is. But he's got a job to do." Another hitch in his breath, but it might have just been a pain reaction; she felt him stiffen, then relax a little. "Should have worn a vest."

"Yes. We both should have."

"Next time, eh?" He coughed and reached up to pat her hand where it pressed against the wound. "Good job, Bryn."

"What, getting you shot?" Her heart was hammering now, and fear was creeping in. "Don't die on me, Joe. I don't want to face your kids."

"Ought to be more afraid of Kylie," he said, and coughed. This time, there was a *lot* of blood—*oh, Jesus*—and she heard distressed breath sounds in his right lung when she pressed her ear to his chest. "Going to be one of those damn tension pneumo things. Check jacket pocket."

She did, fumbling quickly, and pulled out . . . a silver tube with a seal. Her drug, which he kept with him in case of *her* distress. "Joe? Do you want me to give this to you? Will it help?"

"No," he whispered. His lips were starting to turn blue

where they weren't dark with blood, and his breathing was hitchy and painful. "Drain it. Use it as a needle tube."

"Is that safe?"

"Safer than dying—ah, God—" His back arched a little, and when his next breath came, she heard nothing from his right side. The lung had collapsed. Fideli's breathing was shallow and fast.

She ripped the tube open, slid the syringe out, squirted the contents onto the ground in a silvery stream. *Well, there goes a few thousand,* she thought, stupidly, and filled it with air to push out again, just in case. A drop of liquid hissed out, and then the syringe was clean, or as clean as she could get it. She ripped the handle out to leave a jagged opening for air. She checked his other pockets and came up with a rubber glove; she pricked a hole in one finger and jammed it down over the syringe.

Bryn held the penlight in her teeth and counted off ribs, hoping her years-old emergency field medicine still held true. She pressed on the area, took a deep breath, and pushed the needle home. There was a pop as she went through connective tissue, and then a sudden hiss as air pushed out, inflating the finger of the glove as it escaped. Fideli took in a sudden gasping breath, and the glove deflated, preventing air from flowing in to compress the lung from outside. She couldn't do anything about the blood in the lung, but that seemed to be less of an urgent issue.

About thirty seconds later, she heard the advancing wail of a siren, and took Joe's hand. "Hey," she said. "Looks like I won't have to get beaten up by your wife. Much."

He smiled with those pale lips and gave her a thumbs-up, but didn't try to speak.

One minute later, she heard shouting, and left him to lead them back inside. The police came first to secure the scene, and then let the paramedics in. They immediately threw out her makeshift needle arrangement and inserted a catheter, scooped Fideli onto a gurney, and ran off with him, leaving her in the position of explaining . . . everything.

Bryn was, of course, promptly arrested. After all, two people with guns, one shot . . . it looked bad. McCallister didn't show up to make it better, either. She presented the police with a somewhat ridiculous story about checking out the building for a possible investment, along with her bodyguard, and being fired on by an unknown assailant. The facts would actually support that, as it happened, and her gun hadn't been fired. The detectives hated the story, of course, but couldn't argue too much with the evidence that mounted in her support. After six hours in the interrogation room, and another four in very boring custody, she was finally released to her lawyer—someone she'd never seen before, a brusque, harried woman who handed her paperwork and hustled her out to a waiting yellow cab at the curbside.

Patrick McCallister, unshaven and almost unrecognizable in a cap and sunglasses, was driving. He nodded to the lawyer, who tossed an envelope in the window. "There's my bill," she said. "Don't call me again."

McCallister said nothing, just pulled out into traffic. Bryn was monumentally unsurprised to see him, but she was mildly curious about the disguise. "Who was that?"

"Old girlfriend," he said. "Best I could do without ringing someone's bells."

She let that pass. "How's Joe?"

"Out of surgery. You saved his life. The bullet bounced and did some damage in his chest wall; he'd have suffocated before help got there if you hadn't acted. He won't be able to come back to duty for a few weeks, though."

"Not my biggest concern."

"It should be," McCallister said. His face looked exhausted and pale beneath the thick growth of dark stubble. "Round one went to our friend, and he's proved he's dangerous. Very dangerous. Not some rogue accountant with a side business; he's way too good for that. We're rerunning every single employee, but he's hidden this long, and he's going to stay hidden unless we get very lucky. You're still our very best option to uncover him."

"You really think he'll get back in touch. After *this.*"

"This didn't go badly for *him.* He made off cleanly with a hundred thousand in cash, *and* took out your protection. You're alone now, and vulnerable. He'll like that." McCallister's mouth was very tight, and his eyes very dark. "I have to leave you in place, alone. He's watching us. Closely."

That was, Bryn assumed, why she was in the back of a cab. Maximum cover for their meeting. Things were getting too hot for him to risk being linked to her directly.

"Do you think you'd recognize him if you saw him again?"

"I doubt it, but I can try. He was good. If it hadn't been for his contacts, I wouldn't have suspected a thing, and that was only a trick of the light and the angle."

"He can't disguise his height that much."

"That's not a lot to work with."

"I know, but it's what we have to work with, until he gives you something else." McCallister hesitated. "Bryn, we're running close to Harte's deadline. So far, I have nothing to show for it but two hundred thousand lost and a man down. She's not going to be happy. I'll do what I can, but we're almost out of time."

What he meant was *she* was almost out of time. And Bryn knew that. She felt it in every aching muscle. "I'll keep trying," she said. "You know that. I want to live."

He pulled the car over and parked, then reached in his coat pocket and took out a silver tube. As he unshipped the syringe, he said, "Shoulder." She leaned forward and bared skin for him, hardly even wincing at the needle and afterburn this time. You could, indeed, get used to anything. "Tomorrow, you leave the office for lunch and head to a place called La Scala Ristorante. Be there at one o'clock. There's parking in the back. Inside the back entrance there's a men's bathroom. Go in. I'll be in the last stall to give you the shot before you sit down to eat."

"The men's bathroom."

"It's less obvious than my going into the women's room. You can always say you made a mistake. Act embarrassed enough and anyone watching will buy it. Oh, it helps if you're on the phone as you walk in. The restrooms aren't clearly labeled, so it's a simple mistake."

"You think of everything." She sighed, and closed her eyes. She felt deathly tired. "I need to go to the mortuary." Riley's words came back to her. *People never stop dying.*

There were no days off, no breaks from death. Every day was someone's most emotional moment.

"Make it an early day," he said. "Conserve your strength."

The car was making turns, and she recognized the neighborhood. They were close to her apartment. Her phone, in silent mode, vibrated again. Annie was trying to get hold of her, probably frantic with worry.

"I wish I could have a normal life," she said. "Just *pretend* to have one, anyway."

McCallister thought for a moment, then said, "Liam did mention he'd like you to come to dinner on Thursday night. He's making beef Wellington." Somehow, he managed to make it sound as though it were the butler's idea, and not his own.

"I see. And will I be dining with Liam?"

"Of course, if I can get him to sit down long enough. Otherwise, you're stuck with me." He was looking away as he said it, checking over his shoulder for any sign of trouble. "I'll tell him you said yes."

"You may have noticed I didn't actually say that."

He turned and looked at her, and all the pretense just . . . stopped. "Come to dinner," he said. "You just said you'd like to pretend to have a normal life."

"Did you phrase it that way to see if the protocol inhibitor is still working?"

That woke a very faint smile. "Partly."

"All right. Can I bring anything?"

"Anything but your sister," he said. It sounded heartfelt, and she found herself smiling.

"Wow. You sound as if you'd actually met her."

"I wouldn't mind meeting her, except that you already have enough to explain. It would take a lot more to produce a boyfriend with a Bruce Wayne mansion that she's never heard of before. I'm using hypotheticals, of course."

"The mansion is hardly hypothetical."

"I was speaking of the boyfriend part. About our relationship."

"I wasn't aware you thought we actually had one."

That cued him to look away again. "Of course we do. I'm your handler."

"That doesn't sound as sexy as it ought to."

He let out a snort that was remarkably like her dog's, and the brakes eased the taxi to a stop. "You're home."

Bryn made no real effort to get out, other than putting her hand on the handle. She said, "You could have come in to save Joe. You didn't. I know you had your reasons, but it makes me wonder: what if it's me next time? You said you wouldn't let me suffer. I need to count on that."

"You can," he said. "Always."

Bryn stepped out and watched the taxi glide away. Her phone vibrated again, and she let out a tired sigh, jammed her fists in the pockets of her hoodie, and went upstairs to explain things to Annalie.

It didn't go well.

Chapter 10

She just didn't have the energy, after the awful night, to deal with Annalie's questions—valid though they might have been. Bryn abandoned the field, showered, dressed, and stormed off to work with new (if adrenaline-fueled) energy. That lasted through the first consultation with a newly bereaved husband; his wife had celebrated her seventy-fifth birthday and passed away two weeks later of a stroke. He was stoic, but fragile, and Bryn guided him through it with the sad knowledge that he'd probably be a client soon; she could see the resignation in his eyes. He'd lost everything, and he was giving up. Maybe he'd come out of it, but at his age, she doubted it.

After he was gone, and she had time to think, she realized that her head was throbbing and her throat was dry. A visit to the coffee machine helped. Lucy tried to tell her about Joe's shooting, but Bryn was too tired to keep up a pretense of surprise. Besides, with Lucy's connections, she'd find out soon enough that Bryn had been there on the scene.

"I was with him," Bryn said, sipping her coffee. Lucy stopped typing on her computer keyboard and looked up with widened eyes. "He was helping me out, and he got shot for his trouble. I need to go see his wife and kids."

"I think they're all at the hospital," Lucy said. "I was told so, anyway. The nurses say he's not in any danger, thank the Lord. Shot. My God. And you were right there?"

"Yes," Bryn said. "I was right there."

"But what were you—" Lucy checked herself and firmly

closed her mouth. "You know what? That's none of my business, none at all. I'm just happy you're all right."

She wasn't all right, on so many levels, but Bryn just nodded and went back to her office. She could feel Lucy's curious stare on her back. By the end of the day, everybody—including Riley Block, in her prep room inner sanctum—was going to have the unshakable opinion that she'd been screwing Joe Fideli.

God.

When her phone rang, it was almost a relief. It wasn't her private line, just the main switchboard, so she answered with the standard greeting—or tried to.

Annalie interrupted her. "We need to talk about what happened, Bryn!"

"No, trust me. We really don't."

"You were *arrested*! You don't think Mom's going to hear about that?"

"Only if you tell her."

"I wouldn't!" Annie sounded less than convincing, though. "Look, clearly this is not a good time for you to have me hanging around whatever ... stuff ... you're into. . . ."

"God, Annie, do you think I'm a *drug dealer*?" Because that would be gruesomely ironic, all things considered.

Annie chose her words carefully. "I think you may have some kind of a problem you don't want to acknowledge," she said. "I mean, damn, you're working with dead people; it's no wonder you'd want ... some kind of—"

"Oh, so I'm not a drug dealer, just a junkie."

"I'm not *saying* that!" Annie took a deep breath. "Okay, I'm taking the next flight back home," she said. "I'll leave your key with the apartment manager. And I shredded and flushed your apartment codes. Anything else you want me to do?"

"Walk Mr. French before you go running home to tell Mom what a loser I am," Bryn said.

"Bryn, c'mon, you were *arrested*. Many people would consider that a wake-up call!"

"I was innocent."

"You were off skulking around in the dark with a *mar-*

ried man and you almost got shot. I don't know what you think you're doing, Bryn, but whatever it is, it's nuts. *You're* nuts. I always said you were when you went running off to join the army, but now—"

"Says the girl who can't add well enough to avoid over-drafts," Bryn snapped. "Don't hit me up for money any-more. Go crying to Mom; tell her I'm not her golden girl anymore. Maybe you'll get the job."

"Maybe I will!"

"Do it!" Bryn slammed the phone down and concen-trated on controlling her breathing. Damn, no one could push buttons like family, especially bratty little sisters. How *dared* Annie get holier-than-thou with her, especially when the *holier-than* had to be bailed out of trouble six months out of twelve?

The downside is that I have to make my own dinner, Bryn thought, and almost laughed, but she was afraid it would sound too much like a sob. She felt sick and feverish, and was deathly afraid there was something wrong with her. Nanite wrong. *You have another shot coming up*, she reminded herself. *Don't get panicky.*

She drank three glasses of water, signed papers, wrote checks, and finally it was twelve thirty. She told Lucy where she was going, and headed for La Scala Ristorante.

"You know," Bryn said as the needle pushed into her arm, "my sister thinks I'm a junkie, and she'd really think it if she could see me now. Shooting up in a bathroom. A men's bathroom, at that." She closed her eyes and focused on the warm strength of McCallister's fingers where his left hand gripped her, holding her shoulder still. The hot surge of the shot almost took her focus away, but she held on and didn't flinch.

McCallister put the used syringe back in the tube and pocketed it. "You're done," he said, as she pulled her shirt-sleeve down. "Have a nice lunch."

"Wait—"

"I can't, Bryn." But he hesitated, with one hand on the latch of the cramped bathroom stall. There was barely room for the two of them and the discolored curve of the toilet seat. "What?"

"I just wanted to ask . . ." She fell silent as the hinges on the bathroom door creaked. They stared at each other, pressed intimately close, as the unknown man outside un-zipped his pants, grunted, and started splashing the urinal cake. Bryn covered her mouth with her hand, afraid that for some insane reason she was about to laugh. Even Mc-Callister couldn't suppress a smile.

Especially when the man started to sing off-key along with the Italian music piped in over the bathroom speakers. Dear God, he was awful.

McCallister put his lips very close to her ear and whispered, "I think he's got a future on *American Idol*. The wrong kind."

She shook with the silent force of her laughter, and bit her lip until tears threatened. Part of it was the sheer craziness of being so tired and emotionally stretched. The man finally flushed, washed, and the door thumped shut behind him.

Bryn found herself leaning against McCallister, eyes closed. She'd relaxed sometime in the last few seconds. *I trust him*, she thought, and hated herself for it.

"What did you want?" he asked, still in that very soft whisper.

"He's gone. You don't have to whisper now."

"I know." There were volumes of meaning in that, too much for her tired brain to decipher. "You're wondering about Joe. He's fine. Kylie's at the hospital with him. He'll be home in a few days to recuperate."

"She probably hates me."

"She hates me a whole lot more. I'm the one who's re-sponsible for all this." McCallister's slightly beard-rough cheek rubbed along hers, waking all kinds of shivers down her skin. "I have to go. You'll be all right, Bryn. I'll see you for dinner on Thursday."

Thursday was after Irene Harte's deadline, and he knew that. He was trying to give her some kind of hope for a fu-ture.

She appreciated it, but she no longer really believed it.

Bryn stepped back, and he unlocked the stall door and stepped out, then gestured for her to go ahead. She moved fast, and heard him locking the stall back again as she reached for the door handle.

A man pushed it open, and she scrambled away, feeling a surge of panic that heated her face. "Oh, God," she said. "Wrong room. Sorry." She hurried past him and directly into the women's room, opposite, where she lingered for a few minutes checking her hair, makeup, washing her hands, and wishing she'd put on more concealer to blot out the dark circles under her eyes. *Sleep. I need sleep.*

First, she needed food.

As lunches went, it was unremarkable right up until the front entrance bell jingled, and two men in business suits walked up to her table to loom over her. She looked up, frowning, and one of them produced a Pharmadene ID in a fancy flip wallet, like a police detective would carry. "You've got an appointment," he said. "We're your drivers."

"I don't know what you're talking about," she said. It was a busy restaurant—waiters everywhere, diners, cooks, and a maître d' who was currently smiling at a large group of women who'd entered together. "I'm not going anywhere."

"Ma'am, Ms. Harte wants to see you. Right now. Let's not make this a scene."

"If I scream—"

"If you scream," he interrupted her, and bent closer, "we will turn around and walk away, and you will be cut off, do you understand? Completely cut off. No one will be able to help you. It'll take a long time before you stop feeling what you'll be feeling, Bryn."

"Screw you!"

The look in his eyes turned even colder. "Do you want us to walk away? Because we can certainly do that. Ain't nothing to me, lady."

Ah, that closed, choking feeling was her leash being yanked. Bryn stared him down for another few seconds, then reached for her wallet.

The Pharmadene man smiled and said, "Oh, it's on me." He dropped a twenty on the table. "Let's go."

They took her gun as soon as they had gotten her outside. It happened without a fight only because the larger of the two pulled his own weapon first and held it steady on her as his partner searched her. Bryn fumed, but there didn't seem to be any point in trying to go hand-to-hand with men who were obviously very serious about their jobs.

The Town Car they put her in was a duplicate of the one McCallister normally drove, but there was no sign of him. Once they were on the road, Bryn said, "This isn't right. I'm a Pharmadene employee, and I work for McCallister. Call him."

Silence. Neither of them even turned to look at her. "Hey!" she said sharply. "Either you call him, or I do. Your choice."

"Try it," one of them said. He sounded smug, and as she checked her phone, she found it dead. "You'll get service back when we want you to have it. Now shut up. You're not a person. You're a proprietary lab rat."

A plastic barrier went up between her and the two in front. Bryn tried the door handles, but without much hope, and she was right: they controlled the locks. Kicking out the window was an option, but she didn't know whether she was desperate enough to try it. Besides, they were right: where was she going to run? It wasn't like she had a lot of choices.

The ride to Pharmadene left her time to think about what she'd do, what she'd say, but in truth, she had very few plays to make. The goons in the front seat were right: she wasn't a person, not once she was in their custody.

"I'd like to call Ms. Harte," she finally said, leaning up against the clear barrier that separated her from the men in front.

"No need for that," the one who did all the talking said. "You're on your way to see her."

"I need to tell her—"

"Doesn't matter what you want to tell her. Paperwork's been signed. You're done, sweetheart."

An ice-cold panic formed in the pit of Bryn's stomach. She was going to disappear and never be seen again. *Like Sharon.* She didn't want to vanish like her sister, without a word; she didn't want her last minutes with Annalie to be angry. She didn't want her mother to spend her last years agonizing over what had happened to yet another daughter.

She'd given Annie the perfect explanation. *Bryn got involved with drugs. That's probably what happened to her.*

They'd be sad, and they'd be sorry, but she'd be gone. Completely, utterly gone.

I have to get out of here. Better to be on the run than be hauled in there, to die trapped. Maybe Manny Glickman could help her. Maybe Joe Fideli. Running was her only hope.

Bryn twisted and kicked. Her heel connected solidly with the window next to her on the first try, with an impact that rattled all the way up to and through her brain, but she got nothing to show for it, not even a hairline crack in the surface. She kicked again, and again, until the barrier between her and the two thugs in front rolled down, and one of them pointed a gun at her.

"Easy," he said. "You're going to break something, but it won't be that window. Bullet-resistant glass, all the way around. This is our VIP car."

"I'm honored," she said in utter disgust, tugged her skirt down to a ladylike angle, and sat in silence until they'd passed the gates of Pharmadene.

Until all hope was gone.

Damn you, McCallister, what is going on? Where are you? She was starting to think that Joe Fideli wasn't the only casualty of the last twenty-four hours—or the last.

Irene Harte had an office approximately eight times the size of Bryn's; it was so large that there were two conference tables at different points, a sofa-and-chair grouping, a full bar.... It was bigger than most apartments, kitchen included, and as Bryn was frog-marched across the expensive Persian carpet toward the desk, there was no sign of the woman herself. Just an extremely impressive desk—clutter-free, save for two thin folders in a letter tray and a Montblanc pen lying at an angle. The empty leather chair behind the desk could easily have doubled for a throne in a movie about Queen Elizabeth the First. The view from the gigantic panorama windows behind it was breathtaking, and mostly green and unspoiled.

"Sit," Bryn's guard said, and pushed her down in one of the two angled visitor chairs. He stood behind and a little off to the side, ready to counter if she did anything stupid.

Which she was considering, but it would probably be fairly difficult to stab someone fatally with a Montblanc. The pen's shape was a little too rounded.

A concealed door opened to the side, and Irene Harte emerged, trailed by another movie-star-beautiful woman who carried a steaming cup in one hand and a notepad in the other. The cup went on the desk, on a crystal coaster. The pad, and the woman, left the room without even a glance at Bryn or her escort.

Harte nodded to the guard and said, "You may wait outside."

"Ma'am, I don't think it's advisable. She's—"

"I know exactly what Ms. Davis is capable of doing," Harte interrupted, her gaze fixed on Bryn's face. "Go. If I need you, I'll ring Mareen's desk. You may wait there."

"Ma'am." He touched an invisible hat and left. It seemed to take forever for him to cross the office, even at a brisk walk, but Harte didn't move or speak until the door had clicked its latch behind him.

Then she sat back, smiled, and said, "How are you, Bryn? Doing well?"

That was *not* what Bryn had expected. She didn't answer. Harte glanced at the steaming cup on her desk, and her fine eyebrows twitched, then pulled down. She pressed a button on her phone. "Mareen, bring Ms. Davis a cup of coffee. . . ." She paused, looking at Bryn. "Milk? Sugar?"

"Yes," Bryn said. If she was going to die, she might as well have coffee. The whole thing—already surreal—was turning into a French farce. "Are you going to offer me a blindfold and a cigarette, too, or just a last meal?"

"Don't be so dramatic," Harte said. "Mareen, milk and

sugar in that, please. Thank you." She let go of the intercom button and sat back. She tapped her index finger on the desk's surface, slowly. It was the only sound in the hushed room.

Bryn said, "You abducted me for coffee and to ask how I was. You know, most people just phone."

"I'm not most people."

Obviously. "What do you want?"

"I want you to tell me everything you know about Patrick McCallister."

That was a *very* odd request, coming from a woman who had access, surely, to every scrap of information on record about the man. "I don't know anything, really. He likes to be mysterious. Don't *you* know him better? You're his boss."

"Boss," Harte repeated softly, with an odd smile. "Yes, I am. But as you say, he's mysterious. You've been working with him quite closely."

Bryn shrugged. "If by *closely* you mean he tells me what to do, yes." *Calm*, she told herself. *Be calm.*

"It's come to my attention that Mr. McCallister may be involved in . . . questionable activities. Do you have any knowledge of these things?"

"No." That was still the truth. She had no idea what Harte would consider *questionable*, considering what was being sanctioned by her at Pharmadene.

Harte's eyes went flat and cold, like a shark's. "I want you to listen to me very closely," she said. "Condition Sapphire, Bryn. Do you hear me?"

"Yes," Bryn said. She felt nothing. The inhibitor was working, she hoped; if it wasn't, it was going to be a panic-stricken interview on her side, and a very informative one on Harte's.

"You and McCallister have become close, haven't you? Tell me the truth."

"Yes," Bryn said. *Nice to know I can still lie.* Patrick McCallister definitely wasn't close to her; they had an emotional barrier between them the size of the Great Wall of China. She was honest enough to admit that it was partly her own issue.

Harte was moving on. "You've stayed at his family home."

"Yes, while security was upgraded on my apartment."

"And quite recently, you and McCallister took a trip out of town together—quite an elaborate little trip, apparently, one on which he took great pains to evade surveillance. Where did you go?"

Bryn didn't dare hesitate, not for a second; she remembered how it had felt when she'd lost control in the bar. Hesitation would be fatal, and it would betray her completely. "To a motel," she said. "The Hallmark Motor Court Inn. I don't really know what town it was in."

Harte opened a folder, took up the Montblanc, and marked something down without really looking at her. "And what did you do all that time at the motel, Bryn?"

Even with the inhibitors, Bryn felt a little stirring of impulse to blurt it out—the lab, Manny Glickman, the IV, Pansy, the mugging, McCallister's gentle touch on her forehead. She gulped it down and squeezed the arms of the chair as she said, "We made love. Three times. Once on the bed—"

Harte glanced up, eyebrows arched, and then held up a hand. "I don't need the details. Well . . . not yet. Not until I have Patrick McCallister's story to match it against." Her smile was cold, and thin enough to cut. "You went all that way, to a *motel*, to indulge your apparently ravenous sexual appetites for each other. You do know he has a *house*."

"He said we were being watched. And there was something else he wanted there, at the motel."

"Did he say what it was?"

"No," Bryn said.

Harte waited a beat before she said, "Did you do anything else while you were on this little pleasure trip?"

"No." Again, Bryn felt that stirring inside, like something hammering hard against a closed door, struggling to get free. *Tell her. Tell her everything.* She shuddered and held on. How long had Manny said the inhibitors would last? Was she getting close to the time they'd wear off? What if he'd been wrong about the effective dose?

"Did McCallister pay you?"

Bryn blinked. That was the last thing she'd expected. "*Pay* me?"

"Did McCallister give you money in return for sex? Or your silence about such activities?"

"No."

"Well, you wouldn't be the first, although you're certainly his most . . . unusual choice." Harte lifted her shoulders in a graceful shrug. "I suppose he has somewhat perverse taste, considering your . . . condition." She paused and cocked her head, staring hard at Bryn for a moment. "Do you understand what's happening to you, Bryn? Why you can't stop yourself from telling me these very personal things?"

"No." Bryn tried to remember the panic she'd felt before, the internal struggle. Harte needed to see those things. She *expected* to see them.

Mareen entered the room from that same side door she'd used before, set a second cup of coffee pale with milk on the side table beside Bryn, and departed without a word.

"Drink your coffee, Bryn; I wouldn't want it to get cold."

Bryn obediently reached for it and sipped. It was delicious, and the hot liquid made her feel sharper, but more jittery, too. The cup rattled lightly against the saucer as she put it down. *Look at us, so civilized, sipping our coffee from expensive cups while she mind-rapes me. Or tries to.*

"I knew from the moment I saw your revival profile that McCallister had some use for you beyond his stated objectives; he tried to opt you out of certain control features built into Returné for the safety of the company. I countermanded that, in the hopes you'd tell me something more about McCallister's business. It's not your fault, Bryn. You may feel you're betraying him, but I assure you, you're not. You're simply a recording device I put next to him." Harte tapped her fingernails again, thinking, then continued. "Have you seen him meet anyone not associated directly with Pharmadene?"

"Liam," Bryn said.

"The estate administrator. No, not counting Liam. Anyone else?"

"No. Just Joe Fideli and his other security people. No one else."

"Hmm." Harte's eyes lowered to half-mast, making her look deceptively relaxed. "And have you overheard him discuss anything that did not relate to Pharmadene business?"

"No."

"That's deeply unfortunate. I was really hoping you would be more . . . enlightening." Harte sat back and drank her coffee in silence for a moment, and Bryn was just starting to relax a bit when she said, "Are you in love with Patrick McCallister?"

"No!" Bryn said. Too quickly. Too much force. It was an instinctive denial, not a reasoned answer, and Harte speared her with a cold, level gaze. Bryn swallowed and tried again. "I have no feelings for him."

"That, Ms. Davis, means that when he took you to the motel, he did so without your consent. I assume that he coerced you by use of the same command I just engaged. Is that correct? You had no feelings for him, yet you participated in a full day of illicit sex with him, under duress?"

"I . . ." She was caught, dead caught; either she admitted she had just lied, and proved she wasn't conditioned the way Harte wanted, or she dropped McCallister in what was, at the very least, a charge of rape. "It wasn't about love. It was about needing something." That was the best middle ground she could walk, but she could see, with a sinking feeling, that Harte wasn't buying it for a second.

"You should have just admitted it," the other woman said. She straightened and put her cup down, pressed the intercom button, and said, "Mareen, please send Ms. Davis's escort in. I have what I need to know." She went back to her coffee, sipping in ladylike composure. "I have not ended Condition Sapphire, Bryn. You should not be able to lie to me. And the fact that you have tells me that something is very, very wrong here. With you. With McCallister. If you'd simply told me that he'd used the protocols on you, I would have believed you; he's a ruthless son of a bitch, which is why he's valuable to me. If you'd told me you loved him, I'd have believed that, too; he's got that effect on women. But something in the middle . . . no. Not with him."

"I—"

"Don't waste your time. The point is that you've lied to me, he's lied to me, and there's something deeper. Something that threatens me, and the company. And I will find out what that is. Now."

Bryn's guts went tight and cold. The look in Harte's eyes was that of a hawk zeroing in on a rabbit: no mercy, no feeling at all. This wasn't about jealousy, which was somehow what Bryn had expected; this was pure, cold calculation, and she had fallen for it.

The guard who'd brought her in entered the room. "Ma'am?"

"Please take Ms. Davis to level three," Harte said. "Check her in. I'll call down orders in a moment."

"Yes, ma'am."

"And find Patrick McCallister. Now. You don't have to be gentle about it if he resists."

He nodded and started to hustle Bryn out.

"Wait," Harte said. "Let her finish her coffee."

It was time for the false civility to end. Bryn picked up the coffee cup and threw it hard at Harte's face. She missed, but the coffee didn't, drenching the woman in a milky brown, sticky wave from hair to neckline, ruining the teal silk suit.

Harte jumped up, shocked, wiping coffee from her eyes. Too bad it wasn't hot enough to leave scars, Bryn thought; that would have been something. She'd have to settle for the look on Harte's face—comically horrified.

But then it turned into a stiff mask of spite. "So we know where we stand," Harte said. "You're his little spy, aren't you? His slave. He turned you."

"*You* turned me. You made me *this*. I'm not dead; I'm not alive; what am I supposed to do? Thank you?" Bryn was shaking all over with the fury she'd held in for so long, ever since that first raw, primal scream of waking. "I've seen how this ends. Have *you*?"

"Not yet," Harte said. She'd regained her composure; she'd taken a hand towel from a drawer and was blotting the worst of the coffee from her hair and face. The expensive suit was a total ruin. "But I'll be sure to have them record every moment of your deterioration for my home viewing later. Good-bye, Ms. Davis. I hope you enjoy your ... retirement. I'll give Patrick your farewells. You won't be seeing him again."

Bryn kicked and fought, but the guard had all the leverage and muscle, and he was used to restraining angry people; she got in a couple of off-balance shots, but he took them stoically without granting her any chance of escape. After the second elbow to the ribs, he swept her feet out from under her, took her facedown to the carpet, and yanked her arms tight behind her back. She felt zipcuffs being yanked in place, too tightly, and then he grabbed her by the collar and hauled her back to a standing position. "March," he said. "You give me trouble, and I'll give you a beating you're not going to forget."

"I'll heal," she said. She wasn't aware, until she saw herself reflected in a pane of glass, that she was smiling. It was an unhinged sort of smile, half a snarl. She felt like an animal backed into a corner, and that was how she looked.

"Yeah," he agreed. "You would."

And without any warning he hit her with a rock-hard hammer of an uppercut, and she was out like a switched-off light.

Waking up was painful. Her head, first; it throbbed in queasy red flashes. Next, her jaw; she knew that awful grinding feeling. It was dislocated. Bryn worked it gingerly until it snapped back into place with a mind-numbing zap of agony. It, like the headache, lasted only a few minutes, and then the pain faded. *Busy little nanites, burning up energy I can't afford.*

Bryn sat up.

She was in an empty white room. No furniture, not even a cot—just a clean, white, *shiny* room, like a box made of dry-erase whiteboards.

One entire wall of the room was thick, tempered glass. Outside the window, a portable camera had been set up, and a red light showed it was recording. *I'll be sure to have them record every moment of your deterioration for my home viewing later,* Harte had said. She was living up to her commitments.

The only other things of interest about the room were the spray nozzles and pipes across the ceiling, and the drain in the floor. Bryn considered that, and the shiny, slick walls.

This place was designed for easy cleanup.

Stay calm, she told herself. They'd taken her clothes. She was in a baggy, thin coverall, snaps up the front, that rustled uncomfortably with every movement. It, like she, was disposable. There was a number printed on the breast of the coverall: 00061.

Bryn's legs suddenly folded as the reality of it overwhelmed her.

They were leaving her in here to dissolve, under the merciless stare of that camera. Nobody was coming to help her. Nobody would care. She was 00061, not a person. She was a dying lab rat. Once life left her rotted remains, they'd flush the room, disinfect, and throw her bones in some incinerator somewhere.

She'd just vanish without a trace.

Get up, she told herself. *Get up and fight.*

But there wasn't anything or anyone *to* fight. She couldn't fight for her life. She didn't have one. Without the shots, she had no chance at all.

McCallister—

She couldn't count on him, not anymore. Fideli was out of the picture; McCallister was missing, maybe on the run. She had no allies here, no help, and no hope.

They didn't put you in here just to kill you. Harte wants to know what McCallister is up to. They'll question you. When they do, there will be an opportunity.

She didn't really care. The bleakness of the situation was overwhelming.

Get up!

She did, just because it was something to do besides lie down and die.

A careful inspection of the room didn't make her feel any better. There was a door, but it opened only from the outside; there wasn't even a hint of a handle or hinges in here. Bryn tried the drain, but it wasn't nearly big enough to fit her head through, which meant it was useless for escape purposes, even if it didn't narrow below the floor. Plus, a nightmare crawl through a drain full of the decomposing tissues of numbers 1 through 60 . . . No. That was definitely a last resort.

The glass was ballistic quality, and she had nothing to use to break it in any case. Battering her fist against it would only snap her own bones.

As she stared out, she realized that she *did* have a view, after all—of another room, identical to this one, except that it contained a fixed metal table with thick restraint straps. *I guess I didn't fight hard enough to rate that*, she thought. Bryn wasn't sure whether she should feel happy about that, or disappointed, but all that fell away as a briskly walking figure suddenly crossed her field of vision outside.

"Hey!" Bryn yelled, and slapped the glass. "Hey!"

It wasn't one person, but three—two blue-jacketed security men, and a third person being escorted in. He looked nervous. *Very* nervous. Tall, good-looking in that bland *GQ* way; he was wearing suit pants and a crisply ironed white shirt, a snazzy tie, suspenders, but no jacket. She couldn't hear him, but he was talking to his guards, trying vainly to pull away. He had a Pharmadene ID hanging from his belt, one with a green stripe; one of the guards took it, ran it through a scanner, and put the ID in his pocket.

Then they unlocked the room across the hall and hauled the unfortunate man inside.

He screamed and fought when he saw the table, but it wasn't any use, and he wasn't very good at it anyway. He was yelling so loudly now that a faint whisper traveled to her through the glass. When she pressed her ear to it, she could make out some of what he said.

"—can't *do* this! I'm not some nobody you can make vanish; I'm an important man. Do you hear me? I'm a *vice president*, damn it! Take your hands off of me!"

The guards nodded to each other, and in one smooth move had him down on the table. They were a well-coordinated team, locking down his arms and legs in fast, sure motions. He kept on yelling, but Bryn wasn't listening anymore, because a new person had entered the picture.

Irene Harte.

She'd changed into a different suit, and her hair and makeup looked fully restored. Not even a spot showed to prove that Bryn had marked her—and she didn't so much as glance Bryn's way. Her full attention was on the man strapped to the table across the hall.

Bryn didn't need to hear him to know what he said next; his lips were easy to read. *You bitch!* The rest was probably threats, not that it would do him any good; maybe next he'd try to bribe her, if intimidation didn't work. The last thing would be begging.

It didn't get that far.

Bryn had been expecting this to be some sort of interrogation; maybe Mr. Vice President had made a serious security error, or was even the leak they'd been looking for ... but instead of pulling out interrogation drugs, or even a decent torture tray, one of the guards pulled out ...

A clear plastic bag.

Bryn gasped and stepped back from the window. "No ..."

The bag slipped neatly over the man's head, and was cinched in place with a deft twist of the guard's wrist.

"No ..."

She saw it from two angles, like some nightmare ... from where she stood, watching the man's panicked eyes widen under the film of plastic before his breath clouded the bag, and from inside the bag at the same time. Déjà vu. Panic roared up inside her, flattening her defenses. She pressed both hands against the glass, trying desperately to help him, *help him*, because she knew how it felt; she knew the agonized terror that drove him to suck in all the available air and compress the plastic around his skin.

She knew the taste of that toxic panic, and how it felt to gasp for the last tiny bit of oxygen. To watch the diffused light go out.

It hurt—oh, God, it hurt—and it seemed to go on forever as the man struggled, twitched, thrashed, and fought against death.

No one helped him.

When he finally relaxed, Harte looked at her watch. The guards didn't move as the minutes ticked by, waiting for her word. When she finally nodded, the bag came off, leaving the dead man's damp, stark face, eyes wide and bloodshot, lips blue. A trickle of blood came from the corner of his mouth. He'd probably bitten his tongue in his panic.

The guards left, taking the bag with them, and took up posts outside the room. Now a medical team came in, three gowned and masked people who hooked up monitors and oxygen and all the things necessary to saving a life.

Not that there was a life to be saved. Not anymore.

Not until they gave him the shot of Returné.

The scream of his revival penetrated even the solid barrier of the glass to Bryn's death cell. She watched him come back, full of horror and pity and anger, and then, *then*, Irene Harte finally turned and looked at her.

She triggered some kind of intercom outside of Bryn's room.

"You seem to have something to say."

"You have a funny way of retraining people around here."

Irene Harte laughed—a real laugh, full of amusement and little bit of admiration. "I'm consolidating my position, that's all. One thing we cannot have, from this moment on, is any hint of disloyalty. We can't take any risk of harboring traitors and whistle-blowers. Like, I suspect, Patrick McCallister."

"You're killing your own people!"

"I'm ensuring they'll never betray us," Harte said. "From the moment our researchers discovered that this drug could revive and maintain dead tissues, there was no going back. It isn't about a market share; it's about power. Someone's going to have it. Someone will control how this drug is manufactured and used. It will *change the entire world*. Wars will be fought. Whole civilizations will be destroyed, because right here, in these rooms, we have stopped the one thing that man never conquered: death."

There was a glow in her face now, an almost religious

ecstasy that Bryn found scarier by far than the corporate bullshit she'd seen before.

"As long as Pharmadene controls how this gets out, we have a chance to make this change rational. To dispense revival to the people who can make a difference. And that's what we're going to do. Choose who lives on, and ensure their loyalty."

God. Harte made an eerie kind of sense, from a megalomaniac's point of view. If one power—say, Pharmadene—controlled the release of the drug, they could pick and choose the movers and shakers in all areas: politicians, bankers, technologists, the capitalist and political royalty of the entire world. They could manipulate markets, topple—or simply puppet—governments, rig the entire game of life and death in their favor.

And she was right about something else: if Returné got out uncontrolled into the world, it would cause chaos—every grieving parent screaming for his or her children to come back, every husband, father, wife, sister, daughter. Politicians would tilt revivals in their political favor. Armies would become indestructible.

It was a vision of a future in which everybody died, and everyone lived, and nobody really survived. No matter how it played out.

"Pharmadene can still control all this," Harte said. Her voice had gone soft now, and very sure. "We *will* control it. First in our own house; then we broaden our goals to include political and financial leaders immediately after. We're starting with our top ranks today. We'll work our way down through the corporate structure and have everyone on board in the next few days."

The man across the hall had finally stopped screaming, but he was weeping, a desolate and lonely sound. Irene Harte moved to shut off the intercom.

"I'm not dying in here," Bryn said. Harte hesitated, smiled, and shook her head as she flipped the switch. Bryn hit the glass. "Hey! *I'm not dying in here!* I'm going to stop you!"

Harte turned to watch as the newly reborn vice president was led away, and another executive-level victim arrived to take his place.

For two days, the room across the hall saw a steady parade of people, and it was always the same—the indignation, the *don't you know who I am*, the fear, the terror, the death, the scream. Bryn stopped watching. Stopped listening, except to note the scream and keep count of how many had been . . . processed. It went on twenty-four-seven, and after a while she fell asleep. It felt obscene to sleep while people were dying, but all the self-loathing in the world couldn't keep her awake.

She got thirsty first, then hungry.

No one came. She received nothing at all.

On the morning of the second day, she noticed that her skin was starting to get dry. It might have been the lack of humidity in the room, but she didn't think so. The nanites couldn't manufacture water or energy for her muscles; dehydration would render her helpless first.

But what scared her much, much more than the dryness and her cracked lips and parched mouth were the ominous dark bruises that formed under her skin. She woke up from a restless nap on the afternoon of the second day and noticed discoloration on the side of her palm, where it had been resting against the floor. She rubbed at it, and it gradually faded; when she unsnapped the coverall and checked the hip she'd been lying on, it, too, had a bruise.

Lividity.

"No." She massaged the bruise away with trembling fingers. "No, no, this isn't going to happen. It's not." *He promised.*

She couldn't count on him anymore. McCallister was on the run, a fugitive at best. She was inside Pharmadene, in a fortress, and they were killing everyone here, systematically. McCallister would be an insane fool to set foot in this place ever again. He had to cut his losses and run, get help from the government or the military or the FBI or the fucking SEC. *Anyone*, to shut this down before it was too late.

Harte's plan was moving along nicely; someone had posted an org chart printout on the wall that Bryn could just barely make out, and it looked like they'd gotten through the executive ranks. Now there were two rooms in use, one just visible at an acute angle down the hall—two that Bryn could see, constantly processing live people in, revived people out. She couldn't afford to care, not even when one of the women—only a little older than Bryn, pretty—broke free and ran screaming and ended up banging uselessly on Bryn's glass, staring into Bryn's face. In her struggles, she hit the intercom, and for a deadly thirty seconds Bryn had to listen to the woman plead for help, for mercy, for her children.

Then, pathetically, scream for her mom, like a terrified child.

After that, Bryn didn't stand at the window anymore. She huddled in the corner, back to the view, head down.

Waiting.

By day three—as best she could count it—her muscles were starting to shake, and her skin wasn't dry any longer. It was moist, but not in a healthy way. And it hurt. Her nerves caught fire and burned, a low boil at first but growing worse with every breath, every minute.

She had two more days of this, maybe three. Maybe even *four.*

I am not dying here, she told herself. *I'm not.*

But she was, with every second, dying a little bit more.

And the expected interrogation didn't come.

Bryn lost count. It wasn't sleep so much as unconsciousness that took her the next time; she woke up with livid red marks on her blotched skin where her weight had rested, and the torment of her nerves was like a blowtorch being applied all over her body, without respite or mercy. She couldn't stop crying.

Walking was better than sitting. She was starting to lose the ability to do it smoothly; it was more of a stumble now, and she trailed her violently shaking fingers over the wall to keep herself upright as she moved around the room, around the room, around the room. People dying and screaming and dying and screaming and she was going insane, she knew she was, and oh, *God*, it hurt. It wasn't supposed to be this way.

Patrick had promised. *Promised.*

She was halfway through her tenth methodical circuit of the room when something ... changed. A shift in the room's pressure, a *breeze*. Fresh, cool air moving against her skin, stirring her hair.

She sighed and wavered on her feet, then clumsily turned to look.

The door was open, and three masked medical personnel stood there. Maybe Harte was going to show a little mercy. Maybe she was going to end this, after all. Better being cut apart like a chicken than another three or four days of this, and worse.

Bryn tried to walk to them, but her legs gave out, and she fell. Two guards stepped around the medicos and stoically picked her up, dragging her out of the room and down a pristine white hallway. Bryn's head sagged backward. She watched the lights flicker overhead without any real idea about what was happening, until she was lowered into a chair, her damp, filthy jumpsuit stripped off and replaced with a clean one, and a gowned, masked, and gloved woman gave her a shot.

The needle didn't feel like a little stick; it felt like impalement on a red-hot iron, and Bryn screamed and cried and tried to pull away. They held her in place. Another shot followed. Then another.

The woman sighed and stripped her mask down. "That'll do it," she said. "It'll take time for her to come back, though. I'm not sure she's really rational at this point. You'll have to wait for her cognition to return."

Bryn hadn't seen her come in, but there was another woman in the room now, without the mask or gown. She was wearing a suit. Her name was ... was ...

Harte.

"Keep her strapped in, just in case," Irene Harte said. "I'm going to go check progress on the org charts. I'll be back to question her in an hour. Be sure not to give her too much; there's no need to drag this out for another entire week. I need a few hours of lucid interrogation, and then you can put her back in the room until she's finished."

"Yes, ma'am." The woman nodded. She was a pretty lady, with shiny black hair bobbed around her jawline and a mobile, kind face.

And she was *familiar*. Bryn studied her, blinking, trying to force her sluggish brain back to action. The woman started fastening big Velcro restraint straps around her arms and legs, watching Irene Harte as the woman pulled out a cell phone and dialed on her way out of the room.

As soon as the door clicked shut, the woman ripped the restraints open again with furious strength. "Bryn? Bryn, are you with us? Can you understand me?"

Oh. She *knew her.* Flower, some kind of flower. She was Manny's girlfriend. . . .

"Pansy," Bryn murmured. "Pansy Taylor. You shouldn't be here."

"Yeah, no kidding. Nobody should be here. I know it hurts." From the appalled look on Pansy's face, Bryn gathered that she wasn't looking very good. "You're going to be all right. I gave you boosters. You'll feel better soon."

"We can't wait," the other man said, looking toward the door. He also lowered his mask. His face was pale and set, and she knew him, too. Joe. Joe Fideli.

"You were shot," Bryn said.

Joe laughed, but it sounded all wrong. He glanced at her, then quickly away, and she saw muscles jumping in his tight jawline. "I checked myself out once Pat told me you'd gone missing." He moved his shoulder a little, and winced. "I'm not supposed to be getting in any wrestling matches. Doctor's orders, so don't go kicking my ass like you usually do." He sounded like the old Joe, but his eyes were haunted and worried. Not for himself, Bryn realized. For her. God, how bad was she?

Worse than she'd thought. The blowtorch of pain was dialing down a little, but when she glanced down at her hands, she saw how discolored they were, how . . . inhuman.

"We have to move," Pansy said. "We don't have much time left." She nodded to the two security men still in the room with them, and Bryn's sluggish brain woke up enough to wonder why Joe wasn't worried about their overhearing. Pansy said, "Gentlemen: this is a Condition Diamond situation, and I'm invoking your protocols. Protect our escape at all costs; do you understand? Acknowledge these orders. You first."

"Yes, ma'am, acknowledging Condition Diamond. I will protect your escape at all costs," said the first man. He was familiar, too; he was the one who'd taken Bryn to Harte's office, and then to the white room. His partner echoed the same words; then they moved as a team out into the hallway as Pansy took Bryn's arm and got her on her feet.

"Hold on to me," she said. "I know it's not easy for you to move fast. Do your best, okay?"

"Gun," Bryn said, and licked her dry, desiccated lips. "I need a gun." Her voice was hoarse and faint, but steady. Joe reached under his surgical gown and came out with two weapons. He chambered a round in one and handed it to her.

"Point and shoot," he said. "Try not to get me or Pansy. We're the ones around here now who don't get up again so easy."

The guards. Bryn's brain kept chewing away at the question, and finally, she understood. The guards had been killed and revived, probably under Irene Harte's new corporate loyalty program; that left them open to protocol orders, if you knew the keys.

Which Joe and Pansy did. Condition Sapphire made you follow orders, even to confessing to everything you knew. "What's Condition Diamond?" she asked.

"Not really the time, Bryn."

"I want to know."

"All right." Joe exchanged a quick glance with Pansy, who was now holding a gun of her own. "Condition Diamond is a lockout command. Once it's triggered, it can't be countermanded, and the revived will follow that last order to the end, no matter what happens. We programmed it into a few of the security guys along the way, just in case we needed a back door; it's supposed to be reserved for military use only. You haven't got it, in case you were wondering."

"I wasn't," she said. That was a lie. She'd been worried.

Just then, a Pharmadene security man out in the hall noticed their little party, and the two guarding it. "Charlie, I thought you were supposed to keep her in the room—" he said.

That was as far as he got, because Charlie—one of their two guards—immediately fired point-blank into the man's face, and not just once; Bryn counted three shots in quick succession, and then Charlie nodded to his partner and they began taking down anyone and everyone in the hallway with cool, cruel, methodical precision.

Condition Diamond. Whatever their past loyalties might have been, they were owned by Pansy now.

Joe took point, moving as fast as possible to sweep the area ahead of them. He took down three guards who came swarming out of a hallway, checked the corners, and motioned Bryn and Pansy forward. Behind them, gunfire continued to rattle as their rear guard held on. From the sound of it, they were getting shot to pieces.

Bryn said, "You . . . you used them . . . like weapons—"

"I know. I had to." Pansy gasped, staggering under Bryn's almost deadweight. "Believe me, I'd rather not have done it. Harte has the cancel protocols for everything except Condition Diamond; if we expected to get anywhere, we needed to cause some chaos any way we could, and that meant making them into suicide troops. Come on, Bryn—we have to keep moving!"

"Hurts," Bryn whispered. That was an understatement. Her whole body felt as if she were being boiled alive.

"In here," Joe called, and kicked in a door. It was some kind of laboratory, and there were two scientists inside; they both held up their hands and backed off to the walls as he pointed the gun at them. "Condition Sapphire! Down. Down on the ground and stay there!"

They hugged the floor. Joe edged past them to another door, one with a swipe card lock. He looked back at Pansy. "Did you get it?"

"Here." She reached under her gown and handed over a Pharmadene ID, one with a gold stripe. Bryn got a blurred glimpse of it in passing, and she was almost sure it was Irene Harte's. "Hurry. They'll lock it down as soon as she realizes I lifted it."

He dragged it through the reader. The light turned green, and Fideli slammed open the door.

Bullets rang on the metal next to his head, and he ducked.

Bryn pulled free of Pansy, braced both hands on her gun, and aimed over her body to put three rounds in the guard standing at the end of the room. All head shots.

He went down. So did Bryn, in a helpless gasping heap, from the agony of the recoil.

"Damn," Fideli said, and helped her up again. "Nice shooting."

"He's moving," Pansy said. She sounded like she was about to be sick. "His brain's exposed, but he's still moving."

"It'll take him a couple of hours to heal up. He's out of the fight, for now." Fideli kicked the man's gun away, just to be sure, and rolled him out of the way of the door that he'd been guarding.

It was a small loading-dock door.

This time, when Fideli swiped his card, the light flashed red, and a siren began to sound. "She realized we had it," Pansy said. "Unless we can get this door open, we're stuck. We need out. *Now.*" She stripped off the surgical smock, cap, and mask, and pulled out a gun of her own. "Any ideas?"

Fideli shot the card reader into junk, but the door stayed firmly down. He tossed the ID back to Pansy, who stuck it in her pocket. "Not so much," he said. "Retreat?"

"They're coming," Bryn said. She limped off to the side and braced her arms on a lab table. She'd need the support. The shooting she'd already done had taken a lot out of her, and she felt as weak as a little girl. *Water. I need water.*

No time for that now.

Her searching gaze fell on neatly ranked and labeled jars, beakers, and canisters against the wall on racks. "Pansy," she said. "Acid." There was a whole row of it, in a multitude of flavors and packaging. Pansy let out a surprised gasp and ran over to inspect the labels. She grabbed two large bottles, a safety face shield, and thick protective gloves that came up to her armpits.

"Back off," she ordered Joe. "Don't breathe it in." She opened up the first bottle and splashed it in a golden arc over the corrugated metal door that refused to open for them, and kept splashing as it began to hiss and eat through the thick surface. The first bottle emptied. She used the second. A noxious, thick, burning fog filled the room, and Joe and Pansy were coughing and choking on it.

Bryn was, too, but it didn't matter. Like the man she'd shot in the head, everything was temporary. She could burn black holes all over her lungs and it would all be okay in the morning.

She grabbed the gloves from Pansy, who had sunk to the floor to gasp in cleaner air, and began punching at the weakened metal. It sagged and melted, and her blows bent it outward.

Bryn made a hole, then dragged Pansy over and pushed her through it, then went back for Joe, who was staggering blindly through the corrosive air. "Don't breathe it! Keep your eyes shut!" she yelled at him, and he nodded, eyes tightly shut. She shoved him through the narrow opening and dived through after.

There were guards swarming from both sides, but their little escape party was lucky in one small way. . . . A Pharmadene van sat at the dock, back doors open. The driver ran when she pointed the gun at him, and left the keys in the ignition. "Get in!" Bryn yelled. She climbed into the driver's seat and heard the other two clamber aboard; she checked through the wire mesh to be sure as Joe swung the back doors shut and slapped his hand on the van's side.

"Move it!" he yelled back.

She put it in drive and punched it.

Driving straight at the guards was the only way to go. Some got out of the way; two stood their ground, firing right through the windshield. She took two bullets, one in the shoulder, one in the throat, and the pain washed over her in a blinding, crippling wave.

Not going to die. Not here. Not now. I can't.

She held on, kept her foot down, and hit the gates at full speed. The crash almost bounced her out of the seat, but the gates gave way first.

"Tire shredders!" Joe rasped, crawling past her into the passenger seat. "Go off-road; go around!"

She saw the pavement lifting up ahead in a line of black spikes. Automated defenses, designed to stop any cars that made it this far through the gates. Automatic weapons fire was peppering the back of the van, and in the cracked rear-view mirror, Bryn saw that three Pharmadene sedans were headed out in pursuit.

She turned the wheel at the last minute and went off the road. There were low stone walls designed to keep her on the path, but she didn't care about the damage to the van, and the walls hadn't been reinforced; they smashed apart under the van's momentum, and she squeezed by the tire shredders with about an inch to spare.

The first pursuing sedan hit them head-on. All four tires blew, and the driver lost control. The car flipped, shedding glass and one rag-doll passenger.

The others managed to avoid the wreckage, and crawled around the edges before accelerating again in pursuit.

"Still with us!" Joe said. "Punch it! Go right at the intersection!"

She took the turn, barely slowing, and fought to keep the top-heavy vehicle from tipping. In the back, Pansy threw open one of the back doors, opened a box marked with hazardous materials symbols, and began throwing the contents onto the closest pursuing sedan. It must have been more acid, because the hood began to smoke and melt, and the mist pitted and clouded the windshield.

The car veered off and smashed full-speed into a pole, which tilted and crashed, downing power lines in blue-white sparks.

The third car stopped, tangled in the high voltage.

Bryn didn't slow down. Joe kept dictating turns, and finally Bryn eased off the gas as they reached a busier area. "God," she whispered. "It actually worked."

"No, it didn't," Joe said. "They're tracking us." He looked over at her with a strange kind of sadness. "They're tracking *you*. And we're going to have to take care of that right now."

Bryn took in a deep breath. "It's not going to be painless, is it?"

"No," Joe said, and turned to look at the road. "I'm afraid it's not going to be painless at all."

Chapter 11

The pain slowed its rush through Bryn's system to a merely unbearable ache. She tried not to look at her hands, or catch any hint of a reflection, but even so, her eyes wouldn't stay away from seeking out some sign of regeneration.

By the time they'd switched out of the Pharmadene van to another car, her fingers were starting to look human again. Sickly and bruised, but *living*.

She was so grateful that it was hard not to sob again, but she couldn't. Not now. Not when Pansy and Joe had risked so much, and they were all still in danger.

Joe Fideli had all kinds of unexpectedly criminal talents; he could boost cars (a cargo van from a rental-car lot, taken from the "fixed" part of the repair area, which would cause the most confusion and delay), he could circumvent alarm systems (like the one at the veterinary clinic, where he took surgical supplies and animal tranquilizers), and most important, he had an RFID scanner and blank credit cards.

He sent Pansy for a walk at the Westfield Horton mall with the scanner tucked into her small clutch purse, and taught her the fine art of butt scanning. "Men are the easiest," he said, as Bryn rested in the passenger seat of the newly stolen van, downing bottle after bottle of water from a twelve-pack he'd taken from the vet's. "Credit cards are in their back pockets. Just brush the scanner up against them and listen for the tone in the earpiece. A good scan will chime. Get as many as you can in fifteen minutes; then meet us back here."

Pansy hesitated, looking at the two of them. "You're sure? You don't need me to help with this?"

"It's not going to be pretty. Better leave it to me," Joe said. "Go on. Get us some money; we need it."

Pansy went out the back, and Joe watched as she walked across the parking lot and entered the multilevel jumble of the mall. "Bryn? You ready?"

"I guess." She finished the bottle and set it aside. She felt better. Stronger. Almost herself again. "Where do you want me?"

"Here." He flipped levers and laid down one of the rear seats, creating a long, flat space. She climbed over and sat on it. "Lie down."

Bryn complied, trying not to wince, and looked into his eyes as he bent closer. "How bad's it going to be?"

"Nothing like what you've already had," he said. "How's the throat?"

She cleared it experimentally. "Not too bad. I sound like a whiskey bum, though."

"It's a little bit sexy. All right, I'm going to give you a shot. I'm not sure how long it'll last; from what Pat said, painkillers wear off quicker than normal, since the nanites clear them from your bloodstream, but we'll give it a try. I'll work fast."

She nodded and tried not to think about it much. The shot was familiar by now, a bright pinpoint of pain, then a flood of warmth that quickly sank into a blissful warm numbness. "Oh," she murmured. "Nice." Then she couldn't talk at all.

"Yeah, I gave you an elephant load," he said. "Here we go."

He lifted her right knee up. She felt it distantly, like something in a dream, and then he rolled her over on her side. That felt good, too. She smiled and tried to tell him how it felt but her lips wouldn't make words, just bright bubbles of sounds.

His knife cut a slash in the back of her thigh.

Bryn made a wordless sound of surprise, betrayal, and pain; even with the numbness and happy, drugged warmth, she felt the invasion, and kept feeling it as the knife cut deeper, separating muscle, digging, probing. She tried to wiggle away from it. Joe's hand clamped down hard, holding her in place. "Steady," he said. He sounded weirdly out of tune. "Almost there. It's in deep, and I'm going to have to pry it off the bone." She felt another small, bright star of a shot. Another cascade of warmth. This time, it didn't crest quite as high, and it receded much faster, leaving her cold and horribly aware that the knife was in her, moving, *prying*. She whimpered and panted and tried not to scream, and then something happened with a white-hot stab of pure agony and she screamed into Joe's muffling hand and couldn't stop until it began to subside.

"Good," he said. His voice was low and soothing. "You did good, Bryn. It's out. The wound's already closing. Relax now; relax."

She kept on shuddering and whimpering, and a heavy warmth dropped over her—a blanket, smelling of cigars and wet dog. She didn't care what it smelled like. Anything helped.

Pansy came back about ten minutes later. She froze, silhouetted in the opening for a second, then climbed in and slammed the door fast. "God, it looks like a slaughterhouse in here," she said. "Is she all right?"

"She will be. Here." Joe handed her something wrapped in a piece of tissue. "Take that; throw it in the back of a truck that's getting ready to pull out. Go."

She handed him her purse and bailed out again without any questions. Joe took the scanner out and looked at the stored results.

"Hey," Bryn whispered. "Did it work?"

"The scanner? Yeah. I've got six cards I can work with here. It'll get us what we need."

"Can't they trace them?"

"Sure. But we don't use them. We make the clones and sell them on, and use the cash we get paid for it. That's untraceable." He glanced back at her. "You doing all right?"

"Yeah." She swallowed and tried not to think about the mess of her leg. "It still hurts."

"No doubt. I had to take out a pretty good chunk of bone. It'll heal, but it'll hurt while it does. Best thing for you to do is stay horizontal." He uncapped another bottle of water and handed it to her, and helped her sit up to sip. She almost threw it back up, but the nausea passed quickly.

She *was* healing. Another half an hour, maybe, and she'd be almost normal again. McCallister would be impressed with the speed of—

McCallister. Bryn remembered in a horrified rush that she hadn't told Fideli about Harte's orders ... and McCallister wasn't with them. "Joe? Where is he?" Her voice trembled.

"Pat's on the run, like us. I'll get in touch with him and let him know you're okay."

"But he's alive?"

"Yeah. She sent a team to get him. Didn't work out so well for them, I understand. Harte sent one of her revived men after him, and Pat sent him back in boxes." He slid a credit card blank into the machine and pressed buttons. "He'll join us when it's safe."

"It's never going to be safe. Do you know what they were doing in there?"

"Ramping up the program." Joe sounded grim. "Harte was getting pressure from the CEO to go to the military with the drug, and he was going to get his way. She had to move if she wanted to keep control. She did, I guess. That place is a death factory. She addicts everybody, and then nobody can cross her."

"It's worse than that," Bryn said. "They're going after politicians. Bankers. Leaders of all kinds. She's out to take over, Joe. *Really* take over. And she has to be stopped."

"Nice idea, babe, but we had a hell of a time shooting our own way out. I don't think waging a three-person crusade is going to get us anywhere. Four, if we can hook up with Pat. Five, if you count Manny, which I don't." He shook his head. "Best we can do is blow the whistle loud and hard, now that we have you."

"Have ... me?"

"Without you, we're paranoid schizophrenics babbling about the zombie apocalypse. With you, maybe we've got a fighting chance to have someone believe us."

"Is that why you—"

"No," Joe said. "McCallister was going to come get you himself. He said he promised. It would have been a disaster; no way could he have gotten in without being caught, much less gotten you out. Me and Pansy, we're not really on their radar. Well, weren't, until then. I gotta tell you, Pat and I don't come to blows real often, but we did over this thing. He was damn sure going to get himself killed for you." He gave her a long, assessing look. "You do know why, right?" She shook her head, but it was a pro forma lie, and he smiled. "Hey, I'm the last one to point fingers about getting personally involved. I met a girl on a job once. Look how that turned out."

"You mean Kylie?"

"Exactly. Being professional will only get you so far, and then you've got to be human."

Horror flooded her, on the heels of that warm moment. "Joe—your family—"

"They're safe," he said. "Pat saw them moved out to a secure location, as soon as he knew this was going south. Nobody's going to touch my kids, or Kylie."

"I'm so sorry."

"Yeah, well, it's going to take a bouquet of roses the size of the frigging Rose Parade to make this up to her, but my wife knew what she was getting when she married me. And the kids think it's a cool adventure." Fideli shrugged. "Which it is, right?"

Unbelievable. "You got *shot.*"

"Eh, I've been shot for worse causes. And we just rescued you, shot our way out, had a car chase. Plus, there's this whole coming-back-from-the-dead thing. My kids would be *very* impressed."

"I'm very impressed, too."

"Well, it wasn't a clockwork operation, but it'll do. At least you're on the mend."

For now. Bryn swallowed again, miserably aware of her own vulnerability. "Joe . . . I'm going to need another shot," she said. "And one tomorrow. And one the day after. What exactly are we going to do about that?"

Fideli kept his eyes on the credit card machine. "You want me to lie to you and tell you I've got a brilliant plan on that?"

"Would you?"

"Probably not. I'm hoping McCallister does."

Pansy slid the door back, jumped in, and slammed it shut, panting from her run. "Done. I put the thing in the bed of a truck with Texas plates. As far as I know, they'll chase him all the way back to San Antonio," she said, and took a moment to lay her hand gently on Bryn's head. "You doing okay?"

"Peachy," Bryn murmured. "I have a giant hole in my leg, and we were just talking about how much Returné we don't have."

Pansy gave her a slow, delighted smile and said, "You two don't think I'd let you down, do you?" Even Fideli turned to look at her when she said that, eyebrows raised. Pansy picked up a small box from the floorboard. "*Et voilà.*" She opened it.

Inside were vials filled with clear liquid. Seven of them.

"How . . ." Bryn's voice failed her.

"Where do you think I got the shot to give you? I made sure I was the one Harte tapped to pull it from the supply. They had two boxes out on the cart, since they were assembly-lining the staff. I grabbed one. We'll need to pick up syringes—that's all. Oh, and just in case . . ." Pansy handed her a gold-edged Pharmadene ID. "Irene Harte's. It probably won't work, but just in case you ever wanted a souvenir, that's probably the best you can get. Manny won't let me keep it. He'll assume it's bugged."

"Is it?"

"Not anymore." Pansy gave her a cheery smile.

"I'd kiss you if I could get up," Bryn said. "God, thank you."

"No charge. Well, no *extra* charge. Joe's already paying me."

"Paying you . . ."

"I don't come cheap, sweetie," Pansy said. "Manny doesn't like it when I leave him all alone. He's got another batch of inhibitor ready, by the way, so when you take me home, you can get your booster on that, too."

A week. A whole luxurious *week* of life, guaranteed right there.

And what about after that? But for the first time, Bryn felt the tight fist of anxiety in her chest ease, just a little, and as Fideli and Pansy spoke in low, quiet tones, and Fideli pulled the van out to drive on, she finally surrendered to her need to rest.

When they finally arrived at Manny Glickman's lab, hours later, it was chaos. Even Pansy seemed shocked when, as she helped Bryn in the big fire door, she ran into a giant pallet of neatly stacked boxes. "Great," she said, staring at them. "Just great."

"What's going on?" Fideli asked, from behind them.

"Get in and stay right here," Pansy said. "Whatever happens, don't go all Rambo on me, all right?"

That didn't sound good. Neither did the tension in Pansy's voice. Edging around the boxes, Bryn saw why; the place was crowded with boxes stacked everywhere. No more lab equipment; it was all packed. Big machines were crated and secured, ready for transport. The curtains at the back of the big room were open, and more pallets of boxes were stacked there.

"Freeze!" a magnified voice said from overhead, and Bryn looked up sharply to see a figure above them on a narrow catwalk. It was almost obscured by the lights, and she squinted and just barely made out Manny Glickman's form up there.

He worked the action on a pump shotgun, and the crisp *chunk-chunk* sound made them all obey. Even Fideli. Bryn raised her hands in surrender.

"Jesus, Manny, it's me." Pansy sighed. "What the hell are you doing?"

"Moving," he said. "You were supposed to be back four hours ago."

"I told you it wasn't guaranteed, baby."

"Four hours ago."

"You didn't pack all this in the last four hours."

Manny was silent for a few seconds, then said, "Are you vouching for them, Pansy?"

"Of course I am, or I wouldn't have brought them up here, would I?" Her voice was gentle, but as Bryn glanced at her, she saw that Pansy was worried. "It's all right. Trust me. Her tracker's gone, and we weren't followed."

"I thought about blowing up the van," Manny said. "You know that, don't you? You didn't come in the right car. You said you'd be in a red sedan."

"Pansy, what the hell ...?" Fideli murmured. She shushed him.

"We had to improvise. Things were crazy. But we got out, and everything's fine, and I brought you a present." She held up a single vial of Returné. "Enough to run tests on for months."

It was a shiny treat, but Manny failed to take the bait. "Make them sit down on the floor, right now. Hands behind their heads."

"Manny—"

"Now!" His shout rattled the rafters. Pansy sighed and turned to Bryn and Joe.

"Please," she said. "I need to back him off the ledge."

Kneeling down with her stiff and still-healing leg hurt, but it was better than risking Manny going all hair-trigger on them; Bryn was more concerned about Joe, who'd had a very full day for a man with a recently collapsed lung. He shrugged off her silent concern, though, and sat down a lot more easily than she did. By unspoken agreement, they kept their hands in the air.

"Okay, they're down," Pansy said. "Can I *please* come talk to you?"

"If they move—"

"They're not going to move. Can *I?*"

He hesitated for a long moment, and then said, "I'm coming down. Stay there."

His heavy footsteps clanked overhead and down a staircase somewhere in the shadows to the right. When Manny finally came back into the glow of the overheads, he was dressed in black—black turtleneck, black pants, a black tactical vest with pockets bulging with ammunition. He carried the shotgun at a neutral but ready position.

And his eyes were more than a little crazy. He didn't take his gaze away from Bryn and Fideli, except for a very fast glance at Pansy.

He handed her a syringe.

"What's this for?"

"Blood sample," he said.

"She's okay, I told you—"

"Not from her. From you."

"Jesus, Manny!"

This time, the glance he sent her lingered, and was half-apologetic. But still half-crazy. "I need to know that you're still you. They could have revived you. You could be acting under protocols."

She didn't try to talk him out of it, and Bryn thought it was sad that Manny's paranoia was actually quite practical now; she wouldn't have believed that kind of thing two weeks ago, but now, it was surprisingly rational. Pansy just walked over to the nearest flat surface, drew a sample of her own blood (not something Bryn thought she could have accomplished with nearly as much aplomb), and handed back the full syringe. Manny backed up, keeping his eyes fixed on all of them, opened up a box nearby, and took out what looked like a sheet of paper. He squirted a small amount of the blood onto the surface. It soaked in quickly, and a blue ring spread out from the crimson blot.

Manny's body language visibly relaxed. "You're okay," he said. He sounded shaken. "You're really okay."

"Of course I'm okay, idiot." Pansy took the shotgun from him, broke open the stock, and set it aside. Then she hugged him, hard, and kissed him. "Thanks for worrying."

"I always worry."

"Okay, worrying more than normal."

Manny looked over his shoulder, first at Bryn, then Fideli. "I know about her. What about him?"

"He's all right."

"Test him. Prove it."

"Okay. First, we don't need a whole syringe full, right?" She took the syringe from Manny's fingers and disposed of the rest of the blood in a haz-mat container off to the side, grabbed a test sheet from the box, and went to Fideli's side. "Knife?"

"Yo," he said, and took one out of his belt—a big, wicked thing with an edge sharp enough to cut the light. Pansy pressed it lightly to his thumb and smeared the thin crimson line that appeared onto the paper.

Blue halo.

"See?" she asked, and handed Fideli's knife back. "You can get up now. It's okay."

Manny clearly didn't agree, but he didn't argue. "We can't stay here," he said. "I've already called the vans. We'll be moved by the end of the day and in the new location."

"Manny, there's no need to do this. We can stay here."

"No. I need to move. Too many people in and out. It's not secure."

Pansy rolled her eyes. "*Not* what I needed today. All right, we'll move. But first, Bryn needs her inhibitor booster, and then I'll send them on their way."

"All right." Manny pointed at a set of boxes across the lab. "Third carton from the bottom. I packed it underneath the extra saline."

The boxes weren't labeled, Bryn realized—not a single one. "Do you remember what's in every one of them?" she asked.

Manny looked at her. "You can put your hands down," he said. "I'm not going to shoot you."

"Yeah," Pansy said, as she walked toward the indicated boxes. "But only because I took his gun."

"You really remember what's in the boxes. There must be two hundred of them!"

"Two hundred thirty-six," he said. "Not counting the crated machines. Yes, I do."

"What happens when they mix them all up in moving vans?"

"I pay them to make sure they get stacked and delivered in order." His green eyes were less crazy now, and he frowned as he looked her over. "You don't look so great."

Bryn laughed a little. "It's been . . . stressful."

"They were letting her rot," Fideli said, "for science."

"Really?" Those eyes gleamed suddenly. "Did you get any records? Video? That would be very useful."

"Jesus." Fideli raised his voice. "Pansy, you really sleep with this guy?"

"I keep one eye open," she called back, as she restacked cartons—keeping them, Bryn noticed, in precisely the same order as they'd been. "Got it!" She held up an IV bag and needle kit. "Manny, stop being so creepy. It was awful for her. It really was."

He didn't look noticeably sorry. "I'm sure it was, but still, the opportunity to study something like that . . ."

"Yeah, well, I hope you won't have the opportunity to do it on me," Bryn said. "Where do I sit?"

"Over here," Pansy said. She hooked the IV bag on a rolling stand that hadn't yet been packed and pulled over a straight-backed chair. Bryn sat and let Pansy numb the back of her hand, then guide in the needle. It still, as always, hurt, but the cool rush of fluid into her veins soothed things nicely. "Should take about an hour. I'm going to get you some more water. Anything to eat?"

Food. Bryn's stomach rumbled, and she realized that she hadn't really even thought about food for so long, it was an abstract concept. "Uh, anything," she said. "Whatever isn't packed, I guess."

"I'll find something. Joe?"

"I'll have what she's having. Minus the IV." Fideli put his back against the wall and leaned. Now that he wasn't under threat of death, he allowed himself to look tired. He nodded to Manny. "So you're the FBI guy, right? The one Mc-Callister knows."

"You know McCallister."

"Yeah, old friends. I kinda work for him."

"Then I suppose you're all right," Manny said grudgingly. "He'd probably take it badly if I'd shot you."

Fideli grinned, a surprising flash of white, even teeth. "I'd like to think so. Glad I didn't shoot you, too."

Manny raised his bushy eyebrows. "Do you think you could have, before I fired the shotgun?" Fideli stared back. He didn't answer, and he didn't need to, really. Manny nodded and sat down on the edge of one of the wooden pallets. "Interesting."

"Mutual, if you do half the stuff he says you do."

"Interesting that he's talked to you about me, and not to me about you."

"I've known him longer," Fideli said. "And he meant to bring me over here. He just didn't get the chance."

That made them fall silent for a moment. Bryn felt the

anxious flutter in her stomach at the thought of McCallister, still missing, and she knew Joe was feeling it, too. Maybe even Manny was, as well.

Pansy came back with cups of instant soup all around, and by the time they were emptied, the four of them had formed a fragile kind of trust.

For now.

Manny kicked them out as soon as Bryn's IV was finished. So much for trust.

Pansy walked them down to the van. "Sorry about this," she said. "Once he gets in this mood, I can't talk him out of it. We'll move the lab; he'll settle down; things will go back to normal. But I can't take you with us. I can't even tell you where we're going, because he won't tell me either. I'll contact you later." She passed Bryn a bundle of things. "Here. I think they'll fit. You can't run around in some numbered paper jumpsuit and expect not to get noticed."

"Thanks."

Fideli nodded to her, too. "Thanks, Pansy," he said. "Nice working with you."

"You too, Joe. It was good to get out and stretch my legs again." Pansy hugged Bryn, and she hugged her back, surprised but pleased. "You, girl, you take care of yourself. I'll see you in a week for your booster."

"Promise?"

Pansy silently crossed her heart. "Get going. The moving vans will be here soon, and that makes him extra paranoid, even with all the background checks."

"How the hell do you put up with it?" Joe asked, climbing into the van's driver's seat.

"I love him," she said. "And he's not just paranoid. People really are out to get him. And hey, seems like we're all in that boat now, right?" She leaned in to put a kiss on Joe's cheek. "You take care, sweetie. Call me anytime you need a partner in crime."

Bryn buckled her seat belt and rolled down the window as they left the safety and shadows of the warehouse to let a fresh breeze blow through the van. The inside of the vehicle frankly reeked; the smell of her blood made her a little light-headed, or maybe that was the inhibitors taking hold. She was feeling herself again, finally; her leg's ache had subsided, and when she ran her fingers over the back of it, she felt only a faint and fading scar.

"You can change clothes in the back," Fideli said. "I'm not gonna peek."

"You saw it all anyway." She sighed. "It'll be nice to not be dressed in paper."

And it was, very nice, from the soft cotton underwear to the long-sleeved thermal tee and jeans. Pansy had included a pair of slip-on flats for shoes, which would have to do, for now. At least it wasn't cold outside.

Bryn climbed over the seats and buckled herself back in place. "Where are we going?" she asked.

"Safe house up in the hills," Fideli replied. "Strap in; we don't need a ticket when the back of the van looks like a butcher shop died in it."

"Is McCallister there . . . ?"

"I don't know where Pat is," Fideli said. "When he's ready to contact us, he knows my number. We've both got disposable burner phones. It's the best we can do, for now." He was quiet for a moment, watching traffic, watching the rearview mirror. Road noise hissed through the cabin. "You probably ought to know something."

"What?"

"McCallister made me promise something. If I couldn't get you out, or if . . . if you were too far gone, he made me promise to . . ."

"To end things for me," Bryn said. "So I wouldn't suffer."

"Yeah. I thought you'd want to know that." He pulled in a deep breath and let it out, slowly. "These are some fucked-up times if that's romantic, Bryn."

It made her smile, and it made her eyes well up at the same time. She turned her face away and let the wind whip against her cheeks to dry them as tears rolled down. "Thanks," she said. "I did want to know that."

He turned the radio on after that, and surprised her by singing along to it. He had a good voice, baritone, and did a mean version of Harry Nilsson's song about the limes and coconuts. It almost felt . . . normal.

That was something Bryn realized she craved most. Normality. The feeling that her reality was still the same one that all these other people shared, the ones driving on the freeway next to them. They were headed to work or play or home or shopping. They had lives, goals, plans, challenges that didn't include rotting away inside a dead shell of a body.

She envied them all, so strongly that it hurt. Somehow, without ever meaning to, she'd become an alien, stranded in a strange yet achingly familiar landscape.

"Bryn?"

"What?"

"Stop feeling sorry for yourself," Joe said. "My family's stuck somewhere halfway across the country, if not outside the country, and I don't know when or if I'll ever see them again. Deal with your shit and don't wallow in it."

"You—" She bit back her angry retort, and took a deep breath. "I am. I will. I just feel—"

"Yeah, I know," he said, more gently. "Lost. There's a lot of that going around."

A phone was ringing somewhere, a harsh distant buzzing sound that brought Bryn up out of a restless light sleep in a strange bed. Her eyes snapped open, and for a moment she didn't know where she was—a darkened room, with streetlights casting slanted shadows across the carpet through the blinds. The place smelled stale and unlived-in, and she finally remembered that she was in the safe house, a nondescript ranch house with a pathetic straggly lawn and secondhand furniture in the run-down rooms.

The phone was ringing down the hall, where Joe Fideli was sleeping. She heard him answer it, although she couldn't hear what he was saying.

Exhaustion pinned her flat to the bed until she heard a light knock on her closed bedroom door, and she rolled out to swing it open.

"You're dressed," he said. He sounded surprised, although he was still in his clothes, too.

"Yeah, I figured we'd better be ready for anything." That, and being dressed made her feel less vulnerable.

She'd spent way too much time in that paper jumpsuit. "You got a call."

"McCallister." Fideli didn't sound thrilled, and that made her muscles tense in anticipation of the bad news. "Listen, I think you'd better sit down, Bryn."

That *really* didn't sound good. She backed up without thinking about it, and eased down onto the bed. He stayed where he was, talking from the doorway. "He's been tracking down your mysterious supplier, and he says he found him."

"So . . . that's good news, right?"

"Yeah, I guess so."

"Who is it?"

"Some guy named Mercer. Jonathan Mercer. Sound familiar?"

It didn't, but then it did. She remembered, far back at the beginning of this nightmare, that McCallister had mentioned the name Mercer. . . . "Mercer and Sams," she said. "They . . . created the drug. Right?"

"Sams offed himself after Pharmadene started the Returné trials; couldn't take the guilt. Mercer's been quietly working like a good beaver ever since, until about a week ago when he went on *vacation*." That last was said with air quotes. "He dropped off of Pharmadene's radar. Translation: he had a heads-up that the big conversion push was coming from Harte, and he didn't want to end up strapped onto a table with a bag over his head. So he bailed, and they've been ripping up streets looking for him ever since. That's stirred up a lot of information, including the fact that apparently Mercer had been quietly setting up his own production line for Returné."

"He could ruin everything for them."

"The only reason he hasn't so far is that it's in his interest to keep this thing a black-market enterprise. They need to shut him down hard and fast. Mercer's a bigger threat to them than any of us are, but he's also damn smart; we all checked him out and found nothing on him until he bolted."

"Joe," she said. Her fists clenched where they rested on her thighs. "Why am I sitting down? What are you not telling me?"

"Mercer wants to make a deal," Joe said. "McCallister's full resources and protection of his fledgling operation, in exchange for keeping you supplied with the drug."

That wasn't so bad. It was for McCallister, obviously, but ... "What else?"

This time, Joe just gave up and said it. "He has leverage," he said. "He has your sister Annie. She never made it to the airport when she left your apartment, and he says he's going to kill her if we don't take a meeting and make a deal. We've got just under two hours. He wants you there."

Annie. Bryn sat frozen; she'd expected ... Well, she didn't know what she'd expected. She hadn't thought they'd go after her family. She was used to thinking of her people as safely distant, away from all this ... but Annalie had walked into the middle of it. Made herself a target.

And Bryn hadn't seen it coming.

"Bryn? Still with me?"

"Yes." She stood up, feeling unnaturally calm and focused. "When do we leave?"

Joe cleared his throat. "That's just it. We don't. McCallister says it's better to keep you out of—"

"Give me the phone, Joe."

"I can't do that."

"Joe." She held her hand out, staring into his eyes. "She's my *sister*. Give me the phone."

He shook his head and handed it over. "His number's in the call list."

Bryn dialed, listened as it rang on the other end, and heard McCallister's voice say, "Bryn. I thought you'd call."

He sounded tense, but there was a kind of animal comfort to hearing him again, hearing him say her name. She shoved all that aside and said, "I'm going to the meeting."

"You can't do that. He's already got too much leverage over—"

"He asked for me, specifically. You know him; you know how ruthless he is. If I don't show up, I'm signing Annie's death warrant," she said. "I'm getting her back, one way or another."

"You're emotionally involved. Let me negotiate this. He will work with me. He doesn't have a choice." He paused for a bare second, and then continued. "You have to trust me to handle this for you. He could be setting us up, and I can't have you complicating things."

"I do trust you," Bryn said. "But I'm still going. Either you tell Joe to drive me or I will find a way to contact Mercer myself. I'm not letting you shield me anymore, McCallister. Not from this."

That brought an even longer silence, and finally, "Put Joe back on the phone."

"No. You tell *me* where this meeting is. If I let you talk to him, you'll probably tell him to drive me around for a while and knock me out when I'm not looking."

McCallister's laugh was dry and humorless. "You know me too well already. All right. Here's the address." He read it to her, and she burned it into her memory; no chance she'd ever forget it. "Leave Joe out of it. He's putting on a good front, but he's hurting, and I don't want to be responsible for landing him back in the hospital. Or the morgue."

"Just you and me, then," she said. "That sounds right."

"Bryn?"

"Yes?"

He was quiet for so long that she thought she'd lost the connection, and then he said, "I wanted to get you out of there myself. You know that, don't you?"

"I do," she said. All the fight went out of her, and she clutched the phone hard, wishing she could see his face. "You told him to kill me if it went wrong. Thank you."

"I keep my word, Bryn. Always. And I promise, we'll get your sister back."

She hung up the phone and slipped it into her pocket, then held out her hand, palm out. "Keys, please," she said. "You're staying here. If you don't believe me, call him back and ask."

Fideli looked at her for a few seconds, clearly trying to decide whether or not she was insane, and then fished the keys out of his pocket and handed them over. "Go in heavy, and go in hot," he said. "You understand what I'm talking about?"

She remembered the same conversation, back on a sweltering afternoon as she labored under the weight of body armor, ballistic helmet, weapons, and the stare of her commanding officer. *We're going in hot.* It hadn't ended well that day. Too many IEDs, too many snipers on the rooftops taking out their supply convoy. She could almost taste the grit of blown sand. "I understand," she said. "Rest. I'll be back."

He reached in his pocket and took out a silver tube. "Don't forget this," he said. "This one's not coded to a particular administrator. You can give it to yourself if you need to."

"Thanks."

She saw him at the window as she drove away into the night, and wondered whether she'd ever see Joe Fideli again. Wondered whether he'd ever see his family, too.

So much had been torn apart, and she still had so far to go.

Going in hot and heavy.

That pretty much described her entire relationship so far with Patrick McCallister, come to think of it.

Chapter 12

Bryn made a fast circuit of the immediate area around the address McCallister had given her; it was a residential area, which made her worry. She'd thought these types of potentially explosive things went on in deserted buildings, vacant warehouses, open lots ... not on a street with brightly colored playhouses and Big Wheels parked in yards.

There was no sign of McCallister, and she had a horrified thought. ... What if he'd deliberately given her the wrong address? And she'd been dumb enough to fall for it? *No, he wouldn't do that. He'd known I was serious. And that I needed to do this.*

Parking the van behind a closed convenience store two blocks away seemed the best option; Bryn locked it and stepped out into the cool predawn darkness. It was misting, and threatening to rain, but the hoodie that Pansy had given her was enough to counter that. The thin shoes were a pain, though. It was hard to feel badass in Payless.

At least she had the gun she'd stolen from Pharmadene, and a supply of ammunition, thanks to Joe. Not as well stocked as Manny Glickman in his fortress, wherever it was now, but it would do ...

She pulled up short after a few steps, because someone was standing in the light of a street lamp twenty feet away, watching her.

Patrick McCallister.

The damp had matted his hair down in a sleek cap around his head, but she'd know him anywhere; if nothing else, nobody she'd ever met had that quality of coiled stillness to their posture. He was wearing dark clothes and a loose Windbreaker that wouldn't have looked odd if it came with big reflective governmental-agency letters on it, but this one was unmarked.

"How'd you know?" she asked him, not coming closer. He shrugged and put his hands into the pockets of his dark jeans.

"Where you'd park? It was tactically the smartest choice," he said. "So I thought you'd find it."

That spoke volumes about what he thought of her . . . and made her ask, "So where did *you* park?"

"Someplace not as tactically sound, but unexpected," he said. He pushed away from the streetlight and walked toward her, taking his time. "You look good."

"You should have seen me a few hours ago," she said. Without conscious decision, she was also walking toward him. *I should have my gun out*, she thought. *I really don't know what he's going to do.* Maybe he'd knock her out and put her back in the van and go do the meeting himself. That would be typical McCallister.

"How bad was it?"

"Ever seen *Night of the Living Dead*? Like that," she said. "Only you're right. I wasn't craving brains."

"At least that's a bright side."

And then he was right there, a foot away, in her space, with only the gently drifting mist between them. His eyes were wide and dark, and she thought, *He's going to do it now; he'll strike*, and she was ready for that, ready to block a punch. . . .

. . . But not, as it turned out, a hug.

She stiffened for a second, then relaxed into the embrace. "I'm sorry," he said. "By the time I found out they'd taken you, they already had you inside Pharmadene. I didn't have a chance to intercept. When you didn't come out, I knew they were going to let you . . ."

"Decay," she said, very quietly. "I have to face it. I'm dead. I'll always be dead. This, all this feeling and looking alive, it's just . . . just cosmetics." She pulled back and stared at him. "You can't really feel anything for me, can you? Because I'm not really *here*. Underneath, I'm . . . *that*."

"Underneath, we're all *that*," McCallister said. "Everybody's dying, Bryn. You're just maintaining it better than most people—that's all."

"You can't actually believe that."

"I do," he said. "I believed it from the moment I saw you wake up. I knew you were a fighter. I knew you'd break my heart."

He stepped forward, put his hands on either side of her head, and kissed her. His lips were cool, damp, sweet, and urgent on hers, and suddenly Bryn felt wildly out of control, but safe. *Safe.* It felt like such an amazing relief.

"I'm sorry," he whispered, and pulled her into his arms. "I said I'd never let that happen to you, and I couldn't . . . I'm sorry."

"You sent Joe."

"I should have gone myself."

"He did fine. I'm out. I'm . . . as good as new." She felt a flashback to that awful place, the white room, the sound of primal screams, her own silent, implacable dissolution caught in the staring eye of a camera. "I'm fine."

He knew she was lying; she could tell from the way his fingers traced damp lines on her cheek, and the gentle way his lips brushed hers. "I know how you are," he said. "It's in your eyes. They're darker now."

He didn't mean in color; she knew that. Her eyes were haunted. She'd seen that herself, in the scratched mirror of the safe house as she'd showered off the remembered stink of her own death, again and again. It was hard to feel clean now. Hard not to remember how little separated her from dissolution.

"I can't think about this right now," she said. "I'm sorry; I just can't. I have to think about Annie. I have to make sure she's safe."

He hesitated for a moment, looking into her face, and then nodded and stepped back. "Let's do it. But, Bryn, let me do the talking, all right?"

She didn't agree or disagree, just walked with him into the darkness.

*   *   *

The house was halfway up the block, dark just like all the neighbors. There was a play set in the backyard visible through the chain link, and a doghouse, but no dog came out to bark at their approach.

The whole neighborhood seemed eerily silent. Bryn would have expected to see at least one light on, even as early as it was. . . . Early risers existed everywhere, didn't they?

This felt almost like a movie set—dressed, but vacant of human habitation.

McCallister mounted the porch steps and held out a hand to keep her on the sidewalk. The front door was open; she could see the black gap from where she stood. She hadn't seen him draw, but McCallister's gun was at his side, primed and ready to fire.

She drew hers as he eased the door open and stepped inside.

Bryn followed him. She wasn't staying on the damn sidewalk, and he must have known that because he didn't bother to try to tell her again.

"Shut the door behind you," said a man's voice from the darkness, and a light flared on, splashing over pale blue, worn carpet, toys spread in a corner in primary-color confusion, newspapers piled on a chair, a faded floral sofa. . . .

On which sat a man with a round, unremarkable face, short graying hair, and cold, ice blue eyes.

"Mr. Mercer," McCallister said. Bryn shut the door and locked it behind her to ensure nobody would be coming up behind them. Mercer didn't have a gun visible, and they had two; she wasn't letting anyone in to start to even the odds.

"Mr. McCallister," Mercer said, with perfect composure. "I would have expected you to be down at the headquarters getting your shot by now. Surely Irene's chewing nails over your absence. You know how she is about full buy-in from her team."

"You should have been the first one she went for," McCallister said. "If I'd been making up the charts, you would have been at the top of the list."

"I'm glad you weren't, then. I had just enough time to

get my things together and file for my vacation before Harte thought to order my lockdown. That's something my good little corporate-citizen act bought me, at least— vacation time. That and free Krispy Kreme doughnuts once a week at the team meetings. But in fact, Harte was too afraid to order me put into the program at first; she knew I could engineer a vaccine to counteract the revival process and make myself useless to her. Effectively, she would be rolling the dice on whether or not I'd wake up, and she couldn't afford that risk until she was sure she wasn't dependent on me."

Mercer transferred that cool stare to Bryn. "You made it out. I heard they were bringing you in for . . . What do they call it? Observation. Irene likes to have a record of the process on file, to prove that the experimental failures have been cleaned up properly. I'm not really sure she doesn't keep copies. You know, for fun."

"You really are crazy," McCallister said, almost admiringly. "I'd heard rumors."

"Oh, I'm not crazy. Crazy is sticking a gun in your mouth and blowing a hole in your cerebellum, like my old lab partner. I simply chose to stop counting the cost of what we did, other than in terms of what it could buy me. That's eminently sane. Thanks for your two hundred thousand dollars, by the way. I'm very grateful. It's helped me get my new assembly process tooled up in a secured facility. I'm turning out the drug in enough quantities to guarantee steady employment, and that's all I really want." He smiled. "Well, that and destroying the company, and particularly Irene Harte. But that's what I want from *you*, McCallister. In return, I will guarantee your friend Ms. Davis here a lifetime supply of Returné, as long as she makes her wealthy funeral home clientele available to me as customers, as Mr. Fairview did. I have to look to the future."

"I'm not your assassin," McCallister said. "And she's not peddling your drugs."

"Wait. Let's review. You *are* an assassin, as we both very well know; Ms. Davis is in a particularly nasty situation, because her supply from Pharmadene is gone, and even if she managed to secure some on the way out, it won't be much.

It doesn't store well; did you know that? Ineffective in the vials after about a week. Fresh batches are important. So really, there's no bargaining going on here; you're going to do what I want, and she's going to do what I want. Because the alternatives are unthinkable."

"Where are they?" Bryn asked. She raised her gun and pointed it at Mercer's face.

He cocked his head, baffled. "Who?"

"The people who live in this house. The kids."

"Oh, they're in the back," he said. "You're free to go check on them if you'd like, but I promise you, their hearts are still beating. They're just in a very deep sleep."

"And where's Annie?"

"Your sister. Ah, yes." Mercer glanced behind him, toward a rounded doorway that led into a kitchen; Bryn could see a silvery refrigerator and a sink from the angle where she stood. "In there. Go on. I'll wait here. By the way, the kitchen door has been jammed shut."

McCallister started to follow her as she moved, and this time she was the one to give the hand signal. He didn't like it, but he obeyed . . . mainly, she thought, because he knew Mercer was far too dangerous to leave unobserved.

She crossed to the kitchen and stepped inside.

For a second she didn't see anything, and then she heard a scrape, and looked to her left. There was a recessed breakfast nook with a table and chairs. One of the chairs had been turned to face outward.

Annie sat on it, hands tied behind her, legs secured to the wood. She was breathing fast, and her hair was in her eyes, lifting and falling with each rapid gasp.

"Bryn, help," she whispered, but that was all she had time for, because there was someone sitting behind her who slipped a plastic bag over Annalie's head and twisted it tight at the neck. Annie immediately panicked, twisting against her bonds, the bag sucked tight into her open, gasping mouth.

"No!" Bryn screamed, and raised her gun.

"Careful," said the man killing her sister. "I'm just making a point. Look." He loosened the bag, and slipped it up

just enough that Annie sucked in a deep, agonized breath.
"Play nice, Double Trouble. I'm not going to tell you twice."

Double Trouble. Oh, God.

The man torturing her sister was *Fast Freddy Watson*.
His smile was like razors, and there was bitter triumph in it.
"You fucking lunatic," she spat. "Take that off of her. *Now!*"

"Nah, I don't think so; I love watching you squirm," he
said, and snapped the bag back into place. Bryn watched
helplessly as her sister arched against her bonds, sucking
plastic as she tried to breathe. "How's life after death?"

She fired a round right by his head, adjusted her aim. He
ducked behind Annie, spoiling the shot. "Let her go," she
said. "She's your *leverage*, you asshole!"

"Trust me. It's not going to kill her. Just fuck her up a
little bit."

"I swear to *God* I'll shoot you."

"Gotta shoot her first!"

Behind her, she heard McCallister enter the kitchen.
When she glanced back, she saw he'd brought Mercer, and he
had his gun at Mercer's temple. "Let's call this a draw," Mc-
Callister said. "I pull the trigger and you get no more antide-
cay medicine, Freddy. We don't want that, do we? Let her go."

Annie was gagging on the bag. It was misted over from
her breath, and Bryn had that double-vision nightmare
again. She didn't blink as she met Freddy's gaze, just visible
over her sister's head. "I'll put you down, Freddy," she said.
"Don't think I won't."

"I know you would," he said, "but we both know I'll get
up again." He shrugged then, and yanked the bag off Annalie's head. "Whatever."

Annie coughed and sobbed and gasped, tears streaming
down her face, and Bryn came forward, grabbed Freddy,
and shoved him facedown onto the floor. "You got him?"
she asked McCallister.

"Got him." He put a foot on the back of Freddy's neck,
and kept the gun trained on the real threat. Mercer.

Bryn rummaged in the kitchen drawers, found scissors,
and cut Annalie's ties at the wrists and ankles. Annie
pitched forward into her arms, sobbing wildly. *"Shh,"* Bryn

said, and stroked her matted hair. "*Shh*, baby, you're okay. It's all okay."

"No, it's not," Annie sobbed. "It's never going to be okay. Never."

"She's right," Freddy said. His voice was muffled against the floor, but he still sounded creepily sure of himself. "Poor little Annie. Not the first time she's been through that. Right, Annie?"

"What ..." Bryn looked at her sister, scraped the hair back from her face, and looked into her eyes. "Annie?"

Annie whispered, "It happened before. The bag. Coming back. The bag." She was shaking all over, and her face was ice white. If Bryn's eyes were haunted, Annalie's were blind mirrors, reflecting only panic and horror. "He likes it."

Mercer sighed. "I told you not to play with her, Freddy."

"I was bored," Freddy said. "She's fine."

"She's no good to us insane."

"Annie! Annie, look at me. You're safe now. It's all right. Understand?" Bryn hugged her again, and got her to stand up with her. Annie's skin felt damp and cold. Where she'd been tied, it was ...

... Discolored.

"Annie?"

Her eyes weren't just blind; they were ever so slightly cloudy. The whites were discolored.

There were livid red bruises on her skin where it had rested on the chair's arms.

"Annie. Oh, God ..." Bryn felt suddenly, violently sick, and had to fight the impulse to throw up. She turned, screamed out her fury, and pointed her gun at Freddy's head. "You killed her," she said. "You son of a bitch! You killed my sister! You killed her and you brought her back *too many times*!" Burning tears blinded her, and she came close, so *close* to pulling the trigger. That was why there were bruises. Why Annie's eyes were cloudy, even though she hadn't been long out of revival.

Because he'd been using up the nanites too quickly by torturing her.

Mercer said, "I needed leverage, Bryn. Something you

cared about other than your own survival; I couldn't count on you not being ridiculously self-sacrificing, what with your military service background. Now you've got good reason to work with me. Oh, and please don't shoot Freddy; it'll be hours before he's any good to me again."

McCallister shoved him face-first into a wall and held him there, gun at the back of his head. He was tight with fury, and the look he gave Bryn was black with it. "You want me to do it?" he asked. "Tell me and it's done."

Mercer held up a single finger. "As Harte expected, I've taken precautions," he said. "You see, I don't *want* to be one of the zombies. I have a counteragent in my system that will destroy any nanites injected in my bloodstream. If you put a bullet in my brain, it's the end. No revival. No more drugs for your girlfriend or her sister."

She wanted Mercer dead; *God*, she wanted it with every aching cell in her body, but it wouldn't solve anything. Not now. "You can't," she said. "We need him. God help me, we need him. *I* need him."

Down on the floor, Fast Freddy rolled over on his back, looked up at Bryn, and laughed.

"But I don't need you," she said, and shot him in the face.

Twice.

Annie screamed and covered her face with her hands. Then she staggered away and threw up in the sink. Her shorts revealed telltale lividity bruising all along the backs of her thighs.

Bryn stepped away from the spreading pool of Freddy's blood, avoided his still-moving fingers as they reached for her, and lowered her weapon. Without looking up from Freddy's ruined face, she said, "Mr. Mercer. My sister needs a shot. Give it to her."

"You know that won't actually kill him."

"I thought a brain injury renders you unrevivable."

"Only in your first death. Once the nanites have the template of an uninjured brain, they can always put it back together. It just takes time. Do we have a deal?" Mercer asked. "Irene Harte and Pharmadene come crashing down. You act as my distributor. Deal?"

McCallister looked at Bryn for a silent tick of a second, and then stepped back and holstered his own gun. "Deal," he said. "But you get to clean up Freddy." He went into the living room, came back with a soft throw that had been lying on the arm of the sofa, and put it around Annie's shoulders. "Give her the shot, Mercer."

Mercer opened his jacket and took out a slim silver tube. He shook out the syringe and injected Annalie, who watched with dull, traumatized eyes. "I'll need to give Freddy another as well. That's a serious injury; the nanites will wear out much faster than normal."

"Or I could cut him apart and dispose of him in landfills," McCallister said coldly. "I'm leaning toward option two."

"He's a good worker."

"He's a sadistic, murdering son of a bitch."

"Well, everyone has flaws. I need someone I can trust to run the lab, and Freddy's perfect for that purpose. I can control him. Leave him to me. *Your* problem is Irene Harte. She's got considerable ambition."

"Soon."

"Now," Mercer said. For the first time, there was the glow of sincerity in his eyes, and real urgency in his voice. *"Soon* is too late. If you don't stop Pharmadene now, there's no stopping them, ever. Do you understand? It's already gone too far."

"What are you talking about?"

"I'm talking about the summit meeting Irene Harte is hosting tomorrow," Mercer said. "At the Civic Theatre. Secret invitations went out last month via the State Department. Pharmadene is paying for the facilities and running the show, but the guest list includes state legislators, governors, judges, the heads of the FBI and CIA. The *secretary of state* is on that list as a guest speaker. Do you understand what I'm saying? It's the beginning of the end, if they pull it off."

McCallister had gone silent, watching Mercer. Bryn put her arms around her sister, trying to still her shaking. On the wall, a kitchen clock ticked seconds.

"She's going to do it there," Mercer said. "Kill as many

as she can. Revive them. Addict the power players. They'll have no choice but to buy in."

"She can't control this once it starts."

"She can ride the whirlwind, and that's all she wants. This is how it all starts, McCallister; this is how the end of the world happens for us. Tomorrow. I'm just guessing, but I'd think the most effective way would be gas pumped into the auditorium, mass deaths, mass revivals. The first generation of the new order. She's got plenty of people to do it now; everyone at Pharmadene, from the CEO to the secretaries, is protocol-enabled, ready to die for her cause. That's why it has to be now, before it's too late." Mercer checked the clock. "In two hours, they'll be arriving at the Civic Theatre to prep it. You have until people start arriving to take out Harte and stop this."

"God," McCallister breathed. He didn't seem surprised, only resigned; he'd expected this, Bryn realized. He just hadn't expected Harte to move this fast, or this decisively. "He's right. She deliberately left me out of this. She suspected me, or she'd have tasked me with security for the meetings."

Mercer shrugged. "I would have killed her for you, but I believe in employing experts to do these kinds of things. And you're an expert at this, aren't you, Patrick? Isn't that what you did in the bad old marine days?"

McCallister didn't answer. He glanced at Bryn, a fast and apologetic brush of gazes, and then checked the clock. "He's right about the meeting," he said. "I have to go. I have to do this. Take care of Annie."

Every instinct in her rebelled against that, against sending him out on his own . . . and against being left here, with the not quite dead Freddy and the not very sane Jonathan Mercer. But Annie couldn't be on her own. She needed help, shots, and above all, she needed safety. "Take Joe," she told McCallister. "Don't go alone."

He nodded, eyes locked on hers. Then he turned to Mercer and said, "If anything happens to either one of these women, I'll find a way to keep you alive while I cut you apart. Understood?"

"Sure," Mercer said. "Why would I kill my own employees?"

"Ask Irene Harte," McCallister said. One last glance at Bryn, and he was gone.

Bryn pulled the blanket closer around Annalie's shoulders. "I'm taking her out of here," she said.

"Well, it's time we were about our own business, too," Mercer said. "I suppose I'll have to clean up Freddy's brains; I hate to leave a mess for the home owners. Hand me that plastic bag; I need to put it over his head to keep him from leaking. Oh, relax, Freddy; I'll tear an airhole for you."

Bryn turned to get the bag.

She never saw Mercer's blow coming, and never knew how he hit her, or what with, except that it had to be with something big and heavy. She heard a sound that might have been Annalie's choked scream, and then she was down on the cold floor, trying to figure out what was happening, and why, *why* in God's name he'd done that. . . .

Mercer thought she was unconscious, Bryn realized. She should have been, but she guessed she had a harder head than he'd expected. Her body wasn't quite within her control just yet, but she could hear as he pressed buttons on a phone and said, "Irene Harte, please. Yes, I'll hold. . . . Ah, Irene, nice to hear your voice. Patrick McCallister will be at the Civic Theatre in about twenty minutes, thirty at the outside if he stops for coffee and doughnuts. I believe he's going to try to take out your advance crew, and then get you for good measure. That concludes our deal, I believe. You get what you want, and you leave me strictly alone. Bye-bye, Irene."

"You lied," Annalie said shakily. "You're working with her."

"I'm a businessman, and Irene has no real use for me now; it's just as easy for her to pay me as kill me. She can always try to kill me later. McCallister, on the other hand— he's much harder to get, so she's perfectly willing to trade my life for his. And frankly, Annie, my life is really all that matters to me. Now, be a good girl and hit your sister with this pan, very hard, on the back of the head, and I promise not to let Freddy put that bag over your head ever again."

"I can't," Annie sobbed. "I can't. Bryn—"

"You will if you want to live," Mercer said. "I'll count to ten. One, two, three, four . . . Oh, all right, I suppose blood really is thicker than water. Don't cry, Annie; listen to my voice. *Condition Diamond.*"

Annie abruptly stopped crying. The silence, in contrast, was eerie. *Get up,* Bryn thought grimly. She tried, and managed to push herself over on her side. Paralyzed nerves were starting to wake up and scream.

Annalie was staring at Mercer, slowly clearing eyes vacant as a doll's.

"Now," he said. "Take this pan, and hit your sister in the head with it, as hard as you can, until she's not moving anymore."

"Annie—" Bryn whispered.

Annalie didn't hesitate. She took the pan, braced herself, and swung the skillet with brutal force.

It took three hits to crush Bryn's skull.

The last thing Bryn heard, a faint and echoing whisper as she fell into darkness, was Mercer saying, "That's my good girl."

Chapter 13

She woke up to someone screaming, and for a moment she was back in the white room, hearing that awful birth scream through the glass. . . .

. . . And then she realized that she was hearing it full-strength, somewhere a few feet away.

Bryn blinked and rolled over. The agony in her head was like spikes of steel driven deep, and she thought, *That is bone digging into my brain.* No, it couldn't be. The back of her skull felt soft, but not shattered.

Busy little nanites. She *knew* it had been smashed.

She was lying on a blood-smeared kitchen floor, all alone, and there was a woman in a fluffy pink bathrobe standing in the doorway, shrieking like a banshee.

Get up, she told herself. *You have to get up.*

She managed to drag herself to her knees, then up to her feet. The woman stopped screaming and ran. Next stop, 911. Time was running out.

Annie. Mercer had taken Freddy with him; he must have taken Annie as well. *God, Annie killed me.* Or had tried, anyway. Not her fault; she'd been controlled. She wouldn't have done it on her own, not even out of fear.

Bryn had to cling to that. There was very little left to cling to.

Oh, God, McCallister. He was walking into a trap, and—on her insistence—probably taking Joe Fideli with him. She had to stop it. Stop him.

She had to find Annie.

Bryn gasped and lurched for the living room, past the

sofa and the toys. She tripped, hit the door, and bounced off. Locked. Nice that Mercer had been so considerate of the family that he locked up as he left—only he hadn't bothered to move the dead woman on the kitchen floor. The woman in the bathrobe was on the phone, shrieking out the address.

Have to get out of here.

Bryn twisted the dead bolt and made it outside, staggered down the steps, and broke into an off-balance run once she hit the sidewalk. The neighborhood was still quiet, but lights were coming on all over now, responding to the screams.

She had to get out of here, *fast.* At the very least, she'd be arrested for breaking and entering; even if no charges were filed, she'd be held long enough that McCallister . . .

She had to run faster. Somehow, she had to try.

It was ironic that the sun was rising, and it was a beautiful morning; birds were singing in lyrical melodies from the treetops. Morning glories bloomed on the fences. She left fat drops of blood behind her on the sidewalk, but fewer and fewer with each step as the injury's last bleeder sealed itself. Her head ached unbearably, but she ignored that, concentrating on the pounding rhythm of her feet.

How long had she been lying there? How much time had it taken for the nanites to repair her broken skull?

Two blocks up was the convenience store. She dug for the keys and threw herself into the van, fired up the engine and sped away, not caring about traffic cameras or anything else. If she led a parade of cops to the Civic Theatre, fine. The more, the better.

The clock on the dashboard said she was already too late to get to McCallister to warn him, *hours* too late, but she had to try.

She had Joe's burner phone with her, and used it to dial McCallister's number. *Pick up, pick up. . . .*

She got an answer. "Patrick! Patrick, listen—"

"It's Joe," said the voice on the other end. "Bryn?"

"If you're at the theater, get the hell out of there!" she yelled. "Mercer sold us out, understand? Harte knows! She knows you're coming; get out!"

"Too late for that; we're in—" His voice was covered by gunfire, shockingly close. "Got to get Harte and shut this down or all this is for nothing. Stay away, Bryn. Just stay away."

"No! I'm coming!" She hung up and tossed the phone, and drove faster.

There was an eerie sense of quiet at the Civic Theatre, but the entrance to the parking area was manned by men and women in suits and sunglasses, scanning the area with merciless intensity. Bryn took a right turn and drove by, knowing they were tracking the van as it came close to the perimeter. *I'll never get inside. Not against Pharmadene robots.* They were definitely company people; she could see that at a glance. Not all of them were trained security, but they were on alert, and she had no doubt that every single one of them had orders to hold the perimeter against any and all comers. They'd do it. For one thing, they were all revived. Hard to kill.

Like her.

What happened to the other security? The Secret Service should have been here; there should have been other government bodies in place. It was entirely possible that Pharmadene had already overwhelmed the Secret Service, then. And the FBI. And anyone else who posed a threat.

You'd never know guns were being fired inside the building; it looked cool and calm. No emergencies reported at all, or there would have been some sign of police, of ambulances. *Something.*

Bryn moved on, looking for some way onto the grounds. Her panic was mounting; out here, she was useless, and she couldn't help them. If Harte got to McCallister and turned him . . . she could order McCallister to do anything. And he was capable; Bryn knew that. Capable of anything. If someone as essentially peaceful and harmless as Annie could be turned into her sister's killer, just like that, McCallister would be a deadly weapon. No wonder Harte had wanted him so badly.

And Joe. He was already separated from his family, but he was risking something much, much worse, something that would take him away forever, dig a gulf that even love couldn't breach. *If* he was revived. Harte might not even bother.

Bryn had to get in. If nothing else, *she* could kill Harte. She wanted to. She needed to, after that white room, after seeing the horror of that hallway at Pharmadene.

Harte had to be stopped, and like the Pharmadene staff, Bryn would be very, very hard to kill.

I could call the cops, report shots fired. If she did that, though, there was a very good chance that she'd be signing the death warrants of anyone who responded. They could be killed, revived, made to report that nothing was wrong.

But I don't know how to do this alone, she thought in utter despair. *I'm not a spy. I'm not some special ops expert, like McCallister. I'm just . . .*

Just a funeral director. What did funeral directors have that would be of any use at all . . .

Oh, God.

It was crazy, it was insane . . . and it just might work.

Bryn turned the van at the next light and headed at high speed out to Fairview Mortuary.

She tried to call Fideli again, but got nothing except a bland computer voice asking her to leave a message. Either the phone was dead, they were too busy to talk, or McCallister and Fideli had been taken already.

Time was not just running out; it was *gone*. She had no options left. Nothing except this one last, desperate try.

The only car already in the Fairview Mortuary lot belonged to Riley Block. That was fine; Bryn planned to avoid her. This wouldn't take long.

She went in, raced to her locker, and took out the extra set of clothes she kept there—a nice business suit, discreet and dark. Sensible but attractive shoes. She changed fast, rinsed the blood out of her hair, and slicked it back in a severe ponytail. No time for makeup. She made do with pale lipstick.

Then she clipped on Irene Harte's gold-edged Pharmadene badge and went out to the parked Fairview limousine; like all their family transport cars, it was unmarked. She tossed a body bag in the back, and was preparing to pull out when a knock came on the window.

Riley Block was standing there, still in her spotlessly white Fairview lab coat.

Bryn hit the button and rolled down the window. "Riley, I have an urgent pickup to—"

Riley silently held up a black leather wallet and flipped it open. Inside were a gold badge and an ID card.

FBI.

"I'm sorry," she said. "I'd been hoping to break it to you gently." She raised her other hand, and in it was a gun, which she pointed at Bryn's head. "I know it won't kill you, but it'll slow you down. Don't try to drive away. Hands off the wheel, please."

Bryn slowly raised her arms. Riley said, "Keep them up," and walked around the long, gleaming hood to the passenger side, where she got in, never taking her gaze off of Bryn as she fastened her seat belt. "You're going to the Civic Theatre."

Bryn couldn't control her surprise. "How did you—"

"Believe it or not, the FBI's been aware that Pharmadene had something to hide for some time. We traced McCallister's activities and connected him to Fairview, although he hid it very well; we still weren't sure it was a way into their organization, but I was tapped to go undercover and check it out. I've had mortuary experience."

"Joe brought you in," Bryn murmured. *Oh, Joe. God, no.* She couldn't believe it—didn't want to believe it.

"McCallister passed my name along to him," Riley said. "And I was recommended by a former FBI agent whom I worked with in the past, a mutual friend of McCallister's."

"Manny Glickman." Bryn felt the missing piece click into place, and saw the flare of recognition in Riley's dark eyes. "McCallister trusted him."

"And Manny had to follow his own conscience about all this. He knew it was going to go wrong; he tried to tell Patrick McCallister that from the start. He was simply hedging his bets. But of course, it's *Manny*, so nobody believed him. Not at first." Riley shook her head slowly. "I'm not sure whether to be impressed or nauseated by what they've

done. What you *are*. It's an incredible achievement, but . . .
so very wrong."

"I'm not one of Pharmadene's robots," Bryn said.

"I know enough about the capabilities of the drug
they've given you to know I can't trust your word about
that. Or about anything."

"But you know about what they're planning to do at the
Civic Theatre, don't you?"

Riley nodded. "The secretary of state is not coming, obviously. Neither are any government officials. We headed
them off."

"You should have stopped it as soon as you knew. You
could have locked down Pharmadene."

"Oh, we have," Riley said. "The building's empty, although we've got our own people in place to return calls
and give the appearance that things are proceeding normally. Harte made that easier by pulling most of the staff
out to man her Civic Theatre plan. And now all of their
most important people are in a vulnerable place."

Bryn's lips parted in horror, and then she blurted it out.
"You're going to take them out. All of them."

"Most of them in one go," Riley agreed. She had a sad
glint in her eyes, but in the next blink it was gone. "We
have to stop it. You'd say the same. And it's more merciful
to do it this way, one surgical strike, take out everyone at
once."

"How many?"

"What?"

"How many people at the theater?"

"We estimate about three hundred of Pharmadene's
employees," Riley said. "Technically, they're bodies, not living people."

"That's not true. They're like me. They think. They feel.
They *are* alive. They *don't deserve this.*" Bryn swallowed
hard. "Riley, I heard them dying. I heard them screaming.
Most didn't want to do this. They didn't sign up for it—
they're *victims*. You have to help me stop it. If we get Irene
Harte, all of it *can* stop. It can be controlled."

"That's what I thought," she said. "And that's what I ar-
gued for. But it's too late now, and it's out of my hands. In

about thirty minutes, that building will suffer a catastrophic event, and everyone in it will die."

"Patrick McCallister is in there. So is Joe Fideli."

Riley didn't blink. "Let's take a drive," she said.

"Where?"

"Where you were going in the first place. The theater."

"But—"

"Bryn," she said patiently. "You understand, this is a cleanup. And you're a loose end. I'm very sorry—really I am—but this is a national security situation, and we have to take drastic measures. I don't like it, but I have to do what's right."

"You mean that you're going to kill me, too."

Riley didn't try to argue the point. She actually seemed a little sad, Bryn thought. "For what it's worth, I like you. I'm sorry it happened. I'm sorry you got caught up in it. It wasn't your fault, but sometimes things just happen."

Bryn shut her mouth and didn't argue. There was no doubt in Riley's face, and no mercy, either. Like Irene Harte, she was a true believer . . . just on the other side. Broken eggs and omelets, and the greater good.

Bryn wasn't entirely sure she was wrong, and besides, at least it was where she wanted to go.

Where she *had* to go. Because if it had to end this way, at least she'd be with McCallister, where she knew—finally—that she belonged.

The Civic Theatre perimeter was deserted when they arrived. There were buses parked in the lot that hadn't been there on Bryn's previous drive-by, and as she pulled into the parking area close by she saw that the buses were full of people sitting in unnatural stillness.

Pharmadene employees. The ones who'd been on the perimeter.

"How did you do that?" Bryn asked. It was incredibly creepy, as if all of them were already dead.

"The bioengineered protocols," Riley said. "Manny told us all about them." She looked a little pale now, but still very controlled. "You can't blame him for that, Bryn. He was doing the right thing. This was never something that a few independents could handle, no matter how well-meaning they might be."

"McCallister was more worried about Mercer's operation; that was a rogue element."

"He wasn't wrong about that. Mercer's a sociopath. He never had any doubts about what he was doing, because the only thing that mattered was his own profit. We tried to reach out to him and bring him in on our side. He refused."

That, Bryn thought, was because he already had his own ideas of how best to use the drug.

"Bryn," Riley said, very gently. "I'm really very sorry about all this, but I have my orders. Are you ready?"

"Ready for what?"

"I want you to get out and go inside."

Bryn laughed, a bitter bark of sound. "Are you trying to invoke protocol on me? Because it doesn't work. If Manny told you anything, he would have told you about his antidote."

"He did," Riley said. "But I know you a little better than that. You're not running away. You were never running away, were you? You came here to finish something. So go finish it." She hesitated, and looked away. "I was supposed to restrain you and put you on one of the buses. But I can't do that. It doesn't matter where you are anyway. So go in. Find McCallister, if that's what you want to do. It's all I can do to help you."

"Thank you," Bryn said. She got out of the limo, walked up the steps, and opened the Civic Theatre doors.

When she glanced back, Riley gave her a faint, sad smile, and rolled up the tinted window.

The lobby was opulent, but mostly deserted; Bryn glanced around and spotted men stationed at each of the entrances to the theater proper. She walked calmly and confidently toward one of them. "I've got a limousine for Ms. Harte," she said. "She sent for me. I'm to find her and escort her out. She has a critical meeting in twenty minutes."

"I'll have to check," he said, but she was right, the looming black presence of the limousine outside the glass doors was a convincing argument. Bryn checked her watch impatiently and tapped her foot as he pulled out a radio.

"Oh, wow, can I see that?" she asked, and plucked it out of his hands. He blinked, startled, and in the next second she'd reached under her coat, drawn her sidearm, and pressed the barrel under his chin. "Back up three steps, please."

He did it, surprise derailing anything else, and in three steps they were in an alcove safely hidden from the other security people. "Condition Diamond, do you hear me?" Bryn asked, and saw his eyes widen. An eerie relaxation came over his body. "Okay, I need you to take this radio, get on the air, and broadcast an alert that you received a threatening phone call. There's a bomb in the building. The building must be evacuated. Do you understand me? I need you to say it and believe it. I'm depending on you to save all these people. Tell me you understand."

"Condition Diamond acknowledged," he said. "Broadcast radio alert that there is a bomb in the building, and evacuation must proceed. Protocol priorities state that executives must evacuate first."

"Perfect," Bryn said. "After you've broadcast the alert, call Irene Harte's people and tell her that her car is waiting at the front door. Questions?"

His eyes focused on hers, perfectly untroubled, but she knew that deep inside he'd be screaming. She'd felt this. She knew how . . . unclean it was. "Where's the bomb?"

"Basement," she said. That would take the maximum amount of time; typically, it was a maze of machinery and locked rooms. "Start now."

She stepped back and took the gun away from his chin. If the protocol was going to fail, it would do it now, in spectacular Technicolor; he could have been faking it, waiting for his chance.

Instead, he just looked at her and said, "I need my radio, ma'am."

She handed it over.

"This is Ledbetter at the entrance. I have a Level One bomb threat. Device is located in the basement. Initiate immediate evac of executive personnel." He met Bryn's eyes as he said, "Ms. Harte has a private car at the front—get her out here *now*."

He clicked off. Bryn nodded and holstered her weapon. "Mr. Ledbetter, I want you to join the others now and lead them in a search for the bomb. Do you understand?"

"Yes. In the basement." He hesitated. "Is this related to the two men we have pinned down?"

Bryn felt her whole body flush with adrenaline. "Pinned down where?"

"The hallway on the left," he said. "Ballroom."

"Go!"

Ledbetter raced off, looking as committed as if he really *believed* in the bomb . . . which she supposed he did, in a certain sense that was beyond his control. Bryn shuddered. The protocols might create kamikaze bombers and suicidal terrorists, but they weren't likely to produce any brilliant military strategists.

Ledbetter's radio message had poked a stick into the hornet's nest, and people boiled out of the building. Bryn stopped another security man and commandeered his radio as he raced toward the basement, and waited next to the glass doors. Executives arrived in neat tailored suits and expensive shoes, surrounded by assistants and armed escorts; she recognized one as the first man she'd seen converted to Pharmadene's new corporate loyalty program.

He recognized her, too, and his eyes widened. "You," he said, and broke free of his guards to come toward her. "You were there. Across the hall."

"I'm sorry I couldn't help you," Bryn said. She meant it. But the man just smiled.

"No need to be sorry. Best thing that ever happened to me, or to the company. First time in years we're all in agreement on what needs to be done around here." He glanced down at her badge, then back up at her face, a frown grooving his brow. "You're not Irene Harte."

"Ms. Harte gave me her badge to get me into security," she said. "I'm her driver."

He wasn't buying it, and as an executive, he would have knowledge and power to invoke Diamond protocol. He could bury her in bodies in seconds.

The radio suddenly rattled with static in her hand, and Ledbetter's voice came over it to say, "This is a Level One alert. All executives need to be out of the building *now*! We have a credible bomb threat!"

The man's security team grabbed her problem executive by the arms and hustled him out. She heard him saying, "But I don't think she's got the right badge...." They weren't listening.

Diamond Condition. She was starting to love it.

Except that in the next five minutes, she saw dozens of executives flee the building, and not one of them was Irene Harte.

She used the radio. "I need a twenty on Ms. Harte. I repeat, there is no sign of Ms. Harte in the evacuation. Where is she?"

A female voice answered, calm and brisk. "Who is this?"

"Her driver."

The voice turned cold. "I'm her driver."

"Ma'am, I've been assigned to drive both of you out of here as an emergency measure," Bryn improvised. She was probably talking to Harte's assistant, she realized. "There's a bomb in the building."

"No, there's not. We swept it for devices hours ago."

"Ma'am, as a precaution . . ."

"Harte doesn't move from her current position until the gunmen already in the building are eliminated."

There was a final click, and Bryn knew she'd lost the bet. No time to lose now, not if she wanted to actually end this; she abandoned the doors and ran, looking for someone, anyone, in a security blazer. She found one heading for the basement. "Harte!" she yelled at him. "Where is she? I'm her evac driver!"

"Downstairs private meeting room," he said, and kept running in the opposite direction, where she could hear the muffled booms of gunfire. *Two gunmen. Pinned down.* That was McCallister and Fideli.

But she couldn't help them yet.

Bryn raced down the silent hallway, the empty one, all the way to the end, and banged open the door to the stairs. Her heart was hammering now, her palms wet, and she knew there would be someone waiting for her at the bottom. Probably a lot of someones, all intent on stopping any intruders.

She could take some pain, and some injury, but it still frightened her.

This has to be done. And you're the only one left.

There were security men stationed at the bottom of the stairs, inside the door. Both had guns out and trained on her as she rounded the last turn of the staircase, and they didn't challenge or wait.

They just fired.

The bullets took Bryn in the chest and left arm, and she staggered against the wall under the assault. The pain rose and then receded, too fast for it to be a nanite thing; shock, she guessed. She felt woozy and strange, but calm enough as she lifted her gun with her right hand and fired clean head shots.

They went down. So did she, falling the last few steps, but she staggered up, pressed her wounded left arm to her side, and kicked their handguns out of the way into the shadows. They weren't permanently down, but it would take time.

And time was what she needed.

The shots had drawn more security out from their positions in front of the meeting room the security guard had told her about, and Bryn didn't wait this time; she began shooting, fast and accurately. She took four of them out and wounded a fifth, but then something hit her from behind with staggering force. Not a bullet, though.

A chair.

Bryn twisted around and caught the wooden chair as it descended again, using her wounded left arm; it didn't stop it entirely but it reduced the force of the blow. She kicked out, and her assailant fell back, dropping the chair in the process.

Mareen, Harte's executive assistant. She held up her hands in surrender as Bryn aimed at her. "I'm not revived!" she gasped. "I didn't get the shot yet; you can't!"

"No, I really can," Bryn said, but she shifted her aim and took out Mareen's knee instead. The woman went down screaming. Somewhere deep inside, the nicer, kinder Bryn winced and complained, but this wasn't the time for mercy or kindness. It was time to get it done.

The meeting room doors were closed and locked. Bryn kicked, bracing herself, and it took three tries before they flew open.

She went flat to avoid the hail of gunfire that followed, and was only partially successful. She felt more bullets striking, and this time, the shock didn't really protect her as much. The bright, razor-edged net of pain fell over her and tried to pin her down, but Bryn fought her way back out of it. She rolled, stumbled upright, and dropped three men in jackets, one after another. One got her with yet another round, but it was a flesh wound in the upper arm. Still, it made Bryn's vision gray out for a moment.

That was just long enough for Irene Harte to step up and shoot her in the chest, twice, point-blank. This time it *was* bad enough to stop her. Bryn went down flat on her back, unable to breathe, unable to think. The wave of agony was crippling. Her brain seemed to be covered in a red and silver storm—red for the pain, silver for the nanites trying desperately to abate it.

"I knew it'd be you," Harte said, from a great distance away. "Not McCallister. *You.* Because you never understood the good we were going to do here."

Bryn blinked, and the world steadied and sharpened just a little. Irene Harte was standing over her with the gun, staring down. She didn't say anything else as she cocked back the hammer of the revolver and aimed it at the center of Bryn's forehead.

Bryn couldn't breathe, and she couldn't think, but she *could* tilt the gun that was still in her right hand, and with the last of her strength, she pulled the trigger.

She hit Irene Harte in the chin, and the bullet exited the top of her skull in a shattering explosion of blood, bone, and brain.

Harte stared blankly down at her and tried to squeeze the trigger—or at least, that was what it looked like, in that split second of frozen time. But then Harte's eyes rolled back, and she folded like a paper doll, and the shot, when it came, bored into the floor an inch from Bryn's head.

The next security wave poured in, looked at Harte's body, and went still in confusion. Bryn rolled up to her knees. She could breathe only in shallow hitches, and she knew the nanites were working overtime to keep her moving, but it was enough.

Harte had invoked protocols, but she'd specified only that they were supposed to protect *her*. With Harte dead, they had no real direction to follow. Nothing to work for. Nothing to achieve.

Nobody paid attention to Bryn until she gasped out, "Evacuate the building. Get everybody outside. If they resist, knock them out. No killing. Go."

Five security personnel dashed out to do her bidding, and she hadn't even tried to invoke protocols. Her ability to get up wavered when she achieved a kneeling position, so she stayed there for a long few moments, wondering how much time was left, wondering whether she had the strength to make it to McCallister. She wanted to. She wanted to get him and Joe safely away, before it was too late. The FBI would allow them to go. They weren't . . . infected. They were still alive.

Harte was safely and permanently dead. Bryn checked. There was no sign of any nanites trying to heal her wound. Her eyes remained open, fixed, with uneven pupils. Like Mareen, she hadn't taken the shot; she'd wanted to be the puppet master, not the puppet.

Thank God.

It took five long minutes before Bryn could make it to her feet, and another three before she could manage to crawl up the stairs. She left a bright trail of blood behind. The hallways were chaotic now, Pharmadene people with conflicting orders, all trying to carry them out.

Gunfire was still coming from the area where McCallister was pinned down. Someone had given this batch of security personnel orders to take down the intruders, and somehow, even the bomb threat hadn't altered that order.

Bryn made it to the doorway, leaned against the jamb, and methodically put rounds into the backs of six guards who were firing at McCallister's barricade. The last one turned and tried to shoot her, but then he hesitated. She knew him. It was the man who'd escorted her through Pharmadene on her first day.

"Get out," she told him. "Just go. Go now, before it's too late."

He thought about it, raised his gun, and then lowered it again. There was confusion in his eyes, and fear.

Then he ran.

Bryn collapsed.

McCallister lunged forward as he came around the barricade and caught her on the way down.

"She's dead," Bryn said. "Harte's dead. You have to go now. Get out before it's too late; the government's cleaning all this up. Please go. You have to go while you still can. . . ."

"Fuck," McCallister spat. He picked her up, turned, and said, "Joe! We are *leaving*!"

"About fucking time," Joe said. "Harte?" He slid around the barricade, carrying a shotgun.

"Bryn says she's down. Move your ass."

"Hey, you're the one who just gained weight, not me."

McCallister gave him a wild-man grin, and Bryn relaxed against him, thinking, *If we go now, it's all right. Everything's all right.*

They made it to a fire exit. The alarms went off screaming. Bryn had a confused impression of the buses in the parking lot, still full of silent Pharmadene revivals, waiting for the end. *I should save them*, she thought. *As many as I can.*

But before she could, a black limousine pulled up to block McCallister's path, and Riley Block stared at them. She had a semiautomatic pistol aimed right at McCallister's head, and held it there for a long few seconds before she sighed and said, "Oh, fuck it. Just get in."

McCallister threw Bryn inside and dived in after, with Fideli close behind. The limo sped away without even waiting for the door to close.

Bryn turned her head away just as there was a screaming sound from overhead, and a tremendous shove at the back of the limousine, and the world exploded into fire around them.

". . . worst explosion in the city's history," a tinny voice was saying when Bryn swam up out of the dark. "Gas company officials continue to say that the incident is under review, but according to recent information from government sources, gas officials were warned about the dangerous state of the pipes under the Civic Theatre as long as a year ago. Clearly, this could have been much worse had the rupture occurred during a major event. . . ."

Bryn cracked her eyes, widened them, and blinked to try to get things clear again. She was lying in a hospital bed, hooked up to monitors, and a television was playing. The thin flat-screen was sitting on top of a rolling cabinet across the room. She blinked and fixed on the picture, which was of a rolling ball of fire rising up into a cloudless blue sky. Burning buses. A wrecked limousine.

Her wrecked limousine.

She felt surprisingly good, but then she would, wouldn't she? Goddamn nanites. She could have been shredded by the blast and might have come back together again.

Maybe.

An alarm went off on her monitor, and she squinted at it, trying to see what emergency it was sensing. Before she could, the door opened, and a doctor looked in.

No, not a doctor. A woman in a lab coat.

Riley Block, with a livid bruise on half of her face, and a patch over one eye.

Riley turned the alarm off and said, "I've been waiting for you to wake up." She poured Bryn a glass of water and handed it over. "Drink."

She did, almost choking at first, then draining it eagerly. "More." She coughed. Riley poured. "McCallister?"

"He's all right. You got the worst of it—shrapnel through the door. He had cuts and bruises, and Fideli got a broken leg, which he hasn't stopped griping about." Riley touched the patch with one fingertip. "I got this. Glass. It's just scratched, though."

"Sorry."

"Better than losing my life." She regarded Bryn in silence for a second, then sat down on the bed beside her. "Some of the Pharmadene people were caught in the blast, but some got out. You warned them, didn't you?"

"Yes. I had to."

Riley nodded slowly. "I can understand that, but now we're stuck. The government doesn't want to officially acknowledge what happened. Pharmadene's executives have been detained. Their threat is done. The people who made it out were seen and captured on film; their names were recorded. If they disappear now, it looks bad."

"Public relations. What a bitch."

"Right now, they're quarantined for exposure to hazardous chemicals. Just like you." Her smile was crooked, and a little sad. "You've complicated everything, Bryn. But I don't blame you. You were trying to do right. Hell, we were *all* trying to do right. Even Harte, in her own megalomaniacal way."

"So what are you going to do with them? With me?"

"We seized the supplies and the production line for Returné, and quite frankly, we're debating about whether to destroy the lot and let the whole thing die. For now, I would imagine that most of the survivors will be kept on at what used to be Pharmadene, with the story that there was a takeover . . . not too far from the truth. If they talk, their supply of Returné disappears forever. That'll hold almost everyone, and the few it doesn't will just . . . disappear." Riley cocked her head a little. "And a few are going to be released on other conditions."

"What conditions?"

"That they work for us," she said. "We still have a rogue producer of the drug to contend with. Mr. Mercer doesn't seem like the type to just go away."

"He still has Annie," she said. "I have to get her back. You understand? She's my sister, and I have to—"

"I know. Luckily, what I'm authorized to offer you helps us both," Riley said. "You go back to Fairview Mortuary, and find a way to make contact with Mercer again. You get your sister back, and give Mercer to us."

"Not good enough," McCallister said. He was standing in the doorway—leaning, really. Riley had underplayed his cuts and bruises; he looked as if he'd been in a spectacular prizefight, *and* been thrown through a window. "She gets a written guarantee of a permanent supply of the drug from the highest levels. She and her sister."

"I'm not going to bullshit you. There's no such thing as permanent. Theoretically, the nanites could sustain her life indefinitely, after all. We need some natural end to this arrangement."

McCallister looked at Bryn and raised his eyebrows, silently asking. She nodded. "A fifty-year guarantee," she said. "Unless I revoke it first. I always have the right to opt out."

"You mean, commit suicide."

"Something like that. But I control it. Not you." Bryn took in a deep breath. "And the government doesn't own my mortuary, by the way. I own it."

Riley smiled. "How exactly are you going to manage that? Pharmadene was bankrolling you. I've seen your assets, Bryn. You don't exactly have the capital to invest."

Bryn felt a hot burn of anger, and a little bit of shame. Of *course* she didn't have the capital. There wasn't any need to rub it in. "You can buy it and give it to me. My tax dollars at work."

"She doesn't need to," McCallister said. "I've been informed that the McCallister trust has acquired Fairview as part of its very large and varied investment portfolio."

"*You* bought the funeral home," Riley said, frowning.

"Not me. The estate administrator controls the trust's investments. You'll have to talk to him about why he made that decision." McCallister said it straight-faced, but Bryn knew exactly who the estate administrator was. Liam.

Riley's frown intensified, and now she looked very serious. "What the hell are you up to, McCallister? I'm warning you . . ."

"Easy, Riley. I'm not up to much right now, and neither are you." He sighed. "It's been a tough few weeks for all of us. I'm not going to war with the government over any of this, I promise. I just want some peace—for me, for Bryn. Even for you."

Riley clearly wasn't convinced. "You're trying to give Bryn a safety net so she doesn't remain dependent on us."

"Absolutely right. Budget cuts happen, especially in black ops. She can't rely on having you in her corner for long, and we both know it. After all, to you she's an asset, not a person. Give her some hope for her own destiny."

Riley shook her head and smiled. "I thought you were smarter than that, Patrick. None of us controls our destiny. Not in this day and age. Especially someone with her . . . special challenges." She looked straight at Bryn. "I can authorize a fifty-year guaranteed supply of Returné, provided you carry out any assignments you're given to earn it—the first of which is that you track down Mercer and his operation, and shut it down. Agreed?"

"Do I have any choice?" Bryn asked.

"You could see if Mercer's offering a better deal," Riley said, and shrugged.

Bryn met McCallister's eyes for a moment, and then said, "I'll take it. One condition."

"Which is?"

"You're fired from Fairview."

Riley laughed, a sound of real amusement this time, and left.

McCallister limped over and sat down on the edge of Bryn's bed, sighing in relief. She put her hand over his, and their fingers twined together.

"We have to find Annie," she said. "No matter what, I have to get her back. I have to make this right."

"I know," he said. "And we both know that no matter what Riley says, you're running on borrowed time. They won't honor their agreements. You noticed the caveat she slipped in?"

"About assignments?" Bryn nodded slowly. "They'll use me."

"Until they can't use you anymore. Then they'll cut you off." He cleared his throat and looked down. "I know Manny informed on us, but he's our best bet at this point to work on a reverse-engineered replacement for Returné. He's close to cracking it."

"I don't trust him."

"I don't either, but he's the only nongovernment game in town except Mercer, and we need him."

"We," she repeated. She closed her eyes and felt a wave of darkness and despair rise up to choke her from within.

"Why are you even here? Pharmadene's gone. It's over. You can walk away now. You should."

"My family's trust has a significant financial investment in Fairview," he said. "And in you." That sounded calm and clinical, but there was nothing clinical about the way he touched her face, so gently, and when she opened her eyes she saw that he'd dropped his guard. All his armor, split open.

She saw the look in his eyes, and her heart shattered, and healed, and broke again.

"We can't do this," she said. "Why the hell would you want me? I'm not—"

He put a finger over her lips. "You're not dying anymore. I, on the other hand, still am. So I think the question isn't why would *I* want *you*. It's why would *you* bother with *me*? If you intend to, of course."

She stared at him, transfixed by the glow in his eyes, by the emotion flooding out of him, unexpressed but all the more real for that.

"I guess I will," she said. "Bother with you, I mean. I've got fifty years to kill, right?"

"Well, I am a good conversationalist."

"Really. That's all you've got?"

His mouth pressed hers, warm and soft, and his tongue slowly stroked her lips until they parted in a soft breath. "Not all," he murmured. "I have all kinds of skills I can share."

"Oh," she whispered back. "I think I can find a use for you after all, Mr. McCallister."

She felt his lips curl into a smile where they pressed against hers. "Is this an interview?"

"Why, do you need a job?"

His smile widened. "Actually, I do seem to be temporarily underemployed." And then he kissed her again, more urgently this time, and she felt her heart pick up beats and start to race. "What do you say?"

"That depends," she said, and pulled him onto the bed with her, his warmth heavy against her. "How do you feel about the death business?"

He kissed her again, and let it linger. "Actually," he finally said, "I'm starting to like it quite a bit more than I ever expected."

"What about Mercer—"

"Tomorrow," he said. "Tomorrow we deal with that."

"And tonight?" Because it was dark out; she could see that from the glow of streetlights through the shuttered blinds.

McCallister reached over, picked up the control lying next to the bed, and lowered the lights in the room. "Tonight," he said, "we deal with the two of us."

Track List

As ever, I built a playlist for the writing of this book. I hope you might enjoy some of this music, and if you do, please remember to support the artists by buying the tracks and albums.

"Bad Man's World"	*Jenny Lewis*
"Watch Her Move"	*Peter Wolf*
"I Don't Care"	*Fall Out Boy*
"Red Machine"	*Sugar Red Drive*
"Please Remain Calm"	*Cloud Cult*
"Where U At?!?"	*Von Iva*
"Favorite Disease"	*Rev Theory*
"Familiar Taste of Poison"	*Halestorm*
"Gorgeous Nightmare"	*Escape the Fate*
"Save Yourself"	*Stabbing Westward*
"Come On Over (Turn Me On)"	*Isobel Campbell and Mark Lanegan*
"Cross the Line"	*Copperview*
"#1 Crush"	*Garbage*
"Love Is Gone"	*Dommin*
"Loaded"	*Seal*
"Go (Go Your Way)"	*The Kin*
"Criminal"	*Fiona Apple*
"True Love (Hell Yeah)"	*Charm City Devils*
"Hero"	*Godhead*
"Still in the Dark"	*Aranda*
"Breaking News"	*Jack Savoretti*

Welcome to Morganville, Texas.
Just don't stay out after dark.

The *New York Times* bestselling Morganville Vampires series

by Rachel Caine

College freshman Claire Danvers has her share of challenges—
like being a genius in a school that favors beauty over brains,
battling homicidal girls in her dorm, and finding out that her
college town is overrun with the living dead.

Glass Houses
The Dead Girls' Dance
Midnight Alley
Feast of Fools
Lord of Misrule
Carpe Corpus
Fade Out
Kiss of Death
Ghost Town
Bite Club

rachelcaine.com

Available wherever books are sold or at
penguin.com

Available Now

from

Rachel Caine

THE WEATHER
WARDEN NOVELS

ILL WIND

HEAT STROKE

CHILL FACTOR

WINDFALL

FIRESTORM

THIN AIR

GALE FORCE

CAPE STORM

TOTAL ECLIPSE

Rachel Caine

The Outcast Season Novels

Undone

Once she was Cassiel, a Djinn of limitless power. Now, she has
been reshaped in human flesh as punishment for defying her
master—and must live among the Weather Wardens, whose
power she must tap into regularly or she will die. And as she
copes with the emotions and frailties of her human condition,
a malevolent entity threatens her new existence...

Unknown

Living among mortals, Cassiel has developed a reluctant
affection for them—especially for Warden Luis Rocha. As the
mystery deepens around the kidnapping of innocent Warden
children, Cassiel and Luis are the only ones who can investigate
both the human and djinn realms. But the trail will lead them
to a traitor who may be more powerful than they can handle.

Unseen

After Cassiel and Luis Rocha rescue an adept child from a
maniacal Djinn, they realize that the girl is already manifesting
an incredible amount of power—and her kidnapping was not
an isolated incident. This Djinn is capturing children all over
the world and indoctrinating them so she can use their strength.
If Cassiel cannot stop her, all of humanity may be destroyed.

**Available wherever books are sold or at
penguin.com**